Edited by Mirha-Soleil Ross

Introduction by Trish Salah, Afterword by Leah Tigers

Compiled by Cat Fitzpatrick

Published by LittlePuss Press, Brooklyn, NY
littlepuss.net

The zines in this collection were originally printed between 1993 and 1995.
They have been scanned from the original masters in the Mirha-Soleil Ross Fonds in
The ArQuives: Canada's LGBTQ2+ Archives
at 34 Isabella St, Toronto, ON M4Y 1N1, Canada.

The Publisher would like to thank Raegan, Daniel, Tobaron and
everyone at the ArQuives for their invaluable assistance.

Designed and typeset by Cat Fitzpatrick with assistance from Sasha Karbachinskiy.

Printed and bound in the United States

This product is GPSR-compliant for sale in the European Union. Authorised Representative:
Easy Access System Europe Mustamäe tee 50, 10621 Tallinn, Estonia; gpsr.requests@easproject.com

ISBN 978-1-964322-08-7 (print)
ISBN 978-1-9643220-9-4 (e-book)

3 5 7 9 10 8 6 4 2

PRAISE FOR *GENDERTRASH FROM HELL*

"Searing, witty, critical and defiant… It feels just as pressing now as it did in the early 1990s… The pages of *Gendertrash* are filled with poems, essays, rants, fictions, speeches, surveys, interviews, resource lists and personal ads – largely for and by trans people, against the straight establishment, as well as the cis gay and lesbian movement, who were only too happy to throw trans people under the bus in order to gain rights for themselves. Sound familiar?"

—*Xtra*

"A breathtaking archive of our community and our struggle for connection, acceptance and liberation. Within these pages I can recollect the path of my own forming, reflections and refractions of the zines and message boards and chatrooms of my past, laid out like stepping stones to my current self. An absolute vital work for a precipitous time!"

—*Lilly Wachowski,*
co-director of The Matrix

"Riotous… fascinating… The most powerful aspect of this compendium is witnessing the zine grow its readership and outreach via its expanding personals section, letters to the editor, and cross-advertising from other trans publications. It's a remarkable and inspiring record of community-building."

—*Publishers Weekly*

"An unretouched gift for future generations."

—*Shelf Awareness*

"Trans people are often told that 'we have always been here,' but it's rare to see that laid out in a way where we feel lifelike. It's one thing to show idealized images of past figures; it's another to make them feel real."

—*The Needle*

"Beautiful. Powerful. Dangerous. Cold. It would be important to put *Gendertrash* back into print solely as a historical document – evidence that trans people have been uncompromising about the things that matter for a lot longer than you might have heard. But *Gendertrash* is a lot more than that. Everything here is still relevant, vital, even crucial. Also? What a potent reminder to make a zine. You. Today. Interview your friends. Make a zine. What a gift."

—*Imogen Binnie,*
author of Nevada

"There is an alternate history of what we now call trans studies, trans culture, trans literature, one that is not USian and monolingual in its origin stories and normative framework, one that begins rooted in sex-worker, racialized, Indigenous and street active transsexual and transgender people's communities, one that is not "queer paradigmed" in its frame, or oriented towards respectability or institutional legitimation."

—*Trish Salah, Lambda Award-winning author of*
Wanting in Arabic *and* Lyric Sexology, Vol. 1

"Thank the Goddexx for *Gendertrash* and its far-reaching vision, uncompromised ethos, its lust for sharing and also for lust, its wildness and its crucial, lived knowledge. A perfect, angry, art community in a zine; a deeply necessary collection, then and now and always."

—Michelle Tea, Lambda Award-winning author of Valencia *and* Black Wave

"You're doing a print edition of *Gendertrash from Hell*?! I've been hoping for something like this for years!"

—Alice Stoehr, The Irreverent Bookworm (Minneapolis, MN) and author of Sissy Bitches

"It's a dream come true to be able to hold *Gendertrash* after years with the PDF. What a gift to trans life. If theory mutilates and surgery liberates, *Gendertrash* has always been a scalpel."

—Saul Freedman-Lawson, Another Story Bookshop (Toronto, ON)

"Wait, are you serious? Oh dude, this is so big. The era of passing around that one Xanthra Phillippa poem out of context on Insta stories is over. The girls are going to learn... genetics on notice!"

—Joyce Laurie, editor of Picnic

"Who knew, back in the early 1990s, that trans people could love one another like this?"

—Leah Tigers, historian, trickymothernature.com

"Gender's back in town, baby!"

—Lou Barcott, Myopic Books (Chicago, IL)

Publisher's Note

This book reproduces documents from the *Gendertrash* files in the ArQuives in Toronto, primarily Mirha-Soleil Ross Fonds F0033, boxes 7 and 8, with some photographs from boxes 9 and 15.

The pages from the published *Gendertrash* zines have not been reproduced from the zines as published, but instead from the original masters, which are preserved in the archives. The scans of the masters have been rendered into black and white, and the paper texture and shadows have been removed. Some additional retouching has also been carried out – in particular, where possible, the low-resolution photocopies of photographs which are pasted into the masters have been replaced with high-resolution scans of the original photographs. The exception here is issue #4 page 6, which is missing from the masters, and has been scanned from a copy of the printed zine.

Gendertrash issues #1 and #2 were laid out in half legal page format: 7 by 8.5 inches. Issues #3 and #4 were in letter size: 8.5 by 11.5. In order to fit both in a single book, issues #1 and #2 are reproduced at 110% of original size, and issues #3 and #4 are reproduced at 85% of original size, with slightly widened vertical margins.

Additionally, a section titled *Gendertrash* #5 reproduces materials intended for an unpublished fifth issue. Those which had been laid-out for publication, even provisionally, have been remastered in the same way as pages from the printed issues. Some items are also included which were never laid-out. These are reproduced in black-and-white images of the form in which they exist in the archives, except in the case of one barely-legible handwritten document and two interviews that survive only as recordings which have been transcribed.

Contents

Introduction

by Trish Salah

Welcome to gendertrash from HELL!
Make yourself at home.
Maybe you already know your way around?
If not,
you're late!
What took you so long?!?!
We've been waiting for you.

If this introduction were being written by Xanthra Phillippa MacKay, that is how I imagine it might begin. Sadly for you, and for me, it is not.

When did I first read it? I've been trying to remember.

In that first issue of *Gendertrash* there is a photo. It's grainy and dark, and in it, she – a woman – is standing outside La Pyramid/Café Cleo's on the corner of St. Laurent and St. Catherine, in the middle of the street, hip cocked, wearing the tiniest black dress, not quite covering her ass. Her ass is gorgeous. Probably, she is working. The photo, credited to Jeanne B., and, I think, of Mirha-Soleil Ross (aka Jeanne B.), is from sometime before '93, when that first issue was published, sometime before Mirha moved to Toronto. Between '88 and '93 I was usually at Cleo's at least a few nights a week, but we didn't meet then, or if we did, I don't remember it. If we had, I'm sure I would remember it.

I want to say it was Viviane who gave me a copy of *Gendertrash* that first time I met her, over bagels at Beauty's in Montreal sometime in 1995... or else later, hanging out at her apartment? But I don't think so. Maybe it was when I moved to Toronto, in the fall of 1996 – I could have come across a copy at Who's Emma?, the anarchist book/record store and collective space in Kensington Market. Mirha-Soleil and Mark both worked there, around that time. Not in a capitalistically remunerated way, you understand. Maybe it was Xanthra who first showed me a copy one Monday night at Meal Trans? Could be. Most likely, though, I read it in parts, individual articles photocopied and included in the course pack Mirha sold us for the class she taught through the learning exchange at the 519 Community Centre on transsexual and transvestite art, politics and culture, back in '96 or '97. It took me a while, I'm sure, to get all four issues, but I did.

From where we sit, thirty years later, it feels like I've spent half my life trying to convey the importance of the zines you now hold, compiled and perfect bound, in your hands. And not just of the zines in isolation, but of the œuvres of their creators, Mirha-Soleil Ross and Xanthra Phillippa MacKay, and of the zines' other contributors, such as Viviane Namaste and Dancing to Eagle Spirit, and generally of the milieu which made *Gendertrash* what it was, and the work that grew out of it. And yet I still have a hard time conveying what I mean. So let me begin simply, and if that fails, let me begin again.

The first issue of *Gendertrash From Hell* (originally *geNDERtrash FROM HELL*) was published in 1993 out of Toronto, a zine by and for transsexuals, transgendered people, and our communities. The zine was edited, published, designed, envisioned, and funded by two transsexual women who were girlfriends at the time, Xanthra Phillippa MacKay and Mirha-Soleil Ross, with help and support from a bevy of brilliant co-conspirators and other people lucky enough to be in their orbit.

The first "trans studies" classes I taught, through the Toronto Women's Bookstore in 2001, were heavily indebted to *Gendertrash*. For that matter, all the trans studies courses I have taught have been heavily indebted to *Gendertrash* (and to Mirha-Soleil's aforementioned course at the 519).

When I'm introducing myself to students in a trans studies class, I sometimes mention that the first time I attempted a PhD I dropped out, and that that was a good thing. I tell them that I had gone to New York in 1994 to study postcolonial and queer theory with some of the leading thinkers of the day – Edward Said, Gayatri Spivak, Anne McClintock – and that I planned to do my PhD research on the history of the idea of transsexuality and how it was shaped by medical diagnosis and anthropological studies of "other" cultures. That if I had stayed, my research would likely have had less to do with how we have written ourselves into discourse than with how non-trans experts defined us or, worse still, regurgitated arguments about the social construction of gender in which trans lives and deaths were little more than a convenient example.

Instead, I realized I needed to transition, dropped out, moved back to Montreal, went back to hanging out at Cleo's, went on welfare, helped take over a local poetry rag, had coffee with Viviane, moved to Toronto, and got introduced to Mirha-Soleil and Xanthra. At the Monday night drop-in for low-income and street-active trans people in the 519 cafeteria, I hung off every word of Xanthra's jokes – some inspired, some actually "dad joke" terrible – and rants, which were generally scathing, but usually on point. And when I learned she had a radio show! *Psychopathia Transsexualis*!!!

So I took Mirha's "trans class" and attended her performances whenever I could, and felt enormously cool when we were performing at the same events. And then participating in the Counting Past 2: Performance-Film-Video-Spoken Word with Transsexual Nerve festivals and reading *Gendertrash* blew up what I thought I knew about the political work of art, as well as about the art of politics, and blew my mind – omg, it was possible to make art with other trans people, for a largely trans audience!!!

To be clear, I'm aware I'm fangirling, and yes, it goes without saying that I had a massive crush on the two of them then too. And yes, of course there were many fucked-up, imperfect, not great things about those days. But more than anything I studied or didn't study in university, that was my formation and training as a transsexual scholar and activist.

Xanthra's editor's introduction to that first issue is phrased as a Welcome:

> Welcome gender queers
> to the world of gender trash
> our gender world

Though like most print (punk, queer, trans) zines it had a small print run, *Gendertrash*'s contributors, analysis, and readership were broader than most: transsexual, transgender, MTF/FTM, Two Spirit and genderqueer, sex workers, prisoners, poor and disabled folks, artists, grassroots activists of all stripes, service providers, anti-racist feminists, anti-imperialists, anarchists and more. For this audience, *Gendertrash* was both a catalyst and a convening .

As a catalyst, it offered new analytic language for what we might now call the cissexist othering of trans people – Xanthra's preferred formulation was "gender described" people. Instead of evoking trans as identity, "gender description" exposed the naturalized privilege of going unmarked enjoyed by genetics (genetics, as in the "genetic jerk quiz," genetics aka "the cis"). It allowed her to theorize forms of anti-trans discrimination as "genderism" and systemic murderous violence (e.g. systematic exclusion of trans women from HIV services) as "gendercide."

Gendertrash showed receipts for feminist (and) queer organizations that excluded transsexual and transgendered people, especially poor, racialized and/or sex-working trans women, while simultaneously playing gatekeeper with social service funds for HIV/AIDS prevention or sexual violence services or scoring arts and research capital to explore the new vogue for all things "gender." It also challenged, in increasingly militant ways over the course of its brief run, the trend of middle-class trans writers and activists building careers as unelected representatives for "the community."

As a convening, *Gendertrash*'s wager was on trans autonomy and collective liberation, on the possibility and necessity of a trans politics led by prisoners, sex workers, poor and racialized trans people "not on listservs." Mixing manifestos and poetry, visual art and community news, film and book reviews, social research and political analysis, activist interviews and report-backs by as wide a range of trans people as possible, *Gendertrash* was full both of love for our communities and insurgent screw-you: *We'd Rather be Dead Than Genetic*.

In short, *Gendertrash* is not a singular, directed battle cry, but an archive of collaborations between trans people and allies, both locally and transnationally, a project that fed and grew activist, cultural, and scholarly work that reached far beyond Toronto, and far beyond zine world.

As both catalyst and convening, as both singular and plural, what these zines prove, what this archive shows, is that there is an alternate history of what we now call trans studies, trans culture, trans literature, one that is not USian and monolingual in its origin stories and normative framework, one that begins rooted in sex-worker, racialized, Indigenous and street active transsexual and transgender people's communities, one that is not "queer-paradigmed" in its frame, or oriented towards respectability or institutional legitimation. *Gendertrash* is a central, a vital, a still-living part of that alternate history. The zine has been out of print for a long time, but, because "trans people and the internet," there thankfully have been PDFs kicking around online for a while now, and now, thank the goddess, there is this.

Thank the goddess, I say, because we need it now. From its inception, the kind of transsexual and transgender culture and politics animating *Gendertrash* were at odds with, and aware of the risk of, displacement, co-optation, or erasure by queer appropriations of "trans" and trans people who uncritically or opportunistically took their lead from queer politics and communities. By 2005, Mirha-Soleil Ross would say that both the efforts led by a handful of transsexual women prostitutes to create social services for and by transsexual and transvestite people and the efforts "to develop our own language, images and come up with our own symbols to define and articulate ourselves," to fashion "a parallel trans culture," had been "a complete failure." (Viviane Namaste, *Sex Change, Social Change*, 2005. p. 89)

This claim may seem strange, even disingenuous, to make: over the last twenty years we've seen increased, if uneven, at times begrudging, inclusion of trans people in queer and feminist communities, gains in healthcare and social service access and human rights codes, the emergence of trans studies as an academic field, and a transgender literary renaissance.

However, Ross's point then (and similar ones made since by Tourmaline, Che Gossett, Miss Major, Dean Spade...) is that these gains were always already chiefly beneficial to more privileged trans people, and that the price for visibility and inclusion was often paid by those who would not enjoy it or who rejected its terms. That is not to say that there have not been gains. The question, as usual, is for who? Or, has there ever been a hate crime bill passed without an increase to budgets for policing, or a re-inscription of the justness of laws, and the rights of state entities to pass them?

As Mirha-Soleil put it in her, *Yapping Out Loud: Contagious Thoughts of an Unrepentant Whore*, one's position on the question of decriminalizing prostitution likely has a lot to do with whether or not one owns property. More mundanely, the development of trans studies as a field or of trans literature as a corner of the diversity marketplace tends to benefit most those who get to work and play in those contexts in a way that is quite disconnected from the material circumstances of most trans people, and draws upon and contributes to the global (racial, capitalist, colonial) privileging of writing, publishing and research done in English, in the West, in the US.

For my own part, I'd be lying if I suggested I was not profoundly invested in the proliferation of trans literatures and trans knowledges (studies) in the university, as well as against and beyond it. And the very existence of this book, in this form, is an effect of the trans literary renaissance, as is the existence of LittlePuss Press itself. And Trans Studies is home to many of the scholars who critique the field's founding biases and exclusions, as do some of the founders of the field. Some of us are even well compensated for doing so – which is part of the problem if most are not. In any case, from an abolitionist perspective, from an anarchist perspective, from an anti-colonial perspective, the "visibility" and statist inclusion and neoliberal commodification of transness has, in many ways, perhaps most ways, been disastrous for us.

Arguably, the mainstreaming of liberal trans rights politics also facilitated the mainstreaming of radfem transphobia, which has in many places emerged as one prong of a resurgent fascist and imperialist politics that doesn't even bother to hide its fascism.

In Canada, Liberal politicians, at least, are still trying to pinkwash and soft-pedal their own transphobia, as well as their hatred of the poor and of whores, their racial capitalist colonial practices, and their support for occupation and genocide in Palestine. Elsewhere, south of the border, for instance, in the form of the blowhard and smirking fascism of the new American emperor, or across the pond, under the reign of the goblin queen of children's fiction, a gleeful push towards the moral mandating of trans people out of existence is well underway.

This is not to say that liberal trans rights alone are what got us here – to do so would be both self-flagellating and grandiose – but to be clear that recent parlays with liberal inclusion projects and self-representation under capitalism, however understandable, seemingly urgent, even desirable from the vantage of individual embattled, excluded, minoritized lives, also represent choices taken against opposing in a more fundamental way the perpetuation and intensification of the violent (racial, sexual) supremacist logics that underwrite both neoliberal and neo-fascist capitalisms. In this way liberal trans inclusion projects have followed pathways well-trodden by mainstream white/settler feminisms, glb(t) rights organizations and liberal anti-racisms, which in pursuing equality with/in dominant groups both undercut their critical autonomy and relativized their opposition to domination as such.

In this context, *Gendertrash*, itself a wartime text, offers us a user's manual for how to make something from nothing, how to refuse and revolt against the idea that there is nothing t/here, that we are nothing without recognition from somewhere, someone else. *Gendertrash* is an archive of radical analysis and creativity, a living memory of tactics that worked and those that didn't. It suggests ways, in adverse times, not only to survive erasure (the condescending indifference of university feminists, social services, NDP lefties and the queer bourgeoisie; the directed murderous violence of the cops and the randos) but also to work against it through mutual aid and maintaining grassroots knowledges and community relations we are already enmeshed in and/or building. It maps how a generation of trans people, mostly transsexual women and Two Spirit sex workers, started services, provided accessible healthcare and housing supports, fashioned our own arts infrastructures and cultural modes, made spaces for knowing ourselves on our own terms, developed political analyses and cultural voice. It offers a vision, a road map, of how transsexual and transgender people can live, and live well, and of how we can make the world anew, not just on our own or for our friends, but collectively, radically, in relation to all those deemed scum or wretched of the earth by those who would be just as happy to see us gone. It is where we came from. It is also where we need to go.

And, it is not perfect, because nothing is, but it is beautiful, and it wants more for all of us than we've yet begun to imagine.

Toronto, 2025

GENDERTRASH FROM HELL

GENDERTRASH FROM HELL

ISSUE 1

APRIL / MAY 1993

geNDER trash FROM HELL

April/May 1993 *Issue 1 Volume 1* $2.50

i would like to thank the following for their help, support & love:

Morgane & Lisa
V & M
Bev & Ev
Isis
Bruce
J. Moss, MD
Barb & Mac
Maggie's
Niche Computer Club
Elizabeth Ann Electrolysis

finally i would like to give a big hug & kiss to my beatuiful transsexual girlfriend, Jeanne B., without whom none of this would have been possible.

Xanthra Phillippa

please
send us

your opinions
your issues
your writings
your drawings
your articles
your concerns
your stories
your poetry
your photos
your ideas

to: Box# 500-62
552 Church St
Toronto, Ont
M4Y 2E3

gendertrash vol 1 issue 1

gendertrash is published every two months & gives a voice to gender queers, who've been discouraged from speaking out & communicating with each other

editor
Xanthra Phillippa

sexual & political advisor
Jeanne B.

contributors
Bobby Gene
Josepha Alexis
Jeanne B.
Marie-Alexandra
Michael McCartney
Xanthra Phillippa CaiRa Mackay
Ysabel

layout & design
Jeanne B.
Xanthra Phillippa

publisher
genderpress

mailing address
Box #500-62
552 church st
Toronto, Ont
M4Y 2E3

submissions can be typed or handwritten, but should be double spaced & must be legible. please include a brief bio. name, phone # & address are optional. anonymity will be preserved if wished. submission does not necessarily include publication. submitted material cannot be returned, so don't send us originals. submissions may be edited for length or clarity. submission deadline is the 15th of the issue's 2nd month.

any opinions expressed are those of the individual writers

index

gendertrash is devoted to the issues & concerns of transsexuals. **gendertrash** also welcomes input from gender positive genetics.

in addition to issues of gender hate & oppression, **gendertrash** is equally opposed to any other forms of systemic oppression by those who are in positions of power.

<u>welcome</u>

welcome gender queers
to the world of gender trash
our gender world
where we can give voice
to our concerns in/around/about gender
issues
metamorphoses
transformations
changes
loves
lusts
intensities
hungers
nightmares
feelings about ourselves
need to be valid on our own terms
to express ourselves in our own languages
phrases
words
ways
to feel strong being ourselves
to be heard by ourselves
for community
to be who we are
to control our own futures
our own lives
our own bodies
to develop our own gender culture
to plan
build
shape
run
guide all of our institutions real & abstract

?

welcome to a safe place
a space of our own
a place of our own
to rest in
to explore ourselves
our wants
wishes
desires
thoughts
spiritualities
sexualities
feelings
emotions
bodies
free from gender oppressive controls
limits
societally created terrors
Patriarchally induced fears
self hatred
self censorship
a space of our own
of warmth & pride & strength
free from gender oppression & hate
free of the War of the Patriarchy
free from the GenderCide we are currently enduring
free from the oppressive indifference of genetics
free of the prisons of the Patriarchy
for all of us to share with
laugh with
sing with
exchange our personal herstories/histories with
cry with
hear
touch
feel
associate with other gender queers

welcome (continued)

a world of our own choosing
guiding
caressing
loving
touching
tasting
feeling
sensing
experiencing
where we can grow without boundaries
flourish without isolation
spread like fireweed
burn like wild fires without restrictions
fly with our powerful wings
swim using our strong, sleek fins
move
glide freely
swarm
flock
herd
scream
shout
yell
fall
roll
crawl
ooze
slip
slide
play
where we are not victims or victimized any longer
a brand new world untouched by the Patriarchy & its horrors
a whole new beautiful world for us to explore
roam through
make love to
a world that is not owned by one
a few
a world that is shared by all of us
a world of our own

gender queers
please feel welcomed

Xanthra Phillippa

gendercide

gendercide is the name for the deliberate and systematic destruction of gender described people that is currently taking place on this continent.
first of all, no statistics are kept on the number of us who even exist, let alone are attacked or killed or who suicide every year. for example, how many of the teenage suicides that are recorded as being lesbian/gay - related (at least 1/3 of all teenage suicides), really are related to gender identity? to continue, how many of the teenage suicides, where the teenager identified her/himself as lesbian/gay were really gender described (and since this society maintains the myth that the gender described are really a subsection of the lesbian and gay communities, it is quite possible that an adolescent, already confused and upset from dealing with her/his own gender identity, might really believe that they are lesbian or gay and identify themselves as such)? if an adolescent, who is identified as both gender described and either lesbian or gay, commits or attempts suicide, how would it (the suicide) be documented statistically? as a lesbian/gay related suicide? how many of the attacks on, deaths or suicides of gender described youths, who live on the streets, are recorded as attacks on, deaths or suicides of gender described youths? the list of unanswered questions in just this area alone, is huge, far too huge.
and what about deaths, attempted suicides of gender described adults? where is the necessary statistical documentation regarding our lives, like for instance our average life span, our average incomes, housing, professions (including prostitution)? and what about HIV/AIDS and the gender communities?
the complete lack of information in this area, allows the political/medical/pyschiatric/sociological/legal professions to continue to either directly or indirectly participate in the destruction of our lives. this is the gendercide that exists here, that we live under, under whose shadow we somehow have to exist. a gendercide that up until now has been invisible & unacknowledged. and our humyn rights will never be respected unless this gendercide is ended & acknowledged by this genetic society.

Xanthra Phillippa

PASSING (ii)

Passing is something you do
to protect yourself when:

>> the genetics are coming to kill you
because you are gender described

Passing is not a lot of fun
In fact, passing is a nightmare
A horrible, sickening, never-ending nightmare
Passing is what we,
the Gender Described,
do
every single second
every single day
of our lives,
passing ourselves off as genetics
because everywhere
on this continent
in this country
in this province
in this city
being gender described means:
- living without support systems
unless we have money
or friends or family or lovers
who have superhumyn patience & strength
& money & are willing to help us
- risking being caught up
in the current gendercide

Passing means surviving somehow
continuously being monitored
& scrutinized
for the "smallest mistake"
or "fault"
- a scrutiny that few if any
genetics would or could "pass"
without screaming "unfair"
- a scrutiny that is much more detailed
& much more degrading
than any beauty pageant
but is completely accepted
& supported by most
in this society
including those who never
support beauty pageants
or similar tests for genetics
- a scrutiny that will never end
- a scrutiny that we can never ever pass
but only fail
- a scrutiny that, when we do fail,
means that we are help up publicly,
displayed & ridiculed for all to see
- a scrutiny that means we will always be
invisible people in this society
- a scrutiny that means we will always be
amongst the lowest classes in this society
- a scrutiny that makes it impossible for us
to be proud of who & what we are
- a scrutiny that forces us to be ashamed
of our backgrounds,
denying them
instead of being proud of them
instead of affirming them
- a scrutiny that is a continual reminder
of how most levels of this genetic society
really feel about us
- a scrutiny that is unbelievably
damaging to our sense of self
& our self esteem

- a scrutiny that is not restricted to us,
  but is also extended
  to any of our friends, lovers or family
  who still continue
  to be seen publicly in our presence
- a scrutiny that is horribly cruel,
  ridiculing us &
  still treating us like circus freaks
  or the inmates of a horrible zoo
- a scrutiny that makes it almost impossible
  to develop any sort of social attachments
  other than prostitution
  (which is the only profession
  we are allowed to have)
- a scrutiny that is like something
  out of the middle Ages
- a scrutiny that is so insidious
  & societally approved of
  (like tourists gawking at
  lesbians & gays in the bad old days)
- a scrutiny that isolates us,
  destroying any relationships
  that we have surreptiously
  managed to build amongst ourselves
  like communist spy cells
- a scrutiny that only adds
  to the seemingly endless list of
  societally approved oppression
  that we have "enjoyed"
- a scrutiny by genetics of all
  political persuaions
  & orientations
  by people who "can always tell"
- a scrutiny that i find
  incredibly & unnecessarily
  stressful & sickening
  & a strong example
  of our Gender Oppression/Suppression
- a scrutiny that means that
  i can never get on with my life,
  i can never rest from,
  but am always aware of

So these are my questions
For those of you who are & would be our judges:

- why is it so fucking important to you
  to find & proudly parade & display our "faults" so publicly?
- what the fuck did we ever do to you
  to deserve such fucking horrible & gross treatment?
- do you get points for each one of us,
  that you find & turn in? Prizes?
- why do i get the feeling that
  this is only the beginning & that for us,
  the worst is yet to come?

Xanthra Phillippa

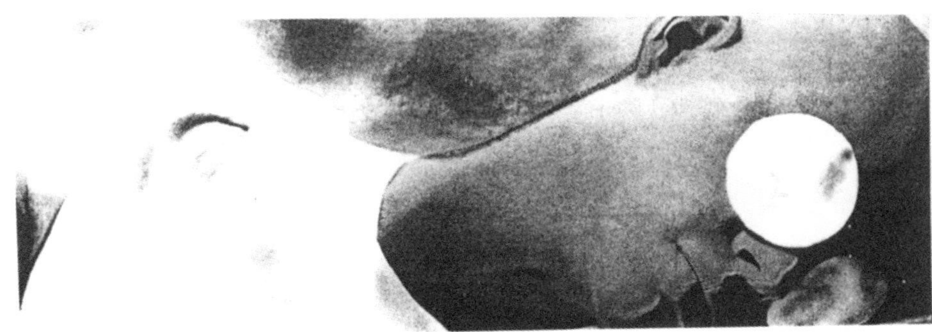

Dancing Wimmin

Jeanne B.

NO MEANS
NO
AND SCRAM
MEANS
SCRAM!
JeanneB.

Safe Electrolysis

[the following was excerpted from the pamphlet of the same name, produced by the health units of East York, Toronto, York & ACT with the support of Metro Council. It was addressed to professional electrologists. These are guidelines that electrologists should be practising.]

What is the Risk?

The risk of catching an infection from electrolysis is very small.

Infections can range from minor skin or respiratory infections to life-threatening blood-borne infections. In any procedure involving close personal contact or exposure to blood, plasma, serum or other body fluids the risk of contracting infection exists. This risk can be reduced by following simple guidelines.

It is impossible to know who is infected even if you ask directly. For this reason, infection control guidelines must be used with every client. In this way, the electrologist and all clients are protected. According to the Ontario Human Rights Code, no one with an infection or illness can be denied access to service or treatment.

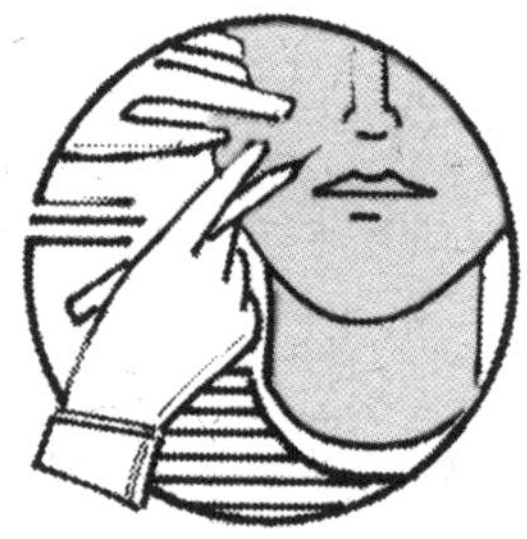

AIDS and Hepatitis B

Hepatitis B is a very hardy virus and spreads in much the same way as HIV, but is easier to get. Many more people are infected with Hepatitis B which can cause serious chronic illness and death.

There have been no recorded cases of HIV or Hepatitis transmission through electrolysis. These guidelines must be implemented to protect the public.

Recommended Procedures

Needles or Filaments/Probes

Sterile disposable needles are a must. These must be used only once and safely discarded in puncture-proof containers.

Skin Care

Before treatment, clean skin with soap and water then clean with an accepted antiseptic product with 70% alcohol.

Use soothing creams from tubes not jars. Keep caps on when not in use. Apply cream to the skin with a fresh piece of gauze instead of using your fingers.

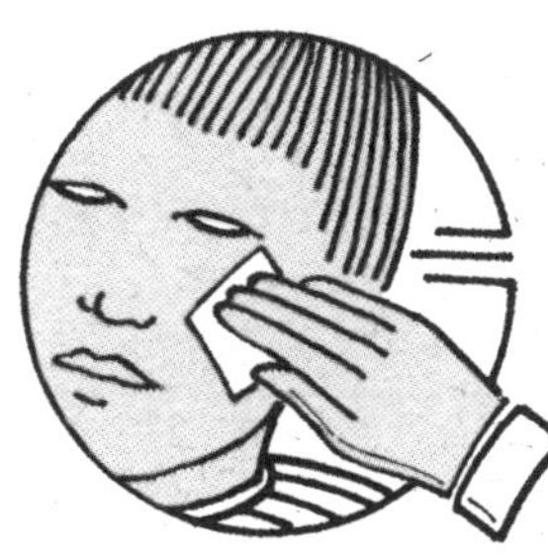

On the rare occasion when the skin bleeds after the insertion of a needle, cover the area with a small pad of dry cotton wool and apply light pressure until the bleeding stops.

Sterilization

All instruments which pierce skin or may be in contact with blood, serum or plasma require sterilization. This includes forceps, scissors, dispensers, including some plastics (check with manufacturer). Always use sterile disposable needles.

To sterilize:

First a) clean instruments with soap and water. Scrub thoroughly to remove any embedded pieces of dirt.

b) immerse instruments in a disinfectant until you have time to sterilize.

Then a) place them in an autoclave for the amount of time called for in the autoclave's instructions.

Or b) place in a dry heat oven following the same procedure as for the autoclave. Note that the intense heat can damage or pit stainless steel.

The best way to sterilize your equipment is with an automatic autoclave so all you have to do is fill it up with water, close it and press a button.

Moderately priced autoclaves are now available and can sterilize your equipment in 30 minutes. All autoclaves should be periodically tested with bacterial preparations available from your autoclave supply company.

Liquid chemical sterilizing solutions are an alternative. They are not the first choice because there may be fumes and they may also damage or pit stainless steel. They are usually glutaraldehyde based and can take anywhere from 10 minutes to ten hours to sterilize. A chemical supply company will be able to give you a choice of sterilizing solutions. Always follow instructions closely when using liquid sterilizers.

Instruments must always be sterilized between clients.

Glass bead sterilizers and ultra violet cabinets DO NOT sterilize well and are not recommended.

General Hygiene

•Always wash your hands, rubbing vigorously for 10 seconds, with dispenser soap before and after each client.

•Use disposable equipment whenever possible.

•Keep everything clean. Clean floors, vacuum carpets and wash surfaces daily or more often if they get dirty.

•If you wear disposable gloves, wash hands before and after removal. Use fresh gloves with each client and be sure to wear gloves that fit properly.

•Disinfect work surfaces daily or more often if they get dirty.

Cuts on Hands

Always wash fresh cuts under running water. Cover any cuts, inflamed or broken skin with a bandaid. Change bandaids often to keep cuts clean.

Disposal of "Sharps"

Needle sticks, piercing or puncture injuries are a proven way of transmitting disease. Be particularly careful when handling sharp or pointed instruments ("sharps"). Place sharps in a commercially available puncture proof container or other secure box or plastic bottle so they can't accidentally cause injuries. It is illegal to dispose of sharps in regular garbage or recycling bins.

for futher information on safe electrolysis procedures or other issues involving electrolysis, please contact:

Canadian Organization of Professional Electrologists (COPE)
416-967-4393

it is very important that your electrologist be operator certified (CCE or CPE designation) & members of either the **Electrolysis Association of Ontario (EAO)** or the **Canadian Organization of Professional Electrologists (COPE).**

THE CRYING GAME

Several people (including **Time** Magazine) have decided that **The Crying Game**is a **gay** film or a film with a **gay** theme. Once again, all the complex issues related to gender, that TV's, TG's & TS's have to deal with, have been dumped under the heading **gay** & thus denied their own & more appropriate category, **gender**.
First of all, even though Dill's gender identity is ambiguous in the film (TV, TG, TS?), she works & lives fulltime as a womyn & is accepted & treated as such by the others in her environment & community, including her lovers. She is definitely not a gay male.
Secondly, the main character is not gay either. Every single gender described womyn knows that gay men are not running after us for sex and/or relationships. This man is spontaneously and strongly attracted to Dill for her female or non-male attributes, not her cock and balls. In fact, the main character thinks she is a genetic womyn & is surprized & upset to find out that she is not. Gay men will have to realize & accept the fact that genetic men who are attracted to us (TV, TG or TS) are not gay, but **gender-oriented** & that their numbers are constantly growing. In other words, we're having a party & genetic gay men are not invited.
Next, because of the many subtle & realistic portrayals of specific gender-oriented situations, we believe that the writer/director, Neil Jordan, intimately knows the reality of gender described wimmin, their lives & their relationships with genetic men. How he got this information is anybody's guess, but unless he is telepathic, we think he got it first hand.
Hopefully this film will help genetic gender-oriented men to admit & accept their attractions to us & others in our community. As an example of this, those of us in the sex trade have already got a number of clients whose curiosity & desire for us has been triggered by **The Crying Game**. Additionally, this film is positive for us in another way:

> it is a much more sensitive & accurate portrayal of a member of the gender communities than **Silence of the Lambs** & other similarly exploitive Hollywood films. Interestingly, **The Crying Game** was made in Ireland.

Finally, we must claim this film as ours. To all the gay men who were/are upset about that or by **The Crying Game** in itself, remember - **The Crying Game** is not a gay film & therefore none of your genetic damned business, so just fuck off.

Best Original Screenplay
NEIL JORDAN

THE CRYING GAME

Jeanne B.
Xanthra Phillippa

The Self Discovery Process

by Bobby Gene

(Being a female to gay male, when I tell family and friends about myself, I have to hit them with a double whammy: first that I am transsexual, and second that I am a gay man. Even some TSs within the community think that this is a silly thing to be. I'm being met with lots of opposition from my mother since I came out to my family, and I am presently working on dealing with the pain I'm experiencing from simply trying to be a "whole" person for the first time in my life. In addition, I fear that I will never be accepted by the gay male community where I feel I belong. Sometimes I just wish I could go back to the womb and be born all over again, this time with the right body. Sometimes I think that would be the only solution that this perfectionist will accept.)

I knew about myself from earliest childhood, like most of us I guess. As a young child (influenced by the world of Disney) I used to think that if I wished hard enough at night, in the morning I'd wake up "correct." It became a nightly ritual, and a secret, great hope. Naturally, it never happened. When I was old enough to realize this could never be, I spent most nights secretly crying myself to sleep due to my frustration.

I was always the "tomboy," had boy buddies, didn't much relate to the girls . . . all the typical stuff, I suppose. I was lucky in that my first teenaged relationship was to a kind, tender, gentle boy who admired my physical strength and mental will and "male" characteristics. Although it was never directly addressed, it was there. I was not yet capable (or educated in the matter enough) to place any sort of label on myself. At that time, a mutual friend of ours commented that "you're like the guy and he's like the girl" which brought a smile to my face. I was with him from the age of 16 to 21. We rebuilt my hot '68 Roadrunner together, and I raced on the streets with the other guys. We lived together in Florida while I went to the University of Miami, and then for three years in San Francisco while I went to the San Francisco Art Institute. In San Francisco I found myself very attracted to the gay male publications and erotica that I came across in street newspaper vending machines. I didn't analyze or understand my attraction for it. I only knew it was quite stimulating to me.

At one point I decided, "Well, this is just too damned painful for me to deal with. They all call me 'she,' they see a 'she,' I have a 'she' body, therefore I must be a she. Knock off this shit. You can't change the body, so change the mind." I was completely unfamiliar with terms such as "transgendered," "transsexual," etc. The only thing I knew was that I was a boy born in a girl's body, and that I could tell no one or they'd think I was crazy. I also knew that I was attracted to boys sexually. I had no idea this meant I was a female-to-gay-male, or that such a concept could even exist. AND, I thought I was the only one.

I was a "freak," and I was quite confused as to what was going on inside of me. So I entered the denial stage. All I wanted was to feel whole. I worked real hard at being a good girl. I even found a guy to whom I was very physically attracted, but who was dominant in the male/female role (unlike my previous relationship), and who was quite heterosexual. I married him, thinking somewhere in the back of my mind during this "sleep period," that through him I could be a real female. I thought I was doing the right thing to help myself. Well, taking the submissive role did not sit well with me, and eventually my true personality had to surface and we were in constant power struggles over every little thing. We're divorced now. He knows nothing about my TSism, but we're friends, and he reflects, "You were much too strong for me." He has since married a real girl who is very into wifehood and motherhood, and I'm happy for him.

We were only married for about a year, but as a result of that marriage I became a "mother" (although I prefer calling myself a parent). I love my son very much. He lives with me. He's 11 now. The first time I went to pick him up from his after school program, one of the kids said to him, as I was signing him out, "Is that your brother?" Thrills. He jokes about such things. He would call me his brother in a teasing manner, without knowing (only sensing my masculinity) what the truth was. When I felt he was old enough to understand without being confused, I sat him down and had a heart-to-heart with him . . . you know, a real "father-son" talk. He took it well. So far, much better than my mother did. I'm lucky in that his love for me is unconditional. He loves me for who I am, not the role society expects of me.

I think my marriage and parenthood were necessary in my development, as it was after the divorce, when my son was about 1-1/2 years old when I "awoke" from my "denial'sleep." I used to take him to a 2-hour-a-day pre-school program, an intro to toddler socialization, and I had to sit outside his classroom with all the mothers. It was like grade school all over again for me. "What are these women talking about???" I did not fit. I actually saw myself as the one "father" sitting there among the mothers. I could not relate at all to their chitter chatter. Although I remained polite, it was obvious I was not one of them. While they talked about recipes, fashion, makeup, husbands, dinners they planned for their in-laws, my mind was on what clients I had to meet and how I'd approach a certain assignment. (I've been a free lance graphic artist since 1979.)

(this article was reprinted from Tapestry magazine, issue 63)

Little by little I strode to really find out what I was, what all these feelings meant. I wrote to Pat Califia who writes the question and answer column of the *Advocate*. In her published answer to me she explained what I am and advised contacting FTM and buying Lou Sullivan's book, *Information for the Female-to-Male Transsexual and Cross-Dresser.* I bought that book and also got the *FTM Newsletter.* I read the book from cover to cover in a record half hour. I was filled with many emotions, from depressed despair at learning that I could be labelled but could never really have correct, functioning genitalia, to elation to learn that there actually were others like me. Especially thrilling to me was the chapter titled "Female-to-Gay Male." I couldn't believe it! So now I know who and what I am, and it's becoming increasingly difficult to deal with as I am at a point where I am living in an androgynous sort of state. I appear male at first glance, but upon a closer look, I am figured out to be female. This creates confusion in people I meet everyday. In addition, I do not like being perceived as a "butch" female. My image of myself is strong and clearly that of a "soft," young male. I am in therapy and go to support groups for FTMs in NYC.

I had a boyfriend who was much like my first, even physically. He was sweet and gentle, and he is gay. All of his erotic stimulation is exclusively derived from male/male. Thus we shared much and had open communication and a fulfilling sex life together. He accepted me and saw me as I wished to be seen. However, after two years together, things started to change. I don't know if it was due to my being in therapy and dealing with some really tough issues, but I started to lose my patience with him and he with me. I realized that he seemed to me to be "penis obsessed" and I found myself feeling more and more inadequate. We had many talks, some of which turned into unresolved arguments. He became somewhat insensitive, and I started to feel that he didn't really fully see me as the man I am after all. We mutually decided to gain some space from each other.

I often sink into depression when I realize what body I am really stuck with. I'm not on hormones yet, although I had a breast reduction (not a mastectomy) before my education about transsexualism and before becoming aware of what I am and what solutions are available to me. I just always hated my once size D breasts which always seemed to attract the most chauvinistic of the heterosexual males. All my life I have locked horns with this type of man. I think I often shook them up when I did something typically male better than they did, then they'd ridicule me and reject me because their own masculinity was threatened. I'm now a size B and wear a tight sport bra to flatten my breasts to look more like pecs. However, I still view them as an eyesore, just unwanted "protrusions" which don't belong on me, and wish to be completely rid of them now.

BOYHOOD

by Bobby Gene

There's something special about being a boy. I'm talking about the "wonder years." The pre-pubescent years, when a boy is a being one and apart from anything else. He's not a man, not a girl . . . just a boy. And there's something unique about the way the world looks upon his boyhood. A boy is endearing, sometimes obnoxious and selfish, but always filled with the magic only boyhood provides. His innocent charm and mischievous nature are the subjects of volumes of Twain's imagination, Disney's fantasy.

And us, the men of today and tomorrow, who were the invisible boys of yesterday, known only to ourselves, we watched the boy rituals move about us, all around us, without us, excluding us from what was also rightfully ours but not granted.

So now we discover we can be men. We travel the road to our lifelong dream of transformation. Our own boyhoods camouflaged and brief, having to be mixed with the responsibilities of adulthood we've acquired over the years. We feel the same boyhood now that we only watched before.

It's okay. Put down your pen, your quarterly reports, turn off your computer, push yourself away from your desk. Kick off your wing tips and tie on your Nikes. Slip out of that suit for a while. Exchange it for your favorite pair of old jeans, which now fit more the way you've always dreamed they should. Take a moment to live the boyhood you missed in the wonder years. Climb a tree. Go fishing with Huck. Take it, it's yours now.

--Pinocchio

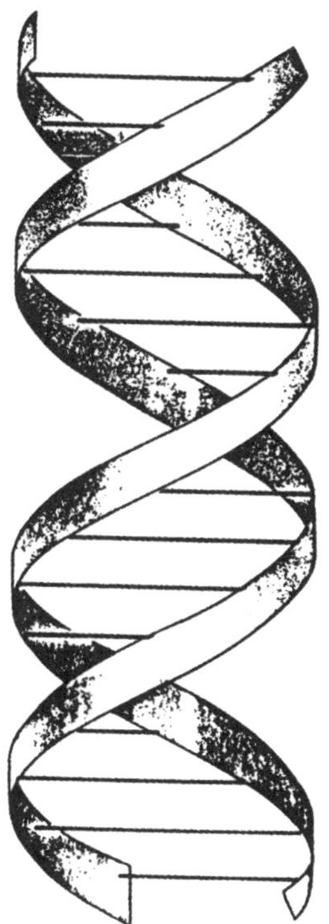

I'm only 5'5", but I am large-boned and broad through the back and shoulders. I bench press about 80 lbs and curl about 60. I am working on attaining more of a "V" silhouette by building up my shoulders, pecs, lats, and biceps. But, I look at the guys at the gym and feel a rush of frustration which comes from seeing

(continued)

their height and their natural "V" shape and narrow hips and lack of hip and thigh fat which they have without even working for it. They were just born with it. Damn! Frustration. Luckily, I pretty much have narrow hips for a female. My son was born by cesarean section due to fetal distress because the doctor said my pelvic structure was not wide enough to birth a baby. I secretly felt very proud about that. I also have a little Adam's apple which I'm quite proud of.

Most recently I have been depressed over the realization that many gay men are quite superficial, and measure a man by the size of what's in his pants. This realization has been the main deterrent in my proceeding with hormone therapy, as I am afraid to turn a "perfect female body" into a "physically deformed male body" and thus doom myself to a life of celibacy. I am in constant agony over having a female body in the first place, but in my mind, I wonder if I could deal with it solely in order to remain "in the sexual running" with men. I don't know. Sometimes it's so bad that the sex part of my future becomes a secondary consideration, and all I want is to look in the mirror and see a man, regardless of what I know is in my pants.

In an effort to "combat" this problem, I put a personal ad in the *Village Voice*, stating what I am and that I seek a gay male who is NOT superficial, who will accept me as I am. I found that most of the male population who reads an ad that says "TS" just assumes that TS always and only means a man who dresses as a woman, completely disregarding the fact that I described myself as a "GWM (TS) who passes as a soft, young boy." I have just begun a writing relationship with only one gay man of the 10 to 15 who wrote to me, most of whom I chose to "educate" in my final reply to their response, explaining to them the differences in the terms "TS" and "TV," that the two are not interchangeable terms, and that they apply to both genders, not only to biological males.

I still talk on the phone to my boyfriend of the past two years, and we see each other every now and then. He claims he loves me very much and can't see a life for him with "no Bobby," but I don't feel the same way about him as I once did. I don't want to feel that I "have to stay" with him because "there will never be any gay man in the world who will accept a gay man who doesn't have a penis." I guess I'm presently "testing the waters" before I make the big move forward in my transition.

I only know one thing for sure: I can't "unlearn" what I've discovered about myself.

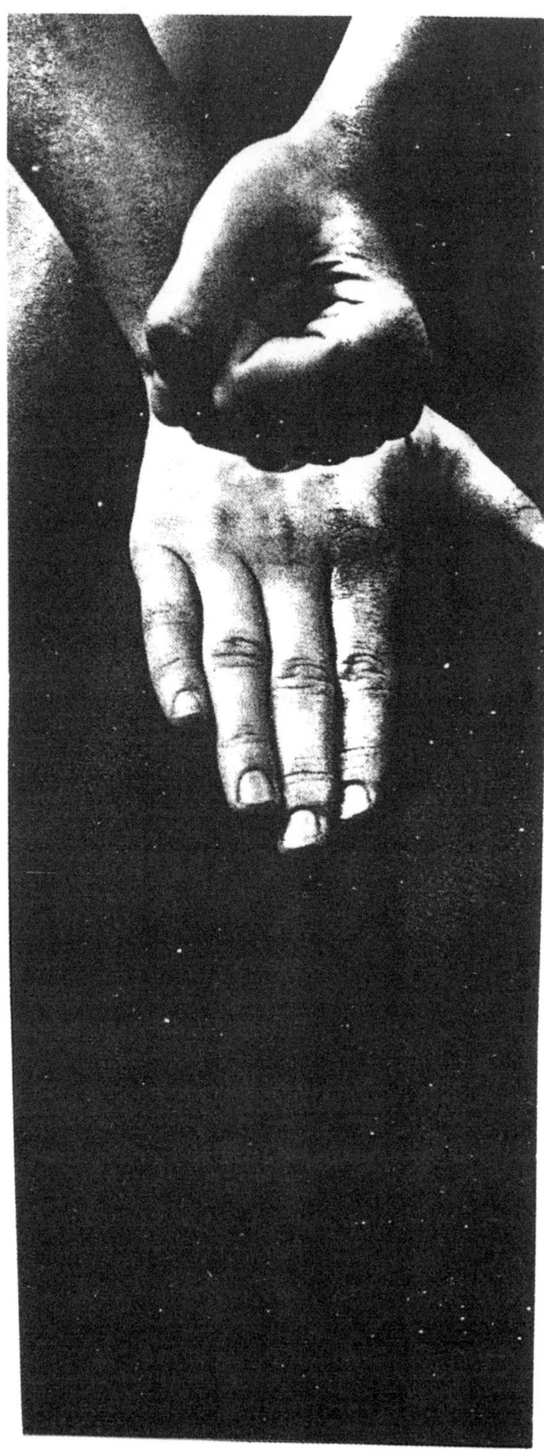

Trannies Speak Out

(opinions recounted at Colby's on Monday, April 5, around midnight)

Since everybody outside of the gender communities seems to think that it's O.K. to call us **trannies**, because, as they argue, we call ourselves **transies** or **trannies**, we decided to ask the people concerned (ie. the **trannies** themselves) how they feel about that.

Question: How do you feel about being called a **Transie, Trannie** or **Drag Queen** by people outside of the gender community?

#1: No, [I hate it] because I'm not a **Transie**. I'm a woman trapped in a man's body with a cock!!!

Ms. Stephanie

#2: I get very offended when someone "outside" calls me a **Drag Queen**, even though I am a Drag Queen (at times). I find the term [**Drag Queen**] is used to be offensive.

Veronica Blake

#3: I would be a bit upset because the labels, **Drag Queen** and **Trannie** don't mean [that] I dress up as a girl every day of my life. Yes, I would be offended.

Inès

Whatever we call ourselves,
Whatever word we choose to describe ourselves
Doesn't give genetics the right to use it...
Just like **Queer** is for Queers only...
That's what reclaiming is all about.

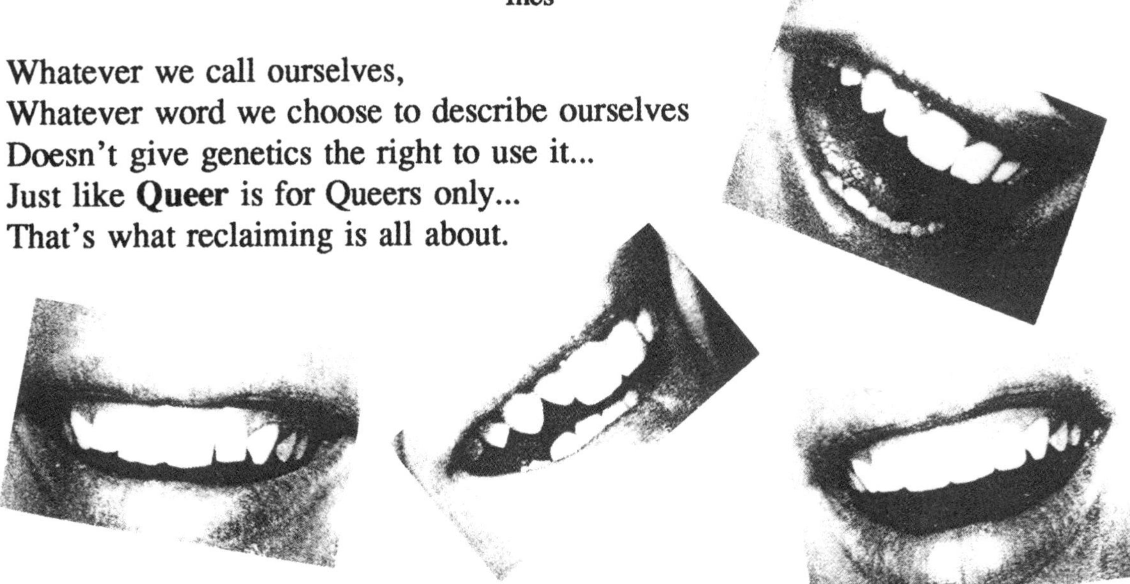

TS Words & Phrases

After having been labelled & ostracized by this genetically defined & controlled society & its institutions for so long, we need to reclaim all those negative words & phrases which are still used to stigmatize us. It is also time to develop our own language & impose it on this gender suppressive society. .

Here is an attempt to start this process:

- **in the pit** (instead of the **closet** of lesbians & gays) is the period of time, quite painful, where we hide our authentic gender.
- **climbing out of the pit** (instead of **coming out of the closet** for lesbians & gays) is the moment when we acknowledge & accept our true selves & begin the liberating process.
- **metamorphosis** (instead of the clinical term **transition**) is the liberating process by which we change literally from caterpillar to butterfly (for this reason it can also be called our **cocoon** stage).
- **persons whose backgrounds are gender described/determined** or **gender described/determined men/wimmin/people** are much more appropriate terms for genetics to use to describe us than **transsexuals, TS's, trannies, transies, males/females to (constructed/artifactual) females/males**. the term **she-male** is appropriate only within the sex trade.
- **members of the gender communities** instead of the clumsy-sounding **transpersons**
- **genetics, genetically/chromosonally described/determined** are non transsexual people.
- **gender oriented wimmin/men/people** are wimmin, men or people who attracted to TS's
- **transsexual lesbians** are usually gender described wimmin who are attracted to genetic wimmin or possibly other gender described wimmin
- **trans dykes** are usually gender described wimmin who are attracted to other gender described wimmin or possibly genetic wimmin
- **transsexual gays/fags** are usually gender described men who are attracted to genetic or possibly other gender described men or both.**
- **gender queers** or **gender outlaws** are what we & only we are, since lesbians & gays seem to think that **queer** means **lesbian/gay (& sometimes bi)** only.
- **gender hatred/oppression/suppression/loathing** (instead of the term **transphobia**, whose origins are obscure & sound genetically inspired) is the oppression we suffer from genetics.
- **that's the way it is** is the phrase we use to describe how we survive in this society.
- **in/into the woodwork** describes how some of us, usually anonymously, try & fit into this genetic mainstream society.

[please note that in general, the word **gender** is much better than the prefix **trans**, which seems to be genetically inspired in its origin]

This is only the beginning. As we continiue to grow, our words & phrases will likewise flourish.

** we still haven't dealt with the many other complex realities such as female to male transsexuals who become gay transvestites or drag queens or male to female transsexuals who identify as lesbians & then cross dress as men, in order to pick up genetic straight wimmin or gay men.

Xanthra Phillippa

The Poetry of Josepha Alexis

when the trees
were teeth
and the sun
was a cunt

photo/Ysabel

floating around
a nipple
i was crying my life

Decriminalizing for Power

a "loose woman",
a student from out of town
with neither loans nor bursaries,
a single mother without a dime,
a transvestite junkie or
simply an ambitious outlaw
Decriminalizing, essentially, to regain our dignity...

communicating,
sharing,
regrouping and
organizing ourselves,
speaking for ourselves without being accused
of "conspiration"
Decriminalizing to end the Fear...

being free to choose financial independence
through selling our bodies,
our beauty,
our sexualities
Decriminalizing to subdue the Stigma...

our freedom, we wish to keep
having control at all times
Decriminalizing and not legalizing
we reject the State as pimp...

the urgency to value our humyn rights:
freedom of expression,
freedom to travel,
to immigrate,
to work,
to get married,
to have children

Respect for our privacy

Decriminalizing to legitimize our profession,
"le vice commercialisé",
in the eyes of the judges,
the doctors,
our families,
our lovers
and this Society...

Decriminalizing to no longer be ashamed
to work the streets...

our heads held high and proud

Decriminalizing to affirm our sexual pleasure...

Decriminalizing for Power

Jeanne B.

Montréal

St Laurent & St Catherine

Outside Cleo's

photo: Jeanne B.

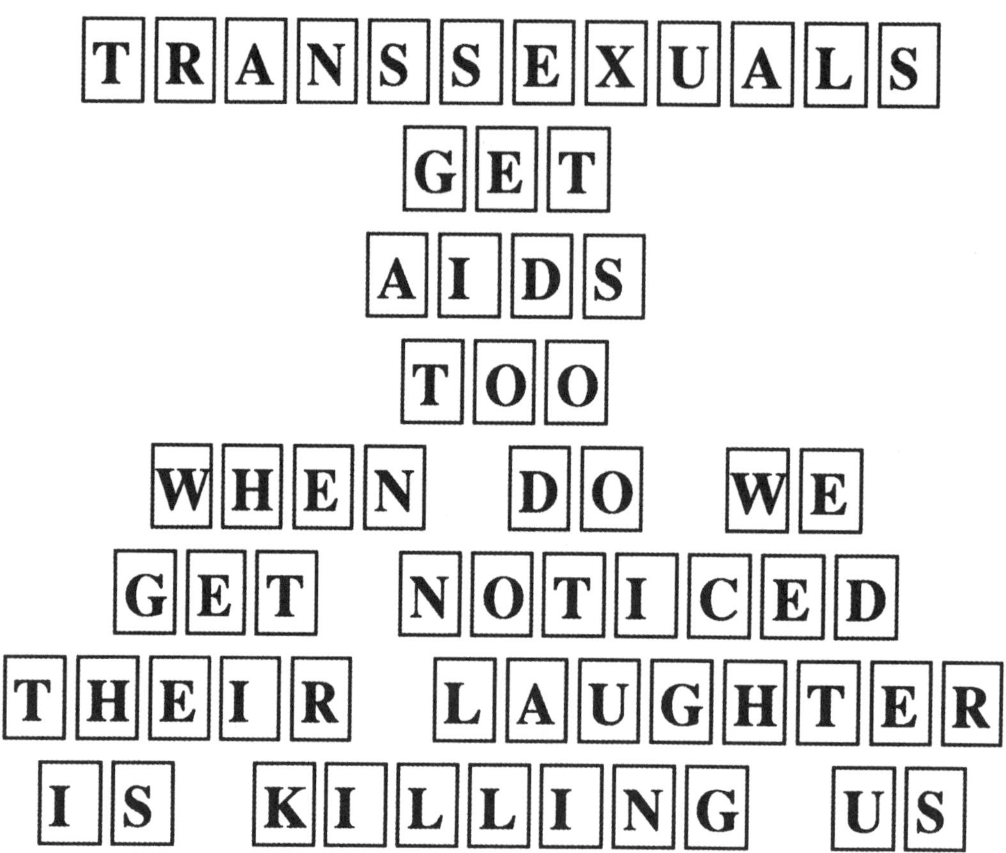
TRANSSEXUALS
GET
AIDS
TOO
WHEN DO WE
GET NOTICED
THEIR LAUGHTER
IS KILLING US

This is what we have	**This is what we need**
ridicule	no more ridicule
isolation	no more isolation
ignorance	no more ignorance
hatred	no more hatred
no studies of our own	studies of our own
no programs of our own	programs of our own
no hospices of our own	hospices of our own
no support groups of our own	support groups of our own

Xanthra Phillippa

Everyone

I, like you, have had to come to know and accept myself as I am. I did not come into this world ready made as "Jack or Jill", very few human beings do. Living a lie is not what I want to do, I haven't chosen my fate, nor have you. So, before you judge me, study, read or ask me about what I'm like or what I'm going through, and then through acceptance and understanding, rather than judgement, can you truly enlighten and accept yourself and others around you and help make your own world truly a more valuable one.

Michael McCartney
February 1st, 1993

photo: Ysabel

Resources

Here are some places that we have contacted or are aware of, that might be helpful to people in our communities. Please let us know if that is (or is not) the case. In addition, we need to know of any other gender resources that are available & might be useful to our communities.

Maggie's Prostitutes' Resource Centre & Safe Sex Project of Toronto
298 Gerrard St. E. (Gerrard & Parliament)
964-0150
- a resource person centre run for & by sex trade workers providing various services such as the Bad Trick Sheet, newsletter, free condoms, lube, etc., video night, library, drop in, legal referrals & workshops, etc
- TS on staff

Toronto Rape Crisis Centre (TRCC)
(now known as Multicultural Wimmin Against Rape)
597-8808 (24 hrs crisis line)
597-1214 (TDD line only)
- a wimmin run collective dealing with people who have been sexually assaulted
- they do not pressure clients to report to the police
- they have no problems with TS clients
- they also run **Take Back the Night** & have no problems with TS's attending

Sexual Assault Care Clinic
76 Grenville (located within but separate from Women's College Hospital)
363-6040
- community oriented & responsive
- do not pressure clients to take any tests
- clients can bring advocates with them
- clients can change their minds at any time
- have no problems with TS's

SOS (Street Outreach Services)
622 Yonge St, 2nd floor
926-0744
contact: Wayne Travers
- deal with street youth
- very aware of the problems of TS youth (esp with shelters & housing)

Transition Support
519 Church St, East Room
- TV, TG, TS & significant other (SO) run support group
- every 2nd & 4th Fridays, 7-10pm

Canadian Crossdressers' Club
161 Gerrard St E
921-6112 (24 hours)
- support, social & educational club for CD's, TS's, TG's, spouses, SO's, DQ's & friends

Hassle Free Clinic
556 Church St, 2nd floor
922-0603 (Men's Clinic)
922-0566 (Wimmin's Clinic)
Wimmin's Clinic Hours 10-3 (M, W & F)
4-8 (T & T)
4-6 (T & T) - non-AIDS STD testing. no appt necessary
- anonymous AIDS testing & counselling
- STD testing & counselling
- health issues
- free condoms & lube, etc
- TS's are respected

Health First ("Walk-In") Clinic
491 Church St
515-0590
- gender positive & supportive health clinic

Original caption: "Male Sexual Pervert" (photograph accompanying Hamilton's article, p. 50; see backnotes).

1894
Dr. Allan McLane Hamilton:
"A class by themselves . . . recognized by the police"

An essay on "Insanity in its Medico-Legal Bearings," in the textbook *A System of Legal Medicine,* included a section on "Disturbances of . . . Emotion."[26]

"Unusual" sexual impulses indicated "mental degeneration," found in the "victim of evolutionary insanity." The behavior of the "sexual pervert need not be conspicuous." The "pervert" was generally "fairly strong intellectually," despite a "complete transposal of his normal appetites."

"Many individuals entertain sexual longings only for their own sex"; but Hamilton refused to specify their "form of gratification." He added:

> In many large cities the subjects of the contrary sexual impulse form a class by themselves and are recognized by the police. The men have their balls, where they dress as women even to the details of dainty underwear.
>
> They adopt the names of women, and affect a feminine speech and manner, "falling in love" with each other, and writing amatory and obscene letters. In New York City alone there are not less than one hundred of these, who make a profession of male prostitution, soliciting upon the streets and in parks when they get the opportunity. Physically, many of these men whom I have examined present the stigmata of degenerative insanity, or else physically approach the female type, and hypo- and epispadias [malformations of the penis] are common. The female pervert or *Lesbian* rarely differs from others of her sex, except that the active agent is gross, wears mannish attire, and cultivates masculine habits.

Other "perverts" were masochists, sadists, and fetishists; other related conditions were "mania hysteria," nymphomania, and satyriasis.

Alberta Lucille Hart as Dr. Alan L. Hart, from the dust jacket of Hart's *These Mysterious Rays* (New York: Harper, 1946).

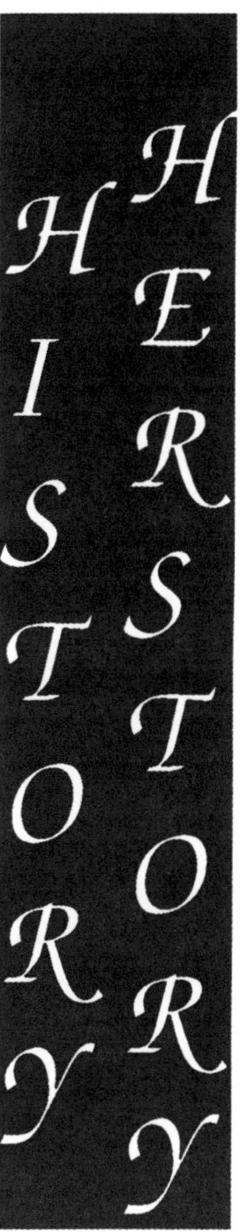

1936, April 12
Dr. Alberta Lucille/Alan Hart:
The Undaunted

In 1917, the twenty-seven-year-old Alberta Lucille Hart adjusted to her earlier erotic and affectional experiences with women by taking steps to pass permanently as a male, Dr. Alan Hart.[50] Hart's early history was recounted (anonymously) in a detailed medical journal article, published in 1920 by Dr. J. Allen Gilbert, a Portland, Oregon, psychiatrist whom Hart had consulted to overcome a fear of loud noises. She ended her analysis with Gilbert by obtaining a hysterectomy, starting to pass as a male, and marrying (in Gilbert's words) a "normal woman" who was "fully cognizant of all the facts." Gilbert's account was excerpted in *Gay American History*, where his subject, whom he had referred to only by the initial "H," was identified as Alberta Lucille Hart—an identification made on the basis of details provided by Gilbert's article.

Further research has now established that the former Alberta Lucille, as Dr. Alan Hart, wrote and published five books, four novels, and a popular account of radiation treatment, a type of medicine in which s/he had specialized.

(reprinted from the **Gay/Lesbian Almanac, A New Documentary** by Jonathan Ned Katz. published by Harper & Row, New York. 1983.)

Marre Alexandra

TSe TSe TerroriSm (herstory)

TSe TSe TerroriSm (1st installment) first appeared in IN YOUR FACE#5, with a slightly different ending. i have decided to change that ending to the one that appears here for the following reasons:

- too many people (male) were vicariously getting off on the violence in the original installment,
  without considering the implications of that violence
- these same people saw the characters (especially molotov cocktail) as one dimensional homicidal maniacs,
  without any real emotions of their own.

Since both of these attributes went completely against my reasons for writing this story, i have decided to change the ending of the 1st installment, without changing (& i emphasize this point) any of of the characters within. They are humyn, with real feelings, concerns, needs & issues, just like those of us who are gender described, outside of the story.

TSe TSe TerroriSm is a continuing novel, in serial form, concerning some members of Toronto's gender described community.

CaiRa

TSe TSe TerroriSm

1st Installment: Fireworks on Carlton

1:00pm, Saturday on the west side of Church, just above Carlton & just after the light rainfall, molotov cocktail, completely in black, hair, eyebrows, leather jacket, skirt, tights & heels, is walking southbound & alone nest to the Gardens. A white Jeep with the top down, pulls up beside her. Four teenaged males. You know the kind.

<<Hey, U. Hey, DYKE? Ha, ha, ha>> [front passenger]

No response from molotov.

<<No, man, <u>IT'S</u> a *guy*. Hey, U, U a guy, eh, faggot?>> [back seat]

Still no response from molotov.

<<What's the matter, queer? Can't talk?>> [front seat again]

molotov crosses the street at Carlton, ignoring the red light & walks along Carlton towards Yonge. The Jeep screeches around the corner, drives past the Gardens, makes a U-turn & stops about 15 feet in front of & facing molotov.

<<Hey, faggot>>

<<Queer>>

<<Dyke>>

<<Gearbox>>

<<Suck my cock, cocksucker>>

<<Fucking faggot>>

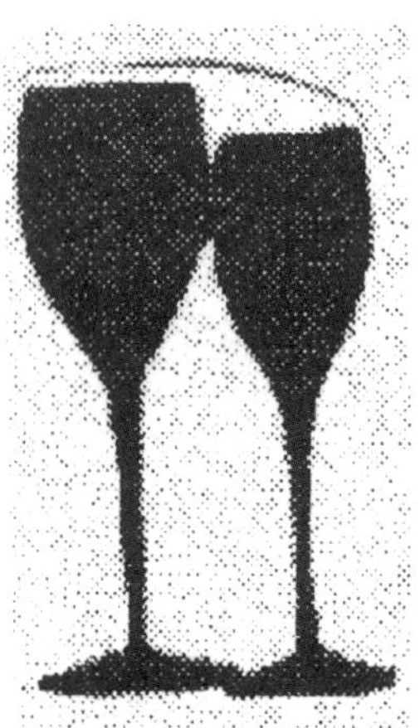

molotov reaches into her purse without stopping & pulls out a purple lighter, cigarette & a large ziplock bag containing a large goblet (see figure on other page) with a pink rayon strip in its mouth. molotov cocktail pulls the goblet out of the bag & lights her cigarette & the strip & tosses the goblet now with flaming strip onto the lap of the astonished front seat passenger. molotov continues walking westward, not once looking back as the goblet explodes into a ball of flame engulfing the Jeep. Two huge Catherine Wheels*, one pink, one blue, as big as suns, rise up out of the fireball, lighting the street, buildings, stores & all the people rushing out onto balconies & pouring out of the restaurants & nearby shops to stare, laugh, applaud, cheer & give deliberately misleading or useless information to the cops, now beginning to arrive in a parade of sirens & lights, to investigate the blackened & smoking carcass that once was a Jeep. molotov continues walking along Carlton towards Yonge. molotov's face is angry, really really angry as she approaches Yonge & Carlton & meets Willow Trees in Autumn, Swordfish & The Scream. No one says anything. Willow looks at molotov's face for a long time & then holds her arms out to molotov. molotov moves into Willow's arms & Willow holds molotov. a strong powerful silence for a lifetime. molotov begins to sob in Willow's arms. Swordfish & The Scream each blow Willow a silent kiss. Willow waves goodbye once with the fingers of her right hand & Swordfish & The Scream walk away in a northerly direction, while Willow continues holding mol, slowly, gently rocking her back & forth & stroking her hair.

CaiRa

Next Installment: molotov & Willow

* A Catherine Wheel is a rarely seen type of firework, looking just like a spinning ferris wheel

TSe TSe TerroriSm

2nd Installment: molotov & Willow

Aeons of time pass. Willow still holds molotov, still rocking her back & forth, still gently & softly stroking her hair. molotov is still sobbing sometimes silently, her head still on Willow's shoulder. Behind Willow, the "street party" (see installment #1) is beginning to end. In the other directions, the evening is darker, quieter, softer, although Yonge St. is still awake.

The sobs gradually begin to subside. Silence, then molotov raises her head, face wet, to face Willow, who offers molotov a kleenex from her jacket pocket. mol accepts, wipes her eyes, face & nose & throws the kleenex in a nearby trash container. She looks around either side of Willow & then at Willow.

<<um, can we, uh, please, go somewhere else? away from here?>>

<<Sure, where would be good?>>

<<anywhere. uh, somewhere quiet, no people, i don't know.>>

<<A restaurant? A café?>>

<<no, i need to be outside. um, i feel too trapped inside. you know?>>

<<Okay. How about the pond behind College Park? No one goes there, so we should be alone.>>

<fine. sure.>>

Willow & molotov start walking, slowly, Willow to the left of mol with her (Willow's) right arm, diagonally around molotov's back. They walk southward on Yonge, west side & circle behind College Park to the Pond, find a quiet bench & sit down. Talking all the time.

<<What happened back there? Are you okay?>> [Willow]

<<yes. it was really horrible, willow, really fucking horrible.

i was walking down church. 4 assholes in a jeep come on to me with the usual genetic/hetero shit <<hey look guys, IT'S a guy>> [in a deep, intolerant male voice], etc, etc, etc, etc, you know the shit, the type. dangerous & stupid & male & white & priviledged. i cross to carlton, south side. they whiz around the corner, like macho-TV-dickhead-land, do a u-turn in front of the donut shop & stop, waiting. a very dangerous situation. very serious. so i open the door, front passenger side & throw in the last one of my special firebombs, right onto their male macho crotches & walk away, while the jeep & four creeps inside go up in flames.

& then - & this is what really pisses me off - & then all these jerks come out of their hiding spots (why am i reminded of the munchkins, the wicked witch of the east & myself as dorothy?) & start celebrating like it's something wonderful & exciting & like i-did-it-all-for-them, instead of the nightmare it really was. it's not a game or a party. i mean, where the fuck were they, when i was being attacked? hiding inside their safe closets, shaking & shivering, but as soon as they see & hear the fireworks, out they come with fucking bells on. those creeps nearly killed, would have killed me for certain - it was that dangerous & here they are, out celebrating. i kill four creeps by setting them on fire because it was necessary. i'd do it again if necessary, but it's nothing to cheer about. it's gross & horrible. i mean, fucking jessica christina, it's a horrible way to die, to be burnt to death, even for creeps like that & i don't care if they would have done it to me, it's still horrible & gross, really fucking goddess-damned

horrible & it's not something i feel like cheering or dancing in the streets for, it's gross, gross, gross & it doesn't solve anything or stop the gendercide or make things better for us (& i mean specifically & only us, gender queers only). we're being slaughtered, really fucking slaughtered & what the fuck makes those fucking genetic cowards think that they can party & jerk off vicariously when one of us (& not them) fight back. what makes them think that they can jerk off vicariously to the violence of that horrible scene. it's so fucking gross & it makes me sick & wanting to throw up & die. & watch tomorrow, they'll have claimed the whole event for themselves (which means for them & not us) & that pisses me off too. as if i don't have enough fucking horrible shit to deal with, i have to fight to take credit for something that really sickens me. i feel like saying to them <<if you get off on violence so much, why don't you do it yourself, assholes, instead of cowering in your cubby holes, waiting for someone to save you & jerking off to the violence of the bloody aftermath?>> >>
<<And of course, the ones on the street were ->>
<<mostly male? genetic males? yes of course, who else are so gross & disgusting & into vicarious violence? & of course, it doesn't matter if they're straight or gay, all genetic white middle class males are equally gross, really fucking gross.
anyways, i felt so fucking angry about the whole scene & even more than that i was really upset about killing those four jerks, so upset that i wanted to throw up & die & that's why i was crying [breath] - & that's why i am crying now.>>
molotov begins to sob again. Willow holds her until mol is ready to continue talking again.
<<what do you want me to do?>> [Willow]
<<hold me, just hold me & stroke my hair, like you've been doing. tell me if you think i'm insane, if i'm some sort of psychotic homicidal maniac, if you still [pause, breath, followed by a sob] like [more sobbing] >>
<<If I still like you? [molotov nods] If i still love you? Yes, molotov cocktail evelyn ann, I still love you. I still like you. Yes I will always like you & love you. Always without conditions or requirements.
[breath] Oh, goddesses, I feel like crying now. However [pause, deep breath] now is not the time.
Okay, my turn for a big speech.
First, I know you're not a psychotic killer at all. Period.
Further, I agree with everything you said. Killing someone isn't glamourous or fun or exciting - it's horrifying & soul destroying - this isn't TV, it's reality. I mean, look at you, you're extremely upset, in shock, you're sickened & you're not about to dance in the street or anywhere else. In fact you probably need to rest for several days until you've recovered. But I agree with you even if it does sound trite: violence never does solve anything. All it does, is create more violence.
Next, I agree totally with your anger towards those bastards, vicariously enjoying & getting off on the whole scene. The next thing that will happen is that the event will be claimed as a major victory for queer - read genetic queer only which means genetic GAY male only - liberation & if you get mentioned at all it will be as a queer (not gender described or transsexual) terrorist. Talk about co-opting. And it is gross & sickening. Okay? Does that help for right now? [a nod of approval] Okay, so let's concentrate on you, now. What about tonight? Right now? What do you feel you need?>>
<<i really would like to go back to the culturalcentre, right now. &, if it's alright with you, um, i'd like to stay with you in your room tonight, um, in your bed & leave the rest til tomorrow.>>
<<Okay. You're sure you can stand my femme-y stereotypically transsexual-designed curtains & interior design? [molotov smiles softly in affirmation] I think it would be fine. And tomorrow we can work out any further problems, as they arise. So let's get out of here & get a cab home.>>
& molotov cocktail evelyn ann & Willow Trees in Autumn do just that, as it starts to rain again.

CaiRa

next installment: the TSTubS

TSe TSe TerroriSm

3rd Installment: the TSTubS

Excerpts from The Scream's journal - three days later:

Well, Goddesses of Amazing Evenings, that was definitely an Amazing Evening, a totally emotionally incredible one. Starting with molotov and followed by Madeline...

[the next section, which deals with the situation on Carlton from The Scream's perspective, has been removed & the reader is asked to read TSe TSe TerroriSm installment# 1 - CaiRa]

Afterwards, Sword & I went to the TSTubS as planned & while we were waiting by the door to get in, I noticed this womyn, red hair immaculately & flawlessly styled & dressed (in a manner that I would kill for but cannot afford & certainly never ever admit to wanting), beautiful face, right out of Vogue & gorgeous red nails. The nails were what I especially noticed, was entranced by: the right ones were long & sharp & I could feel them on my skin, while the left ones, which were just as exciting but in a completely different way, were short, the same length as her fingertips. She was fascinating, no she was gorgeous, really gorgeous.

Sword & I entered, split & I went to my room (#8 - with my favourite vases - the black ones with the Blue Herons) on the 2nd floor, shut the door, had a shower, felt really clean & refreshed, put on my kimono (I know they're really kitsch, but I love them), made some tea (mandarin orange), opened the door, sat down on the futon sofa, had some tea & looking up, saw her there, in the doorway, no longer in her 'street clothes', but instead in a beautiful white camisole.

She came in, sat down, had some tea & exchanged names with me (hers was Madeline - yes based on <u>that</u> Madeline from <u>that</u> book & I was surprised & impressed that she knew the picture where my name comes from & the painter** who painted it), while my nerve endings were jangling (which I have always felt to be really exciting & important). We discussed limits & other things in definite but non-specific terms & ways.*

& then of course we made love. It was wonderful, it was amazing, it was incredible, it was indescribeable, completely different from anything I have been used to, before this & Madeline was/is amazing & yes goddesses, we're going out somewhere sometime soon & I pray to all the goddesses who I can think of, to make it happen really, really soon & I could easily go on & on and on & on about her I probably will & yes I think & hope & feel that yes I, The Scream, Am In Love.

** <u>that</u> book is the infamous childhood book, <u>Madeline</u> by Ludwig Bemelmans*

*** the painting is <u>The Scream</u> by the Norwegian painter, Edvard Munch*

MADELINE

story & pictures by
Ludwig Bemelmans

I'm not going into details (except for one), because it isn't important to me who did what to whom. It's too male & it just isn't me & it's one thing that I am learning about myself & learning to deal with while on this Journey of Exploration. Anyways that's enough polemics for one journal entry. After all I'm not exactly talking to an unsympathetic audience.

To continue with the important thing that I want to talk about: I was sitting on the sofa with my arms by my sides & Madeline softly & gently undid the sash of my kimono. The way the kimono hung down made my arms feel different, much different & so I stretched each arm out straight. My arms felt like wings, like they had become wings, beautiful wings, the most beautiful wings ever & they were mine & even more than that, they were & are a part of me, my wings & they made me beautiful (or so I thought at the time), but no, I realize now with tears of denied truth streaming down my face, it only brought out the beauty that was always there inside of me. That I had spent a whole lifetime searching for in others, but was afraid to acknowledge in myself.

Until now.

I was finally able to say that I am beautiful.

& not only was I beautiful, I felt strong, a strong womyn. & it was so important & incredible & powerful & I am crying now while writing this, it is so important to me & my life. I have always wanted wings: butterfly wings, bird wings, just wings, beautiful wings. I have wanted to fly so desperately for so long, watching the swallows, the swifts, the terns & the hummingbirds perform. I have wanted to be one of them so badly. Or like the eagles or the albatrosses soaring high above the land & oceans. I still remember as a young girl, seeing this huge manta ray, beautiful black & white, fly out of this tiny canal in Florida, fly out of the water effortlessly on these huge wings, way over my head, fly up & then down in a slow, graceful arc & just as gracefully return to the water. Everything else except for me, it seemed, could fly. Why else would I go into paleontology studies at U of T to specialize not in dinosaurs or wooly mammoths like the other students (mostly boys I've noticed. Boys with the same world view as male engineers)? Why instead would I want to specialize in early Mesozoic birds & (even more importantly & hopefully) Mesozoic pterosaurs, if I didn't imagine myself as a beautiful & huge Pteranodon, floating over the Cretaceous world, ever since I was six years old?

So finally I had my wings & even though I felt really foolish, I flapped my wings experimentally & cautiously a few time & then throwing caution & myself to the winds, I flew, I flew, I flew around the room. & I was beautiful. & I felt beautiful. Finally.

I landed in front of Madeline. & kissed her & held her wrapped up in my beautiful wings & told her what a beautiful gift she had given me & what it meant to me & thanked forever & ever and ever & ever. And I cried then, just as I am crying now, because it was so wonderful. And she held onto me for a lifetime & finally I started to giggle hersterically & she giggled too & together & alternatively we recited that verse about Madeline from that book (see facing page) - the one that inspired Madeline & gave her, her name - while continuing to make love & giggle uncontrollably.

And it still is beautiful to see it on these pages. Scream, Scream, Scream, I am beautiful. & I still feel beautiful. Beautiful & Strong & Powerful.

CaiRa

Next installment: The morning after

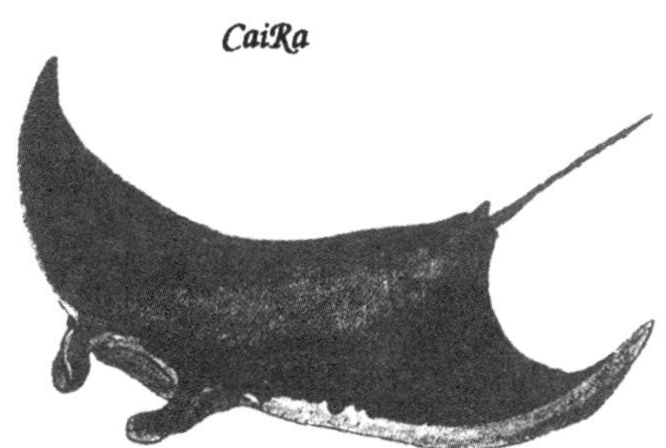

Atlantic Manta Ray
Manta birostris

MEETINGS & UPCOMING EVENTS

April 25
March on Washington for Lesbian, Gay, Bisexual & Transgender Equal Rights & Liberation
PO Box 34607
Washington, DC
20043-4607

May 12
gendertroublemakers Premiere
a video by Jeanne B. & Xanthra Phillippa
at the Euclid Theatre,
as part of the opening of Queer Sites
call 978-4274
Julia or Fadi for details

May 13
Spew III (a queer- & genderzine festival) at Buddies in Bad Times
call 978-4274 for details

GROUPS

Canadian Crossdressers' Club
921-6112 (24 hrs)

Transition Support
meets every 2nd & 4th Fridays
at 519 Church St., East Room
from 7-10pm
TV, TG, TS & SO (significant others) run support group

Fetish Nites
1st & 3rd Thursdays
at Boots
592 Sherbourne St.
921-0665

ISSUES & CONCERNS FOR THE FUTURE

here is an incomplete list of issues that we will try to deal with in future issues of **gendertrash**

TS's & anonymity
TS's & politics
spaces & places of our own
TS parents
TS youth
TS's & isolation
TS's & medicine
TS her/history
true gender positive behaviour
reaching our community
TS's & HIV/AIDS
TS run community centre
TS's & prostitution
TS's & racism
TS's & the queer communities
TS's & employment
TS's & housing
TS run SRS clinics
electrolysis
TS sexuality
TS's & social supports
TS's as a separate gender
TS's & our lovers
TS's & our families
linking with other groups
TS's & the police

please let us know of any other issues that you would like to see discussed in **gendertrash**

CLASSIFIEDS

Classifieds are a way to communicate with others within the gender communities. They do not have to be only personal ads, but can also be advertising for such things as services, groups, etc. Classifieds are free for individuals (including sex trade workers) & not-for-profit groups. Please send in your classified ad (please not too long) & before the 15th of the issues's 2nd month & we'll try to print it in the next issue.

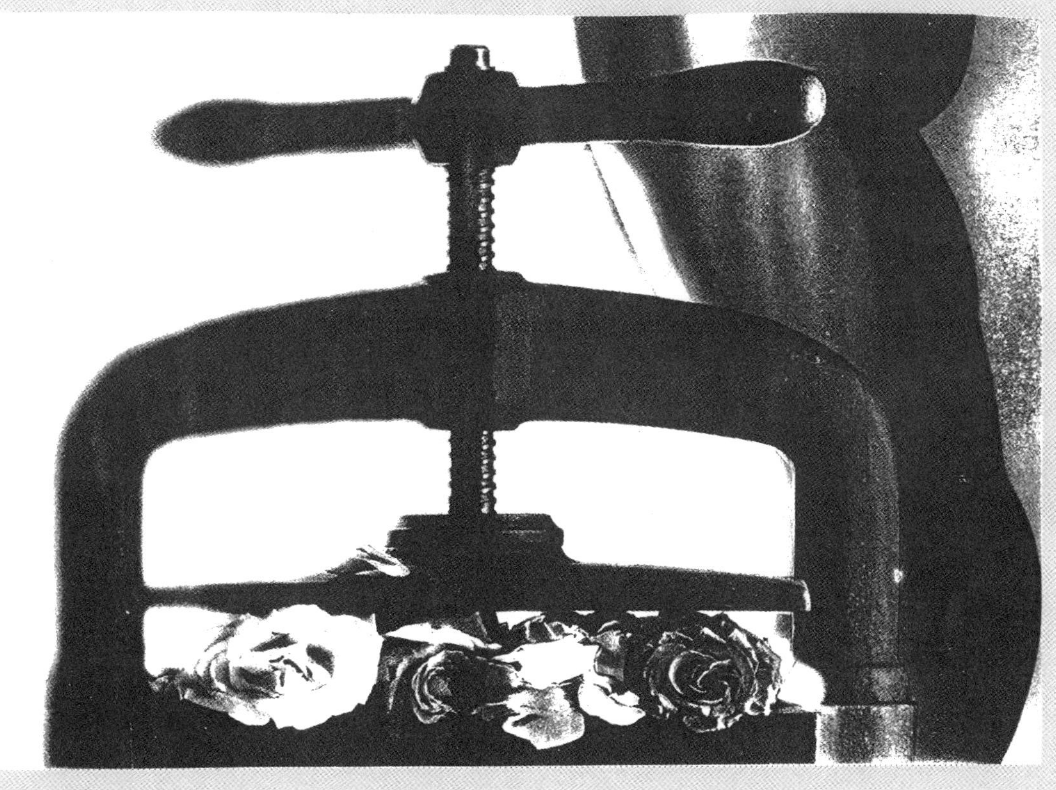

CAUSE WE'RE JUST AS

QUEER AS DYKES AND FAGS

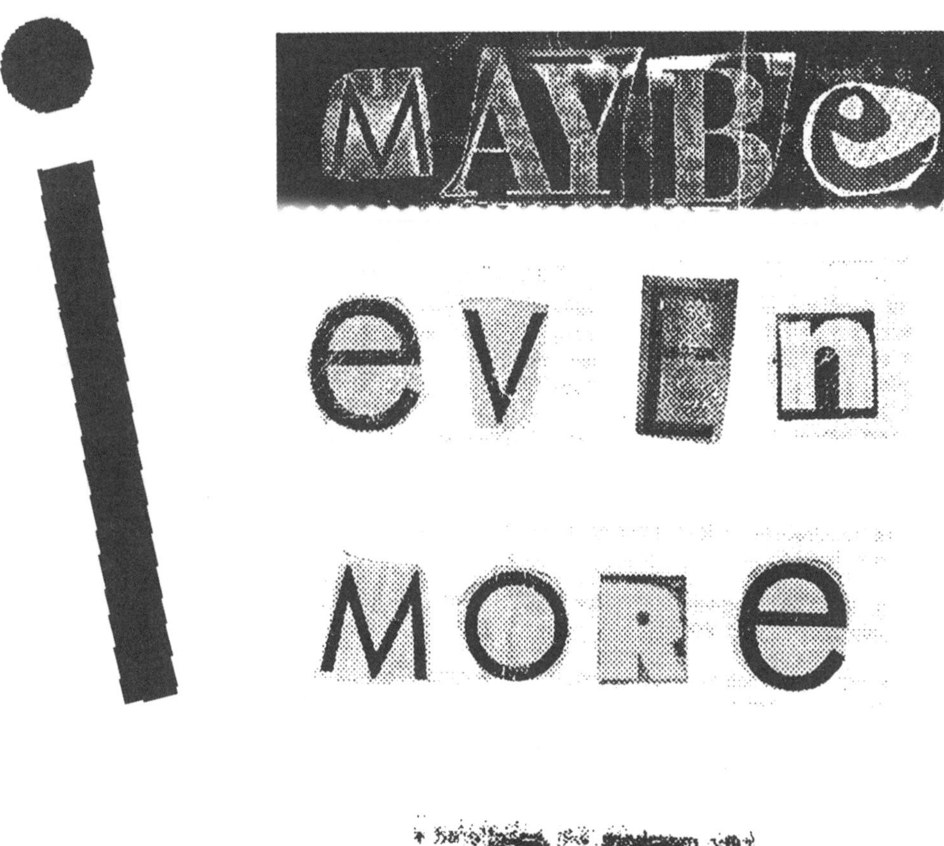

!

GENDERTRASH

ISSUE 2

FALL 1993

Fall 1993 *Issue 2 Volume 1* $4.00

Thanks

to: ***V, Davina Anne Gabriel** & **Janis Walworth** for providing us with the material about transsexuals at MWMF & **Gender Myths**.*

***Kiwi**, who acted as our personal researcher.*

***Mylène** & **Françoise**, who sent us every single article on **Le sexe des étoiles**, ever published in Québec.*

everybody who submitted material, sent letters or expressed their support.

& everyone who purchased our first issue

Donations

*Because **gendertrash** is run by a few starving individuals & funded entirely out of their own pockets, it is essential to ask for donations of money, resources (such as printing, paper, envelopes, address labels, stamps and so on) & equipment (computer, software, etc).*

Thank you
*from **gendertrash***

Submission

We are presently working on an upcoming issue about **transsexuality & sexuality**. We'd love to receive your pictures, drawings, thoughts, pillow stories, ideas, concerns (hot or cold), articles & sweet dreams.

Talk to us about love or sex or both.

We especially encourage submissions from transsexuals, who love other transsexuals. Gender-oriented genetics (ie attracted to TS') are also requested to submit.

gendertrash vol 1 issue 2

gendertrash is published 3 or 4 times a year & gives a voice to gender described people, who have been discouraged from speaking out & communicating with each other

editor
χanthra ρhillippa

political & production process supervisor
Jeanne B.

contributors
Encephalitis Red
Jeanne B.
Mylène P.
Norma
χanthra ρhillippa CaiRa
Isis
Kiwi
Françoise L.
Janis Walworth

about the covers
Front photo - Petra Chevrier (model)
Hill Peppard (photographer)
Back cover - Encephalitis Red (artist)

image processing
Petra Chevrier

layout & design
Jeanne B. χanthra ρhillippa

publisher
genderpress

mailing address & phone number
Box #500-62,
552 church st.,
Toronto, Ont
M4Y 2E3
1-(416)-929-2350

submissions can be typed or handwritten, but should be double spaced & must be legible. please include a brief bio. name, phone # & address are necessary for verification purposes only. anonymity will be preserved if wished. submission does not necessarily mean publication. submitted material cannot be returned, so please don't send us originals. submissions may be edited for length or clarity.

index

gendertrash is devoted to the issues & concerns of transsexuals. **gendertrash** also welcomes input from gender positive genetics.

in addition to issues of gender hate & oppression, **gendertrash** is equally opposed to any other forms of systemic oppression by those who are in positions of power.

Theory mutilates
Surgery liberates!

NO YOU CAN'T

To all those
genetic gay men
who all say that they understand our anger &
where it comes from
while continuing to transie-bash us,
deny us our distinctiveness,
ridicule us,
call our lovers **gay**,
take all **our** M->F heroines & herstories for their own &
speak for & over us
i just want to say **no you can't**

To all those
genetic lesbians
who want to be part of the gender described communities
while still defining themselves as genetic wimmin &
TS wimmin as genetic males,
who continue to label all **our** F->M heroes & histories as theirs
under the guise of reclaiming
i just want to say **no you can't**

To all those
genetics
who have refused to accept our gender identities,
who insist on identifying us by societal gender codes,
who insist that we are agents of the patriarchy &
who use their power & priviledge to deny us any public access
where we might try to contest their messages of hate
i just want to say **no you can't**

To all those
genetics
who insist on treating us as poor suffering victims
while refusing to do anything of real substance to prevent
or end our victimization
i just want to say **no you can't**

To all those
liberal genetics
who want to talk about us
being able to go to a genetic wimmin-only festival
but who won't talk about us having emergency shelters
rape crisis centres &
transie-bashing hotlines
that can really support us
at those times when we really need them
i just want to say **no you can't**

To all those
genetic psychiatrists & their kind
who insist on keeping control over our lives,
who continue to maim us
physically,
emotionally,
socially &
psychically,
in the names of their gender hating theories
stained with our blood
i just want to say **no you can't**

To all those
really politically liberal genetics &
their organizations
who, realizing that transgendered rights are the next big fad
think that they can appear politically okay
by tacking the word **transgendered** at the end
of their group's title,
while doing absolutely nothing to promote transgendered rights &
everything they can to prevent, hinder &/or
limit acceptance of those rights
i just want to say **no you can't**

To all those
organizations
that call themselves **queer** in order to appear more inclusive
but are really just for lesbians & gays & their issues only
i just want to say **no you can't**

NO YOU CAN'T (continued)

To all those
emergency support agencies
who say that we can come to them in times of crisis
while knowing nothing about us or
refusing to learn about us & our specific needs,
without any gender described people on staff or
at most one for appearances only,
who insist that if we do go to them for support
that we keep our backgrounds completely hidden &
who then wonder why we don't feel safe or welcomed by them
if we call them at all
i just want to say **no you can't**

To all those
others, too numerous to mention
who i have left out
but who have attacked us in equally numerous ways,
who have made our lives a nightmare of an endurance test,
denying us our gender identities,
control over our lives, bodies & culture
i just want to say **no you can't**

To all those
gender described people
who continue to follow their true gender paths
with strong gender described courage,
despite the vast array of genetics who oppose us
at every single point of our lives
i just want to say **yes you can**

xanthra phillippa
with gender described
love, support & editing
from jeanne b.

A **Transie** Story

(a **transie** story for **transie**-haters who still insist on calling us **transies**)

i went to the **transie** variety store
got a **transie** newspaper
& a **transie** chocolate bar or **transie** bar
i ate the **transie** bar
i decided to get a **transie** coffee
& a **transie** muffin
so i went next door to the **transie** donut shop
& did just that,
while reading my **transie** newspaper
afterwards i decided to go home
on the way, i was **transie**-bashed
(because we **transies** don't get queerbashed)
& then **transie**-gang-raped
while all the **transie** haters
laughed at me
& my situation
& applauded the **transie**-bashers
& **transie**-rapists
somehow i got home to find myself evicted
by my **transie**-hating landlord
the Ontario Human Rights Commission refused
to hear my claim,
because **transies** aren't covered
by their legislation

hope you find this really funny
ho ho ho

Xanthra Phillippa

Star Wars
The Empire Strikes Back

*Intro: **Le sexe des étoiles** (based on the novel by Monique Proulx - directed by Baillargeon, script by Monique Proulx) was the opening film for the 17th annual Montréal World Film Festival, receiving widespread approval from francophone Québec critics. This article was submitted previously to various mainstream publications in Montréal, but was refused (another example of how we are censored & prevented from speaking for ourselves).*

At the end of the film, **The Crying Game**, Dil the transsexual, in legitimate self-defense, kills Jude, who got her man with her authentically genetic "tits and ass". Jude is a violent, insensitive woman who has a gun on the brain, lacking it somewhere else.

Due to this movie achieving a certain success, Monique Proulx & Paule Baillergeon, have decided to avenge all the Judes of this planet. The film presents the passage from childhood to adolescence of a young girl whose father has suddenly decided to "change sex". This so-called transsexual is presented as a caricature of a woman, pre-occupied with preening herself, sewing, seeking a handsome & rich man to take care of her and hopping from drag queen bar to drag queen bar - in two words, an egotistical & irresponsible being who's ready to sell his daughter if he needs to. The scriptwriters have neglected to tell us how this brilliant scientist has been able to live in New York City without a penny or especially how he's been able, all of a sudden, to become such a monster. B-grade westerns are not cluttered with such details.

In an interview with Le Devoir, Paule Baillergeon said " Remove the transsexual and you have a story that everyone lives". A question naturally comes to our minds: why then did you put him there? Because, like certain newspapers know only too well, freaks sell. You don't have to justify their presence, you just show them.

Where does this hatred come from? A certain group of feminists accuse transsexuals of reinforcing feminine stereotypes, putting the accent on appearance, which is not essential in a woman, and behaving in fact like teenage girls. Transsexuality is a transition phase, at the conclusion of which a person defines themselves as a man or a woman with a transsexual past. During this transition,

these people pass through a stage where they imitate role models, like teenagers. Some stay teenagers longer than others, just like in the standard population. But teenage girls are still women.

The intentions of Monique Proulx & Paule Bailargeon were not honourable: They used a minority they know little, if anything, about for their own purposes (such as the advancement of their own careers), while reinforcing widely-held anti-transsexual prejudices & hatred. First of all, choosing a very masculine looking man to play the character of Marie-Pierre is offensive in itself. Why not choose a woman to play the role (like Vanessa Redgrave in **Second Serve**) or why not simply a real transsexual? Answering that there were no transsexuals able to play the character, reminds us of the response given to women, who were asking why there weren't more female company presidents.

We see that there was a deliberate motive in excluding us: Marie-Pierre is finally a man dressed up as a woman. This motive of exclusion comes from transsexuality's perceived threat to society's notions of gender identity.

Who are they to decide who is or isn't a woman? A woman isn't only an "ass and tits"... she's not just a menstruating being either, as is suggested at the end of **Le sexe des étoiles**. Post-menopausal women are women too.

Behind this abstract debate, there are some human beings who have survived this transition, who are trying to be part of this society & who weren't lucky enough to be able to change their workplace. On a daily basis, they face the scorn of jealous people, scorn that is subsidized by the contributions of the NFB. Since the impact of the cinema on public opinion is very strong, have Proulx & Baillargeon stopped to consider the effects of their film on transsexuals with children?

But nobody has to worry, those transsexuals won't be doing demonstrations like other groups did outside **Basic Instinct**. The price would be too high. The subject matter demanded research, understanding & respect, which Proulx & Baillargeon have chosen to ignore. For that reason, **Le sexe des étoiles** is not comparable to **The Crying Game**, with which they're trying to compete so pathetiquely.

Mylène P.
Françoise L.

(translated from the French by Jeanne B. & Xanthra Phillippa)

Hi Hi Hi Genetics!

Welcome to the Genetic Jerk Quiz

take this simple & easy test to see how much of a genetic jerk you really are

Ready to start?

Okay here we go Just check off the answer that describes your feelings

---

	Yes	No
Transsexuals are victims	☐	☐
Transsexuals are rapists	☐	☐
Transsexuals are traitors	☐	☐
Transsexuals are just self mutilated transvestites or drag queens/kings	☐	☐
Transsexuals are all male-to-female	☐	☐
Transsexuals are anti-social	☐	☐
Transsexuals are selfish	☐	☐
Transsexuals are dangerous	☐	☐
Transsexuals are poorly adjusted	☐	☐
Transsexuals are psychologically unbalanced	☐	☐
Transsexuals are fucked up	☐	☐
Transsexuals are power, glory or attention-seeking	☐	☐
Transsexuals are really just lesbians/gays who can't handle their orientation	☐	☐

	Yes	No
Transsexuals will always be male/female no matter what they say	☐	☐
Transsexuals are uncaring	☐	☐
Transsexuals are asexual/asensual	☐	☐
Transsexuals are gross	☐	☐
Transsexuals are freaks	☐	☐
Transsexuals are ridiculous	☐	☐
Transsexuals are homophobic when they complain about their treatment by lesbians & gays	☐	☐
Transsexuals are cute/funny	☐	☐
Transsexuals are this years's political fad	☐	☐
Transsexuals are cool to be with	☐	☐
Transsexuals are sad	☐	☐
Transsexuals are depressed	☐	☐
Transsexuals are suicidal	☐	☐
Transsexuals are unrealistic	☐	☐
Transsexuals are impractical	☐	☐
Transsexuals are incapable of forming interpersonal relationships	☐	☐
Transsexuals are psychotic killers	☐	☐
Transsexuals are trying to take over the Lesbian-Feminist Movement	☐	☐
Transsexuals are apolitical	☐	☐

SCORING

(count all yes' as 1 & no's as 0)

0-5	**c'mon give us a break - who are you trying to fool**
6-10	**pretty bad, better work on it, really hard**
11-15	**real genetic jerk - time to learn how to think**
16-20	**genetic creep**
21-25	**what are you doing, reading this zine? Go read one for genetic bigots**
26+	**a total genetic pig - you should be on display somewhere**

HOPE YOU ENJOY BEING A BIGOT

Conversation with Tristan

the following conversation was aired as part of ***Transsexual Perspective****, a one-time radio show on CKLN, at the beginning of July, 1993*

Jeanne - We would like you to talk about the situation for FTM's in Montréal.

Tristan - Recently, we just started a group here and we tried to make the other FTM's realize that, you know, from a surgical point, it's very hard here to obtain the last surgery.

We tried to make it clear to the guys that if they don't stick together & do something about it, the doctors won't wake up one morning & say: "Hey let's do operations for FTM's".

If we want to improve the quality of the life that we want to live, we'll have to get together to start committees, researching... start to talk about what we want & write down what we need... get our lives better...

The guys now understand why we have to get together once in a while so we can start the process of going ahead a little bit.

Jeanne - How is it in terms of resources right now, whether it's in Montréal, the rest of Canada or the States? Is it getting better?

Tristan - The resources are practically non-existent yet.

We almost don't have anything written on us. You can see that most of the books written, are usually about MTF's. You can get a lot of information about MTF's, but on FTM's, you get just a little tiny piece at the end of the book.

Usually what we see, is after the transition, the new man is going into life and isn't looking back. He doesn't want to have anything to do with it anymore.

What we're trying to explain to them is that they don't need to go back. Helping others has nothing to do with going back to the transition. It's just putting yourself more ahead. It's helping you living your life now. It's helping you not to forget who you are and where you come from.

Involving yourself doesn't mean showing your face to the world. You're showing your face only to people who are looking up to you.

Jeanne - Right, that's one of the problems with TS'. Many of us want to be discreet, to totally pass off as genetic & not be visible or speak out. At the same time, because we want to be discreet, we don't get anything in return, in terms of our health, in terms of resources. It's very important, 'cause in the transition, we all need role models.

Xanthra - What about the relationship with the MTF community?

Tristan - It's weird... That's a good issue, you're bringing up...

I guess, well... I'm gonna be frank with you, when there's a whole bunch of guys together, they have this tendency to say "we have nothing to do with them". That's the way they think because usually they say "we're dealing here with men stuff".

And this is a social thing. They think "female matters have nothing to do with male matters". Even TS' have a tendency to think that way.

I tell the others that "it's not good to think like that. The crisis that you're going through right now, is similar to what they go through. We should stick together..."

It's not an issue of competition; it's more that they don't understand what the others are going through.

Xanthra - Do you perceive that this misunderstanding or lack of understanding is coming from MTF's also, so that they're not communicating with FTM's?

Tristan - Well you're making a good point. I never thought of it that way. It might be. I can't possibly answer that question. Because it's like too open, you know.

Jeanne - The question is more, socially do they get along well together? I mean, outside of cruising each other? (laughter)

Tristan - Yeah sure, but I really think that it depends on the group. Because you could have two groups that get along really well & suddenly, you know, after a couple of months, there are new people & it doesn't work any more. I think it has to do with individuals more than groups.

Xanthra - Can we ask about what surgeries are now available for FTM's?

Tristan - Yes, sure. You have different sort of mastectomies now available & the surgeons are getting very, very good at them now. You can get high quality for a better price now. It sounds a little bit like business, but it is a business.

Xanthra - We've always got to think about money.

Tristan - Yes and now we are setting up a surgery committee for FTM's here in Montréal. We brought a urologist, we also have a plastic surgeon, one of the greatest in the world, Dr. Ménard. He's not doing any FTM SRS' right now, but he's researching it.

He's supposed to meet with & assist with the surgeon who does it in California. That's where most of us go right now, because there's no one doing it in Montréal.

Jeanne - And what about the results?

Tristan - Well, the results are not that fantastic from what I've heard. What I've seen seems to work great for me, but, you know, it has so much to do with the physical health and background of the patient, that the results are different from one person to another.

What Dr. Ménard said is "bring me something that works, something that will improve the quality of life & I'll do it". That's why we started the committee here. We're doing a lot of research & are planning to be able to get the surgery in Montréal for next year maybe*.

That's also why we tell the guys "if we don't stick together & yell for what we want, we'll never get anything".

* in a recent phone conversation with Dr. Menard's office, we were told that FTM SRS' will be performed by Dr. Menard within six months. They have already started the waiting list for the surgery. For more information, please contact Dr. Menard at 1-514-229-5656.

Xanthra - You have a child. Can I ask how old she is?

Tristan - She's 2.

Xanthra - That's a great age. 'Cause she's very young & you don't have to explain to her what you're going through right now.

Tristan - Yes, but you know, eventually I'll have to explain to her what I've been through. It's been a very difficult issue for me, because I was asking myself "am I gonna tell her or not?" The dilemma is still there. Sometimes I feel like a liar and people say "never lie to your child".

She's now starting to ask "where is Mommy?" What do you answer to that... I finally found one: I said "Mom is in our hearts." For now she's taking it, but in a few years, she'll want to know "yes, but where?" I bet when the time will come she'll be ready. I've always believed that when children are old enough to ask questions, they're old enough to have the answers...

"MISTER... JES KEEP YOUR JUNGIAN ANALYSIS TO YO'SELF... YOU HEAR?" GROWLED MRS. BOTHAM

courtesy of ***Boy's Own****, No. 9, May 1*[st]*, 1993*

Transsexuals and AIDS: The State of the Research

by kiwi

How much do we know about transsexuals and AIDS? We all know that AIDS affects the transgendered communities greatly, but what kind of research is being done? What still needs to be done?

If you do a computer search for all documented articles on AIDS, spanning scientific, medical, and sociological journals, you will find 34, 304 entries. This means that since about 1982, 34,304 articles have been written about AIDS - some of these are research studies, some are descriptive articles, all deal with AIDS.

Of these 34,304, how many deal with transsexuals? 4. More than a decade into the epidemic, and we have 4 srticles on the subject. Normally, when you use this AIDS database (CD-ROM, available at most University libraries now), you can correlate issues. So if you want to find out about education programmes for bisexual men, you cross-list these terms. In this case, you would come up with 88 articles. But in the case of transsexuals, you can't cross-list it with anything! The references are so scattered and seemingly insignificant, that you can only access them by typing in **transsexuals**. Forget trying to find an article on education programmes for transsexuals, forget trying to distinguish between pre- and post-operative transsexuals, forget trying to account for the crossovers between transsexuals and sex trade workers. 4 articles is all you get.

Some of the research which is available is quite cool (and desperately needed!). Here's a summary:

1 - **Efficiency of health education programme of AIDS awareness among transsexuals** Singapore Medical Journal Feb 1990 31., pp. 33-7. Claims that of 71 transsexual subjects interviewed, there is an increased awareness of AIDS, but not much change in safe sex practices.

2 - **HIV seroprevalence and its implications for a transsexual population**. International AIDS Conference, June 4-9 1989, 5: p.748. Shows an HIV seroprevalence of 21% among transsexuals, prostitution incidence of 75%. 58 transsexuals interviewed.

3 - **Transsexuals - don't think about them and they go away ... and die!** (cool title) International AIDS Conference, Jul 19-24 1992. 8(2): D452. Basically states that TS and TV populations have been overlooked in the available research.

4 - **HIV and North American Aboriginal Peoples** InternationalConference on AIDS, June 16-21 1991 7(1): 357. Survey of HIV incidence in aboriginal populations. 5% of people interviewed were transsexuals, but TS' indicated a 25% HIV infection rate.

Transsexual Womyn Expelled From Michigan Womyn's Music Festival

WALHALLA, MI - Four postoperative male-to-female transsexual lesbians were expelled from the 18th annual Michigan Womyn's Music Festival (MWMF) by festival security staff on the third day of the event. The four womyn, who had undergone sex change surgery from 2 to 14 years earlier, and a nontranssexual supporter attended the festival to raise consciousness among the participants about the festival's policy of excluding transsexual womyn, the unclear and contradictory statement of policy in the festival literature, and issues of gender in general. Womyn opposed to transsexuals at MWMF attempted to silence them by destroying their educational materials.

Left to right: Nancy Burkholder, Rica Frederickson, Wendi Kaiser, Janis Walworth, and Davina Gabriel next to banner put up across from MWMF main gate. 8/13/93

photo by unknown festival participant

The five womyn arrived at the festival on Monday, August 9, and none encountered any difficulty gaining admittance to the festival. One of the transsexual womyn was Nancy Burkholder of New Hampshire, who had been expelled from the festival in 1991; she purchased her ticket at the front gate without incident. The other transsexual womyn were Davina Gabriel of Missouri, Wendi Kaiser of Maine, and Rica Fredrickson of Pennsylvania.

The next day, the five womyn set up a table at which they distributed literature and buttons and asked womyn who opposed the exclusionary policy to sign a petition seeking its repeal. The four transsexual womyn freely discussed their experiences as transsexuals with festival participants who approached the table.

On Tuesday and Wednesday the five did workshifts in the kitchen, at the medical and emotional support areas, and at the Sober Support tent. Transsexual womyn provided medical care, including taking a hemorrhaging womon to an area hospital in the middle of the night, extended a helping hand to those in need of friendly support, and prepared food. They also attended concerts, ate meals, took showers, and shopped in the crafts bazaar with other festival participants, without incident.

At approximately 4:30pm on Thursday, Janis Walworth of Massachusetts, the nontranssexual member of the party, and Kaiser, who were staffing at the literature table, were approached by two womyn, one of whom identified herself as MWMF security coordinator. She told Walworth that the transsexual womyn were in violation of the festival's "womyn-born womyn" only policy, and that they must therefore leave the festival. Walworth replied that it was not clear that the transsexual womyn were in violation of the policy as stated, since they all identify as womyn-born womyn.

The security coordinator went on to say that some of the festival participants had complained about the presence of transsexual womyn at the festival, asking security to remove the transsexual womyn from the land and vowing to take matters into their own hands if security did not do so. Security felt, therefore, that it could no longer guarantee the safety of the transsexual womyn. In addition, the security womyn were reluctant to assure Walworth that she would continue to be safe at the festival, since she had been seen staffing the literature table and associating with the transsexual womyn.The festival catalogue calls upon womyn who attend the festival to dialogue and listen to one another and explicitly states that "violence against womyn in any form is not acceptable in this community, on this land". However, no apparent action was taken against the womyn who threatened Walworth and the transsexual womyn.

The security coordinator pointed out that members of the party had been openly discussing their transsexuality at the literature table, thus alerting many womyn to the fact that there were transsexuals on the land. She implied that if they had not revealed their transsexuality to anyone, they would not have been asked to leave - in effect, "don't ask, don't tell".

The four transsexual womyn returned to their campsite and packed up their belongings. However, they were delayed in leaving the festival grounds until approximately 11:00pm because so many womyn stopped them on their way out to express support. A contingent of leatherwomyn offered to guarantee the safety of the transsexual womyn at their campsite for the duration of the festival and strongly attempted to dissuade them from leaving. However, the transsexual womyn collectively decided to honor their agreement with security and declined the offer.

Michigan Womyn's Festival (Continued)

Davina Gabriel in the MWMF communal shower.
photo by unknown festival participant

Upon leaving the festival site, the transsexual womyn set up camp across the road on National Forest land. The following morning, they set up another literature table, along with neon pink banners proclaiming "Transsexual Womyn Expelled From Festival" and "Too Out To Be In!" A steady stream of womyn came out from the festival to spend time with the transsexual womyn and express their support; they brought vegetables, soda, hamburgers, fried chicken, flowers, and encouragement. Throughout the remainder of the festival, the transsexual womyn continued to distribute literature and buttons and to talk with womyn about gender issues and the exclusionary policy. Festival participants who visited the transsexual womyn reported that sentiment inside the festival was overwhelmingly supportive of their participation in WMWF, and there was outrage at their expulsion.

Inside the festival, nontranssexual womyn helped staff the inside literature table, and Walworth conducted two sessions of a workshop entitled "Confronting Transphobia", as well as a workshop on gender and shamanism which had been scheduled to be presented by Gabriel.

On Friday evening, the transsexual womyn were joined by a fifth transsexual womon, Riki Anne Wilchins of New York City, who flew in to present her workshop, "21 Things You Don't Say to a Transsexual". Although Wilchins had originally planned to enter the festival, she chose to remain outside with the four expelled transsexual womyn. Womyn inside the festival who wanted to attend Wilchins' workshop unanimously agreed to move the location to the area outside the front gate. Approximately 75 womyn walked the mile to attend the two workshop sessions.

Saturday morning, when the literature table inside the festival was left unattended for a short time, all literature, buttons, display racks, signed petitions, and completed survey forms, as well as a donation can and personal property, were stolen by undetermined individuals. A womon reported seeing some of the buttons deposited in a portable toilet, which Walworth reported to MWMF security in hopes of avoiding damage to sewage pumps.

Also on Saturday, Walworth and Laura Ervin of Massachusetts, who had travelled to the festival with Burkholder in 1991, met with feminist author Kay Leigh Hagan, who was acting as an official representative of the festival producers, and the security coordinator. At that meeting, Hagan disclosed that the festival producers, Barbara Price and Lisa Vogel, are the sole determiners of festival policy and that she did not anticipate that they would change the antitranssexual policy in the near future.

Transsexual women ready to depart after being told by Security that they had to leave the Festival.
photo by unknown festival participant

Results of 1992 Gender Survey at Michigan Womyn's Music Festival

by Janis Walworth

A total of 633 surveys were collected. There were about 7500 women at MWMF, so this represents a response of approximately 8.4%. The survey asked, "Do you think male-to-female transsexuals should be welcome at Michigan?" *Yes* responses numbered 463 (73.1%) and *no* answers totaled 143 (22.6%). Twenty-seven surveys (4.3%) had indeterminate responses such as "I'm not sure" or did not answer this question. The margin of error is 3.8%.

Given these results, the chance that the majority of 7500 MWMF participants believe transsexuals should *not* be admitted would be less than 1 in 100,000. This calculation assumes that our sample was randomly selected, which it certainly was not. It is probable that women in favour of transsexual inclusion were more likely to fill out surveys than those against it. On the other hand, many would-be Festigoers were not here to fill out surveys precisely because they objected to the anti-transsexual policy. Our impression as we talked to women and asked them to fill out surveys was that most had stopped by our table by chance or to learn about gender issues. Fewer came specifically to fill out surveys, and both positive and negative views were represented in this group. However, even if *half* of the *yes* are attributed to the bias of the sample and eliminated from the calculation, there is still a better than 999 in 1000 chance that most Festigoers would welcome transsexuals.

The reasons Festigoers gave for wanting to *exclude* transsexuals (with numbers giving these responses) were:

They are not women . . . . (23)
They are not women-born women . . . . (16)
They make others uncomfortable . . . . (15)
They have been socialized as males . . . . (12)
They have had male priviledge . . . . (10)
They think like men . . . . (8)
They have male energy . . . . (7)
They have penises . . . . (6)
They have different life experiences . . . . (6)
They are biologically men . . . . (5)
People shouldn't change their sex . . . . (5)
They have not been girls in the patriarchy . . . (4)
They are oppressors . . . . (4)
They behave like men . . . . (4)
They have not been oppressed as women . . . . (4)
They are too feminine . . . . (3)

Reasons given for *including* transsexuals were:

They are women	(75)
They identify as women	(67)
They have made a commitment to womanhood	(38)
They have been through enough	(35)
We should not oppress others	(32)
They have chosen to be women	(26)
We should be inclusive	(30)
We should not judge an individual's choice	(20)
They can benefit from the women's community	(19)
Internally they are women	(17)
They are oppressed as women	(11)
They are living as women	(11)
They share women's goals and perspectives	(10)
They are not threatening	(10)
We should encourage diversity	(8)
We cannot determine who is transsexual	(8)
Gender is in the mind	(8)
They have given up male priviledge	(7)
They deserve our support	(7)
Their condition is not their fault	(7)
We can learn from transsexuals	(6)
We have no definition of "women"	(5)
Legally they are women	(4)
We should all unite	(4)
Their socialization is not so different from ours	(3)
They have been no problem in the past	(3)
It's behaviour that's important	(3)

In both the above lists, multiple responses were recorded when respondents gave more than one answer. Responses given by only one or two people were omitted.

Of women who were in favour of transsexual inclusion, 48 specified that only those who have had genital surgery should be welcome. Of the 27 who gave equivocal answers, 9 stated that those who have had surgery would be acceptable. Six of those against inclusion cited the fact that transsexuals have penises as a reason to exclude them, suggesting that even some of these women might not object to postoperative transsexuals.

Call for Submissions

Davina Anne Gabriel, editor of TransSisters, is collecting material for an upcoming anthology about transsexual wimmin, who have experienced discrimination in feminist communities or at feminist events. Anyone interested can contact her through TransSisters, 4004 Troost Ave, Kansas City, Missouri, USA 64110.

MWMF Survey Results (continued)

In answer to the question, "What is the best way to determine whether an individual is a male-to-female transsexual?" there was a considerable range of opinion. Of the 227 responses, 126 were from those against transsexual inclusion, 86 from women in favour of inclusion, and 15 from those without a clear opinion about inclusion.

Ask them	(50)
Trust them to be honest	(39)
Don't know	(26)
Announce the policy clearly	(21)
Check their genitals	(18)
There is no accurate way to tell	(14)
Driver's license or picture ID	(9)
There is no dignified way to tell	(9)
Self-identification should be sufficient	(9)
We shouldn't try	(8)
Surgery should be complete	(5)
By their behaviour	(4)
Genetic testing	(3)
Birth certificate	(3)
Written exam or questionnaire	(3)
Medical certificate	(3)

In addition, two each were in favour of interviews, having a friend vouch for them, and intuition. One each endorsed a doctor's physical exam, a medical/psychiatric history, testosterone levels, and bone structure. A few stressed that no crossdressers (male, it is presumed) or female impersonators should be allowed. Two said transsexuals would be acceptable if transition was begun, and one said "we should educate transsexuals to respect our boundaries". Of the 126 responses from those who did *not* want transsexuals at MWMF, the majority favoured publicizing the policy, trusting transsexuals not to show up, and/or asking them if their sex was in question; very few recommended any type of testing or objective verification of sex.

Overall, the survey results indicate that there is a great deal of confusion and disagreement about the locus of gender, the relationship between gender and sex, the definition of woman (or womon), the meaning of woman-born woman, the nature of transsexualism, who MWMF should be for, how an anti-transsexual policy should be enforced, and who is the victim and who is the oppressor. The results strongly suggest that the majority of Festigoers would support a "no penis" policy that would allow postoperative male-to-female transsexuals; that they want the policy to be unambiguously stated and well publicized; and that they oppose invasive verification of sex.

Results of the questions that asked about *female-to-male* have not been tabulated in detail, but 80% of respondents were against their inclusion, 10% in favour, and 10% undecided.

Grayce Elizabeth Baxter

(born 1966 - murdered 1992)

A year ago, Grayce Elizabeth Baxter was killed by one of her clients. TS and TV girls, who knew her as well as those who didn't, are still in shock. She was a role model for many of us and her disappearance has left us with unanswered grief and pain.

Where is Grayce?

Missing call girl had drug problem, pal says

By Jim Rankin
TORONTO STAR

A friend of missing Toronto prostitute Grayce Baxter says the 26-year-old woman had a drug problem which may have played a role in her disappearance three weeks ago.

"I don't know if anybody knows, but I know Graycie, and she's a drug addict," said Mary, who says she's known the high-priced prostitute for about six years.

Mary, who didn't want her real name used, is also a prostitute and lives within sight of ...'s waterfront World ... condominium. ... into crack ... in a

Client of transsexual charged with murder

By Lisa Wright
TORONTO STAR

A man described by police as a former client of a transsexual prostitute missing for the last month has been charged with first-degree murder in her death — but the body has not yet been found.

Grayce Baxter, 26, who lived in a condominium in the World Trade Centre at the foot of Yonge St., disappeared the morning of Dec. 8 after visiting a friend in Mississauga.

Baxter, be-...

Baxter

days later.

"We have sufficient evidence to lay a charge," said Detective Sergeant David Clark of Metro police, who refused to elaborate on the proof investigators had gathered.

Detectives Jim McDermott and Tony Warr of the homicide squad are heading the investigation and have been interviewing her clients.

They are still seeking clues that will lead them to the location of the victim's body.

Grayce Baxter was born a male, Grant, and had a sex change operation seven years ago before starting a career as a call girl.

Metro police yesterday ar-

Missing hooker 'into bondage'

collage by Jeanne B.

Self Blessing Ritual

BLESSING YOURSELF IS A RITUAL OF POLITICAL AND SPIRITUAL SYNTHESIS. TO DO SO ENCOURAGES REVERANCE, ESTEEM AND BODY-KNOWLEDGE. IT SUPPORTS RESONANCE WITH OTHERS IN THIS WORLD AND BETWEEN THE WORLDS. BLESSING YOURSELF MEANS TAKING POWER OUT OF THE HANDS OF THE CHURCH OF THE GREAT MAN AND PLACING IT IN YOUR OWN. BLESSING YOURSELF IS A JOYFUL AND REBELLIOUS ACT! BLESSING YOURSELF IS SEXUAL, DELIGHTFUL AND CONFIRMS IN RITUAL YOUR OWN DIVINITY.

circle yourself with safety... calm yourself, ground and centre. maybe light a candle or imagine the moon; full and bright. hold your heart in your mind's eye... breathe into her deeply. relax and let go. with spirit water or perfumed oil or wine or bodily fluid

ANOINT - YOUR CROWN - TO CONNECT WITH THE UNIVERSE, THE ONE LOVE SONG OF LIFE... ANOINT YOUR THIRD EYE - JUST ABOVE AND BETWEEN YOUR EYEBROWS, THIS IS THE PLACE OF INNER KNOWING. TRUST YOURSELF AND HEAL YOUR INJURED INSTINCT. <u>YOU</u> KNOW.

YOUR EYES*... TO SEE YOUR OWN BEAUTY AND THE BEAUTY OF THE NATURAL WORLD... COLOUR, SHAPE, TEXTURE AND GORGEOUS FORM BLESS AND ANOINT YOUR NOSE... YOUR GUIDE. ACCEPT THE WONDERFUL SACRED SMELLY-NESS OF ALL YOUR BODILY ESSENCES. THOU ART GODDESS, GOD! YOUR MOUTH... THE PLACE THROUGH WHICH YOU NOURISH THE BODY!

YOUR THROAT... THE PLACE OF GIVE AND TAKE, WITH WORDS, SONG, SPEAK YOUR MIND - SPEAK YOUR PEACE... SAY YOUR NAME AND REMEMBER WHO YOU ARE!

MOVE DOWN, DOWN TO YOUR HEART... BLESS YOUR HEART... TO BE OPEN, TO BE STRONG WITH PASSION AND MERCY...

YOUR BREASTS, TO BE FREE OF DISEASE, FORMED IN STRENGTH AND BEAUTY! YOUR GENITALS, YOUR WOMB, YOUR SEX.. TO RECEIVE PLEASURE WITHOUT GUILT, TO BRING FORTH LIFE OR NOT WITH RESPONSIBILITY - AS SHE BROUGHT FORTH THE UNIVERSE...

NOW REMEMBER TO ANOINT YOUR KNEES, THEY'VE SERVED YOU SO WELL. THEY HOLD YOU ERECT AND ALLOW YOU TO BEND AND LASTLY YOUR FEET... TO WALK IN BEAUTY, TO BE TRUE. LET NOTHING STOP YOU OR TURN YOU ASIDE.

breathe deeply... charge yourself with strength, health, presence and mindfulness feel your pain or bliss, let whatever you might be feeling be released, cry to the earth mother who sustains and nurtures us all.

OPEN THE CIRCLE - RELEASE THE POWER - IT IS SO!

* - DO NOT USE PERFUMED OIL ON MUCOUS MEMBRANES
IT BURNS LIKE MAD

Hooker of the Year:

Justine Piaget

presentation and interview by jeanne b.

There are a number of pervasive anti-prostitute attitudes amongst some transsexuals, most of whom happen to be white, "well-educated" and middle-class. This is especially true, amongst those whose careers have already been established and were therefore safe enough when they began their gender journeys.

What these would-be well-heeled and well-integrated citizens forget, is that most transsexual prostitutes started living as women at a very early age (sometimes as early as twleve), making it difficult for them to continue within the structure of traditional education and/or careers.

For decades, prostitution has provided many TS's with a decent and empowering way to earn a living and made necessities (such as electrolysis, SRS' and cosmetic surgery) a reality despite their astronomical costs.

It is time for the larger transsexual community, to start looking at certain TS prostitutes as role models. We make up a very large and important part of transsexuals as a group.

We are strong, courageous, intelligent, self-motivated, insightful and clear-sighted individuals whose stories and lives should not be silenced in order to gain mainstream acceptance.

jeanne For how long have you been working in the sex trade?

Justine For about nine years.

jeanne Have you always worked as a girl?

Justine Yes.

jeanne Where did you work, mostly? In bars, as an escort, on the streets?

Justine I worked on the streets for about 80% of the time, then I started to work independently on my own as an escort.

jeanne Where have you been working?

Justine First I started in Edmonton, then I went on to Calgary then back to Edmonton. Then I spent about two years in Vancouver and then back to Edmonton for another year. And then on my way to Toronto, I got arrested in Calgary, so I stayed in Calgary for six months. And then I went to Toronto - that's the first time I came to Toronto in 1987. Since then I've been living in Toronto except for a year and a half in Montréal. I've gone all across Canada.

Hooker of the Year (continued)

I've met a lot of hookers during my travels. And for at least 8 years, I've lived in the hotel scene.

jeanne Since I've known you, you've worked inside. Do you consider this a sign that both your job and your life are more stable now?

Justine Yeah. Because with the phone you have to be more stable. You have to stay home. It's not that I want to. If it was my choice, I'd pick the street over the phone, 'cause it's more fun, more entertaining to go out a lot. But I like money. Basically that's why I work the phone.

jeanne How's money compared to a couple of years ago?

Justine Five years ago, before the recession, it was very, very good; you could make a lot of money. At the beginning of the recession and during the recession, we were not really that affected. But after the recession, now, we are very affected. It always hits us at the very end, not during the recession. But during or after, there are always clients for us out there.

jeanne Where are you from?

Justine Edmonton, Alberta. I was born in a small town. My mother passed away when I was seven. I left home when I was very young. I started to live on my own and don't have any contact with the rest of the family now.

jeanne Ever had any bad tricks?

Justine When I first started, I never had a problem because I was so young and usually always told my clients that I was a transsexual or they knew because of the area I was working in. I never really liked pulling straight dates, 'cause I was so scared all the time and I'm not a big strong person...

But in Vancouver, I had one bad client. He was in the English Bay area. I took him to a parking lot and he tried to rape me but I ran away.

Then when I moved to Toronto, I had one bad client. His kick was to beat up the girls. So I did my service, I was about to leave and then he beat me up with a pipe, really badly. He broke my nose, gave me two black eyes, stuff like that... For the next weeks, I had to wear tons and tons of make-up and I looked really awful... Two black eyes, a busted nose...

In Montréal, I had to cut a guy's balls, just about off...

Over the phones, I haven't had any bad clients.

jeanne Do you think it's more dangerous out there for TS prostitutes rather than for genetic women or boys?

Justine Yes, there are lots of girls out there who don't tell the clients what they are,

"In Montréal, I had to cut a guy's balls, just about off..."

so lots of clients will get angry, whereas for the boys or genetic women, their clients know what they're looking for and what they want.

jeanne Do you see that more and more men are specifically attracted to transsexuals, especially since **The Crying Game** came out?

Justine Yes, when **The Crying Game** came out, I was very surprised to receive a lot of calls from men, saying "I just saw **The Crying Game**". There has always been a big clientele of men that are just into transsexuals.

jeanne What do you think about those men who are specifically attracted to us? Do you see them as gay, straight or do you think that their orientation is definitely a separate one?

Justine I don't understand how a man can be sexually attracted to a TS. Tits and dick... I just don't understand that. [laughter] Seriously, even though I'm a transsexual, I don't understand and I never will.

jeanne I can [laughter]...What about safe sex practices amongst transsexual prostitutes?

Justine Prostitutes have always always always used condoms even before AIDS for the simple fact that we're selling sex. When AIDS came out, we just started to double bag. Personally, even in my private life, I've "safetened up". But there's still a lot of dirty girls out there, especially transsexuals. We have to work so much harder, it's easy to lose self-respect.

jeanne What about AIDS? Have you seen many TS' dying around you, during the last nine years?

Justine Yes, because transsexuals are so hard into the booze and into the drugs. That's basically what we live for, the party life. A lot of transsexuals have died for the simple fact that they just kept partying, partying and partying... They got sick, they realized that they had the HIV virus, they got very, very sick and they didn't care about themselves anymore.

jeanne Why do you think TS's party, party, party and are so much into booze and drugs?

Justine Because it's so much harder for transsexuals than for genetic women. We're transsexuals and we have to go out there, fool the clients and pretend to be genetic women. That's why they're always drunk and high on drugs, they feel better, you know what I mean. They can do the job better. But finally after years of partying, you simply get hooked.

jeanne Is there a lot of competition within TS and TV prostitutes?

Justine Yes, definitely... The girls will always and always fight over clients.

"He's my client!"
"Well I saw him first."
"He was looking at me!"

It'll still be there for 20 years to come and 20 years back. It's a rivalry. Queens will always be queens. There will always be another little younger prettier one coming to Toronto every five years. The queens will always gossip. They always talk over the phone, you know.

jeanne Now talk to me about that contest you won at Colby's.

Justine <u>Hooker of the Year</u>. It was organized by the Trillium Monarchist Society. It was a camp title. There were five contestants.

jeanne What were you asked to do?

Justine There was a "Question & Answer" part, a "Lingerie or Streetwear" parade, then evening gown parade and a talent show.

jeanne What did you win?

Justine A trip to San Fransisco. I'm going in February. And I'm very happy.

jeanne How do you work now?

Justine I quit working on the streets about 2 years ago and started working the phone. Basically it was just NOW magazine where I got started. Then I expanded into other magazines for a total of nine, which is the best you can do. I just stay home. I just answer the phone. The phones ring and I make a lot of money and I'm very happy now.

jeanne What's the recipe of your success?

Justine (laughter)... the recipe of my success is sex, drugs, rock 'n' roll (laughter)... No... if you want to do what I'm doing, you've got to be very serious. It's dedication more than anything. When you're sleeping at 12 o'clock at night and you hear the phone ring, it's automatically instinctive to get up and answer and try to sell yourself.

You've got to remember that on the street, they see you, they know what you look like. Over the phone they don't know what they're getting. You've got to provoke them, get them into it. You've got to try to sell yourself as best as you can to get them over here.

You have to be a disciplined workaholic and try a little harder than others. And staying home, which is the hard part.

jeanne And the surgery?

Justine Right now, I'm happy and content the way I am, living as a transsexual, but I would like to live as a female within the next ten years.

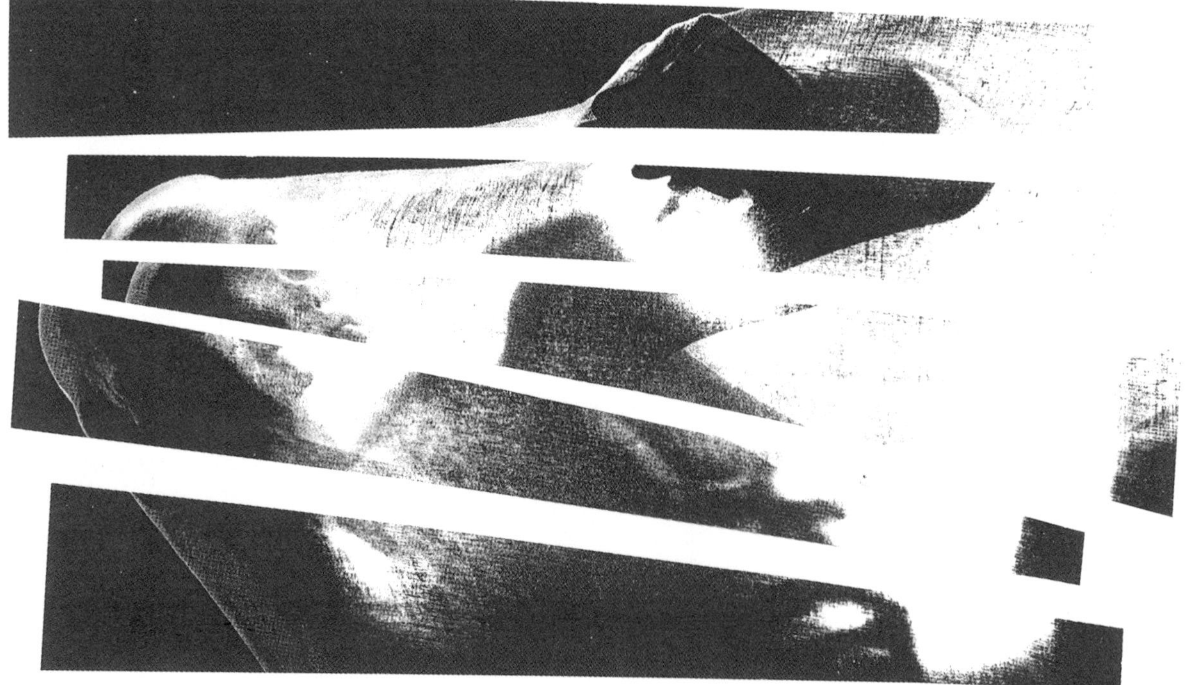

Queer Sites
Toronto, May 1993

by kiwi

Queer Sites was an academic conference devoted to studying *queer* issues. But unfortunately, throughout the weekend it became all too clear that the current use of *queer* only refers to lesbians and gay men.

By far the worst example of this was keynote speaker Elizabeth Grosz. For those unfamiliar with the idea, *keynote* speakers are academics who have generally gained a reputation for themselves in their area of study. They are usually paid a handsome sum of money to talk, and their presentation is designed, in many ways, to set the tone for the next few days.

Grosz is an Australian who has written extensively on French feminist theory and psychoanalysis. In her talk, she maintained that the current use of the word *queer* ignores lesbians. As a corrective measure, of course, she suggested that we get back to the *irreducible difference* of two sexes. This *irreducible difference* she claims, is something that every lesbian and gay man knows.

Clearly for Grosz, only genetic men and genetic women have the right to claim the categories *gay* or *lesbian*. After her talk, I asked Grosz how she could claim to make sense of all non-heterosexual relations through two sexes. For example, if a chick with a dick is fucking a chick with a dick who is at the same time fucking a hermaphrodite, how do we slot these people into one of two sexes? And why would we want to, anyway? What does it mean to develop a theory of desire which elides transgender specificity?

Grosz' only response was that she *often* gets into trouble for her view of transsexuals (she seemed entirely ignorant of the word *transgender*, never once using the term). She thinks that male-to-female transsexuals have fantasmatic relations to what they imagine *women* to be. She went on to say that once many transsexuals have their sex-change surgery, they discover that *womanhood* was not what they thought and are profoundly unhappy. In a move which was all too predictable, Grosz said that was why so many post-operative transsexuals killed themselves. It was enough to make a transgender throw up.

As if this display of intolerance and stupidity wasn't enough, Grosz also made an off-the-cuff remark about bisexuals. She quipped that bisexuals *want to have their cake and eat it too, and then spend the rest of their lives complaining about oppression when they find out they can't*. Sadly, at least half of the monosexual audience laughed and clapped when they heard this.

Not all of the conference was this bi- and trans-phobic. There were several cool presentations on transsexual, transgender and bisexual issues. And Grosz' speech was important because it reminds us that lesbians and gay men can't deal with bisexuals or transgenders. Bisexual and transgender communities would do well to work together in educating the monosexual masses about our diverse realities.

Maybe at the next queer theory conference in Canada, the keynote speaker will be a transgender bisexual. We should be so lucky!

"LOOKING AT" TRANSVESTITES: MARJORIE GARBER'S VESTED INTERESTS: CROSS-DRESSING AND CULTURAL ANXIETY (New York: Routledge, 1992)

by kiwi

Marjorie Garber's recent book on the transvestite is undoubtably one of the most comprehensive academic books on the subject of transvestism. She examines the representation of cross-dressing across an incredible variety of historical, cultural, and political spaces - from the Kabuki theatre to the Renaissance stage to David Bowie.

In the academy, Garber's work has been well recieved. Having attended many "queer theory" conferences over the past year, I can state with confidence that she is frequently cited, and that her project is widely endorsed.

In the popular press, too, Garber has recieved rave reviews. The Nation for example, declares that Vested Interests is destined to become "the bible" of transvestite study. Favourable reviews have appeared in the mainstream newspapers, the lesbian and gay press, and even transgender publishing (Tapestries, Dragazine).

What is all the excitement about? Garber argues that most academic studies of transvestism tend to appropriate the category "transvestite" to one of two genders (men or women), thereby eliding the specificity of this sexual/political site. She maintains that these kinds of studies are limited because they "look through" the transvestite. In contrast, Garber suggests that we begin to "look at" transvestites. This gesture (looking at) means that the local position of transvestism will not be appropriated into a binary gender framework.

The argument is a seductive one. Indeed, Garber would seem to set herself up as one of the few academic researchers who is capable of thinking about the specificity of transgender realities. But let's take a closer look.

While Garber is surely adept at a detailed examination of the representation of transvestism, she demonstrates a sustained inability to conceive the viability of transvestite identities. Consider the second section of the book - "Transvestite Effects". The collocation sums up everything - transvestism, for Garber, is an effect of representation. It is not a viable identity unto itself. In more than 400 pages, not one drag queen's voice comes through.

It's not like Garber doesn't actually consider transgender culture. She mentions magazines like Tapestries, yet examines this magazine alongside movies like The Silence of the Lambs with virtually no discrimination of the political differences embodied in these images. They are both representations of transvestism, for Garber, irrespective of the different political circumstances which engender their very appearance.

And what are the political claims of this research? The readers of Vested Interests had better ask this question, because Garber certainly doesn't. An example: Garber documents that a male-to-female pre-operative transsexual in law school experienced harassment from her fellow students in relation to bathroom issues. Living full-time as a woman, this person obviously did not want to use the men's bathroom. Her genetic women colleagues did not feel it was appropriate for her to use the women's washroom - she still had that dick. In the interim, this transsexual used the lavatory of an administrator.

Now, I'm certainly glad that Garber brought this case to my attention: it's important and reminds us all how much education still needs to be done around transgender issues. But consider Garber's final statement on the issue: "I do not know what ultimate solution, if any, was found." How Garber can merely state this so nonchalantly, without any sense of the role she could play in effecting political change, is a worrisome situation. Presumably, if Garber is a Harvard intellectual working on transgender issues, she could have a considerable amount of political clout when it comes to these kinds of questions. But she remains silent: no mention of organizing a public forum on transgenders and the law, no letter of support to the administration, no attempt to contact the transsexual woman.

Oh Marjorie! For someone who claims not to appropriate transgender issues, it seems that all you can do is "look at". You DO work at Harvard - I'm sure that you could afford a tape recorder to get out in the community and talk with some of us (It's a scary thought, eh? Much safer to keep looking at...)

I've got news for you, honey - we're tired of being looked at, and it's academic researchers like you who we despise! 400 pages, and all you can say is how interesting we are. Well, fuck off and die because that's the same kind of appropriation we experience all the time - in straight society, in gay male culture, now in the academy. "LOOK, EVERYBODY: DRAG QUEENS! THEY'RE SO FUN!"

Your "looking at" book has no doubt furthered your career, Marjorie, but where has it left transgenders? How is it that you can claim The Silence of the Lambs is "In one sense determinedly politically correct - Buffalo Bill is not a transsexual and gender identity clinics are exonerated from even associative blame" (P.116)??? You're so busy looking at us, you can't stop to think about some of the things we need - progressive social policy, inclusive education programmes, supportive gender identity counselling.

VESTED INTERESTS (continued)

Reading Vested Interests, I have to admit I feel embarrassed to be an academic. If this is all the University can offer transgender communities, I say forget it! But don't give up hope - there are some cool academics out there. As academics and activists interested in transgender liberation, we should read Vested Interests (don't buy it, though, it's way too expensive!) But let's read it with an understanding of what we don't want. And let's be noisy and obnoxious about what we DO want. Let's all go tell Marjorie, and everybody else who thinks her work is cool:

STOP LOOKING AT US, AND START SPEAKING WITH US!

It's time academics like Marjorie Garber are held accountable for their politically irresponsible research. Get ready, Marjorie - transgender fury is also inside the academy. I hope you are its next victim.

select bibliography (transgender positive research):

Harold Garfinkel Studies in Ethnomethodology. Englewood Cliffs, New Jersey: Prentice Hall, 1972

Suzanne Kessler and Wendy McKenna. Gender: AN Ethnomethodological Approach. New York: John, Wiley and Sons, 1979

Keesler, Suzanne. **The Medical Construction of Gender: Case Management of Intersexed Infants**. Signs Vol. 16, No. 1 (1990): 3-26

Stone, Sandy. **The Empire Strikes Back: A Posttransexual Manifesto.** In Kristina Straub and Julia Epstein, eds. Body Guards: The Cultural Politics of Gender Ambiguity. New York: Routledge, 1991, 280-304.

Deborah Feinbloom, Michael Fleming, Valerie Kijweski, Margo Schulter. **Lesbian/Feminist Orientation Among Male-to-Female Transsexuals**. Journal of Homosexuality Vol. 2, No. 1 (Fall 1976): 59-71

In Memory

Kelly

(1970 - 1993)

She is missed
by her friends,
family
and sisters
across Canada

FROM MALE TO FEMALE

SEX CHANGE OPERATION (SRS)

by Norma

Thoughts leading up to - including - and afterwards

I am a biological male who is a male-to-female transsexual. A transsexual is a person who thinks that society has placed the wrong role (gender) on him/her, because of what that person has between their legs (sex). I am a 55 year old male, and I am going to have what is commonly called a Sex Change Operation. After years and years of switching gender roles (working as a male by day, and living off the job as a female), I decided to make the switch to the female role full time, as gender switching was taking its toll of me, emotionally and psychologically and I preferred the female role, feeling at peace with myself, the world, and people, in that role.

In January, 1989, I decided to prepare for living full time as a woman, so in February of that year, I started electrolysis and female hormone therapy, under a doctor, and I also became a patient of a psychiatrist, in case of any problem encountered during and after the switch. By January, 1990, I decided to make the switch full time, so I approached the company that I was working for, for 10 years, to see if I could start working on the job as a female. They were not too happy at that idea, to say the least, and realizing that I could no longer work as a male during the day, then switching to the female role after work, I left the company on good terms, and got a good reference from them in my female name, so that I had some work history as a female.

By that time I had officially changed my name, and ID over to my female name, and was ready to take my place in the world as a female, if only in gender form (at that Point in time), for better or worse, hopefully for the better, of course. After a period of unemployment, I started working in an office with a girl friend of mine, and as time went by, and I found myself comfortable around people in the female role, I found myself thinking more and more about Sex re-assignment surgery, so in January of 1991, I decided to go for it. I wanted to feel "complete' as a woman, so after getting the necessary papers together to qualify for the operation, I contacted a Dr. Menard in Montréal, Quebec, who does the operation and arranged an interview with him.

There is only one doctor in the whole of Canada doing the surgery, and that doctor is Dr. Menard (at the time of this paper). The only other doctor doing it close enough to Toronto is a Dr. Biber, who operates out of Trinidad, Colorado, and his price is $10,000 (US), and the price for Dr. Menard is $5,800.00. As I am not going through the Gender Clinic at the Clarke Psychiatric Institute, Toronto, I have to cover the cost myself. If I was on their program, the Provincial medical plan (OHIP), would pay the cost of the operation, but as I said, I have to pay the full cost, but I did not mind, in order to feel "complete".

January, 1991

The consultation date that I had with him was the 22nd of January. The woman in me was happy. I realized that I was on the threshold of a monumental event in my life, but one that I know is the right event that will make me the way I feel that I should have been from the start. This is **NOT** a sex thing with me, as I know that the surgery is not going to make me 21 or beautiful or change the way that some people look at me or feel about me, as they will not see my genitals.

What I will achieve is a sense of "completeness", of wholeness, of joy. I have to undress every day and it is a very painful thing for me to be confronted, day after day with that thing between my legs, hanging down, reminding me that I have the body of a male, but the soul and feelings of a female.

I will feel better in the bathtub, and will not be afraid to strip in front of women, and it will make me feel better seeing "F" on my driver's license, passport, etc., instead of "M". A male and a female cannot survive in one body. It is impossible. One has to go, and in my case, it has to be the male - **Norman is now Norma, and I have to be Norma all the way.** When the last vestige of maleness goes via the operation, then and **only then** will I feel that I am a "complete" woman. At least, cosmetically.

Tuesday, 22nd. January, 1991

I left Toronto for Montréal at 9:30 am, arriving there at 12:20 pm. I made a call at the Montréal Head Office of the company I had worked for in Toronto to straighten out something, then I went directly to Dr. Menard's office, but he was in surgery when I arrived, so I had to cool my heels for an hour or so before I got to see him. He introduced himself and then we talked. He was a very nice man, and he answered all my questions, and he told me about the operation, and what I could expect. We then agreed on a date for the surgery, and I paid him the required retainer, and I left, floating on air. I was one step closer to my dream. I went back to the station, had something to eat, then caught the last train back to Toronto.

Due to the female hormone therapy and electrolyasis, I now pass well as a woman, and I have also had vocal chord surgery to raise the pitch of my voice, plus an Adam's apple shave. As far as my voice is concerned, it is not sounding female, but my throat is still healing, so all I can hope is that when it is healed, my voice will say "female". The date settled on for the surgery was February 25, and I have to stop taking the female hormones until after the operation. The reason is because the hormones change the clotting time of the blood which could be dangerous during the surgery. I start back on them two weeks after the operation. Although the surgery is on the 25th, I have to go down to Montréal on the Sunday, the 24th because I have to check into the clinic the day before.

Sunday, 24th. February, 1991

11:00am. I got a taxi to Union Station in Toronto, riding on air, so to speak. I was on the last leg of my journey from male to female, which due to many of life's twists and turns, had spanned the years from 1956 to the present. The woman in me was happy. Strange to say, though I was as calm as anything. It was because I had every confidence in myself being a member of the female gender, plus every confidence in Dr. Menard's work.

From Male to Female (continued)

I arrived at Union Station, and got in the line-up for the Montréal train. The line-up was long and crowded. It seemed all of Toronto was going to Montréal. I wondered if they were all going to Montréal for a sex change operation (ha ha - some TS humour there), but of course I knew that I was the only one. Besides, Dr. Menard would not have room in his clinic for all of them.

12:40 pm. I left Toronto for an appointment with destiny. During the first leg of the trip, from Toronto to Kingston, I got talking to a young girl sitting next to me. She was very beautiful, and her name was Mimi. I envied her. She was everything that I wanted to be. She was very nice, and in the course of talking, I told her the reason for my trip to Montréal. She seemed very interested, and I explained to her, something about transsexualism and transsexuals.

She got off at Kingston, and I was sorry to see her go. She was a wonderful person to talk to, and very understanding. I like to educate people, if they'll listen to me, about transsexualism, so if they meet someone else like me in the future, they will understand, and know what pain that a person like me is going through, and not be afraid or upset by them.

5:40pm. I arrived in Montréal, got off the train and headed for the a restaurant. I was very hungry, and I knew that I would not have a meal before I went to bed that night. I then took the subway to Dr. Menard's clinic. I was greeted at the door by the receptionist named Claire, and after filling out some forms, I unpacked, and settled in. At 11:00pm., after a fleet enema and a shower, I had some tea and cookies and went to bed. Claire asked me if I needed a sleeping pill, but I said no. I was very tired from the journey, and I went to sleep, right away, and peaceably, knowing that next day, I would be rid of this thing that hung down between my legs, which made me a part of the male gender - (Ugh).

Monday, 25th. February, 1991

I woke up feeling hungry, but was not allowed to eat. The operation was scheduled for 11:00am. (Oh boy! goodbye Norman - hello Norma time). I found out that I would be the only TS done that week. Dr. Menard always does the surgery on Mondays. The other days, he works out of a local hospital, but checks in now and again to make sure that everything is OK. I was prepped for surgery, and then I was wheeled into the OR, and the last thing I remember was being jabbed in the rear end by a needle, and Dr. Menard talking to me. The operation lasted three hours, I was told afterwards.

I woke up feeling like someone had parked a truck between my legs, but I was not hurting. Later on I would, but at this point in time, I was not due to what had been given to me. The word for the next day or so was "discomfort", with a captital "D". I had to stay on my back for the next day or so, because it was more comfortable that way, and there was not a damn thing I could do about it. Even turning on one's side was out of the question. The diet they gave me was very bland. They did not want anything coming out of my rear end for a day or so. I was also hooked up to a catheter tube, so I could not get up. They wanted to make sure that my urinary system worked as that had been altered internally.

Tuesday, 26th. February, 1991

I woke up feeling not too bad. I wondered what my vagina looked like. I guess I will just have to wait. I had some tea and dry toast, then I lay back, marvelling at modern surgery and what it could do. The woman in me was happy that the male hormone factory was out of commission **permanently**, and when she looked at herself in the mirror, she would see a **feminine** contour down there, not a male one. Lunch and supper were more substantial. I also received a lovely bouquet of flowers from my TS friend in London, Ontario, Karen. The flowers sure were a welcome sight, and they smelt good too.

Wednesday, 27th. February, 1991

I woke up to breakfast - happy day - I can get out of bed today. I am sure tired of laying on my back all day. After being washed, I got up and went to the bathroom to empty my catheter by myself. The rest of the day consisted on walking, sitting, and laying down. In the afternoon, I met a local TS named D. She puts up TS' who come to Montréal for surgery by Dr. Menard. The clinic closes down on the weekends, and the "new" woman has to stay somewhere - hotel - friends, etc. D had surgery herself three years ago, and she supplies comfort, support, advice, etc. She charges $50 a day. As it turned out, it was a wise choice. I did not relish staying at a cold hotel with no support, or comfort. We girls have to stick together, you know.

Thursday, 28th. February, 1991

I was sore between the legs, so I stayed in bed all day.

Friday, 1st. March, 1991

After lunch, I was picked up by D. I would be staying with her until Tuesday, the day I would be returning to Toronto, providing that there were no complications from the surgery. I would be checking back with the doctor on Monday. During Thursday and Friday, the local anaesthetics had worn off, and by the time D had picked me up, the pain and soreness in that area was so intense, that when we arrived at the apartment and I was shown to my room, I just curled up on the bed and sobbed my heart out. D came into the room, got on the bed and cradled me in her arms. She said "cry Norma, cry. I understand, but don't worry. The pain will soon be all in the past." Imagine if I had been in a cold hotel room with no one to comfort me. It scares me now to think of it. There were two other problems that night which she solved. I was glad I was with someone who knew what to do. I met a genetic woman there too. I found out afterwards that she lived there with D and that they were man and wife, originally. Who cares, anyway? All I knew and cared about was that they were comfort and support for me in this difficult time of my life.

Saturday, 2nd. March, 1991

Took post-op instructions from D, which made things bearable. Most of the time, I was on my back, taking it easy. I phoned a few biological women friends in Toronto to let them know that I was alright.

Sunday, 3rd. March, 1991

Took it easy - a lot of soreness - watched TV. D had a video of the story of Christine Jorgenson. The movie was very emotional for me, especially a scene in which his homosexual boss tried to rape him, thinking that George (at that time), was gay. I bawled my eyes out, yelling for him to stop attacking George (he did not achieve his purpose). D was highly amused at my reaction. She knew that it was the after effects of the surgery that was making me so emotional. What she did not know is that I despised men. The average male has his brains between his legs.

From Male to Female (continued)

Monday, 4th. March, 1991

I checked back with Dr. Menard. He took out the packing from the new vagina. The packing was actually a condom filled with gauze. He then inserted the stent, which is actually a chopped down dildo, about 3-4 inches long, and about 1 inch in diameter. The instructions are for you to keep this thing in your vagina, 24 hours a day only removing it to go the bathroom.

Tuesday, 5th. March, 1991

It is evening now, and I am home. I unpack, then strip to take a bath. I look at myself, naked in the mirror. I see the female contour between my legs, and the woman in me is pleased at the sight. It is very sore down there, and feels swollen, and looks it, but as I said, I am very pleased. Dr. Menard does good work. Now starts the post-op procedures, of dilating the vagina with the stent, lots of sitz baths, and sleeping with the stent in the vagina.

15th. March, 1991

It is now the 15th of March, and I have been following the instructions faithfully. Things are proceeding OK, and I am being checked weekly by my own doctor. He says that Dr. Menard has done a good job, and that it would fool anybody. That pleased me. I do not sleep through the night due to the soreness, but I will survive, I am sure.

I got an infection in the urethra area, and I am taking antibiotics for it. My doctor phoned Dr. Menard who said that it was normal. Afterwards, I found out that it was due to me wiping myself the wrong way, after I had passed stool. My doctor said that you are supposed to wipe yourself from front to back, not vice versa. He said that if you go from back to front, you carry some of the stool over to the urethra area, and some of it gets into the opening in the urethra, and infection starts. It took a month or so to get rid of it, and it was very uncomfortable down there, especially when I went to pee.

Saturday, 27th. April, 1991

The soreness has gone now, although the urethra area is still swollen a little, and very sensitive, but that will pass soon. I now have my paper from Dr. Menard, certifying that my sex is **FEMALE**, and I am happy. I now can get the sex category changed from male to female on my passport, driver's license, etc. The paper does not guarantee that my future will be a bed of roses, for now I face what every woman has to face in this life, as regards to society and the work place, but the woman in me feels "complete" now. I am now a member of the "weaker" sex and no more a male in a skirt. From now on, my birthday, as far as **I'm** concerned is now February 25th, because on that day, **NORMA** was born.

This is the end - and the beginning

WARNING

To all TS/TG/TV/she-male/she-boy/he-she prostitutes in Toronto

On Monday, November 29th around 9:00pm, a girl, who advertises herself as a she-male in NOW magazine, received a phone call from a man, calling from the phone booth, outside the Pharma Plus drugstore at Church & Wellesley. The man, who spoke quickly, but in a nice & charming manner, arranged a date at her place for 15 minutes later.

When he showed up, he was wearing a blue full-length sleeved pair of coveralls, a light green shower cap over his face, surgical gloves, black police/combat shoes (Doc Martin-style) and carrying a Pharma Plus bag. As soon as he got inside her apartment, he pointed an automatic revolver at her, pushed her on the floor & told her "put your hands behind your back & I won't hurt you". He then covered her eyes with nylons & taped her hands together with surgical tape.

At this point, two friends, who were in an upstairs bedroom, heard the girl crying & came downstairs, scaring off the man. They think he was trying to steal her TV, VCR, etc.

The guy is around 5'10", medium build.

Be Safe.

TSe TSe TerroriSm

Installment #4: The Morning After

From the living room couch of the TScommune & cultural centre, Swordfish & Turquoise Sky are watching the TV intently.

<<Welcome to **Transsexual Views**. I'm r.a. bradlee>> show host, seated at her usual position, at the base of the Y-shaped table <<today's show: should genetics be allowed to present transsexuals or discuss transsexuality in their books, movies, videos, etc? In other words, should transsexuals & transsexuality be discussed or talked with or about by transsexuals only?

To discuss these issues, we have Millicent P Randall, author of *My Life, Myself* and Michael Freeman, well known transsexual rights activist>>, indicating both guests, each seated at the top ends of the "Y" - each with a mug, bearing the show's name, in front of them - Millicent is on bradlee's right <<and as usual our phone lines will be open to viewers, wanting to express their views on the subject or ask questions of our two guests.

Okay, who would like to start?>>

<<I don't mind starting first>> Randall <<We've all heard this rhetoric before: how no one else but transsexuals should be allowed to speak on the subject or use transsexual characters in their movies or their books, etc, etc, etc, or having anything to do with transsexuals. Well I disagree entirely. Yes there have been problems with genetics writing about us or speaking about us or using transsexual characters in their artistic creations, but censoring them is not the way to get them to understand us and our issues.>>

<<Mmm hmm>> Freeman <<This isn't going to surprise anyone, but I totally disagree with that statement of yours in every single way.

Why should we trust genetics anymore? They've had every chance and all they've shown us, is how much they hate and despise us. And saying <<no you can't do that, it isn't nice>> isn't going to stop their bigotry or stop their hate material. We need to be stronger and act stronger and that means stepping on some genetic toes.>>

<<Yes>>Turquoise in the home audience.

<<Frankly>> Freeman continuing <<I feel that saying, that we & only we are able to talk about us or transsexuals or write books about us or make movies about us, is not enough by itself: True Transsexual Liberation will require much much more.>>

<<But that is censorship>>

<<And what is it called when a whole group, a whole culture is censored and prevented from either responding to genetic hate material or from even commenting about the subject itself? What you are saying is that it's okay to muzzle an entire group, but it's totally inappropriate to stop even one bigot from disseminating their anti-transsexual propaganda?>>

<<It's a matter of how we organize ourselves. We should never resort to the tactics of bigots, otherwise we are no better than they are.>>

<<That's simply not true: it's not us who have attacked genetics; it's us who are being attacked. This isn't about censorship - it's about being attacked & protecting ourselves from those attacks. I have no problem restricting the power and priviledge of any genetic, who use that same power & priviledge to try & destroy us. Bigotry is bigotry - it's not a right. It's not okay - it is disgusting & it needs to be stopped. What you & others like you are saying is that transsexuals are worthless.>>

<<Well I totally disagree. What you're preaching is the same as those genetics that you despise. And one other thing, by not censoring their work, this anti-transsexual propaganda, as you call it, is brought into the open and not hidden.>>

<<And what good does that do? Great, so we can see the bigotry. Why, do we need more proof that it exists? At what point does it become too much? When do we say <<no that's enough, we're not going to take any more>>? When we're all dead?>>

<<exactly>> Turquoise again.

<<We have all>> Freeman continuing <<every single one of us, suffered enough & put up with enough. It's time to stop being so goddamned nice about it & say **fuck off & die**.>>

<<I agree, but we need to have it out in the open where we can confront it and show it for what it is.>>

<<That would be nice in a perfect world, but this isn't anything like a utopia, where everyone respects everybody else, and acts according to nice, neat logical rules and so on. We live in a real world, where power means everything, where only power and not logical

TSe TSe TerroriSm (continued)

debate is respected & acknowledged. Therefore, we have to act in a realistic and practical manner, not in some nice philosophic manner, which only aids our oppressors. Nice debate won't help us, but it will keep us oppressed and suppressed. I've got to admit; I'm curious. You're aware of the anti-transsexual hate of genetics - >>

<<Some genetics. Some genetics aren't trying to hurt us. I know lots of genetics who aren't trying to attack us.>>

<<So what? It's in the structure of genetics, their society, their culture, their language, it's in everything they do. And debating about who is and who isn't an anti-transsexual, is a waste of time: anti-transsexualism is buried deep in this genetically-run society, in this genetocracy.>>

<<*Genetocracy* sounds like an invented word.>>

<<So what, all words are invented and there's nothing wrong with us inventing words & language with which we can really express ourselves, free of gender hating concepts. Why are you so gender-hating? Are you trying to be genetic? Because no matter how hard you try, you'll always be a transsexual.>>

<<Sorry to interrupt you both>> host <<but we have a caller from Toronto. This is Tim Finland. Go ahead>>

<<Hi. I'm a published writer and I must say that I agree with Ms Randall. Censorship is an act of fascism.>>

<<I have a question for you: are you a transsexual?>> Freeman

<<I don't see what that has to do with it: censorship is an abominable act that cuts across all gender lines.>>

<<In other words, you're not. My answer to you is that you don't know what the fuck you're talking about. You have no knowledge of what it's like to be a transsexual and therefore what we go through. Not only that but you have your own channels to express your viewpoints and I suggest you use them and not ours. Goodbye>>

<<I must say I find your attitude very vicious and very rude.>>

<<Good, then it shows that we are accomplishing something, because politeness won't get us anything, except killed. As I have said many times before, I don't discuss our issues

with nontranssexuals especially bigoted ones who use the word *fascist* to label anyone who criticizes them in any way.>>

<<What a fucking jerk>> Turquoise Sky <<He doesn't care about anybody but himself. Because he's a *"published writer"*. And Randall [pause], she acts just like a typical genetic bitch.>>

<<I'm trying to watch, so please shut up>> Swordfish.

<<But it really bothers me a lot, when we get shit like this from another TS. I mean, we expect this from genetics, but not from one of us.>>

<<So what's the big deal? Why should TS' be perfect? Can't TS' be assholes as well? Or is that just another genetic priviledge? Get used to it, because TS' are just as fucked up as anybody else. And now, I would like to watch this show, okay?>>

<<But this is important. Anti-transsexualism destroys a lot of our lives.>>

<<And how many lives are being saved by your temper tantrums?>>

Silence.

<<You're pissed off at me, aren't you?>> Swordfish.

<<Yes>> Turquoise <<How can you just sit there and not be affected by it? And how can you be so fucking awful to me, when I'm obviously upset by it?>>

<<Listen, I've learned not to let anyone control my anger. 'Cause if they can control my anger, they can control me. Also I like being relaxed. And I've learned that nothing is going to change in the next few seconds. Anti-transsexuals are going to continue in the same way that they have all along.>>

Big big soap-opera-like pause.

Turquoise gets up calmly and without making a performance of it, leaves the room. Swordfish continues watching the show.

Next installment: **Nightmare on Maitland**

(with irreplaceable help from Jeanne B.)

Other Interesting TransZines

Boy's Own
the FTM newsletter
FTM Network,
BM Network,
London, UK
WC1N 3XX

Crosstalk
The Gender Community's News & Information Monthly
PO Box 944,
Woodland Hills, CA
USA 91365
1 issue/$7(US) 1 year(12 issues)/$48(US) 2 years(24)/$72(US)
Non-US subscribers add $12(US)/year
make check or money order payable to Kymberleigh Richards.

Notes From the Underground
from Gender Mosaic
PO Box 7421
Ottawa (Vanier), Ontario
Canada K1L 8E4
1-613-749-5203
1 year/$15(Cdn)

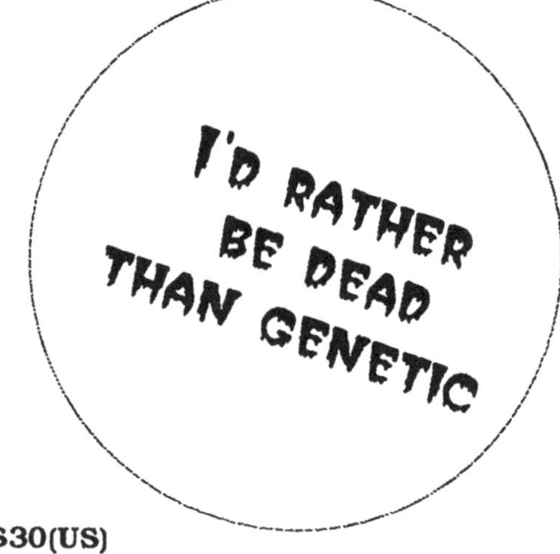

TNT
Transsexual. News. Telegraph
Suite 288,
584 Castro,
San Francisco, CA
USA 94114-2588
1-415-703-7161
sample issue/$4(US) 4 issues/$15(US) 8 issues/$30(US)
make checks payable to Anne Ogborn
free to the institutionalized or prisoners

TransSisters
The Journal of Transsexual Feminism
c/o Davina Anne Gabriel
4004 Troost Ave,
Kansas City, Missouri,
USA 64110
single issue/$3(US) or $4(Cdn) 6 issues/$18(US) or $24(Cdn) Back issue (#1)/$4(US) or $5(Cdn). Make all cheques or money orders payable to Davina Anne Gabriel

TRANS - P.O.R.S. OF Montréal

post-operation residence services
PO Box 613, Station C
Montréal, Québec
H2L 4L5
1-514-526-5892

TRANS-P.O.R.S. is a community service created by Dr Yvon Ménard and the National Foundation on Transsexualism. They provide room and board, with special care and support for people (both FTM and MTF) coming to Montréal for SRS surgery or any other adjusting surgery. For more information, contact TRANS-P.O.R.S. at the above address.

subscriptions

current issue . . . . $4 Cdn/US
1st issue . . . . $3 Cdn/US

free to prisoners and the institutionalized

please send money in cash, stamps (Canadian only), IRC's, cheques or money orders.
(cheques or money orders should be either left blank or payable to Cash.

Donations gratefully accepted.

genderpress
box #500-62,
552 Church St.,
Toronto, Ontario
M4Y 2E3

TRANNIES OR TRANSies

Then WE'LL caLL You

stupid DICks & WEE Wees

time for you to grow UP

Gender Myths

This two-sided sheet of "Gender Myths" was included with *Gendertrash* #2 as a loose insert, folded in half. As mentioned in the *Gendertrash* #2 front matter, it was provided by V. Davina Anne Gabriel and Janis Walworth, who had been distributing it at the Camp Trans protest at the Michigan Womyn's Music Festival.

GENDER MYTH #1

Although male-to-female transsexuals have surgery to change their anatomy and take female hormones, they still act like men.

FACT: Some male-to-female transsexuals act in ways many consider to be masculine; some don't. The same can be said of nontranssexual women. In fact, some types of "masculine" behavior in nontranssexual women are applauded in the lesbian and women's communities, while the same behavior in a transsexual woman is taken as proof that she is "really" a man. Labeling behaviors as masculine and feminine is of little practical value and only reinforces gender stereotypes.

GENDER MYTH #2

Male-to-female transsexuals are not women-born women (or womyn-born womyn).

FACT: No one is born a woman. Most of us who ended up as women started out as girls. The paths we took to womanhood are many and varied. Most male-to-female transsexuals felt like girls from as early as they can remember, just like most nontransexual women. Although many nontranssexual women struggle with the changes associated with becoming women, most become women without consciously attempting to. This fact doesn't make our paths any better, more natural, or more valid than transsexual women's paths.

GENDER MYTH #3

Male-to-female transsexuals have been socialized as men, and this socialization cannot be changed.

FACT: The messages given to each person about the roles of males and females in society are a little different, and these messages may be experienced in very different ways. Many transsexual women felt that the male messages they were given were inappropriate. Many felt inadequate to meet the demands placed on them to "act like a man." Nontranssexual women feel they have a choice to become aware of and reject parts of their sex-role conditioning—so do transsexual women.

GENDER MYTH #4

Male-to-female transsexuals are trying to "pass" as women. They try to make themselves as much like nontranssexual women as possible.

FACT: Male-to-female transsexuals *are* women; they don't need to pass. They don't necessarily want to hide or eliminate their differences from nontranssexual women, although the threat of ostracism leads many to do so. Some transsexuals are proud of their particular route to womanhood, feel that they have learned a lot from the journey they have taken, and value the unique qualities they bring to the women's community.

GENDER MYTH #5

Transsexuals take jobs away from other women because they had access to better training when they were men.

FACT: By making the transition from male to female and staying at the same job, some transsexuals have forced employers to change rules restricting women's positions and salaries, thus opening doors for other women. Many transsexual women seek out qualified women to hire. Furthermore, by holding jobs not traditionally thought of as appropriate for women, these transsexual women bring the message to the general public that women are capable of performing "men's" jobs.

GENDER MYTH #6

To lessen the power of patriarchy in our lives, we must purge our community of everything male, including women who once had male anatomy.

FACT: By emphasizing the distinction between male and female, we reinforce the idea that there are exactly two distinct sexes. This is the very concept that permits sexism to exist, because discrimination would be impossible if women were not readily distinguishable from men. If we wish to deflate the power of the patriarchy, the most effective thing we can do is encourage the blurring of gender lines and expand our thinking beyond the male-female dualism.

GENDER MYTH #7

Most women can easily prove they are not male-to-female transsexuals, if they are challenged to do so.

FACT: There is no simple way to prove you are not a transsexual. There are no apparent physical characteristics nontranssexual women have or lack that distinguish them absolutely from transsexual women. Birth certificates and other documents show an "F" for both. Chromosome tests may reveal an XY pattern for a nontranssexual woman. Hormone levels do not distinguish transsexuals from nontranssexuals. Even inspection of the genitals may not provide definitive proof of your gender history.

GENDER MYTH #8

Male-to-female transsexuals have been raised as boys, have never been oppressed as women, and cannot understand women's oppression.

FACT: Some male-to-female transsexuals were raised as girls for portions of their lives, appeared to the world as girls, and were treated like girls. Some were beaten and raped both by outsiders and by their own family members because of their belief that they were girls or their desire to become girls. For most, the difference in the way they were treated when they appeared as men and after they began appearing as women brought sexism into sharp focus.

GENDER MYTH #9

Women's space is not "safe" space if male-to-female transsexuals are allowed.

FACT: Women's space is not safe whenever anyone in it behaves in threatening or disrespectful ways toward another. Transsexuals are no more likely to behave this way than nontranssexuals. We should exclude individuals who behave badly rather than exclude an entire group because some of its members act in offensive ways—*any* group could be excluded on this basis. Most importantly, women must take responsibility for their their own feelings of being unsafe when others are *not* acting in threatening ways.

GENDER MYTH #10

Transsexuals have surgery so they can have sex the way they want to.

FACT: How or with whom a person wants to have sex is rarely a major factor in the desire for sex reassignment. Usually, people undergo reassignment in order to make their bodies conform more closely to the way they feel inside—their gender. Whether a transsexual is attracted to men or to women usually doesn't change with surgery. Although no figures are available, probably a third of transsexual women are straight, one third bisexual, and one third lesbian. Sexual orientation is not related to gender identity.

GENDER MYTH #11

Male-to-female transsexuals are trying to take over the lesbian community.

FACT: Most transsexuals who identify as lesbians are focused on their own personal growth and happiness—just like most nontranssexual lesbians. Those who feel strongly about their right to participate in women-only events may become activists for their cause and hope to influence the lesbian community. On the other hand, being overly sensitive to issues of power and wanting to avoid controversy, many transsexuals repeatedly decline to take leadership positions and abstain from participating in decision-making votes.

GENDER MYTH #12

The sex assigned to a person at birth is that person's "real" sex.

FACT: Sex is assigned at birth on the basis of a cursory glance at the baby's genitalia. In about 5% of births, there is some ambiguity in the sexual organs, and mistakes can be made. In other cases, internal genitalia, chromosome patterns, hormone production, and secondary sex characteristics that develop later may be at variance with the person's external anatomy. Sex is arbitrarily assigned by the patriarchal medical system, and there is no reason to assume that it is any more correct or real than what a person experiences.

GENDER MYTH #13

The lesbian and women's communities have nothing to gain by including transsexuals.

FACT: Transsexual women bring many valuable qualities to the women's community. They bring skills usually taught only to men into the women's community and pass them on to other women. Many are active feminists, increase opportunities for women, and seek to hire and promote women. Those who have made it through transition must have intelligence, persistence, and a sense of humor. Many also bring a spirituality that has been possessed historically by cross-gendered members of various cultures.

GENDER MYTH #14

Nontranssexual women have the right to decide whether transsexuals should be included in the women's community.

FACT: Each individual has a right to claim her own identity. While being adamant about having this right for themselves, some members of the women's community would deny it to others. Just as each woman must come to her own conclusion about whether she is a lesbian, each must know her own truth about being a woman. Transsexuals can and do include themselves in the women's community and the lesbian community without permission from nontranssexuals.

GENDER MYTH #15

Transsexuals are guilty of deception when they don't reveal right away that they are transsexuals.

FACT: There is no standard of disclosure that requires transsexuals to reveal their medical history, just as lesbians do not need to mention their sexual orientation immediately on meeting someone. The circumstances in which this is considered an important fact to know vary from person to person. The individual meeting a transsexual may collude in the "deception" by assuming she or he is a nontranssexual. If it's important to you to know, take responsibility for asking.

GENDER MYTH #16

Male-to-female transsexuals are considered men until they have sexchange surgery.

FACT: Although male-to-female transsexuals appear as men during some part of their lives, most never consider themselves men. They have felt like females for their entire lives. The change from male to female is a change in external appearance of sex-related characteristics, not a change in gender (how a person feels inside). This transition takes place over a period of several years, and sex-reassignment surgery is only one part of it, together with living as a woman, taking hormones, and resocialization.

GENDER MYTH #17

People can be categorized as transsexual or nontranssexual—there's no in-between.

FACT: There are nearly as many categories as there are people. There are transsexuals who have had or plan to have one, two, or many surgeries to make their bodies conform more closely to their gender, and those who will never have surgery. Some people feel comfortable expressing both genders. Some refuse to identify as either gender. Some people (male and female) enjoy cross-dressing, but their gender is congruent with their sex. Some conform to gender norms; some flout them. The possibilities are infinite.

GENDER MYTH #18

Women who want to become men have bought into societal hatred of women or are hoping to take advantage of male privilege.

FACT: Female-to-male transsexuals don't want to become men—they *are* men. The reason they want to change their bodies to become more male appearing is because that's how they feel inside. If they gain male privilege, it is tenuous; whatever they have gained is lost if they are discovered to be transsexuals. If transsexualism were based on misogyny, there would be far more female-to-male than male-to-female transsexuals. In fact, their numbers are thought to be about equal.

GENDER MYTH #19

A person's "true" sex can be determined by chromosome testing.

FACT: Although most persons identified as male at birth have XY chromosomes and most of those identified as female have XX, there are many variations that can occur. Some "women-born women" have XY chromosomes, a fact that may be discovered only when they are tested to qualify for athletic competition. Other patterns, such as XXY, XYY, and XXX (no, this does not make you an amazon) can also exist. Some individuals have what is called mosaicism, in which some percentage of cells have an XY pattern and the remainder have XX.

GENDER MYTH #20

Transsexualism is unnatural—it is a new problem brought about by sophisticated technology.

FACT: Throughout recorded history there have been people whose gender identity did not match their anatomic sex, and there is evidence that sex-change surgery was performed thousands of years ago. In some cultures, transgendered individuals were held in high esteem as shamans. Today, surgery—from liposuction to sex reassignment—allows many people to have a physical form that is more congruent with their inner sense of themselves and the way they want to appear.

GENDER MYTH #21

"Real" women, certainly those who belong to the lesbian community, rejoice in their womanhood and have no desire to be men.

FACT: There are people who were assigned as females at birth who identify as men, and many of them become part of the lesbian community. Most would be labeled butch lesbians. Many are afraid to reveal their desire to appear more completely as men, including taking testosterone and undergoing surgery to remove their breasts and construct penises. (Transsexual men are apparently permitted at Michigan because they are "still women" according to the Festival doctrine of immutable sex.)

GENDER MYTH #22

Now that Festival policy has been made clear, there are no transsexuals at Michigan.

FACT: Festival policy is far from clear. The brochure states that the Festival is for "womyn-born womyn." Many transsexuals include themselves in that category. While some transsexuals have no desire to participate if they know they are unwelcome, others are here and will continue to come because they have a right to be at any event open to women. No statement has been issued about whether female-to-male transsexuals are welcome at the Festival.

GENDER MYTH #23

Transsexuals have caused trouble at Michigan, resulting in their expulsion.

FACT: According to Festival organizers, transsexuals have been attending MWMF for many years, and 1991 was the first time a transsexual has been expelled. Nancy Burkholder was expelled because she said something that made a woman suspect she was a transsexual, not because her behavior was offensive. In fact, Nancy had participated fully in the 1990 Festival without incident. There is no evidence that transsexuals have ever caused trouble at Michigan. Seeing transsexuals as trouble-makers is once again blaming the victim.

GENDER MYTH #24

Nontranssexual women at Michigan don't want male-to-female transsexuals here.

FACT: Although Festival organizers claim that the policy excluding transsexuals reflects the sentiment of the community at large, many nontranssexual women support the rights of transsexual women and want them to be included. A survey of over 600 women at the 1992 MWMF showed that 73% of those surveyed thought male-to-female transsexuals should be welcome at the Festival; 23% thought they should not be welcome and 4% were undecided. Only 20% would welcome female-to-male transsexuals, who are apparently permitted.

GENDERTRASH

ISSUE 3

WINTER 1995

winter 95 issue # 3 $6.00 (US/Can)

gendertrash

issue # 3

gendertrash (ISSN 1198-8419) is published 4 times a year & gives a voice to gender described people, who have been discouraged from speaking out & communicating with each other.

editor Mirha-Soleil Ross
production dir. Xanthra Phillippa

contributors
Marie Alexandra, CaiRa, Vernon Maulsby, Ki Namaste, Xanthra Phillippa, Mirha-Soleil Ross, Marisa Swangha, Linda Taylor, Janis Walworth, Riki Anne Wilchins

covers
front cover: Linda Taylor photographed by M.S. Ross
back cover by Encephalitis Red

layout & design
Mirha-Soleil Ross & Xanthra Phillippa

published by
genderpress
Box 500-62,
552 Church Street,
Toronto, Ontario
M4Y 2E3
(416) 929-2350 (voice)
(416) 929 2804 (fax)
call first on voice line to set up fax

printed in toronto

Contents

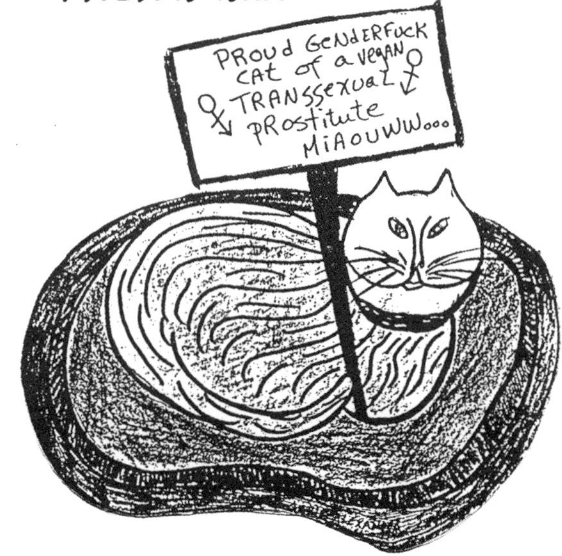

cartoon by Marie Alexandra

You can pick up *gendertrash* at:

Baltimore, MD
Lambda Rising
241 W. Chase Street

Boston, MA
Glad Day Bookshop
673 Boynton Street

Cambridge, MA
New Words
186 Hampshire Street

Montréal, Qué.
L'Androgyne
3636 boul. St. Laurent

La Librairie Alternative
2035 boul. St. Laurent

Ottawa, Ont.
Mags & Fags
286 Elgin Street

Peterborough, Ont.
Marginal Distribution
Unit 103, Lower Mall,
277 George Street

Philadelphia, PA
Giovanni's Room
345 South 12th Street

Rehoboth Beach, DE
Lambda Rising
39 Baltimore Avenue

San Francisco, CA
A Different Light Bookstore
489 Castro Street

Seattle, Wash
Beyond the Closet Bookstore
1501 Belmont

Silverlake, CA
Circus of Books
4001 Sunset Blvd

Toronto, Ont.
Glad Day Bookshop
598A Yonge Street

This Ain't the Rosedale Library
483 Church Street

The Toronto Women's Bookstore
73 Harbord Street

Vancouver, BC
Little Sister Bookstore
1221 Thurlow Street

Transition Boutique
1351 Adanace

Washington, DC
Lambda Rising
1625 Connecticut NW

We're always looking for new bookstores, gender boutiques & other gender-positive establishments to carry ***gendertrash***. If you are one of those or know of a place that might sell ***gendertrash***, please contact us at: (416) 929-2350.

Submissions: We welcome transsexual (both ftm's and mtf's), transgender and intersexed people to send us photos, drawings, poetry, essays,cartoons etc. Gender-positive genetics are also encourage to submit. You can submit a written piece on either a 3.5 or 5.25 floppy disc (IBM format, HD DS). Submissions may also be typed or handwritten, but should be double spaced & must be legible. Include your name, address and phone number. Put your name and the title of your piece on every page. Mention if your piece has been published somewhere else. Please, for Christina's sake, include a brief bio so that we and our readers can know a bit more about you and the colour of your underwear. Also include a picture if possible (mention who took it) or any other kind of artwork to accompany your piece. Anonymity can be preserved, just tell us the pseudonym you want to use. Submission does not necessarily include publication. Submissions are all subject to editing for length and clarity so don't freak out too much about grammar and spelling. We'll try to repair it the best we can. Don't forget a S.A.S.E. if you want your material to be returned.

letters...

Thanks, thanks, thanks...

Thanks for your latest issue - it was great! Excellent articles - very intelligent - and nice lay out. I was most impressed!

yrs
Carl Alessi
St Clair, PA

More thanks, questions & comments...

Xanthra -

I finally picked up your zine and loved it. I also saw you and Jeanne B. at the Euclid [last year] and loved that too. I am a dyke who does lesbian and gay history and was wondering:

- did you know that the real first Canadian ♀ doctor was a woman who passed as a man? and so was the first woman member of Parliament...
- I was wondering, do butch and fem dykes fit into/under your umbrella? I mean women who adorn themselves according to one particular gender, be it male or female, and still identify with their biological sex?

Another interesting comment I have is that it is interesting that you have a feminist consciousness unlike the majority of the gay male population - I hope you find the kind of empowerment I, and many other women have found, by seeing the world thru feminist-coloured glasses, and I feel a greater kinship to your community for it.

Thanks, and I look forward to your next issue.

Elise Chenier
Toronto, Ontario

Our response:
Thank you for your letter.
To answer your first question - no, we weren't aware of the first Canadian ♀ doctor or first member of Parliament being "passing women". But we wonder if they really were women or just FTM transsexuals or transgendered people living in earlier times. We believe that many people from the past who have been labelled as "passing women", were not women at all. They have just been recently reclaimed by the lesbian/feminist community as role models, using questionable methods of analysis. Using present day socio-economic analysis to interpret transgender behaviour in people throughout history who have been classified as "biological women" is not sufficient, but suspect and produces very simplistic results. The notion of gender and what it means to be a woman or a man differs not only from one individual to another, but also across time and culture. Unless we can read these people's intimate diaries or their thoughts or speak to them directly, it is next to impossible to know how they identified themselves (man/ woman/ both/ neither or something else).
As far as butch/fem goes, the answer to your second question depends on what you mean by the term "umbrella". There is an infinite multiplicity of possible gender & transgender expressions & butch/ fem is certainly one of them. The transgender liberation movement will be beneficial to a great number of people with different backgrounds. The main concern that we (& many other transsexuals) have is that it is becoming way too general & will end up emancipating everybody except us. Transsexuals have a herstory/history of being left out or literally dragged through the mud not only by mainstream society but also by lesbians/ gays and feminists. We should keep in mind that not so long ago it was (& still is in some cases) politically okay in certain alternative & left-wing circles to be anti-transsexual. Transsexuals have a unique perspective on gender and should therefore be at the core of any movement dealing with gender or transgender issues (including feminism).
Finally, yes, feminism has had an immense & mostly positive impact on how we perceive ourselves, the rest of the world, and how we live our lives. The reason we have a feminist consciousness unlike the "majority of the gay male population" is simple: we are neither gay nor male.

Mirha-Soleil
Xanthra Phillippa

Greetings from Berlin

Thank you so much for your package...

I really like the idea of *gendertrash*. While the german groups and organizations are desperate for an alternative publication... we (in Hamburg/ Berlin) are planning a magazine called "Genderexpress" (German-wide). With the situation of surgeries. Lea, the BdT and I have already talked and written to many doctors in Germany, Switzerland and Great Britain.

This project called "Information standards in OP Methods" was started by me in order to stop TS's running all over Germany like chickens without heads, because of the confusion that exists around medical jargon, which can make a truly well thought decision impossible.

Dr. Biber is no stranger to us. We were all really shocked at how he does his surgery - he was presented on RTL TV last year.

Dr. Waltraud Schiffels and the BdT will also publish a book this year with a real description of all the methods currently available in Germany. We will also discuss Hormone Therapy since many people in Germany have died through overdose. Since the so-called reunification of Germany, we have started looking at the crimes committed against TS in the old East Germany. We will talk about what happened to our group here in Berlin in September 1992, when Dr. Dörner was looking for test-tube-transsexuals in order to show that Homo- and Transsexuality can be prenately prevented with hormone shots...

The idea that transsexuality is not a sexual orientation - in comparison to homosexuality- is unknown to those East doctors, who crippled TS's in their concentration camps called DDR. (GDR)

Well, as you see we are getting busy - looking forward to submit vital information regarding methods in Germany and Europe, to you. For your next issue I will enclose the listing of all known German groups. Feel free to publish my address - the office of the BdT (Bundesvereinigung der Transsexuellen) <Federal union of the transsexuals!

I believe that it's rather interesting for you to see that we have numerous methods and Doctors in Europe - in comparison to North America...

All our love from Berlin,

Uwe Klaasen
Berlin, Germany

Uwe's address is:
Mindener Strasse 15
10589 Berlin
Germany

If anyone wishes a copy of the list of groups that Uwe sent us, please send us a SASE.

In Spirit

Greetings! I just had to drop a line, and thank you from the bottom of my heart for issue #2 of *gendertrash*. I'm not sure if I can find the words to properly express the gratitude within me. To actually be able to read, to hold in my hands a magazine that speaks what is in my heart and mind, it is a feeling of joy and empowerment beyond my wildest dreams and prayers.

The pieces on the MWMF struck me the most powerfully, and the most personally. Nancy's plight at the festival (as reported in **Gay Community News**) was responsible to a great deal in my own,now very vocal openness. My response to a "rabid" radical feminist that supported Nancy's expulsion, was the first time that anger overrode my fear, so that I was able to speak out on what I saw as a blatant injustice. I've never let fear silence me again.

As you know, I'm a TV, and a prisoner. All of my life, I have had to hide, both my need to crossdress, as well as my love for transsexuals. To be honest, I would join their ranks in a heartbeat if possible.That's a deeply hidden secret I've hidden in my heart all of my life. I feel safe admitting it to you folks.

I truly loved the Genetic Jerk Quiz and plan to make any person I may want to get seriously involved with take it.

Vogel and Price (producers of MWMF) have been lying their asses off for years! The simple truth is that they don't want TS's there, regardless of the opinions of the festival participants. As long as they are in charge, the problem will remain. Perhaps it's time for us to have a festival of our own, one where all womyn are welcome. I suspect that such a festival would leave Price and Vogel sitting in the woods by themselves.

Enough out of me. Again my heartfelt thanks.

Vernon Maulsby
Graterford, PA

Happy Housewife

I have recently had the good fortune to come across your wonderful "zine". I am impressed. I wish you the best of luck in continuing your work.

I can relate closely to the lifestyle your magazine describes. Although I am presently a suburban housewife, my history is colourful. I can honestly say that I've been there. The scene in Ottawa is not as heavy as it may be in Toronto, but it has had its moments.

Hopefully, we can keep in touch. Again, I wish you and all the people that put that magazine together the best of luck. Do keep in touch

Diana R. Coultridge
Gender Mosaic
Orleans, Ontario

Transphobia at the Vancouver Women's Bookstore

Dear Xanthra

I am writing to you in response to our phonecall a while back. I work at the Vancouver Women's Bookstore and spoke to you on the phone about the possibility of selling *gendertrash* in the store. I said that i would present it at the next meeting in the hopes that the other women would be in support of carrying *gendertrash*.

I am sad to say that the meeting went exactly as i thought it would. While some of the women said that they would take a look at the magazine, others felt that they couldn't support it because:

1) transsexuals are homophobic because as men, they do not acknowledge their attraction to men.

- or -

2) they have a stereotypical idea of what women are - feminine, make-up, dresses and so forth.

- or -

3) why are women expected to 'take in' transsexuals - it's always the women that have to do this work.

I am sure that you've heard these kinds of ignorant comments before. This issue is only one of many issues that I am in disagreement with over the 'collective'. I believe that if we are to have a solid 'movement' - it must be inclusive and it means autonomy - or people's right to choose on all levels and issues.

(continued on next page)

letters cont'd...

I am taking a leave of absence from the bookstore for a couple of months but i will take up the fight to have *gendertrash* in the women's bookstore when i return.

Kirsten McIlveen
Vancouver, BC

editor's note - if anybody wishes to see gendertrash (or any other ts/tg magazine) at the Vancouver Women's Bookstore, they are urged to write or call the store to tell them that they are tired & pissed off at this old 70-ish transphobic bigotry.

Inclusion Problems at the Int'l Gay & Lesbian Archives

We wrote the following letter after receiving a request for a free subscription from J.H.on behalf of the IGLA. The 2nd letter is their response:

Thank you for your request.
The only problem we have with your project, as you have described it, is that it does not seem to include transgendered people. So we are wondering if you really know about the nature of our magazine. *gendertrash* is entirely devoted to the issues and concerns of transsexuals and transgendered people, many of whom do not identify as lesbian, gay or bisexual.
In addition, we believe that TS/TG communities are not subsections of the lesbian and gay communities. We have unique cultures of our own despite the intersections between our herstories/histories.
Therefore, we would like to know how TS/TG people are covered in your Mission statement and in your archives (we noticed that we are not mentioned in your title). If we are not included in your literature, etc., well, it's never too late to start. This would greatly stimulate us and other TS/TG's to donate material in the future.
We hope to hear from you soon.

Jeanne B.
Xanthra Phillippa

Dear Jeanne & Xanthra:
Thanks for sending copies of *gendertrash* to the International Gay and Lesbian Archives. I'm a volunteer at the Archives, so I have no decision making power regarding the name and mission of the Archives, but I gave a copy of your letter to the Board President. I recently got a similar note from a Bisexual organization & passed it on. The Board members (once again) decided not to adjust the name of the Archives. My understanding is that they've decided that since the Archives is dedicated to collecting all materials "related to" Gay and Lesbian life and issues, that this is inclusive of Bisexuality and Transsexualism.
I'd like to spend a minute explaining why I wrote to you and felt that *gendertrash* needed to be included in the Archives' collection. Researchers come to the Archives so that they can find not only what the mainstream press has to say, but also what each of the many communities that make up the larger movement have to say. Without publications like *gendertrash* being in the collection, I have this great fear that someone will just assume that transgendered is the same as gay and bisexual is the same as lesbian and that liberal democrat is the only version of any of us. Having your publication in the collection allows someone 10 to 100 years from now to see the difference between an insider and outsider covering transsexual issues.
As the person who does the filing in the clippings and newsletter files, I felt we have a fair to middling coverage of the outsider point of view dating back to the days of "changelings". I felt the insight provided by transsexuals defining themselves was missing so when I read about your publication I was anxious to expand what we can offer by including your efforts. I hope to find myself filing future issues of *gendertrash*.
Regards,

Jeff Hagedorn
North Hollywood, Ca

PS I very much enjoyed reading the 2 issues that were in your package.

*Patrick Daniel Johnson, who was originally charged with the 1st degree murder of Grayce Baxter (**pictured above**), plea-bargained in April to 2nd degree murder and was sentenced to 25 years in penitentiary. He will be eligible for parole in 10 years.*

Grayce Elizabeth Baxter was a very successful transsexual escort, working in Toronto. She disappeared in December, 1992 & her body has never been found.

Don't Touch Me - I'm Electric
TS Epileptic

DISABLED TS NOT WANTED

I found out that I'm not a real transsexual anymore
even though I & everybody else
thought I was

Because, according to some self styled experts
from some Pure Ableist Middle Class TS Fantasy Land,
epileptics aren't really true transsexuals;
it's just the side-effect of all
the anti-epileptic pills we have to take

Of course these experts have no neurological or neuro-pharmacological training
to base these judgements on,
just their own anti-epileptic prejudices

Obviously I must have been wrong when I thought that my epilepsy
was a result of the stress of being a transsexual

I guess I better get rid of my neurologist
because he never mentioned
that what I thought was transsexuality
was really just a psychological side-effect
of the pills he prescribed me

Instead he only checked to see
if the estrogen was having any effect at all on my seizure activity

So I guess I don't belong to the True Transsexual Community
because the community for which I have been searching for all these years
is one that would welcome me
& others like me
as we are
without hesitation

Xanthra Phillippa

Investigating Women's Shelters

by Mirha-Soleil Ross

The inclusion of TS women in women's shelters has been an issue within social service agencies and our community for many years. While many social workers have expressed their frustration at their inability to find adequate emergency shelters for TS women in crisis, very little has been done to:

1 - document the inaccessibility of shelters to TS', so that we can convince funding bodies of the need for TS specific services.

2 - urge women's shelters to establish clear, unambiguous policies regarding TS women & make them public so that we can have an official record/listing of the actual resources available to the TS community.

3 - confront ignorance & obvious cases of discrimination against TS' when they arise (eg "we don't take TS' because they're men").

Because we believe that the collecting of such information is vital for our community, we decided to go ahead and do the job ourselves. Having transsexuals rather than non-transsexuals leading this kind of investigation was also another factor that encouraged us to create the survey. Far too many times in the past, the non-inclusion of transsexuals within women's shelters has been used by some people to attack feminists. We feel very uncomfortable when genetics (especially men) use us to deal with their own personal problems with feminism. We are perfectly able to defend ourselves and don't need any non-transsexual to protect us, much less throw invectives at feminists in the name of our oppression. Whatever problems exist between genetic and transsexual women, they should be solved between us.

We prepared the following covering letter & questionnaire & sent it (with a S.A.S.E) to 20 women's shelters in the Metro Toronto area.

Dear XYZ

We are writing to ask you to complete the following questionnaire.

We are two transsexuals who have been active in the transsexual community for several years. One area that has especially concerned us is the lack of an official list of emergency shelters where transsexual women in crisis can go in Toronto. This has been confirmed by many groups and agencies in this city who work with transsexual clients on a regular basis.

The primary reason for making such a questionnaire is to create a clear and unambiguous listing of shelters where transsexual women in crisis will be accepted and safe. Such a listing would help to evaluate the needs of Toronto's transsexual community in terms of resources and eventually to fill in the gaps.

Another rationale for this questionnaire is to have a record of how transsexuality is perceived by agencies working with women, both collectively and individually.

Even though we are critical of policies excluding transsexual women, our intentions are constructive. As stated above, the purpose of this questionnaire is to create a practical resource base of transsexual-positive shelters for our community. We will compile the information received and share it with the groups and individuals who need it. As well we intend to publish the results in an upcoming issue of gendertrash.

In order to facilitate the compilation of responses, we would appreciate it if you could return the questionnaire on or before April 15th.

Thank you very much for your time and energy. If you have any questions or concerns, please contact us at the above number.

Mirha-Soleil Xanthra Phillippa

The Questionnaire

Identification: In this section, we asked the shelter's name, address, phone number, & the name & position of the person answering the questionnaire. We then asked if they could send a copy of the shelter's mandate or mission statement when they would return the questionnaire.

(i) Funding

We asked if the shelter received funding from the federal, provincial, Metro Toronto or Toronto governments. We also asked about other sources of funding. As well we had a part labelled "cannot answer this section for the following reason(s)". Finally there was a place to list their comments.

(ii) Clientele

1. Does the shelter accept transsexual women as clients?

>yes - without restrictions

>yes - with special restrictions (the following were listed: the client must pass as a woman/the client must live full time as a woman/sex reassignment surgery (genital

surgery) must be complete/the client must identify as a woman/the client must be discreet about her transsexual background/ others(please list)
>no under any circumstances (plus reasons) each case is dealt with individually
>other
>comments
2. Have you ever had any requests to take transsexual women in your shelter (yes/no)?
>if yes (a) approximately how during the last year (1993) & (b) approximately how many were referred by other social agencies
>comments
3. To your knowledge, have there ever been any transsexual women as clients at the shelter (yes/no/don't know/uncertain/cannot answer this question for the following reasons)?
>if yes, can you give an approximate number during 1993 & approximately how many were referred by other agencies
>comments
4. Does the shelter have a written policy regarding transsexual women as clients (yes/no/a policy is in the process of being written)?
>comments
5. If the shelter accepts transsexual women, is there a policy protecting the confidentiality of their backgrounds?
(iii) Employment
1. Would you accept a transsexual woman working at the shelter (yes - any specific requirements/no - reasons)
2. Does the shelter have a written policy regarding transsexual women as employees? (if yes could you include a copy of the policy)
(iv) General Information
1. Does the shelter have a written policy prohibiting discrimination on the basis of gender identity? (if yes could you include a copy of the policy)
2. a) We are unable to answer this survey for these reasons
b) We do not wish to answer this survey for these reasons
3. Would you like to receive the results obtained from this questionnaire?
4. Further comments, suggestions and/or concerns.

List of shelters:
Anduhyaun Residence
Emily Stowe Shelter for Women
Ernestine's Women's Shelter
Homeward Family Shelter
Interim Place
Interval House
Nellie's
North York Women's Shelter
Our Lady of the Resurrection House
Redwood Shelter
Salvation Army Evangeline Shelter
Shirley Samaroo House
Society of St Vincent de Paul - Rendu House
Stop 86
Street Haven at the Crossroads
Women in Transition
Women's Habitat of Etobicoke
Women's Residence
Woodland Residence
Yellow Brick House

Results

Several weeks after sending the survey to the shelters, we still had received very few responses. So we sent another letter to the shelters who hadn't mailed back the questionnaire. We offered to forward them another copy if they hadn't received it or had lost it.
As of August 1994, a total of 5 questionnaires had been returned to us, from the following shelters:

Interim Place
North York Women's Shelter
Rendu House
Stop 86, YWCA of Metropolitan Toronto
YWCA Woodlawn Residence

We also received phone calls from women working at Emily Stowe and Ernestine's Women's shelter. They said that they felt they didn't know enough about transsexual women at that point to be able to answer the survey adequately. They nonetheless said that this was an area they were very interested in and asked us to send them educational packages and/or meet them to discuss the issue.
Another woman contacted us, this time from Homeward Family Shelter. She told us that they deal with families (with or without a father) and since they provide a separate room for each family, it was irrelevant to them whether or not their clients were transsexuals.

Questions re: TS women as clients

In responding to the question whether or not the shelter accepts transsexual women as clients, Stop 86, North York Women's Shelter and Rendu House answered yes, with special restrictions. North York specified that the client must identify as a woman whereas Stop 86 indicated that sex reassignment surgery must be complete. Rendu House specified both restrictions as a condition to take TS women in and stated that their reasons for those restrictions were "because women here live in close quarters and [have] histories of abuse from men." Interim Place answered that each case is dealt with individually. The YWCA Woodlawn Residence answered "other" and that "Woodlawn House is for women only, the facilities at Woodlawn are common in that all residents share bathrooms, kitchen, lounges, laundry room etc. and some sleeping accommodations."
In response to the question "Have you ever had any request to take TS women in your shelter?", North York Women's Shelter, Rendu House and Stop 86 answered yes. Interim Place answered no and Woodlawn Residence didn't answer. North York Women's Shelter said that they've had requests to take, and have had TS women as clients in the shelter in the past but none during 1993. They declared having no policy regarding TS women in general nor one specifically protecting the confidentiality of

their backgrounds.
Rendu House said that, as far as they are aware, they had only one request during 1993 to take a TS woman in the shelter. She was referred to them by another social agency. They also said that as far as they are aware, there have been TS women as clients at the shelter but none during 1993. They declared that they have a written policy regarding TS women as clients, including one protecting the confidentiality of their backgrounds.
Stop 86 said that they had approximately 3 requests to take TS women in their shelter during 1993, one of which was referred to them by another social agency. Responding to the question "to your knowledge, have there ever been any TS women as clients at the shelter?", they answered "No. We have had request for referrals from TS women whose genital surgery was not complete." But to the question "if yes, can you give an approximate number during 1993?", they answered "one." As far as a written policy goes, they said that a general policy regarding TS women was in the process of being written and that the shelter has a confidentiality policy for all clients.
Interim Place said that they don't know if they have ever had TS women at the shelter. They also stated that they have no policy regarding TS women in general or specifically protecting the confidentiality of their backgrounds.

Questions re: employment
Concerning TS women as employees, North York Women's Shelter wrote that they would accept a TS woman working at the shelter if she identified as a woman. Rendu House also wrote that they would accept a TS woman working at the shelter if "she was as well qualified as other applicants." Stop 86 didn't answer clearly yes or no but just wrote "if the surgery phases were totally complete. Our policies are developed by the YWCA of Metropolitan Toronto." Interim Place and YWCA Woodlawn Residence didn't answer that question.
None of the shelters have a policy re: TS women as employees.

General Information
None of the shelters have a written policy prohibiting discrimination on the basis of gender identity. North York Women's Shelter commented

"Thank you for your questionnaire. This is an area that we need to explore further regarding our policies and our commitment to an inclusive service delivery."

Rendu House wrote

"I agree that there is a need to provide shelter service to transexuals. We would welcome a transsexual woman (within our limitations as outlined in our policy on complete sex-change.) As I noted, this policy is in fairness to the women we serve. But it is an extremely sensitive topic to broach with someone, and causes discomfort for all involved. We would not approach a person unless there was cause for concern and the safe feeling of the house was affected. we might ask for verification (papers or medical proof) as proof. We would never do this ourselves (try to verify.) The integrity and the dignity of the person is a priority. If we could not accommodate a transsexual woman, we would refer her to women's residence and hope that they could put her up in a motel room. We would strive for fairness in employment and hire based on qualifications and skills needed to serve our residents. Good luck. Sorry for the delay"

Comments
The response to this survey was too small to perform any kind of statistical analysis. This wasn't the idea behind doing that questionnaire anyway. The motives for creating it were explained in the covering letter that we sent to the shelters as well as in the introduction to this article.
So what does this survey and the responses tell us? First, it shows that transsexuality is becoming an issue that is finally beginning to be taken seriously, within certain women's shelters. The comments from certain women who answered the survey taken with the fact that some shelter workers expressed a desire to educate themselves about transsexual issues, clearly demonstrate that they are trying to honestly deal with the sometimes difficult and complex questions that surface alongside the integration of TS women in the larger women's community.
One of the main concerns of non-transsexual women, when we talk about TS women's access to women's spaces (and many women answering the survey mentioned it), is safety. It is safety that is often used as a justification for exclusion or limited inclusion. Although no one answering the survey explicitly said that they are worried about the safety of the actual residents (ie: the non-transsexuals), it is often implicit in some of their responses and also in some conversations we had with them. I don't understand where this fear comes from. It is as if there were hordes of TS women attacking non-TS women all over this continent. I do not know of one documented case of a TS woman assaulting a non-TS woman. On the other hand, I know of many cases, on a personal as well as on a public level (and not just on Geraldo or Jerry Springer either) in which non-TS women have verbally and/or physically assaulted TS women. If I have fear and concerns for anyone's safety in a shelter, it is for an isolated TS woman, not for a non-transsexual who doesn't have to prove to anyone that she is a woman. This concern was echoed to us by a worker from Ernestine's Women's Shelter.
Even the argument that TS women should be excluded for their own safety is not acceptable on a long term basis. Just like for any other form of prejudice and discrimination, if some non-transsexual women are threatening the safety of a TS woman because she is a transsexual, it should be dealt with immediately and efficiently. The non-transsexual women should be confronted about their own ignorance and violence. I don't see why TS women should be restricted from access to such vital services because of somebody else's transphobia and hatred.
Another point that I really think is crucial to address in any discussion concerning TS women access to women's shelters, is the requirement of complete

genital transformative surgery for inclusion. I think this is crucial because that's what this whole issue is all about. It revolves more around the inclusion of pre/non-op TS women since the exclusion of a post-op TS woman may be easier to challenge on legal grounds. Some women's shelters with a commitment to an inclusive service will accept TS women but will only include TS's who have undergone an SRS. This policy is politically problematic when we know that the TS women who need those shelters' services the most, are the ones who are probably the least likely to have the priviledges required to get an SRS. It means that, right off the top, transsexual prostitutes and transsexuals with a criminal record will be penalized since they are still systematically excluded from gender identity programs, the only path to take to get the costs of an SRS reimbursed. It means that HIV-positive transsexuals and transsexuals living with AIDS will be excluded since most surgeons won't perform an SRS on them. It means that transsexuals who are a bit too young to get an SRS or transsexuals who are still uncertain about what they are or want even if they look, behave, talk, walk, smell, piss and shit like women will be excluded on the basis of a "genital issue". It also means that transsexuals who don't fit the narrow criterias of Harry Benjamin (Sacro-saint détenteur du dernier mot sur la nature des sexes et la destinée de nos organes génitaux), will be excluded. And what about transsexuals who can't have a major surgery for health reasons? Or transsexuals who refuse to have an SRS for political and/or cultural and/or spiritual reasons? Or the transsexuals who are justifiably concerned about the very poor quality of many SRS's? Or simply transsexuals who are further disadvantaged socially and therefore economically because of race, class, age, disability and/or others, and can't afford 10 to 25 thousand bucks in order to conform to the suffocating standards of gender currently in vogue in this society? All of the above and many others will be deprived of a very vital service because they can't or don't want to get an SRS for whatever reason. I would also like to add that in my experience, every single time I came across a transsexual woman who needed the services of a shelter, she was a pre or non-operative transsexual.

I do not have any miracle solutions. I deeply believe that the inclusion of TS women in women's shelters is a very complex issue that should be dealt with carefully, step by step. There is no doubt that a key factor for success in resolving this matter will be the education of the shelter directors and workers. It is only after these women take steps in getting to know more about transsexuality, in examining, acknowledging and confronting their own anti-transsexual feelings and ideas that they will be able to really deliver decent services to our community.

One could ask and wonder if we consider that this questionnaire was worth doing and if we reached our goal. As far as keeping a record of how transsexuality is perceived in women's shelters, I think that the fact that so many shelters didn't even bother answering the survey is in itself a very significant testimony of the importance given to transsexual issues in these establishments. On the other hand, as I already mentioned, the sincere interest and good intentions of many others regarding this question, was very encouraging in developing future discussion and cooperation with them. We are no more advanced than before in terms of getting an official listing of transsexual-positive shelters since we recieved such small and vague responses. In order to get that "official" listing of shelters, we will have to reiterate our demand that <u>all</u> women's shelters establish <u>clear</u> policies regarding transsexual women. Policies such as "women only", or "women-born women only", or "biological women only" are not acceptable because they are far too equivocal and imprecise, and allow far too great a variation in interpretation.

Finally, I would like to state that the whole question of TS women in women's shelters is a perfect example of how TS's are defined, controlled and regulated by non-transsexuals, whether they be psychiatric authorities demanding that we fit <u>their</u> pre-conceived and prejudiced notions of gender or non-transsexual women deciding whether or not to include us and under what circumstances. It shows very clearly the real lack of control we have over our own identities and just as clearly why we need to take charge of every single facet of who and what we are. Hopefully, the day will come when we will have transsexual specific services, when we won't need to package ourselves in such a degrading way, and when we won't need to conduct this kind of survey. That day, we will have finally proven to ourselves and this society that our lives, transsexual lives, are worth it.

Photo of Mirha-Soleil Ross
by Xanthra Phillippa

Realizing that she could never be a second Marlon Brando, Mirha-Soleil Ross quit acting school in 1991 to become a street prostitute. She is québécoise; her first language is Joual; she's been pro-animal rights/vegetarian for 9 years and she lives with her dog, two cats, five turtles and TS soulmate, who patiently helps her juggle her attraction to men and her love for TS women.

Born to tell

by Linda Taylor

I'm a sixteen year old transsexual.
I've been a transsexual
for about three years now.
I remember when
I first came out as
a transsexual;
it was as if
I were a criminal.
Everyone kept looking at me
and whispering.
They all had
one thing to ask::
"Are you gay?"
Truly I said yes.
I didn't care
what anyone
thought of me,
because I learned
that I can't please everyone.
I found out that
being gay was hard,
but being a transsexual was even tougher.
But anyway,
who said life
was going to
be easy.
For me to be strong,
I have to believe in myself.
I can't let people put me down.
Sexuality is a big thing for me;
it's like the more I get deeper in myself,
the more my sexuality
seems to get the best of me.
I'm not saying I'm all sexual,
but of course we are all sexual people,
no matter who we are.
In school, sexuality is never spoken.
I hope my school takes sexuality,
but till then i've got
to let them
see the meaning of love.

photos by M.S. Ross

♦ *Linda Taylor is a gorgeous, intelligent, and very funny Indian-Jamaican sweetheart living in Toronto.*

Davi

a true story
by Vernon Maulsby

I've always loved, or wished to be loved by, transsexuals and it all began with Davi.

We met in our early teens. He had just been thrown out of the parochial school he'd been enrolled in, something about being caught in a school dress once too often. He wore it on his first day in public school, and I must admit that he looked great in a white blouse, dark blue and green checked dress and knee socks. When I saw him across the room, something changed in me forever. Davi smiled at me, just for a second, and his hazel eyes locked onto mine. The smile was a brave one, it only slipped a touch when the teacher, finally aware that Davi was a boy, had him sent home. Every lover of mine since has had hazel eyes.

Seven years went by, years of hiding my "difference". It stayed hidden, buried so deep that only the pain showed. Years of hazel-eyed, out-of-bed before dawn, one night stands, episodes that were total lies in themselves. I continued to hide, to pretend to be so butch that no one would ever suspect that I, six feet and over 200 pounds, cried most nights, because I didn't dare to reveal the woman within me, the woman I am meant to be. Seven years of hidden woman's years, then Davi reentered my life.

At that time, I was working in an electronics factory, openly out as being gay, while in truth lying my ass off about who I really was. Then I saw Davi. He was totally transformed, long-to-the-shoulders blond hair, a truly magnificent bosom, and a walk to die for. What I recognized were the eyes, the same eyes that bewitched me so long ago. When she saw me, her face lit up and my name came instantly out of her mouth. Davi was living as a woman then, going through years of stuff before the surgery. Everyone in the factory thought her a gorgeous woman, and were a bit miffed when we became a couple.

We lived together for about a year, one that taught me that love was possible. I gave my heart without reservation.

After her surgery, something happened; she began, ever softly, to leave me, not just me, but anyone who reminded her of her pre-surgery days. Yes, I'd been warned of the possibility, by my smarter, wiser sisters, but I had held on to the slim hope, up to the second I came back from work to find her gone. The faint scent of perfume, and the memory of her eyes were all that was left to me.

I saw her again, about a decade later, looking truly smashing; she had a truly handsome guy, and they looked rather meant for each other. This time, when our eyes met, her hazel eyes looked through me, leaving a chill in its wake.

♦**Vernon Maulsby is a transgendered prisoner from Pennsylvania.**

TS Womyn Enter MWWMF

photo by Mariette Pathy-Allen

Women from Camp Trans buying tickets at the MWMF front gate.

(HART, MI.) — Six openly transsexual women were allowed to enter the 19th annual Michigan Womyn's Music Festival near Hart, Michigan, on Saturday, August 13, 1994, following a week-long protest of that event's "womyn born womyn" only policy. The six transsexual women were: Zythyra Anne Austen of Winchester, Va.; April Fredericks and Riki Anne Wilchins of New York City; Rica Ashby Frederickson of Philadelphia; Davina Anne Gabriel of Kansas City, Mo.; and Jessica Meredith Xavier of silver Springs, Md. Accompanying the transsexual women were several nontranssexual supporters who were also taking part in the protest, including authors and activists Leslie Feinberg and Minnie Bruce Pratt, both of Jersey City, N.J., and one intersex individual, Kodi Hendrix of Kokomo, In.

The protest of the festival's policy of excluding transsexual women from attendance was the third consecutive and largest action staged against the policy since Nancy Jean Burkholder was expelled from the 16th annual festival in 1991. Thirteen transsexual women — with their friends and supporters, including 12 nontranssexual women, one transsexual man, one nontranssexual man, and one intersex person — camped out during the week or the festival and took part in a variety of activities designed to inform festival participants about gender issues and to protest the festival's exclusionary policy.

The transsexual women at Camp Trans who did not enter the festival were: Hannah Blackwell of Kansas City, Mo.; Nancy Jean Burkholder of Weare, N.H.; Nancy Anne Forrest of Philadelphia; Wendi Lynn Kaiser of North Berwick, Me.; Lynn Walker and Krissy Withers, both of New York City; and Arlene Wolves of Ashland, N.H.

The protesters began setting up their camp, including a large, bright green banner proclaiming, "Camp Trans: For Humyn-Born Humyns," before festival participants began arriving on Sunday, August 7. The following day, protesters began distributing a schedule of 29 activities consisting of workshops, speeches, meetings, readings, concerts, religious services, games, and meals, taking place at Camp Trans over a four-day period, to women in their cars waiting to enter the festival. Also distributed to festival participants was a joint statement addressing the need for respectful and constructive dialogue on the issue by one of the transsexual protesters, Riki Anne Wilchins, and lesbian musician Alix Dobkin, a supporter of the festival's exclusionary policy, who has been actively involved in the festival since its inception.

Protesters received an overwhelmingly positive response, and only very slight negative reaction, to their presence and their flyers. They continued to distribute their literature to women arriving for the festival throughout the week, as well as to the many women who came out from the festival to visit them. Festival workers at the gate engaged in a variety of tactics throughout the week apparently designed to harass protesters and prevent them from distributing their literature to arriving participants.

The first activity, scheduled to take place on Wednesday, August 10, was a community meeting on the issue of transsexual inclusion, which Alix Dobkin had agreed to attend. However, Ms. Dobkin sent a message to Camp Trans on Tuesday, August 9, stating that she had changed her mind and that she would not be attending because it might appear that she was in support of the protesters' position. The community meeting, which was attended by approximately 20 festival participants, was held without Ms. Dobkin and sparked a thought-provoking discussion. Workshops were also conducted on self-defense, androgyny, transsexual sexuality, disability rights, transsexuals and the military, sadomasochism, female-to-male identity, gender bending, and other topics.

Protesters were joined on Wednesday by lesbian comedian Mimi=Freed of San Francisco, who performed stand-up comedy and conducted a workshop entitled "The joys of Marginalization" the following day. A good-humoured weenie roast was held Thursday evening, which drew about 25 festival participants out to enjoy relaxed conversation and indulge in meat and chocolate, comestibles not served by the festival kitchen. — ***ed.'s note: oh those poor little oppressed and oh-so-victimized meat and chocolate eaters*** —

Also on Thursday, Charlotte Manheimer of Cincinnati, Oh., a 68-year-old non-transsexual lesbian, attempted to enter the festival in order to visit a friend but was not immediately allowed to enter because she refused to disclose whether or not she was a transsexual and refused to agree to the festival staff's condition that she "respect" the exclusionary policy. Because she was over 65 years of age, Ms. Manheimer was eligible to attend the festival free of charge. Staff offered to escort Ms. Manheimer to find her friend but were reluctant to issue her a festival wristband. After a two-hour period of deliberation among festival staff, Ms. Manheimer, who travelled to the festival for the express purpose of demonstrating support for the transsexual women taking part in the protest, was given a wristband and allowed to enter the festival unescorted and without disclosing whether or not she was a transsexual.

Acclaimed authors and activists, Leslie Feinberg, Minnie Bruce Pratt, and James Green joined protesters on Friday, August 12. Ms. Feinberg is well-known for her popular novel *Stone Butch Blues*, and Ms. Pratt for her poetry. Mr. Green is a postoperative female-to-male transsexual and the publisher and editor of the *FTM Newsletter*, which is the most widely circulated publication in the world specifically addressing female-to-male transsexual issues, as well as the director of the FTM Support Group in San Francisco. Mr. Green conducted two workshops on female-to-male experience and identity at Camp Trans. Each was attended by 20 to 30 festival participants.

The highlight of the scheduled activities was a speech entitled "Sisterhood: Make it Real!" delivered by Leslie Feinberg in which she discussed the necessity for the women's movement in general, and the Michigan Womyn's Music Festival in particular, to adopt an "all women welcome" policy. Approximately 150 festival participants came outside to hear Ms. Feinberg's address, making it the most well attended event at Camp Trans during the course of the protest.

This was followed by a concert by the Celtic Transsexual Modal Band from Hell, consisting of Arlene Wolves and Beverly Woods of Beyond the Pale, Zythyra (formerly Seth Austen), and Jessica Xavier. Hammered dulcimer, keyboard, and guitar blended exquisitely, but the highlight of the concert was the original "Ballad of Nancy B.," which retold the story of Nancy Burkholder's expulsion from the festival in 1991.

Later in the evening, Ms. Feinberg and her lover Minnie Bruce Pratt conducted a recreation of their joint reading originally performed at the 1992 Out/Write Conference, which consisted of selections from *Stone Butch Blues* and Ms. Pratt's upcoming book *S/he*, to be published by Firebrand Books in February 1995. Ms. Pratt conducted further readings from her book the following morning.

Another of Friday's highlights was the wedding of two festival participants, Kym and Becki, performed by transsexual minister Lynn Walker. James Green and Leslie Feinberg stood up for the couple in a lantern-lit ceremony attended by everyone in Camp Trans and several visitors from the festival, and accompanied by Camp Trans musicians.]

On Thursday, Riki Anne Wilchins, who is a member of the New York City chapter of the Lesbian Avengers, was invited by Lesbian Avengers inside the festival to attend their scheduled meeting on Saturday, August 13. Ms. Wilchins agreed to attempt to enter the festival as an openly transsexual woman in order to attend the meeting if the Lesbian Avengers would provide a contingent to escort her, which they readily agreed to do.

photo by Mariette Pathy-Allen

Leslie Feinberg addressing a Lesbian Avengers meeting inside the Festival.

On Saturday morning, in an attempt to obtain clarification or the "womyn born womyn" policy, protesters requested to meet with Communications coordinators Lucy Tatman and Sue Doerfer. They were asked whether Leslie Feinberg, James Green, and Kodi Hendrix would be permitted to buy tickets without violating festival policy. Leslie Feinberg introduced herself as a person who was born anatomically female but who passes and lives as a man and has a driver's license showing her sex as male. She asked whether she would be welcome to enter the festival. Ms. Tatman said that "the festival would prefer not," a statement she retracted after Ms. Feinberg declared that she would tell audiences on her upcoming book tour that she had received confirmation that she "is not welcome at the Michigan Womyn's Music Festival."

Kodi Hendrix then informed Ms. Tatman and Ms. Doerfer that he was born with both male and female genitalia and asked whether "only half of [him] could come in." James Green stated that he had no desire to enter the festival, and was only there "in support of [his] transsexual sisters," but wanted to know if he would be considered a woman by the festival owners using the same logic by which they consider male-to-female transsexuals to be men even after sex-change surgery. Ms. Tatman and Ms. doerfer were unable to provide answers to either of these questions. Protesters then requested that they receive clarification of the policy regarding these three individuals from festival owners Lisa Vogel and Barbara Price.

Less than an hour later, Ms. Tatman and

Ms. Doerfer delivered a message from the festival owners declining to further clarify the term "womyn born womyn" and stating that it is up to each individual to decide whether or not she is included in that definition. Communications coordinators also assured protesters that no one attempting to purchase a ticket would be harassed and that none of them would be asked by security to leave the festival, because it was "no longer a security issue." The decision was then made that protesters who wished to enter the festival would attempt to enter to purchase tickets when the Lesbian Avengers sent their contingent out to accompany Ms. Wilchins inside for their meeting. Ms. feinberg, who had previously stated that she would not enter the festival until her transsexual sisters were allowed to attend, decided to enter if the transsexual women were also allowed to enter.

Upon approaching the box office, the contingent of protesters presented a statement to the box office staff declaring that their group consisted of transsexual women, nontranssexual women, an intersex person, and transgendered women, and that each of them interpreted the term "womyn born womyn" to include them. None of the protesters were refused tickets or asked questions regarding their medical history or their commitment to uphold festival policy. The protesters were then surrounded by the contingent of Lesbian Avengers and escorted to the scheduled meeting, with a number of other festival participants joining the contingent along the way.

At the Lesbian Avengers meeting, both Ms. Wilchins and Ms. Feinberg spoke at length regarding the festival's exclusionary policy and received an overwhelmingly positive response. After the meeting, the protesters, again surrounded by Lesbian Avengers and joined by numerous other festival participants, conducted a parade through the festival grounds chanting "Support Our Policy: All Women Welcome!" As promised, no one in the Camp Trans contingent was asked by security to leave the festival.

Following their return to Camp Trans, the decision was made to strike camp because of impending severe thunderstorms and forecasts of rain throughout the night and into the following day, and because it was felt that the protest action had been highly successful. However, protesters still feel that the wording of festival policy as "womyn born womyn" only remains unclear and that it is still uncertain whether openly transsexual women will be allowed to attend the festival without fear of expulsion in the future. Unless there is further clarification of these issues in the interim and the festival abolishes its "womyn born womyn" only policy, activists say they will continue their protests next year.

photo by Mariette Pathy-Allen

Members of Camp Trans and supporters.

The MENACE in Michigan

by Riki Anne Wilchins

this article first appeared in Village Voice on September 9,1994. It is reprinted here with the permission of the author.

Last night's rain is gone, and the afternoon sun is burning off the haze. We crossed red-clay county road separating our tents from the wood posts, wire fences and candy-colored tents of the Michigan Women's Music Festival. There are six of us, gender outlaws all, queued up like so many ten-pins before the smiling woman in the ticket booth. The Michigan Womyn's Music Festival is about to meet the transexual menace.

The rather outlandish moment had its genesis in the summer of 1991. A transexual woman, Nancy Jean Burkholder, was accosted by Security guards near this very gate. The producers Barbara ("Boo") Price and Lisa Vogel stated a policy of "womyn-born womyn only". They interpreted this to exclude transexual women, and had Nancy evicted.

It's unlikely the participants in that anonymous late-night drama anticipated the chain reaction it would ignite. Within days, women across the country were talking about the eviction. Author and activist Gayle Rubin called it "the cause celebre'" of '91 Festival. As Rubin writes in her essay "Of Catamites and Kings", "After decades of feminist insistence that women are 'made, not born', after fighting to establish that 'anatomy is not destiny,' it is astounding that ostensibly progressive events can get away with discriminatory policies based so blatantly on recycled biological determinism."

In fact, the complexities of lesbian politics have always made the Borgias look like Ozzie and Harriet. And lesbian transphobia was hardly unique to Michigan. As early as 1972, a transexual woman was forced out of the prototype lesbian organization, Daughters of Bilitis, and as recently as 1991 the National Lesbian Conference banned "nongenetic women". But the festival is one of the country's oldest and most visible gatherings of lesbians, with 7000 to 8000 attendees. For many transexuals, it is a unique symbol of lesbian culture. More importantly, the festival is closely identified with radical lesbian separatists, feminists who embrace Mary Daly's and Janice Raymond's theory that transexual women were merely (I am not making this up) surgically-altered men created by patriarchal surgeons to invade "women's" space. For these reasons, the decision to admit "womyn-born womyn only" carried a special sting.

There have always been lesbians opposed to any women appointing themselves "gender police," judging who can call themselves female and which queer identities are deemed acceptable. "Despite theoretically embracing diversity," notes Rubin, "contemporary lesbian culture has a deep streak of xenophobia [responding with] hysteria, bigotry, and a desire to stamp out the offending messy realities. A 'country club syndrome' sometimes prevails in which the lesbian community is treated as an exclusive enclave from which the riffraff must be systematically expunged."

Lesbians in early feminists C.R. groups were told they weren't "real women", butch-femme and S/M lesbians have been attacked for invading women's space with oppressive, patriarchal influence. The result has been an unrelenting struggle within lesbian-feminism against the politics of exclusion. True to form, the posse accompanying six gender queers into this bucolic vortex included '50s "passing woman" Leslie Feinberg, '70s feminist Minnie Bruce Pratt, S/M sex outlaws from the '80s, and the '90s answer to Queer Nation, the Lesbian Avengers. What earthly power could stand against such a formidable and unholy alliance?

I could trace my own presence at Michigan back to 1978, when I began divesting the male trappings forced on me from birth, transitioning into someone nontransexuals could recognize as female. In the process, my female lover and I metamorphosized from another nice, straight couple to a couple of militant ho-mo-seck-choo-alls walking arm-in-arm in broad daylight down the mainstreets of Cleveland Heights, Ohio.

How is a transexual woman a lesbian? I can no more explain it than breathing, no more describe it than a smell. How is anyone a lesbian, except that their gender identity is female and they are attracted to women? I had know I was female from childhood, and even before surgery made such things possible, desire had long since etched my dreams with soft butches and strong arms, their weight on my back and their insistent, taxing presence inside me. In all this I was not along, for of 13 transexual women in Camp Trans, 11 were lesbian-identified.

So I knew the name for what I was, and I knew I belonged with other lesbians. But the women's community greeted us less like prodigal sisters returned to the fold and more like something they had just discovered after 6 months in the back of the communal icebox. Following a decade of fruitless efforts to claim my place in the lesbian movement, and sick of being harassed in parties, bars, and groups, I left for good. What was the point of tossing back brewskies with my oppressors or fighting for a liberation which excluded the likes of me?

During the years of my premature retirement, transexuals began finding their own voices. A transexual woman today is much more likely to claim her right to define as female whether or not she has had surgery or is perceived as adequately feminine. Along with this newfound pride came outrage at our relentless oppression. Activist organizations with names like Transgender Nation and The Transexual Menace have sprung up across the country. We've zapped the Gay Games, Stonewall 25, various startled city councils, and, I blush to add, the Village Voice.

News of Nancy's expulsion reached my ears like a gunshot across water. I looked at the last 16 years of my life, my interminable struggles on the fringe of the lesbian community, put on sensible shoes, and headed for the fray. This bitch was back.

I joined them in 1993, after Nancy and three transexual friends had again attempted to attend the festival. And security again had asked them to leave, maintaining that radical separatists were threatening violence, and that their safety on the land could not be guaranteed. When S/M women stepped forward to insure their safety, security asserted the producer's "womyn-born womyn only" policy and insisted the transexuals leave. The four women did, but we refused to pack up and go home. Instead we set up camp directly across from the main gate and lobbied our case with anyone who would listen. Camp Trans was born, and in four days over 200 festigoers stopped by to offer support, food, water, and attend two impromptu workshops.

Camp Trans was about to become a staple of the Michigan festival, with or without official sanction. In June of this year, a fund-raiser was held in New York. For the first time a transexual event drew mainstream gay organizations, from the Lesbian Avengers to the Gay and Lesbian Alliance Against Defamation, along with mainstream queer activists like Ann Northrop, Minnie Bruce Pratt, and Amber Hollibaugh. If there is such a thing as a queer Weltanschuung, it was definitely moving in our direction.

Over $5000 was pledged to send a bunch of gendertrash rejects to the Michigan woods. Plans were laid to fly nationally recognized queer activists from around the country, including transgendered author Leslie Feinberg, for 25 workshops between August 10 and 14, when attendance at the festival would peak. Two thousand schedules were printed and distributed as part of our plan to draw as many women as possible to Camp Trans ("for humyn-born humyns").

So now it is Saturday afternoon and our workshops, including the first annual "Mary Daly Memorial Volleyball Game: Surgically-Altered She-Male Scum vs. the World" have drawn over 400 festigoers. One is Hillary Smith, a Lesbian Avenger from Portland, Oregon and she, bless her subversive little heart, has recognized my Transexual Menace t-shirt. "Didn't I see you at an Avengers' meeting in Manhattan? Why don't you come to the national meeting inside?"

"Sure," I flip back, "why don't you just send me some escorts?"

(continued on next page)

(continued from previous page)

"How many?", she replies, not missing a beat.

We have checked with Festival Security about this, and been told that Boo and Lisa's "womyn-born womyn only" policy stands. But, unlike past years, each of us must interpret it for ourselves. And that is how the six of us, three pre-operative transexuals, two post-operative, one intersexed individual (with both male and female genitals) happen to be here. I suspect our lives and identities are far more complex than any policy could possibly anticipate. I also suspect our grinning, excited escorts are enjoying this more than pigs in shit.

I love these strong women, but suddenly the idea that we need protection feels surreal and sad. There are sounds of nervous laughter, bad jokes, and a lot of affection going down the 40-person chain. I am wide-eyed; I have wanted to go to Michigan since 1978, and I am seeing it for the first time. Mostly it is just by acres and acres of forest, tents, campsites, and women looking up with reactions as varied as they are: astonishment, confusion, laughter, applause, raised fists, smiles, angry glares, indifference.

After what seems like forever, we head up a short rise to the Avengers' meeting area. This is the first time a mainstream, national lesbian group has supported transexual women, and the scattered applause, growing to a real ovation as we come into full view, is an incredible rush. I have never seen so many young, hip dykes with good hair and straight teeth in one place and they are all, for gosh sakes, clapping for *us*.

Afterwards, fearing an angry confrontation for which we will undoubtedly be blamed, there is general consensus that, having done what we came for, we ought to just declare victory and get the hell out of Dodge. I prefer Hillary's suggestion: go to the kitchen area and sit down and eat, just like we're normal people and belong there, which, damn it, we do. We compromise: March back out crossing the packed kitchen area at dinnertime.

Coming around a bend, I see an opening about the size of a football field with, I don't know, 800, 1000, who knows how many women in it. For a moment, it looks like the entire lesbian nation is spread out, eating, carrying food, leading children, or serving dinner. One woman, dressed entirely in studded chains and leather and sporting an enormous black strap-on, is cavorting along our path. She is going wild as we approach and I stride up, grasping her dildo firmly and ask "Excuse me, can we talk?". I see women all over turning now to stare at us, and, my palms suddenly moist, I breathe sotto voice: "*we* are going to *fucking* die".

You think people's mouths only drop open in cartoons or sitcoms, but I assure you their jaws actually do go slack in real life. As we're walking festigoers see us, momentarily freeze, then just as abruptly spring back to life, trying to grok who and what we are. Applause breaks out, the odd raised fist, a few waves, and finally lots and lot of smiles. Almost without exception, these women support our cause. By now we are all beaming as well; I myself am grinning like an idiot at anyone within range. I am suddenly aware, clearly and precisely, that lesbian politics is changing: fundamentally, irrevocably, visibly right before my eyes.

How do I feel? Being transexual is like a tax: you pay it to get a job, rent an apartment, find a lover, just exist. Phrases like "women-born women only", "biological women only", "genetic women only", "no dogs allowed" or whatever exclusionary formula is in vogue cut deeply. With each hurt I hear anew Alice Walker's admonition *never* to be the only one in the room, and recall that as a transexual woman, I am *always* the only one in the room. But not today. Today I have sisters: protecting me, standing beside me, honoring my presence. Mostly being here feels just like coming *home*.

♦ ♦ ♦

Riki Anne Wilchins is a bisexual or lesbian, transgender or transexual, man or woman living in New York City or Greenwich Village. Her hobbies include Transexual Menace, the Lesbian Avengers, overthrowing binary economies and attacking any other political structure which oppresses her or just really pisses her off. Riki Anne Wilchins can be reached at : **Riki@pipeline.com (E-mail address).**

photo of Riki Anne Wilchins at MWMF '94 by Mariette Pathy-Allen

Don't call me mister 'Cause I'm a TS Butch

So
I don't wear dresses or makeup
Well that doesn't make me mister
'Cause I'm a TS Butch

And so what
If I don't have painted nails
High heels or a purse?
That doesn't make me mister either
'Cause I'm a TS Butch

You see
I wear pants, not a skirt
And an ordinary shirt
and that still doesn't make me mister
'Cause I'm a TS Butch

In the morning
When someone calls me on the phone
And I answer
In a deep and tired voice
That doesn't make me
A sir or a mister
'Cause I am what I am
And that's not a man
Simply a Butch
A TS Butch

When I hold my TS femme
Tight at night
Under covers
And kiss her neck, her shoulders
Stroke her hair and her body
This is a TS Butch touching her
This is a TS Butch holding her

And even if I get scared sometimes
Wondering what the fuck am I
Just because I don't do
All those femme things
TS' are supposed to do
Or because
I get depressed sometimes
And question my identity
That still doesn't ever make me mister
'Cause I'm a Butch
'Cause I'm a Butch
A strong TS Butch

Xanthra Phillippa

♦ *Xanthra Phillippa hates writing self-descriptive bios, feeling that people have more important things to read than a list of her kitchenware.*

photo of Xanthra Phillippa with Olga the Rottweiler by M.S. Ross

Subscribe to:

"Hopefully this zine will cause a lot of us to reexamine our preconceptions about sexuality, gender and politics." — *Lynna Landstreet, **Xtra***

Buttons	quantity
Stop Violence Against Transsexuals Now!	
Don't touch me: I'm electric TS epileptic	
Don't call me TRANNIE shitface	
'Mary's Fight Back	
Make Love not Steak	
Bi Bi Love	
We don't need balls to play	
Drag King	
This Transie's Angry	
Sex Change	
Blatantly BI	
Trans Curious	
100% TransGendered	
Gender-Fuck Me	
I love 'em butch	
Feminists for TransGender Liberation	
[no to] genderphobia	
Just say No to transphobia	
Butchy Femme	
F2M Queer	
TS Butch	
Have a safe GenderFuck	
Trans Dyke	
Trans Fag	
Gender Outlaw	
Gender Queer	
Transsexual Hooker	
The Empire Strikes Back	
Transsexuals get AIDS too	
Transgender Fury	
I love Transsexuals	
TS lives under TS control Now!	
Theory Mutilates Surgery Liberates	
Only a Transsexual could love you	
Employment Equity for Transsexuals	
I have big feet - So what???	
Woman-born Transsexual	
I'd rather be dead than genetic	
Transsexuals for Animal Liberation	
Nobody knows I'm a Transsexual	
Decriminalize Prostitution Now!	
Pissed Off Transsexuals United	
Gender Liberation	
Polysexual	
Poly gendered	
Gender Oriented	
gendertrash	
total number of buttons	
price (buttons are 1/$2, 3/$5, 10/$15 or 25/$25)	
s/h ($1 on all button orders under $10)	
total buttons	

"A man wanting to be a woman is like

" A Man wanting to be a woman is like a white person wanting to be Black"

WHITE FEMINIST STATEMENT

I have many problems with this ignorant racist statement.

First: It implies that <u>all</u> transsexuals are white, that <u>all</u> transsexuals are MTF and that being a woman is like being Black. But most of all it negates the millions of lives of transsexuals/transgendered peoples of FIRST NATIONS, AFRIKAN and ASIAN descent, who are the world MAJORITY of transsexuals.

An Afrikan/Asian/Native "man wanting to be" an Afrikan/Asian/Native woman is not "like a white person wanting to be black", it is like a "man" of a certain color wanting to be a woman of the same color as "he" already is. GENDER is not like RACE.

Second: If we follow the logic of that statement, a "woman" wanting to be a man is like a Black person wanting to be white. NO. A Black "woman" wanting to be a Black man is not "wanting to be white", she wants to remain Black but affirm her gender.

I also think that this statement (A man wanting to be...) is a diversion created by the white feminist community. By accusing other white folks of "wanting to be Black", they, once again, avoid dealing with their own ferocious racism.

From claiming to have been Black in another life (peuh-leeezz!), to stealing from Native spirituality, to desperately wanting to own/adopt/have a child of color, white feminists are very good at their "wanting to be Black" game.

a white person wanting to be Black"

White women cannot relinquish their gender-constructed-monopoly-on-victimhood, they are so oppressed, how can they oppress anyone? Don't get me started on this.

I want to end this piece by saying that transgendered peoples have always existed, sometimes treated as sacred beings (in traditional FIRST NATIONS beliefs) and sometimes treated as witches and burned (in oh-so-civilised Europe). Maybe it is this euro-tradition that white feminists are trying to keep alive today, even though historically they have suffered from the same source as transgendered peoples. Why can't they see transsexuals for the warriors against genderism that they are?

So next time you want to say: "A man wanting to be a woman is like a white person wanting to be Black", ask yourself "**Why would I want to say such obnoxious racist crap for?**" And if you still want to say it I suggest you join the thousands of your sisters already members of Aryan Nation.

Marisa Swangha

photo of Marisa Swangha at Lesbian & Gay Pride Day in Toronto by M.S. Ross

Marisa Swangha is a BLACK, GENETIC WOMAN of AFRIKAN, CHEROKEE and SOUTH-ASIAN descent.

Genderphobia: Where Separatism joins Patriarchy

by Janis Walworth

(this article first appeared in LesCon, summer 1992. It is reprinted here with permission of the author.)

I used to consider myself something of a separatist—not in an extreme way, but I certainly minimized my contact with men and actively opposed the patriarchal system (as I still do). However, I find I must break ranks with separatists on the issue of transsexuals (used here to mean only postoperative male-to-female transsexuals). Separatists' insistence that transsexuals are men is a denial of reality and reflects ignorance on the subject of transsexualism as well as a failure to get to know many of these people personally.

Interestingly, both separatism and patriarchy rely on the ability to distinguish clearly between the sexes. In fact, the differences are not so clear. In our society, babies are assigned a sex at birth based on a cursory examination of external genitalia, and it is assumed that gonads, chromosomes, and hormones, as well as the later development of secondary sex characteristics, gender identity, sexual orientation, and gender role, will all match this assignment. However, this is a schema imposed on the world by human minds—nature is not so neatly composed.

This becomes evident when we try to obtain objective criteria with which to differentiate transsexual from nontranssexual women. Anatomically, careful observation by a trained observer is necessary to make the distinction, and even that will not distinguish a transsexual from a nontranssexual woman who has had genital surgery as the result of cancer or to correct a birth defect.

Genetically, there are many variations in sex chromosomes. Not all women have XX and not all men have XY. Some people assigned as females at birth who have never questioned their sex have XY chromosomes. Some transsexuals have an XXY pattern or have a certain percentage of their cells with XX.

Hormone levels also do not distinguish between transsexual and nontranssexual women. There is considerable interindividual variation and some overlap between male and female levels. Postmenopausal women and those who have had their ovaries removed are still women, although their hormone production pattern resembles men's.

Secondary sex characteristics are not a reliable guide to sex. Flat-chested women may have smaller breasts than overweight men; women body builders have more muscle than most men; and the latest thing at Michigan last summer was to let your facial hair grow—an amazing number of women sported beards and moustaches.

Legally, postoperative transsexuals are considered women. All their legal documents, including birth certificate, driver's license, etc., are changed so that from a legal point of view, they are indistinguishable from nontranssexual women.

In terms of gender identity, most transsexuals have felt like females as long as they can remember, just like most nontranssexual women. They react to having a penis just the way I would if I suddenly woke up tomorrow morning with one. As far as social behaviour or gender role, the transsexuals I know are no more or less masculine or feminine than the dykes I know. It is fascinating to me that some members of the lesbian community rejoice in the natural expression of masculine characteristics in nontranssexual women as a form of defiance against patriarchal gender norms, but any trace of masculinity in a transsexual woman is taken as proof that she is "really" a man.

Some lesbians argue that transsexuals have been socialized as males and therefore can never escape behaving in masculine ways. In discussing this with transsexuals, I have found that most of them felt uncomfortable with the male socialization others attempted to impose on them. Some actively rejected it, while others tried to conform to expectations, only to feel like failures. Furthermore, some transsexuals were actually raised as girls from an early age.

Many transsexuals who were trained as adults to behave in masculine ways—being authoritative, decisive, unemotional, uncommunicative, etc.—have consciously rejected that training. Contrary to the paranoid fears some separatists and others have expressed about transsexuals taking leadership positions in the lesbian community, I have seen them time and again step back from positions of power and remove themselves from decision-making bodies.

Some have argued that transsexuals haven't been oppressed as women all their lives and so cannot really understand what it means to be a woman in this society. Certainly there is a wide variation in the amount of oppression nontranssexual women have experienced. Transsexuals have often been treated badly for wanting to be women, and the contrast between the way they are treated before and after assuming a feminine appearance brings sexism into sharp focus. In fact, many of the transsexual women I know are feminists and are actively working for women's rights.

The fact that transsexuals have lived in a male role has allowed them to take advantage of male privilege in school, job opportunities, etc., and this is a point of contention for some nontranssexual lesbians. My view is that most of us have taken advantage of vicarious male privilege at some point in our lives—I went to college on what my father earned as a male. Transsexuals should not be asked to erase their experience in the male role any more than I should be asked not to use my college education. There is no doubt that some of us have had more opportunities than others. The essential question is whether we use that advantage to aggrandize ourselves at the expense of others or whether we use it to improve the status of women who did not have those opportunities.

Finally, transsexual women define themselves as women. We in the lesbian community value highly the right to define ourselves as we see fit and to have that definition respected by others. I think we should extend that same respect to anyone who self-defines as a woman. Whether we argue for inclusion of transsexuals in our groups or for restricting our activities to so-called women-born women, we should acknowledge that transsexual women are women and refrain from the offensive practise of using masculine pronouns to refer to them (which some extremists insist on doing).

On a personal level, I am privileged to know quite a few transsexual women and to count several of them among my good friends. They have enriched my life considerably. Although I hate to make generalizations, most of the transsexual lesbians I know are intelligent, have a great sense of humour, and possess an intense spirituality. They are more aware of sex and gender issues than most women and can view social inequities with a unique perspective. In their quest for wholeness, they are struggling with the same issues many other lesbians are dealing with—self-esteem, childhood sexual abuse, parental rejection, alienation from mainstream society, sexism, job discrimination, etc. In addition, transsexual women have fought and sacrificed to make their anatomy match their gender identity, a congruence most nontranssexual women take for granted.

Of course, there is as much diversity among transsexuals as there is among any other group, and I don't expect to like every transsexual woman I meet. Most dykes I've talked to, if they are aware of knowing any transsexuals, have based their opinions of transsexuals on just one acquaintance. Just as we deplore the judgement of all lesbians based on the behaviour of the few who are the most outspoken and obvious, we in turn should not judge transsexuals on that basis.

In short, there is little reason, other than our own prejudice and fear, to believe that transsexual women are anything other than women. I, for one, prefer to accept the truth of transsexuals' own experience of themselves above a determination of sex at birth that is based on only a fraction of the characteristics that make up one's sex. Unquestioning acceptance of this rather arbitrary assignment of sex at birth, which is sanctioned by the patriarchal system, endorses the right of the partiarchy to define the truth of our experience for us.

I believe we should include transsexual lesbians in our community, not because there is nowhere else they belong or because there is no reasonable way to distinguish between them and us or because it may be illegal to discriminate against them, but because we owe it to ourselves. We can grow by confronting our internalized genderphobia; we can partake in the fullness of womanhood by embracing all its aspects; and we can help deflate patriarchal power by welcoming the expression of the gray areas of gender.

Janis Walworth is a gender activist and researcher. She has been involved for 4 years in the effort to open the Michigan Womyn's Music Festival to transsexual women. In 1994, she created Full Circle of Women, a yearly conference for woman-identified persons of all body shapes. She is currently earning an MS degree in Counseling.

Janis Walworth at MWMF, 1992. Photo by Irene Walworth

Divers/Cité?

The Rhetoric of Liberalism

The following text was supposed to be given at Divers/Cité, Montréal's lesbian/gay/bisexual/transgender pride march in July 1994. Although I was the ONLY bisexual or transgender invited to speak, the organizers eliminated me from the the speakers list, due to "time constraints." It goes without saying that numerous lesbian and gay political speakers addressed the crowd that afternoon (focusing mainly on the elections to be held in the fall). The biggest irony of these events is that this speech addresses precisely the kinds of exclusions enacted by the organizers of Divers/Cité. Despite the liberal rhetoric, Montréal's pride parade is only about lesbians and gay men. Just because people can say the words "bisexual" or "transgender" doesn't mean they understand monosexuality. Maybe if they had a chance to hear this speech, they would.

I've been asked to talk about bisexuals and transgenders. Who are we, and why do we claim our right to speak here today?

There are a lot of myths about bisexuals — that we can't make up our minds, that we're obsessed with sex, that we're really straight, or that we're really gay. The truth is, we organize our erotic lives in a variety of ways. Some of us are monogamous, some of us have multiple partners, some of us sleep mostly with one gender, and some of us have relations with men, women, and transsexuals. Some of us choose not to be sexual with other people. As bisexual activists, we defend all of these choices — because we know what it is to be told your sexuality is not valid, and because we believe that there is no one correct way to live desire. A rejection of compulsory heterosexuality also means questioning the sanctity of monogamy, the valorization of couple culture, the mistaken belief that there are only two sexes and two genders, and the erroneous assumption that people who are not sexually active would be if they could find a partner.

One of the most common myths about bisexuals is that we transmit HIV. A recent issue of a local lesbian magazine is filled with comments from lesbians about how they're not at risk for HIV because they don't sleep with bisexual women. We are tired of this bi-bashing, and we reiterate that safe sex is about what you do, not the label attached to the body you fuck.

As bisexuals, we've learned an important lesson from the lesbian and gay communities — we need not feel ashamed of the persons we choose to love, have sex with, and/or welcome as friends. Ironically, as bisexuals, we must often reiterate this same lesson to lesbians and gay men when we tell them about our opposite-sexed and trans-sexed partners. Our desire does not respect the artificial borders of language and identity, and we do not fit into your hetero- and homo- boxes. This is not the refusal of choice, fence-sitting, or of being politically uncommitted. This is a challenge to your limited categories of sexuality and gender, and it is something we defend fiercely and celebrate. Passion deserves no apology.

I am also here to talk about transgendered people. The word "transgender" refers to those people who live outside normative sex/gender relations — transsexuals, drag queens, passing women, hermaphrodites, the intersexed. Those of us who dare to reject compulsory sex/gender relations are faced with life and death issues, of pain and struggle to live our bodies as we choose. While lesbians and gay men fight for insurance benefits and tax-breaks, transgendered men and women live in a world with no guarantee of basic human rights. We lose our children, our jobs, our homes, and sometimes our lives. Transsexuals in prison are incarcerated according to their "original," biological sex — which means assault, rape, and often, the transmission of HIV.

Transgenders are also ignored by the police. When the body of Marcia Johnson surfaced in the Hudson River, the New York police said that she'd killed herself, even though witnesses report that she had been harassed by a group of people at the precise spot her body surfaced. When Grayce Baxter disappeared in December of 1992, the Toronto police waited two months before beginning their investigation. And when Tammy Ross was found hung in her apartment here in Montréal, the morning after she'd been working the streets, the SPCUM said that she'd killed herself. If this is the first time you've heard these names and these stories, think about that for a moment. Transsexual sex trade workers are too far removed from the suburban middle class, too marginalized to warrant media coverage, activist demonstrations, or commemorative ceremonies.

Transsexuals, like lesbians and gay men, are also harassed by the cops — just ask the girls on the corner of St. Laurent and Ste. Catherine. Since August 1993, obscenity legislation — the so-called "kiddie porn law" - is being used against sex trade workers, especially those who are young. If you think that this doesn't affect you, because you're over 18, or you're not a sex trade worker, think again. Until prostitution is decriminalized, until youth can explore desire to its fullest, you do not have the freedom to do what you will with your body.

Transgenders and sexual minorities share a common history. Pre-Stonewall public spaces were seized by sexual and gender outlaws — drag queens, lesbians, stone butches, gays, and sex trade workers. Remember today that Stonewall happened when a passing woman — a woman who dressed and lived as a man — resisted arrest, when she was supported by Puerto Rican drag queens and transsexuals. Do not rewrite this history to claim that white gay men helped a lesbian, and do not trivialize it with the statement that these gender outlaws were upset because of Judy Garland's recent death. These people fought back because, like most poor people, they were tired of being treated like shit, and they had nothing else to lose.

While sexual and gender outlaws share a common past, times have changed. Here in Montréal, lesbian bars routinely eject male-to-female transsexuals, even when these individuals live as women and identify as lesbians. Gay male bars refuse entry to women, drag queens, transsexuals, and men in lipstick. Gay men are particularly fond of calling themselves "straight-acting." Since straight men don't fuck other men, this phrase can only mean that these individuals consider themselves "masculine," "real" men. Which makes one wonder how much respect these gay men have for nellie faggots, transsexuals, or for that matter, women.

We as transgendered people ask the lesbian and gay communities the following questions: Why have you forgotten our common history? Why are you, like your straight counterparts, so uptight about gender? Are you so desperate for civil rights that you will sell out the very people who, historically, faced the most police violence and harassment? And although some of you here today can say the mantra of "lesbian, gay, bisexual, and transgender," what have you done for transsexual liberation?

In 1973, homosexuality was removed from the list of psychiatric disorders, a move which was hailed as a significant victory for the modern lesbian and gay movement. We need to celebrate these moments, but we must also think about their repercussions. In 1980, transsexuality entered the same list of psychiatric disorders from which homosexuality was removed. Currently psychiatrists decide who is a "real" transsexual and who is not. If you are a male-to-female transsexual who loves other women, or a female-to-male who loves men, you must lie about your desire, and pretend to be heterosexual. This issue affects lesbians and gay men, you see, because psychiatrists only sanction transsexual men and women who are heterosexual. The battle with psychiatry is not over.

As bisexuals and transgenders, we have a great deal to teach the lesbian and gay communities — about alternate ways to organize our erotic lives, about honouring sex trade workers, about living our bodies as we choose. We struggle for a world with a thousand million sexualities and genders — an infinite combination of bodies and desires. There are no easy answers, and if it appears to be politically useful, we respond with the statement that our lives expose the limitations of those lines. Do not mistake fluidity for fickleness - we fuck gender and sexuality because they're already fucked.

All of this means that as bisexuals and transgenders, we don't just want to be included in some willy-nilly liberal rhetoric of "diversité," "a queer family," or "children of the rainbow." We do not just offer new or different names to call oneself. We pose a fundamental challenge to the ways in which gender and sexuality are organized in this society. Just as lesbians and gay men refuse the narrow options of compulsory heterosexuality, we refuse to be trapped by a hetero/homo, man/woman split.

Bisexual and transgender activists demand more than having our names tacked onto the end of the phrase "lesbian and gay." We are tired of being stuck at the end, and we are more tired of people saying these words in a meaningless way. We do not accept the liberal argument that we must fight for lesbian and gay rights now, and that, maybe one day in the future, other sexual and gender minorities will have their turn. We want it all, and we will settle for nothing less. This is not a utopian dream, this is a committed activist programme. In a world where transsexuals who are HIV-positive are denied sex-reassignment surgery, in a world with no useful AIDS education for bisexuals, and in a world where gender outlaws face the threat of physical assault daily, I for one cannot mobilize my energies to fight for same-sex RRSPs. Some of us non-heterosexuals face issues more pressing than the accumulation of capital; do not be fooled into thinking that the ballot box and the legal transfer of property equal "freedom."

So as we celebrate together here today, let us realize that the issue is not lesbians and gay men deciding to let bisexuals and transgenders into "their" communities. The deeper issue is whether or not lesbians and gay men are willing to learn from the lives and experiences of bisexuals and transgenders. Because we insist on including all kinds of sexual and gender minorities, because we publicly defend sex work, and because we do not limit our struggle to securing insurance benefits and tax breaks for middle class couples, we politicize the middle ground of lesbian and gay activism. That is our contribution to contemporary sexual and gender politics, and it is that courage, determination, and resistance that we should honour, affirm, and celebrate today.

— merci—

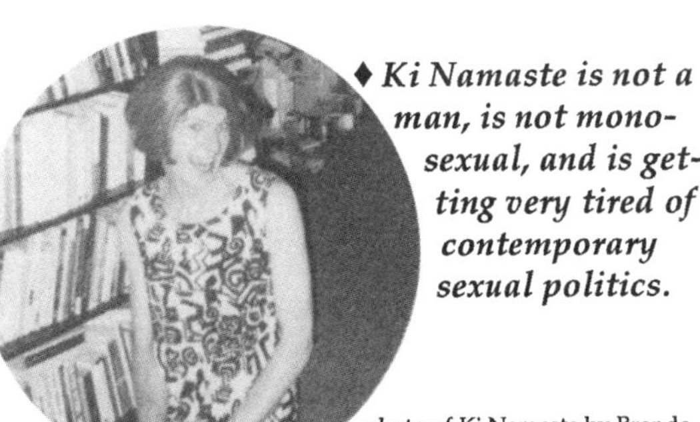

♦ ***Ki Namaste is not a man, is not monosexual, and is getting very tired of contemporary sexual politics.***

photo of Ki Namaste by Brenda

Installment: Nightmare on Maitland
©1995 CaiRa

For those of you who can't remember back to the last installment (because it's been so long ago), Turqouise Sky & Swordfish have just had a BIG argument and now our story starts.

Turquoise is walking towards the door, without saying a thing. Her anger shows on her face. Swordfish is equally silent, not even looking in her direction.

Meanwhile, at the very same time, across town, No More Strange Names, Bruce & Kathy enter Our Place. Lee Phelps is headlining. They get a table in the balcony, at the front, on the left side. No More order juice, Kathy a beer and Bruce, as usual, coffee.No more is talking about the latest movie, she & her lover have just seen & Bruce is about to reply when the MC comes out & announces Lee Phelps. There is a pause & then she comes out. She is wearing black pants, a white shirt, a black blazer and not much makeup.

Lee << Hi, everyone. I'm Lee Phelps.Yes, I know, what kind of a boring name is that - Lee? Why couldn't you pick a normal name like Serena Sunlight or Radiance Extravaganza - these are normal names. For transsexuals. But not *Lee.* [Pause] I know it's weird but people really do look at me strangely when I tell them my name. You know, that *you-can't-really-be-a-transsexual-not-with-a-name-like-that* look. So now I say something like I'm sorry, but in the support group I went to, all the really normal TS names like Elegantia dell'Ivory were all gone & this was all that was left, so that's what I was stuck with.

Actually I really like my name, Lee. It's sweet, it's nice, it's calm, it's beautiful. It's a name in which I can hear a million angels singing *Oh most beautiful Lee.* And I reply *It's me, beautiful me.* So how could I not have a beautiful name like that?

Now here's something else to think about when you're searching for that perfect name: [echoed voice] have you ever noticed how many genetic women have names that sound like something out of *Star Trek* or *Lost in Space?* Okay first lesson in passing - those of you who have decided that passing is not politically correct, please shut your ears & fasten your seatbelts 'cause we're going to crash - all or almost all genetic women have names like Jill, Barb, Pat, Bev, Sally, Susan & so on. Leaving out Moonunit Zappa, not one have names like Galaxia Tremendia, Palatia Dementia Powderpuff or Cassandra de Tupperware. So if you really want to pass, forget those names that sound like your great aunt's tea set & check out something nice & simple. Unless you really have to have a name that weighs the same as the amount of makeup you use.

Back outside the TSculturalcentre. Turquoise has just stepped outside, slamming the door shut. She walks down the steps and onto the street, heading toward Jarvis. There is nobody on the street, only parked cars - not a very exciting evening. Turquoise keeps walking with angry steps, talking to herself.

Our Place. Okay here's one we all know. You send away for that SRS package they promised (can you imagine them on those Home Shopping Networks - *operators are standing by & if you order before midnight tonight,...* [laughter]) & you're looking through all these pictures & booklets in a package affectionately known as *the SRS kit,* where they tell you things like *this surgeon does such a good job it would fool a gynecologist* & all you can think about is *Where's The Clit?* or *How Come There's No Clit?* (Big pause) And you can't find a single picture, not a single word about the clit.

And you're thinking *what's going on here - don't they know basic female anatomy, you know like right on top of the lips, there's supposed to be the clitoris? And it's not there. And this is supposed to fool a gynecologist? Give me a break. This wouldn't fool my Aunt Mildred.* [Big laughter]

And this starts you thinking *okay what else have they left out 'cause I'm not paying $15,000 for a big surprise.* It isn't like there's an SRS repair company down the street [laughter]. And if there was, they'd probably want two psychiatrists' letter, a note from your mom, your teacher and so on just to make an appointment.

Getting back to TV, how about this for an idea? Forget about the problems around the standards of care, the DSM-IV, the real life tests, what lipstick will really go with your spiffy dinner plates & all those truly important issues & concerns. How about doing it like this? To get your surgery, or anything else, you have to go on a specially designed TV game show. *Okay, for the car, the house, that free trip to Europe, plus all the surgery you've ever dreamed of, in 25 words or less, what is gender? Let's ask Ms Clock, how much time does she have? Alright, you have one minute to answer, starting now. Time is ticking.* [pause] And of course if you're wrong - *Aww, I'm sorry, that's not the right answer. The correct answer is... However don't worry because no one goes away a loser because everybody gets a home version. Thanks for being a wonderful guest & maybe we'll see you again on* *This Is Your SRS*. *[pause again]* What do you think? Wouldn't that be better? Of course it would.

So now let's talk about Janice Raymond. I know what you're thinking *oh please not another bad-old-feminist-theory-&-theoretician joke*. Hands up everyone who was actually thinking that. Uh huh, I thought so. Okay I know this is supposed to be comedy, not nightmare city, but it's not my fault. Really. Look [she pulls out a long sheet of paper]. See, right here, in my contract. *Must do at least one bad-old-feminist-theory-&-theoretician joke.* So don't jump on me & let's just get it over with as soon as possible.

Okay, so how many of you have read that horrible old chestnut *The Transsexual Empire*? Yes that's right - the book that made Anti-Transsexualism a household phrase.

Here's my absolute favourite part. How we're not really women because we swear too much. Okay all you genetic women, watch out, the Swearing Police are here with their meters; over 50 swear words or phrases per minute & you lose your genetic status. But here's the best part, the part I really love; this whole idea comes from a **male**, yes **male** doctor. Perfect for a Radical Lesbian-Feminist document, right? Didn't anyone else notice this apparent problem? And it's right at the beginning where you can't miss it either. I mean swearing too much, goddamn, shit, piss, fuck - whoops, better watch out or I'll be spotted as one of those [dun da dun dun] **Transsexual Imposters**.

Or how about this - after calling us *male-to-constructed-females* & all kinds of other nasty things for over 300 pages, she says *well, yes transsexuals have suffered too.* Well thank you oh so much Ms Raymond, that makes us feel oh so happy. And may we offer you a big *fuck-you-very-much* to you, too?

Of course there's her famous one: Her Solution for Transsexualism - (low echoed voice) *we'll mandate them out of existence.* Mandate them? What does that mean? And what about that *out of existence* - that has a really ominous & forever feel to it. Sort of like the way the terms *electric chair* and *lethal injection* do. How many of you would feel safer jumping off the CN tower without a parachute?

Okay we're almost done. Let's look at Janice's survey. How many of you think that the 14 transsexual women used in her book were selected at random or because they had certain attributes: like emerald green eye shadow going right up over their foreheads, five foot eyelashes dripping with mascara or seventeen inch high heels? (laughter)

Turquoise on the street. A small black car turns the corner, behind her, moving slowly forward. There are two passengers. The car moves up slowly behind & to the left of Turquoise, who is still too angry to notice. The car moves slowly forward until it is almost beside her.

Our Place. Okay now that I've got that out of my system, let's talk about political action. Ready? Okay here we go. We've all seen how some other groups handle their political problems and I think that we can learn from them, by avoiding their mistakes. So here's my suggestions: next time we have to deal with anti-transsexual genetics trying to curtail our rights, we kidnap the Pope or at least a couple of high ranking bishops or right wing heads of state, bad politicians & cover them in really bad makeup & short skirts, so they look like the worst drag queens of all time & make videos of them & broadcast them all over the world & say we won't stop until we get what we want. Or threaten to kidnap their kids & turn them into *Transsexuals Just Like Us*. And we can use our sisters who belong to the TS Women Football Leagues to kind of drive home

(continued on next page)

(continued from previous page)

the point. You can bet that we'll get what we want immediatly & their objections will vanish, in minutes, not years or decades. So we won't have to spend hours in our meeting rooms, whining about *The Way Things Are*. I think it's worth a try at least.

So, anyways, I have a question - in these days of destroying all the labels - who isn't transgendered in some way? *Transgendered* no longer just means transsexuals, transgenderists, transvestites, drag queens & drag kings, straight crossdressers & genderfuck & people like that - now it seems to mean practically anyone. I'm just waiting for the moment when someone like Preston Manning can claim that he's a member of the Transgendered Community. What do we have to do - issue identity cards like *this card entitles the holder to all the benefits & priviledges of the Gender Community & to claim membership in said Community for one year*? What's going on here? Doesn't anyone else think this is just a little crazy, strange, bizarre or just totally fucked up? Does any man wearing an earring get to claim transgendered status? C'mon let's get real here. This is just getting a little too much.

Speaking about labels - how about the incredible proliferation of everybody's favourite pronoun *trans*? Have you noticed? Like someone can be ***trans***-phobic, ***trans***-positive or ***trans***-incredibly-negative? Why stop there? How about ***trans***-indecisive or ***trans***-wishy-washy or ***trans***-uncertain? Or ***trans***-mostly-undetermined or ***trans***-unsure-exactly-what-is-going-on. Then there's ***trans***-incredulous-&-shocked. And ***trans***-inclusive & ***trans***-exclusive? And why stop there? Why not ***trans***- on other words? The sky's the limit. We could have ***trans***-schools, ***trans***-cars & ***trans***-buses & ***trans***-trains, even ***trans***-cities & ***trans***-towns or even ***trans***-countries. Of course it would give right-wing crazies something else to attack, claiming that it was just another form of political correctness or ***trans***-correctness, as they would no doubt put it. But we wouldn't let them stop us - we'd have ***trans***-shopping malls & ***trans***-department stores. We wouldn't go shopping - we'd go ***trans***-shopping & ***trans***-buying on our ***Trans***-credit cards (or ***transie*** cards, as we'd probably call them) in our ***trans***-worlds.We wouldn't have pets; we'd have Timmy the ***Trans***-Hamster, Gigi the ***Trans***-Rat & Sammy the ***Trans***-Guinea Pig, not to mention Bobbi the ***trans***-parrot. [molotov is actually visibly laughing at this point.] We'd spend our ***trans***-times in our ***trans***-houses, in our ***trans***-backyards & possibly even in our ***trans***-pools. And maybe we'll watch our ***trans***-TV shows. The ***trans***-possibilities are ***trans***-endless. And I think with that, I'm going to say good night. So good ***trans***-night.>>

Let's see what's happening with Turquoise. The passenger opens the window. Turquoise keeps going. The passenger says something unintelligible.

<<What the fuck do you want?>> screams Turquoise <<Just fuck off & leave me alone.>>

The car stops. The passenger reaches behind and gets something out of the back seat. The car starts, slowly aiming toward Turquoise. Turquoise keeps walking toward Jarvis...

Next installment: Nightmare on Maitland Part Two

♦ ***CaiRa has been writing <u>TSe TSe TerroriSm</u> for what seems almost an eternity now. She hates pictures of herself, which is why there isn't one here.***

PASANEWS

Toronto based PASAN (Prisoners with HIV/AIDS Support Action Network) has recently "recognized the need to develop an understanding of the specific issues facing transsexual and transgendered prisoners (both around the prison situation in general and HIV/AIDS in particular) and eventually write an appendix to the PASAN Brief to address these issues."

So far, they have been in contact with Laura Masters of TransEqual who sent them a document entitled "The imprisoned transgenderist." The 12 page document offers some good insights about the social circumstances that lead TS/TG's to end up in (male) jail and the lack of consideration and brutality they are forced to endure once there.

PASAN also contacted Wayne Travers of SOS (Street Outreach Services) who is known for his work with TS/TG youth.

Here's a condensed version (excerpted from the minutes of PASAN's general meeting) of the presentation he did for them, May 6 1994:

> *Most of SOS's TS/TG clients who get arrested are charged with minor offenses (possession, communicating) and therefore end up with minor time. However, some of their clients have done or are doing federal time. It is Wayne's experience that TS/TG prisoners receive different levels of treatment depending on the level of incarceration they're facing (ie. county, provincial, federal). Often the first reaction of TS/TG's when put in provincial prison is to hide their identities for fear of persecution. They then only "come out" gradually to see how the guards and the other prisoners will react. In the federal system, TS/TG prisoners are often locked in a separate range - but it's often the same range in which sexual offenders are placed. Guards often view all TS/TG prisoners as prostitutes and expect them to sexually service the men on the range, which the guards like because they see it as keeping the population quiet.*
>
> *TS/TG prisoners have a variety of specific needs which are often denied within the prison (ie. access to hormones, women's clothing, make-up and counselling of their choice). Wayne knew of only two TS/TG prisoners who have access to hormones, and both those times access came only after lengthy battles.*
>
> *Wayne has experienced many barriers stopping TS/TG prisoners being released into halfway houses. Even if eligible for release, halfway houses often refuse to take TS/TG's because of their identity. Halfway houses often view TS/TG's as disruptive influences. Even if admitted to a halfway house, TS/TG's are usually the first to be removed if there is a problem in the house. Wayne's experience is that if there is trouble in the house, the TS/TG is viewed as the "cause" of the problem whether or not that individual is [the] one actually being disruptive.*
>
> *In terms of HIV/AIDS, Wayne's experience is that his clients tend to hide their status. A major reason for this is that there are no doctors who will agree to do surgery on TS/TG's if they are positive. Because of this many TS/TG's either won't test at all or won't disclose. If they have had the surgery, post-operative transsexuals are at increased risk of contracting HIV because [their]vaginas don't lubricate naturally so there is an increased risk of tearing of the skin. Wayne's experience is that a very high percentage of his TS/TG clients are positive (maybe as high as 70-75%)."*

As a result of this information coming to light, PASAN has decided to set up a working group to write a draft appendix to the PASAN Brief. The working group will get in touch with TS/TG prisoners to get their input. If you have any information to give them, PASAN can be reached at:

PASAN, 517 College Street, Suite 327,
Toronto, Ontario, M5G 4A2
phone: (416) 920-9567
fax: (416) 928-2185
toll-free (in Ontario) 1-800-263-9534
PASAN accepts collect calls from prisoners.

gendertrash

Canadian Directory of organizations, resources & services for the gender community

Symbols

NS
non-TS/TG/TV specific group

P
non-TS/TG/TV specific group **with** written policy prohibiting discrimination on the basis of gender identity

☑
information about the group has been recently confirmed by us

The following was compiled to give as large a listing of Canadian resources as possible. Some of the groups/organizations listed are not specifically for TS/TG/TV persons, but may still offer valuable services since they are known to be familiar with members of the gender communities.

The inclusion of any organization here, does not necessarily stand as a stamp of approval by gendertrash. We believe that it is each individual's responsibility to decide for her/himself what is or isn't in her or his best interests. However, your comments about the quality, both positive & negative, of the services that you received from any of the providing groups would be appreciated & will be kept on file.

If you want your group or any group that you know of, to be listed here, please contact us at genderpress.

Alberta

Calgary

Illusions Social Club (☑)

✉ **Illusions**, 6802 Ogden Rd. SE, Calgary, Alta, T2C 1B4

☎ (403) 486-9661

contact: Barbie

➔ TS/TG/TV/SO support group, meeting twice a month in Calgary & once a month in Edmonton

see Publications

Edmonton

Crossroads

☎ (403) 474-7421

contact: Maureen Reid

➔ provides various services for sex workers in general (AIDS education, safe house, pimp prevention, legal help, etc.) They have a big TS /TG clientele.

B.C.

Kimberley

Canadian Organization of Professional Electrologists (COPE) (NS/☑)

✉ **COPE**, 410 Aspen Rd., Kimberley, BC, V1A 3B5

☎ (800) 665-COPE

fax: (604) 427-2573

➔ COPE provides a registry of electrologists in Canada who subscribe to their high level code of professional and ethical conduct as well as standards of hygiene and sterilization.

Vancouver

Cornbury Society(☑)

✉ **Cornbury Society**, Box 3745, Vancouver, BC, V6B 3Z1

➔ Non-profit support group for heterosexual cross-dressers & their families.

Foundation for the Advancement of Trans-Gendered People's Equality (FATE)(☑)

✉ **FATE**, 1-1727 William St, Vancouver, BC, V5L 2R5

☎ (604) 254-9591

contact: Jamie Lee

➔ Promotes the well-being of transgendered individuals as well as public education & awareness. Provides advocacy for people on welfare. Registered as a non-profit organization.

see Publications

Gender Dysphoria Clinic (NS/☑)

✉ **Gender Dysphoria Clinic** c/o Vancouver General Hospital, 715 West 12th Ave, Vancouver, BC, V5Z 1M9

☎ (604) 875-4100

→ Full gender identity clinic with several groups/ meetings, including Explorers, FTM's,etc. Child psychiatrist for TS parents. Drop-in & other services available.

High Risk Project (☑)

✉ **High Risk Project**, c/o Zenith Foundation, Box 46, 8415 Granville St, Vancouver, BC, V6P 4Z9

☎ (604) 879-2426

contact: Sandy Laframboise

→ The High Risk Project serves TS/TG/TV people who are HIV+ or at risk of getting infected. It operates a drop-in out of the Vancouver Native Health Centre (449 East Hastings Street) Mon-Wed(1-4:30pm) & provides free hot meals on Tues night to TS/TG/TV street prostitutes at 223 Main Street. As well, the High Risk Project provides an opportunity for socialization. Because it is entirely run by volunteers & is unfunded, donations are welcome. They are tax refundable & must be made out to: DEYAS/Zenith Foundation "High Risk".

Zenith Foundation (☑)

✉ **Zenith Foundation**, Box 46, 8415 Granville St, Vancouver, BC V6P 4Z9

→ Charitable non-profit foundation, whose objectives are to work toward improving the security & circumstances of people with gender dysphoria. Both FTM & MTF are welcome. Operates several committees, including housing & the high risk project. First contact by writing.

see Publications

White Rock

Transsexual Support Group

✉ c/o Dr Angela Wensley, 14905 32nd Avenue, White Rock, BC., V4P 1A4

☎ (604) 536-2053

→ Inclusive rather than exclusive support group for transsexuals and their families.

Manitoba

Winnipeg

Prairie Rose Gender Club

✉ **Prairie Rose Gender Club**, PO Box 45091, Regent Postal Outlet, Winnipeg, Manitoba, R2C 5C7

→ Club provides support, social activities & education. Write for info.

Village Clinic

✉ **Village Clinic**, 668 Corydon Ave., Winnipeg, Manitoba, R3M 0X7

→ General health & STD clinic. TS/TG's welcome.

Nova Scotia

Halifax

Stepping Stone

✉ **Stepping Stone**, 2224 Maitland St., Halifax, N.S., B3K 2Z9

☎ (902) 420-0103

→ User-directed street outreach programme for sex workers including transgendered youth.

Ontario

Cambridge

Society for the Second Self (Tri-Ess Society)

✉ **Tri-Ess Society**, PO Box 28002, Cambridge, Ont, N3H 5N4

→ nature unconfirmed at this time

Ottawa

Gender Mosaic (☑)

✉ **Gender Mosaic**, PO Box 7421, Vanier (Ottawa), Ont., K1L 8E4

☎ (613) 749-5203

→ Social, support & info. group for TS/TG/TV people.

see Publications

FACT - Ottawa

✉ **FACT**, Box 9155, Ottawa, Ont., K1G 3T9

☎ (613) 238-1717 (between 7-10pm)

→ TS support group

Mississauga

Monarch Social Club

✉ **Monarch Social Club, PO** Box 386, Stn A, Mississauga, Ont., L5A 3A1

☎ (416) 949-6602

→ Social, support & info. group for TS/TG/TV people.

St Catharines

TransEqual (☑)

✉ **TransEqual**, 165 Ontario St. #609, St. Catharines, Ontario, L2R 5K4

☎ (905) 688-0276

contact: Laura Masters

→ TransEqual "hopes to ensure that each transsexual & transgenderist has appropriate legal recourse available to them... when their equal access to society is withheld". TransEqual is a TS/TG - rights advocacy group.

Toronto

Education Against Homophobia (NS/☑)

✉ **Education Against Homophobia**, c/o John Campey (trustee), Toronto Board, 155 College St, Tor, Ont., M5T 1P6

☎ (416) 516-4948

fax: (416) 397-3114
attn: Marlene Ziobrowski, EAH, c/o John Campey's office

contact: Marlene Ziobrowski

→ The group is composed of parents, teachers, trustees & students to try & deal with the issues & concerns of lesbian, gay, bi & transgendered students. The group exists primarily for lesbian, gay & bi students, but have included transgendered students in their mandate.

Canadian Crossdressers' Club (☑)

✉ **Canadian Crossdressers' Club**, 161 Gerrard St. E, Tor, Ont., M5A 2E4

☎ (416) 921-6112

→ Provides a safe atmosphere for CD's & DQ's to dress up & meet others with similar interests/lifestyles.

see Publications

Gender Identity Clinic (NS/☑)

✉ **Gender Identity Clinic**, c/o Clarke Institute of Psychiatry, 250 College St, Tor, Ont. M5T 1R8

☎ (416) 979-2221 ext 2221

→ To get an SRS reimbursed by OHIP, you must go through the Gender Identity's two year program & be approved by them for surgery. They also have a Wed afternoon support group for people in the program.

Hassle Free Clinic (NS/☑)

✉ **Hassle Free Clinic**, 556 Church St, 2nd floor, Tor, Ont., M4Y 2E3

☎ (416) 922-0603 (M)
(416) 922-0566 (W)

→ **Hassle Free** is a STD clinic, which provides anonymous HIV/AIDS testing & counselling (by appointment only). TS' are welcome at either clinic.

Women's Clinic - M,W,F (10-3), T & Th (4-8).

(continued - next page)

(Directory continued.)

STD drop-in (no appointment necessary) - T & Th (4-6). Appointments required at all other times.
Men's Clinic - M & W (4-9), T & Th (10-3), F (4-7), S (10-2). No appointment necessary except for HIV/AIDS testing.

Human Sexuality Program (NS/☑)

⊠ **Human Sexuality Program**, c/o Student Support Services, Toronto Board of Education, 155 College St, Tor, Ont., M5T 1P6

☎ (416) 397-3755 (ask for the Human Sexuality Program)

contact: Tony Gambini

→ This is primarily a counselling service for lesbian, gay & bisexual students, but they have included transgender students in their mandate. They have a support group for lesbian, gay, bi & transgender students (LGBST) who are experiencing personal difficulties, etc.

Maggie's Prostitutes' Resource Centre & Safe Sex Project of Toronto (P/☑)

⊠ **Maggie's**, box 1143, Stn F, Tor, Ont., M4Y 2T8

☎ (416) 964-0150

→ A resource centre run by & for sex trade workers, providing condoms, legal info, AIDS info, referrals, etc. Drop-in (M-W, 12-6pm) & office at 298 Gerrard St E., 2nd floor.

ReproMed Ltd. (NS/☑)

⊠ **ReproMed Ltd.**, 2333, Suite 209, Tor, Ont. M6R 3A6

☎ (416) 537-6895

fax: (416) 537-4301

→ ReproMed Ltd. is a medically-oriented lab serving those who desire to have some measure of assurance against possible loss of their reproductive capabilities. They specialize in the cryopreservation of human spermatazoa for future clinical application and the providing of cryopreserved donor semen specimens to physicians (for artificial insemination).

Sex Workers Alliance of Toronto (SWAT) (NS/☑)

⊠ **SWAT**, box 1143, Stn F, Tor, Ont., M4Y 2T8

☎ (416) 964-0150

→ A political action group working for the rights of all sex workers.

Sexual Assault Care Centre (NS/☑)

⊠ **Sexual Assault Care Centre**, 76 Grenville St, Tor, Ont., M5S 1B2

add (same as above - in Women's College Hospital)

☎ (416) 323-6040

→ The Sexual Assault Care Clinic provides services for the sexually assaulted.

Street Outreach Services (SOS) (NS/☑)

⊠ **SOS**, 622 Yonge St, 2nd floor, Tor., Ont., M4Y 1Z8

☎ (416) 926-0744

fax: (416) 926-9552

contact: Wayne Travers

→ **SOS** is an agency that assists youth, (16-24) involved in prostitution, to make informed choices in their lives, whatever their goals might be. They deal with TS/TG youth on a regular basis. Drop-in (M-F 10-6). Legal, medical, welfare & AIDS counselling available.

The 519 (P/☑)

⊠ 519 Community Centre, 519 Church St, Tor, Ont. M4Y 2C9

☎ (416) 392-6874

→ All purpose resource centre for mostly lesbian/gay groups. Has other resources like free legal clinic, queer bashing hotline, etc which can be useful. People who work there are somewhat aware of problems that transgendered persons may face.

Toronto Rape Crisis Centre, now known as Multicultural Women Against Rape (NS/☑)

⊠ **Multicultural Women Against Rape**, Box 1143, Stn F, Tor, Ont., M4Y 2T8

☎ (416) 597-8808 - this line may be picked up by their answering service, especially at nights

TDD: (416) 597-1214

business: (416) 597-1171

fax: (416) 597-9648

→ **Multicultural Women Against Rape** is a collective of non-transsexual women, providing support for victims of sexual assault (including TS/TG persons). They also run **Take Back the Night** & have no problems with TS', who identify as women, attending.

Transition Support (☑)

⊠ Transition Support, c/o 519 Community Centre, 519 Church St, Tor, Ont. M4Y 2C9

☎ (416) 392-6874 (messages can be left only if necessary)

→ Support group open to all members of the gender communities.

women's counselling referral & education centre (WCREC) (☑)

⊠ **WCREC**, 525 Bloor St. W., Tor., Ont., M5S 1Y4

☎ (416) 534-7501

→ WCREC has an extensive listing of feminist-oriented therapists. They try to match each client with the appropriate therapist. They also have a crisis line and seem to be receptive to TS women.

Québec

Montréal

Association Des Opérées - és en Chirurgie Esthétique (ADOCE) (NS/☑)

⊠ **ADOCE**, CP 230, 5135 Jean-Talon est, Mtl, Qué., H1S 2Z2

☎ (514) 327-8148

contact: Rachel Boutin

→ cosmetic surgery info. & doc. centre. ADOCE provides extensive info on all types of cosmetic surgery. They also provide info on surgeons (both good & bad) in Québéc.

membership — $35/year

Association Québécoise des Travailleuses - eurs du Sexe (AQTS) (NS/☑)

⊠ **AQTS**, CP 5028, Succ. C, Mtl, Qué., H2X 3M2

☎ (514) 527-5320

contact: Claire Thiboutôt

→ AQTS is a support group for sex workers as well as a political organization of sex workers & sex worker rights advocates dedicated to the decriminalization & deregulation of prostitution & other types of sex work.

Centre d'Action Communautaire auprès des Toxicomanes Utilisateurs de Seringues (CACTUS) (NS/☑)

⊠ **CACTUS**, 1209 Ste-Dominique, Mtl, Qué., H2X 2W4

☎ (514) 954-8869

→ **CACTUS** is a needle exchange, condom distribution and AIDS information centre. A group of specially trained male & female nurses are on hand to offer support, references & first aid. Situated in the red-light area, downtown Montréal. Open from 9:15PM to 4AM.

Human Sexuality Clinic (☑)

⊠ **Human Sexuality Clinic**, c/o Montréal General Hospital, 1547 Ave. des Pins ouest, Mtl, Qué., H3G 1B3

☎ (514) 934-8013

fax: (514) 934-8204

→ The Human Sexuality Clinic operates a gender identity clinic & offers various services including therapy, hormones & SRS referrals.

Fondation Nationale du Transsexualisme (☑)

⊠ **Fondation Nationale du Transsexualisme**, PO Box 613, Stn C, Mtl, Qué., H2L 4L5

☎ (514) 526-5892

fax: (514) 526-1060

contact: Delphée Martin

→ The foundation exists to help anyone, experiencing gender dysphoria or dealing with transsexuality, to go through his/her transition in harmony with his/her values, beliefs & customs.

Dr Yvon Ménard, Chirurgie Plastique et Reconstructive (☑)

⊠ **Dr Ménard**, 1003 Boul. St-Joseph est, Mtl, Qué., H2J 1L2

☎ (514) 288-2097

fax: (514) 288-3547

→ Dr Ménard offers a wide range of plastic & reconstructive surgeries, including SRS for both FTM & MTF patients.

Projet d'Intervention Auprès des Mineures - eurs Prostituees - és (PIMP) (NS/☑)

⊠ **PIAMP**, CP 5028, Succ. C, Mtl,Qué., H2X 3M2

☎ (514) 527-1267

→ **PIAMP** is a team of street outreach workers, doing advocacy work for street youth. They also run a drop-in, in downtown Montréal.

TRANS-PORS (Post Operation Residence Services) (☑)

⊠ **TRANS-PORS**, 2006 Sherbrooke est, Mtl, Qué., H2K 1B9

☎ (514) 526-5892

→ Community service created by Dr Ménard & the Fondation Nationale du Transsexualisme to provide room & board, with special care & support for people (both FTM & MTF) coming to Montréal for SRS or any other type of adjusting surgery.

Québec

Dr Denys Chabot (☑)

⊠ **Clinique Dr Denys Chabot**, 1281 Place de Mérici, Québec, Qué., G1S 3H8

☎ (418) 682-8810

→ Dr Chabot is a cosmetic & plastic surgeon, offering several types of surgeries including MTF SRS. He is considering doing FTM SRS at a later date. He has been on medical leave for at least a year, but should return to work in the fall of '94.

Être Femme: Québec Transsexual Association Inc (☑)

⊠ **Être Femme**, 84 Boul. des Alliés, Québec, Qué., G1L 1Y2

☎ (418) 529-1152

contact: Mme Viviane Bélanger

→ Support group for FTM & MTF transsexuals. Provides referrals for therapy, hormones, etc. Works in close collaboration with the Centre Hospitalier de l'Université Laval. They also work with a local detoxification centre (Domaine de l'Hêtrière) for people with addictive & compulsive behaviours.

TransEqual Goes Online

You never know who you will meet in cyberspace! Now you can network electronically with TransEqual, and lots of transgendered people from all over the world.

Patrick Riley, system operator of the Writer's Resource Group BBS, in St. Catharines, Ontario, has just set up a "Friends of TransEqual"conference, and is also carrying a number of international FidoNet Echo-Mail conferences that are germane to Gender Orientation and Sexual Orientation issues. The BBS also has areas for a wide range of other topics, and has a private message area for one-on-one e-mail.

The *Friends of TransEqual* area is a special conference that cannot be read by the BBS's general callers. This special area is intended to facilitate a round-house discussion of the social, legal, ethical, and moral issues surrounding Canada's transgender community. It will also be used for a series of special projects, including discussions of TransEqual's activities, and "talks" with invited guests.

The Writer's Resource Group is at 1-905-685-1016, and can accommodate modems from 1200 to 14,400 baud. Access to the special areas is free with your paid membership in the Writer's Resource Group BBS. The membership fee is $25.00 per year (cheap at twice the price) and you will be responsible for your own long distance bill. To save money call at night and use packet-mail with an offline reader.

When you log on the first time, you must complete a new user sign up. Enter your CD-name when it asks for your alias. This way nobody can connect your real name with the name you use in the message areas. When it asks who referred you, you say "Laura Masters", and then leave a "Comment to the Sysop" requesting access to the transgender areas. Everything should be on-line for you the next day, and all you will need to do is select the areas you want to read, from the "Combined Messages" area.

If you need help getting started, call me on the TransEqual hotline (1-905-688-0276) and I'll happily do what what I can.

Laura Masters

Publications & Newsletters

Boy's Own
The FTM Newsletter

Boy's Own is published quarterly by the FTM Network, BM Network, London, UK, WC1N 3XX. Write for subscription information.
Provides a forum for FTM's to discuss issues of concern.

The Channel

The Channel is a newsletter published by ETVC, PO Box 426486, San Francisco, CA, USA, 94142. (510) 549-2665. If no answer, call (510) 849-4112, Telzey. Membership is $20(US)/year, which includes 1 year subscription.
Available only to members, helping professionals or through club exchanges.

Chrysalis Quarterly

Chrysalis Quarterly is published 4 times a year by the American Educational Gender Information Service (AEGIS), PO Box 33724, Decatur, GA, USA 30033-0724. (404) 987-8312. Subscription rates: $36(US)/year - within the US; $46(US)/year - outside the US.
Publication dedicated to in-depth exploration of gender issues & designed for both consumers & caregivers.

City Lights

City Lights is a newsletter published by the Metropolitan Gender Network, 561 Hudson St., Box 45, New York City, NY, USA, 10014. (718) 461-9050. Write for subscription information.

Cross-Talk
The Gender Community's News & Information Monthly

Cross-Talk is published monthly. PO Box 944, Woodland Hills, CA, USA, 91365. (818) 907-3053, (818) 347-4190 (fax). e-mail: kymmer@xconn.com. Subscription rates: $54(US)/1 year - US, $96(US)/2 years - US. Non-US subscribers add $12(US)/year.
Contains many articles of interest to the CD/TV/TG/TS communities.

Cross Port

Cross Port is a newsletter published monthly by Cross Port, PO Box 54657, Cincinnati, OH, USA 45254-0657. (513) 474-9557 (Shelbi). Subscription rates: $8(US)/year.

The Crystal Chronicle

The Crystal Chronicle is a newsletter published monthly by the Crystal Club, PO Box 287, Reynoldsburg OH, USA, 43068-0287. (614) 224-1165. Subscription rates: $8(US)/year.

Damaged Goods

Damaged Goods is published by Nygel Wesly Daggers, 584 Castro St. #251, San Francisco, CA, USA 94114-2500. Each issue costs $3(US).
Alternative transgender zine.

Destiny

Destiny is published quarterly by FATE, 1-1727 William St, Vancouver, BC, V5L 2R5. Destiny is free, but donations & postage are welcome.

Devil Woman

Devil Woman is a newsletter published by the Diablo Valley Girls, (DVG), PO Box 272885, Concord, CA, USA, 94527-2885. (510) 849-4112. Membership fees are $10(US)/year, includes subscription.
Available only to members, helping professionals & through club exchanges.

Dragazine

Dragazine is published two times a year and can be reached at: Dragazine, PO Box 691664, West Hollywood, CA, USA, 90069. Single issues are $5^{95}(US) & two issues $10^{95}(US).
Dragazine is designed to appeal to those that enjoy the art of crossdressing either as the audience or the Drag Queen that's teaching your children 1st grade.

DQ International

DQ International is published quarterly by Canadian CDC. Canadian CDC, 161 Gerrard St. East, Toronto, Ont., Canada, M5A 2E4. (416) 921-6112. $20(Can)/issue includes tax & postage.

Gender Quest

Gender Quest is a newsletter published bi-monthly by Phoenix Transgender Support, Phoenix, PO Box 18332, Asheville, NC, USA, 28814. (704) 259-9428. Subscription rates: $7(US)/year.

Girlfriend!

Girlfriend! is available for $4(US)/issue. Send money to Box 191781, San Francisco, CA, USA 94119.
Girlfriend! is a drag zine. The **Girlfriend!** calendar also available for $7(US).

In Your Face!
The Journal of Record of Transexual & Transgender Activism

In Your Face's mission statement is to cover all actions by transpeople and friends around the country. It is published 2 times a year. Free. Contact Lynn Walker & Riki Anne Wilchins, 274 W. 11 St. - #4R, NYC, NY, USA, 10014. (212) 645-1753.

IXΣ

IXΣ is a newsletter published monthly by **IXΣ**(Iota Chi Sigma). **IXΣ**, PO Box 20710, Indianapolis, IN, USA, 46220. Membership is $23(US)/year, which includes 1 year subscription. Back issues are $2(US)/issue. Checks should be payable to "cash" or "bearer".

Journal of Gender Studies

The Journal of Gender Studies is published twice a year by the Human Outreach and Achievement Institute, 405 Western Ave., Suite 345, South Portland, ME, USA 04106. Subscription rates: $16(US)/year.
This is the official publication of the Institute.

Lipstick and Lace

Lipstick and Lace is a newsletter published by Girl's Night Out. Write for subscription information to GNO c/o Barbara Fortune, POB 350369, Brooklyn, NY, USA, 11235-0007. (201) 794-1665, ext 202.

New Men And Women of Minnesota

New Men and Women of Minnesota is a newsletter published quarterly by the New Men and Women of Minnesota, PO Box 6432, Minneapolis, MN, USA, 55406-0432. Membership fees are $25(US)/year which includes 1 year subscription.

Notes From the Underground

Notes From the Underground is published bi-monthly by Gender Mosaic. PO Box 7421, Vanier, Ontario, K1L 8E4. (613) 749-5203. Subscription rates: $15(Cdn)/year.
Contains various articles relevant to the gender communities.

PPOC Girl Talk

PPOC Girl Talk is a newsletter published monthly by the Powder Puffs of California (PPOC), PO Box 1088, Yorba Linda, CA, USA, 92686. (714) 779-9013 weekdays, 9 to 9 pm (pacific time) & leave message. Subscription rates: $30/year for non-members.

Reflected Images

Reflected Images is a newsletter published quarterly by Reflections, PO Box 4002, East Dedham, MA, USA, 02026. $4(US)/issue. (617) 323-6082.

The Southern Belle

The Southern Belle is a newsletter published monthly by Sigma Epsilon, Tri-Ess, PO Box 272, Roswell, GA, USA, 30077. They don't sell their newsletter, but are willing to trade it with other newsletters.

Tennessee Vals

Tennessee Vals is a newsletter published monthly by Tennessee Vals, PO Box 92335, Nashville, TN, USA, 37209. (615) 664-6883 voice mail. Membership $25(US)/year includes 1 year subscription.

TNT
Transsexual - News - Telegraph

TNT, 584 Castro St., Suite 288, San Francisco, CA USA, 94114-2588. (415) 703-7161. Subscription rates: $15(US)/4 issues within the US & $20(US)/4 issues within Canada. All checks payable to Anne Ogborn.
Political publication that aims to cover the many issues affecting TS/TG persons (besides shopping and makeup), while promoting transsexual pride.

TOPS
Newsletter for Transsexual Sex Industry Workers

TOPS is published quarterly by the Ongoing Network - Transsexual Outreach Project (ON TOP). All correspondence should be addressed to ON TOP, PO Box 11-412 Manners St.,Wellington, NZ, phone 64-9-3666-106. Write for subscription rates.
Provides a forum for transsexual sex trade workers to communicate with each other about their various issues & concerns.

The Transgenderist

The Transgenderist is a newsletter published monthly by the Transgenderist's Independence Club (TGIC), PO Box 13604, Albany, NY, USA, 12212-3604. Membership is $40(US)/year which includes 1 year subscription.

TransSisters
The Journal of Transsexual Feminism

TransSisters is published quarterly by Skyclad Publishing Co., 4004 Troost Avenue, Kansas City, Missouri, USA, 64110. (816) 753-7816 - phone & fax (call first to set up fax). e-mail: davinaanne@aol.com. Subscription rates: $18(US)/4 issues within US, Canada & Mexico; $19(US)/4 issues outside those countries. Back issues available for $6(US) within Canada, US & Mexico; $625 outside those countries. All checks payable to Davina Anne Gabriel.
Provides a forum dealing with issues of transsexuality from a feminist perspective & exists to promote dialogue, understanding, co-operation & reconciliation between the feminist & transsexual communities.

The TV\TS Tapestry Journal

Tapestry is published quarterly by the IFGE. Box 367, Wayland, MA, USA 01778. (617) 899-2212 (617) 899-5703 (fax). Individual copies: $12(US). Subscription rates: $40(US)/1 year - regular subscription (US), $55(US)/1year - 1st Class (US), Canadian & overseas (surface) $65(US)/1 year - overseas (air). Subscribers receive a personal listing free of charge for the duration of their subscription. Regular subscribers are considered voting members of IFGE.
Primary publication of IFGE.

The Zenith Digest

The Zenith Digest is a newsletter published quarterly by the Zenith Foundation, Box 46, 8415 Granville St., Vancouver, BC, Canda, V6P 4Z9 (604) 261-1695. $3 (Cdn)/issue, payable to the Zenith Foundation.

The Cutting Edge of Feminist Journalism

TRANSSEXUAL WOMYN AT THE 1994 MICHIGAN WOMYN'S MUSIC FESTIVAL

Plus: Leslie Feinberg on Making Sisterhood Real ✱ The Power of Naming ✱ Gordene MacKenzie's *Transgender Nation* ✱ Beyond Patriarchal Power ✱ Transsexual Theory vs. Reality ✱ Transsexual Dykes to Watch Out For ✱ Elitism ✱ Transsexual Lesbians Expelled from Australian Lesbian Confest ✱ and more

Current Issue

"TransSisters gets more interesting, more literate and more articulate with every issue. I can see it maturing before my eyes, and it's a wonderful feeling to know that such a publication is possible." -- Sandy Stone, author of "The Empire Strikes Back: A Posttranssexual Manifesto"

"Some of the most hostile and damaging criticisms of transsexualism...have come from the feminist community, and TransSisters confronts these issues head-on. Because Davina positions the magazine in the breech of the cannon, it has potential to cause great change. TransSisters ... [is] ... on the leading edge of the politics of transsexualism." -- Dallas Denny, Chrysalis Quarterly

One year (four issues): $24.00
Sample Issue: $6.00

To order use order form on next page ☞

TransSisters

The Journal of Transsexual Feminism

The Cutting Edge of Feminist Journalism

Back Issues: $8.00 each

Issue # 1

Mission to Michigan: Transsexual Womyn at the Michigan Womyn's Music Festival

Issue # 2

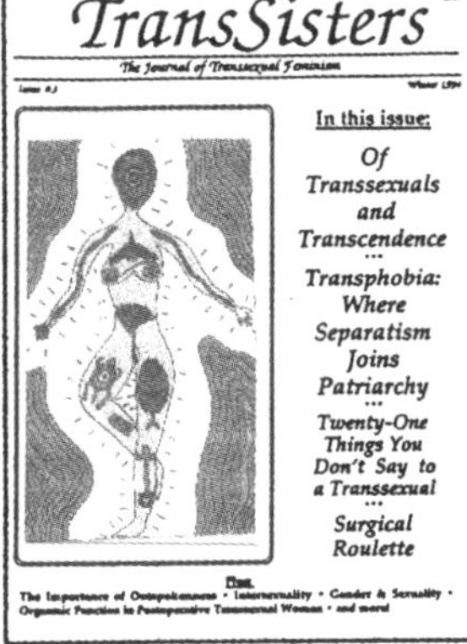

Issue # 3

Issue # 4

Issue # 5

FIRST ANNIVERSARY ISSUE

Issue # 6

- ☐ Please send me ____ sample issue(s) of *TransSisters* @ $6.00 each (current issue only)
- ☐ Please send me ____ one year subscription(s) (four issues) of *TransSisters*. @ $24.00 each.
- ☐ Please send me ____ copies of back issue # 1 of *TransSisters* @ $8.00 each.
- ☐ Please send me ____ copies of back issue # 2 of *TransSisters* @ $8.00 each.
- ☐ Please send me ____ copies of back issue # 3 of *TransSisters* @ $8.00 each
- ☐ Please send me ____ copies of back issue # 4 of *TransSisters* @ $8.00 each
- ☐ Please send me ____ copies of back issue # 5 of *TransSisters* @ $8.00 each
- ☐ Please send me ____ copies of back issue # 6 of *TransSisters* @ $8.00 each
- ☐ Enclosed is a contribution in the amount of ________________ to *TransSisters.*

(New subscriptions begin with next issue. To receive current issue, order sample issue. Outside U.S.A., Canada & Mexico add $0.25 per single issue & $1.00 for each subscription ordered)

Total Amount Enclosed: $ ____________ (U.S. funds only)

Name ____

Apt. or Suite # ____________ Address ________________________________

City ____

State / Province ____________________ Zip / Postal Code ____________

☞ **Please Make Checks or Money Orders Payable to Davina Anne Gabriel**

Mail to: Davina Anne Gabriel; 4004 Troost Avenue; Kansas City, Missouri 64110

PERSONALS

HOW TO PLACE AN AD

It's free!!! Just send us your ad with your name, complete address & phone number. All of these will be kept in our strictest confidence, babykins. And then all you have to do is wait by the mailbox for tons & tons of letters requesting your personal (& we're talking very personal) attention.

TO ANSWER AN AD:

Place your letter in a sealed & unstamped envelope. Write in pencil and in the top right corner of the envelope, the drawer number of the ad you are responding to. Next put the envelope(s) plus $5.00 for each contact (in cash or cheque/money order payable to genderpress) in another envelope & mail it to us at:

"*gendertrash*/personals"
box 500-62,
552 Church St,
Toronto, Ontario
M4Y 2E3

Please remember: no money no response. *gendertrash* can't live only on good intentions.

The editor & publishers of *gendertrash* assume no responsibility or liability for any meeting(s) resulting from these services.

❦❦❦

Bi-Curious
Post-op TS woman, single, french speaking, socially active, good natured, early forties, curvaceous. Recently found myself attracted to women. Would like to practise my english and explore my bisexuality with transsexual or genetic women. - *Québec City # 170*

Exploring Mind
Sincerely sadistic masochist (and a real sweetheart besides). Actually just an actively exploring and curious mind trapped in the body of a statuesque, ice-blue-eyed & make-up-fluent girl-type guy(?) with firm, ripe bosoms. I'm all of it and none of it - if you're similar or can in any way relate, let's talk, okay? - *Toronto # 210*

Femme Seeks Butch
Desperately wants strong short-haired, no dress, no makeup, no purse, no high heels, good looking butch type, pre/non/post-op TS woman for great hugs, play fighting & outdoor fun. I'm a bright & cute 20ish TS femme - *Toronto # 150*

French Man
Straight, but open-minded French genetic man, late 30's, attractive, business type, seeks good-looking & intelligent MTF TS for ongoing relationship. Discretion & respect a must. - *Toronto # 230*

Gender Oriented Genetic
I am a gender-oriented genetic man who is drawn to TS's. Also am a bit of a cross-dresser. I would like to find a cute, smart TS who seeks a lover/friend/or relationship. I have many cultural interests from A to Z (abnormal psychology to art to avant garde novels). My favourite author is Jack Kérouac, father of the beat generation and son of French Canadians - pacifist, Zen seeker, jazz disciple, etc. - *Pennsylvania area # 100*

Gender Outlaw
Gender outlaw into zines alternative music, cats and 90210. Seeks funky TS/TG/TV/DQ who doesn't shop from Tapestry (and also can't afford to) for dancing, demos, researching TG history, hanging out & ? Way bilingual, way bisexual too. - *Montréal # 160*

In Search of a FTM
Genetic woman, french, 25, red-head, mature & insightful, seeks sensitive, politically aware, intelligent, sexy FTM with a sense of humour, who likes children, for friendship and more... - *Montréal # 120*

Party Girl
French crazy smoking, drinking, wild partying genetic girl wants to meet TS/TG girls with a brain for friendship, watching TV, eating junk & nights out. - *Toronto # 270*

Sexy Femme TS
Beautiful model-type transsexual, 25, tall, slim, sexy, feminine figure, long curly brown hair, blue eyes. Seeks cute young (18+) guy for friendship plus ? - *Toronto # 190*

TS Angel
Young but mature MTF Angel. Very beautiful, soft, sweet and sincere, but strong and assertive. Seeks unattached, intelligent, pro-feminist, non-smoker, vegetarian, attractive man for stable relationship, based on affection not garter belts... - *Toronto # 130*

TS Lesbian Wanted
Non-transsexual lesbian, trans-curious, presently living in Montréal but planning to move to another planet soon. Would like to correspond with and/or meet a soft-core feminist transsexual lesbian. Must be open-minded, love kids and travelling. - *Montréal # 110*

TS Man Wanted
Would like to meet a very masculine, confident, passable FTM for friendship and/or more. I'm a very feminine attractive 25 year old TS woman. Must be caring and open minded. - *Toronto # 150*

TS Woman Wanted
40 years old TS woman would like another intelligent, mature, political, vegetarian, non-smoker, non-drinking, quiet TS woman, 30-40, for friendship. Operative status unimportant. No makeup sessions nor lingerie parade, please.- *Toronto # 160*

Le Babíllard

- HIV/AIDS SURVEY: Ki Namaste from Montréal, is co-ordinating a survey designed to assess the impact of HIV/AIDS on TS's, TV's, DQ's and other gender outlaws living in Canada. The information gathered will be used to develop AIDS education programs and social services for TG people in Canada. If you would like to participate in this survey, would like to know the results or any other information, please contact : Ki Namaste, CP 423, Succ. C, Montréal, Québec, H2L 4K3.
- MWMF: Plans are already under way for next year's protest against the Michigan Womyn's Music Festival. For information & greatly needed donations please contact Davina Anne Gabriel, 4004 Troost Ave., Kansas City, Missouri, 64110, USA.
-FULL CIRCLE OF WOMEN, a conference for woman-identified persons of all body shapes. Essex, Massachusetts, March 31- April 2, 1995. Contact: Janis Walworth, PO Box 52, Ashby, MA 01431 USA
- TRANSGENDER PRIDE PROJECT: Leslie Feinberg (author of Stone Butch Blues & Transgender Liberation) is soliciting tax-deductible donations to publish her historical & cross-cultural research on transgender, tentatively titled Transgender: A History of Resistance. Checks should be payable to the Column Foundation, c/o William Sachs, Esq., Suite 830, 7 Penn Plaza, New York, New York 10001, USA. Please clearly mention that this contribution is to be used for the Transgender Pride Project.
- NATIONAL TRANSEXUAL HEALTH CONFERENCE: NTHC will be held in New York City by & for TS/TG people in April, 1995. For further information please contact Monica Pedone (212/213-6335), Lynn Walker (718/836-6215), Riki Anne Wilchins (212/645-1753) or Barbara Warren c/o Lesbian & Gay Community Center (212/620-7310).
- ICTLEP: the International Conference on Transgender Law & Employment Policy, Inc., is holding its 4th annual conference June 14-18, 1995, in Houston. They are also looking for donations. For further information, please contact them at 5707 Firenza St., Huston, Texas, 77035-5515, (713) 723-8368, (713) 723-1800 (fax)

I
love
Transsexuals

GENDERTRASH

ISSUE 4

SPRING 1995

spring 95 issue # 4 $6.00 (US/Can)

gendertrash

issue # 4

gendertrash (ISSN 1198-8479) is published 4 times a year & gives a voice to transsexual/transgendered people, who have been discouraged from speaking out & communicating with each other.

editor Mirha-Soleil Ross
production dir. Xanthra Phillippa

contributors
Marie Alexandra, Christine Tayleur, Lofofora Contreras, CaiRa, Sandra Laframboise/Debarah Brady, Xanthra Phillippa, Mirha-Soleil Ross, Selena Anne Shephard, Michelle

front cover
Janou, Montréal 1991. Photographer unknown.

layout & design
Mirha-Soleil Ross & Xanthra Phillippa

published by
genderpress

Box 500-62,
552 Church Street,
Toronto, Ontario
M4Y 2E3
(416) 929-2350 (voice)
(416) 929 2804 (fax)
call first on voice line to set up fax

Contents

Submissions: We encourage transsexual (both ftm's and mtf's), transgendered and intersexed people to send us photos, drawings, poetry, essays, cartoons, etc. Gender-positive genetics are also encouraged to submit. You can submit a written piece on a 3.5" floppy disk (ASCII text file - PC HD/DD format). Submissions may also be typed or handwritten but should be double spaced & must be legible. Include your name, address, and phone number. Put your name and the title of your piece on every page. Mention if your piece has been published somewhere else. Please, for Christina's sake, include a brief bio so that we & our readers can know a bit more about you & the colour of your underwear. Also, include a picture if possible (please mention who took it) or any other kind of artwork to accompany your piece. Anonymity can be preserved; just tell us the pseudonym you wish to use. Submission does not necessarily guarantee publication. Submissions are all subject to editing for length and clarity so don't freak out too much about grammar and spelling. We'll repair it the best we can. Don't forget a S.A.S.E. if you want your material to be returned.

TRANSSEXUAL SISTERHOOD IS POWERFUL!!!

cartoon by Marie Alexandra

letters...

Dear Mirha-Soleil & Xanthra:
I wanted to write to tell you how impressed I was by issue #3 of *gendertrash*. The format & articles were certainly challenging & thought provoking. I also want to take this opportunity to thank you for the support you have given us as an organization through your patience & teaching.
You and your magazine have made a difference to us in the way we think, and the manner in which we offer service. Your contribution has also had a positive impact on at least one individual who has made use of our Centre. We want you to know that your caring & constructive influence has not gone unappreciated. Truly this individual would not have made the gains she has without your support.
I imagine the struggle in which you are involved can be tiring & often frustrating. As you move forward, please know that your efforts have & will continue to create change.

Irwin Elman
Supervisor/Facilitator
Pape Adolescent Resource Centre (PARC)

Dear *gendertrash*:
Yours is the magazine I was imagining creating after becoming hep to the 'zine scene several years ago and sensing, well, a gap, a space, an unfilled opening. Congratulations on your first, second and third issues welcome & long overdue arrivals.
I've noted a certain maturing in tone in issue #3 as befits the subject matter of the Michigan Womyn's Music Festival's TS inclusion/exclusion issue vs allowing TS's to self-define, as a reflection of society's jaundiced eye towards us as actual breathing, feeling persons and not merely as walking genital question marks.
The survey regarding Women's Shelters' accessibility to TS wimmin was also rather sobering. It gives one pause to reflect for a moment, or two or three, on just how easily we can slip through the holes in the social safety net...
That said, however, I must say how much the initial two issues' generous soupçons of irreverent wit & self-righteous anger served to help empower my thinking not only towards myself but to fellow travellers as well.
I showed the Genetic Jerk Quiz to someone who I thought pretty much knew the score, at the time, and he said, "Wow, they sound really angry..." he himself sounding somewhat baffled by the thought of a TS having anything to be angry about. "They?" I asked. It was cathartic... eventually.
That spark helped bring me to now: unencumbered (stripped & deprived I would have said at that time) by a (mis) understanding lover-boy; alone-but-not too lonely, looking towards a future & present of my own, rather than serving as a footnote to another's.
To know that I'm not the only one who finds this a bit confusing, sometimes arbitrary & mind-boggling road to tread, to be able to laugh at the absurdities & speak out against mindless & thoughtless indignities has helped imbue me with a sense of strength & pride of self & I thank you both, Mirha-Soleil & Xanthra, for your efforts in creating a voice & a forum where we & our friends can speak about our selves, ourselves.

Sincerely yours,
Dale Anderson

Dear Xanthra:
Thank you for the latest issue of *gendertrash*. You do a remarkable job with it. Thanks for the buttons; they arrived just in time for me to wear the "I'd Rather Be Dead than Genetic" one last weekend at the conference in Northridge.
What I liked most about *gendertrash* is how radical you are. Issue #3 seemed a bit less angry than nos. 1 & 2 (loved the electric epileptic transsexual poem). Please don't lose your edge.

Sincerely
Dallas Denny

Dear Xanthra:
Two and a half years ago, when I was media relations co-ordinator for Buddies in Bad Times Theatre, someone suggested I call you to ask if you would be interested in speaking with a journalist from *The Toronto Star* who was researching a piece about transsexualism, drag culture and cross-dressing. You answered a resounding NO and said that your experience with the non-TG press had left you mistrustful of their ability and interest in sensitively addressing and furthering transgender liberation issues. I don't know if *gendertrash* was in the works back then (Issue #3 is my first), but may it stay and stay! It's a tremendous read that has elaborated my understanding of your objections and my admiration for the courage of transgendered people who live and write out their experiences with pride.
I wish you and Ms. Ross the best of enterprising luck and will watch the stands for Issue #4.

Fanfully yours,
Robin Williamson

AEGIS suggests Electrolysis to Avoid Problem of Hair in Neovagina

The Problem:

Vaginoplasty using the penile and penoscrotal inversion methods, with or without skin grafts or skin flaps, can result in a neovagina which is lined with hair-bearing skin. As the hair grows, the vagina can become choked with hair. Not surprisingly, many transsexual women find this extremely embarrassing.

Some sex reassignment (SRS) surgeons do not appreciate the extent of this embarrassment. During a presentation given at the October, 1993 meeting of the Harry Benjamin International Gender Dysphoria Association, one prominent surgeon remarked that although his procedure sometimes results in hair-bearing vagina, his patients do not seem to mind. Reports we have had from transsexual women indicate, however, that they *DO* care.

Our Recommendations:

We recommend that surgeons doing male-to-female SRS become aware that hair-bearing vagina is extremely embarrassing for their transsexual patients, and to provide them with materials educating them about the problem and indicating where they should consider having electrolysis to avoid hair-bearing vagina.

We recommend that electrologists be aware that transsexual women who are seeking SRS have legitimate reasons for seeking electrolysis in the perineal area.

We recommend that persons seeking male-to-female SRS who have excessive hair in the pelvic region consult with the surgeon they have selected in order to determine which skin will eventually be inside the vagina so that they can decide whether electrolysis is desirable and so they can schedule electrolysis and surgery accordingly.

All parties should keep in mind that electrolysis is a gradual process, and that it can take a year or more to completely clear an area

- from the American Educational Gender Information Service

The Rainbow Book

The Ontario Directory of Community Services for Lesbians, Gay Men, Bisexuals, Transsexuals, Transgenderists and Transvestites

published by: the Coalition for Lesbian & Gay Rights in Ontario, 519 Church Street Community Centre, Lesbian Gay Bi Youthline, and Project Affirmation.

The best thing about this book is its subtitle "the Ontario Directory of Community Services for Lesbians, Gay Men, Bisexuals, **Transsexuals, Transgenderists and Transvestites**" (emphasis added) because first we're there and secondly we're not dumped into a poorly-fitting category like "others." Transgendered people come in all shapes, forms, and from very different backgrounds/gender persuasions. Therefore the more names genetics use to describe/include us, the better represented/included we are.

Unfortunately, there are not a lot of listings of support groups for the transgendered in Ontario (*quelle surprise!*). This is not the fault of the writers/researchers, but reflects the ability of transgendered people to provide support groups or create political organizations in the same numbers and specificity as do lesbians and gays (ie. "Lesbians and Gays Who Prefer Pepsi to Coke With Their French Fries").

Some of the organizations listed are not specifically for members of the communities targeted by the Rainbow Book (including but not limited to rape crisis centres, shelters, HIV/AIDS, youth groups, health services). However, we assume them to be positive towards those communities, since they are listed there. This constitutes a problem because not all groups/resources that are lesbian/gay-positive are necessarily trans-positive. There should be a section in the Listing Entry Form where groups or service providers are explicitly asked whether they are open to or knowledgeable about TS/TG/TV's.

And what about those social service agencies that may come in contact with TG/TS/TV people and try to help? Will this book give them any valuable information? The answer is a qualified yes - if they rarely deal with transgendered people, the Rainbow book will provide them with a handy little guide. Otherwise no, because the few groups listed are sure to be well-known to them.

— reviewed by Xanthra Phillippa

High Risk Project
Vancouver

Dancing To Eagle Spirit *talks with* ***Mirha-Soleil*** *about addiction, recovery and her involvement with the street transsexual community*

Doing this interview with **Dancing To Eagle Spirit** was a bit odd because we are both Francophone, yet we did the interview in English in order to avoid exhausting hours of translation. She and I usually spend more time on the phone laughing like thunder and telling each other about our last spicy sex-adventures than eloquently discussing some nebulous points of transsexual politics.

Nevertheless, I was very glad to interview her for *gendertrash*, for I believe she is amongst those pioneers who, realizing the extent to which their own people have been neglected, take matters into their own hands and, by the same stroke, empower all of us.

Mirha-Soleil: First of all, why don't you tell us who you are and where you're from?

Dancing To Eagle Spirit: My given name is Sandra Laframboise, but my native name is Dancing To Eagle Spirit. That's the name my elders acknowledge in Sweatlodge and that's the name they will acknowledge in the Pipe ceremony next week.

My family is originally from Maniwaki reserve in Québec. I'm Métis, Algonquin Cree. I was born in Ottawa, raised in Ottawa until the age of 12, lived my life on the streets of Montréal as a hooker from 12 until the age of 29. I prostituted myself in Ottawa, Montréal, Toronto, and Vancouver which was mostly transitional.

M-S: How old are you now?

DTES: I'm 35. I'm old.

M-S: You had worked in the sex trade since you were 12?

DTES: I started as a male and prostituted myself as a boy. My first customer was for 5 bucks and I quickly changed over within the first years. I prostituted myself as a male for about 3 years and I started crossdressing around the age of 15 and working on the market where females were hanging out.

M-S: At that time were you working openly as a transsexual?

DTES: No, as a female. I wouldn't tell the clients. I never told the clients. I just gave them blow jobs, car dates. If the guy wanted to lay, I would ask for extra money, would tell him to wait a second, and I would turn myself on my tummy. I would grab my penis, lay on my front and let him lay me in the butt. So I never told them. Sometimes the guy would know and say: "I know what you are, so just don't worry about it." But most of the time they never knew. I always had that risk, that fear of being discovered and being beaten.

M-S: When did you move to Vancouver?

DTES: I moved to Vancouver in 1987. I never worked the streets in Vancouver; I worked the papers. I advertised in the national and local papers.

M-S: When did you stop working as a prostitute?

DTES: I stopped working the 18th of June, 1989. I went to detox on that date, and I cleaned up. I was doing drugs, cocaine. I was a freebase addicted person as well as a prostitute. I went to a treatment centre, had a spiritual experience and never went back to prostitution, drugs or alcohol after that.

M-S: Do you mind talking about this spiritual experience?

DTES: Oh no. I can talk about my spiritual experience. First of all, my recovering treatment was run through the Salvation Army. They have a Christian-based philosophy in which Jesus Christ basically died for your sins. For a long long time, I had felt that there was a God up there; I had felt a connection. Being clean, sober and being in an environment where I was accepted for who I was (NOT knowing I was transgendered of course) led me to believe in the experience of the Holy Spirit. I felt that the creator was inside of me, guiding me. At that time, I believed it was the Holy Spirit and Jesus Christ, and I truly practised those philosophies. But there was always something missing. Being Métis, Algonquin, Cree and white, there was always that side of me, the native side of me that I wanted to start searching for. Being a transsexual, I always wondered, "what if they knew?" In the Bible, they talk against homosexuals but what if they knew about me being a TRANSSEXUAL? So I started coming out, really out and being open about who I am. Eventually the pastor used that in the Salvation Army against me. At that moment, I knew I was getting abused by the church, not by God but by the church. I felt religiously abused and left the church shortly after that. This was from '89 to '91. I had lived with the SA for two years when I quit them in '91. I had already started school and had gotten some funding for school. I rented a place, found a part-time job on the weekends as a health care giver and started to learn how to live with myself. I started to deal with my issues from the past with the drugs, the alcohol, and my background which is quite dysfunctional - I mean my father raped me, beat me, emotionally fucked me up; my mother abandoned us to his mercy and had multiple lovers in front of us... So I started dealing with those issues.

M-S: How is your relationship with your parents now?

DTES: Well, they're comfortable with me because I say: "ok, what you did to me when I was young was cruel, but my alcoholism is my problem not yours." So I take away their guilt and their shame by saying that. They always blamed me for being the black sheep 'cause I drank and I was on the street. They kept saying: "well, we were good parents; we never did anything wrong." Well, excuse me but I'm a transsexual, I'm an ex-IV drug user, ex-prostitute; my brother and my sister are both alcoholics. It's like...

M-S: Do you feel that being a transsexual has something to do with the way you were treated by your parents when you were young?

DTES: Not the fact that I'm a transsexual but my alcoholism yes. It has something to do with it. The

transsexuality itself is something totally out but they've used that against me; they've used that to shame me, to ostracize me, to segregate me, and to hurt me 'cause they themselves don't understand it. So I take their shame away from them. I can't forget what happened, but I have to look at them as spiritual human beings; that's my responsibility in my recovery.

M-S: What happened in 1991 when you broke with the SA?

DTES: I went totally gay. I hung out with a totally gay crowd. So I went from one extreme to the other until I found a balance.

M-S: You were living as a woman then?

DTES: Oh yeah. I've been operated for 15 years. I've been a complete sex-change for 15 years now.

M-S: You talked a lot about your spiritual experience with the SA. Since you left them how did your spirituality evolve?

DTES: Well, I was on a spiritual search. I was brought up Roman Catholic and knew that there was something wrong with me, because I was persecuted for being an indian. So I started to study different philosophies. I went Muslim in 1991. I wore the Hadjeb, the veil to hide my face.That lasted for 9 months and it was great. I was madly, passionately involved with a Muslim man who was mujahideen. It was great. I was just living my experience to the fullest. This was what I felt; this was what I was looking for. Let's go learn about it. Let's go live it. And whatever happened, I'm grateful, because it's a lesson I've learned. After the Muslim period, I went a little bit Zen Buddhist and read about that a little bit, started learning how to meditate and started getting in touch with my centre, learning about the chakras, the crystals which are part of our culture as well. And that took all together about another 3 years which brought me to the "Redroad" as I call it, which is my native culture. And when I got there, that felt good, that felt right, that felt balanced. It incorporated all my knowledge 'cause it incorporates everything. It teaches respect of the environment and of yourself. It teaches that introspection is respect and that you can't have respect if you don't have introspection. It teaches all that and that's what created a balance for me. I had a bit of trouble with being a transsexual but in our culture, we're called Two-Spirited and everybody has a place in the circle 'cause we believe in the circle. Everything is circular, and what you put out comes around, so we have to respect each other at the community level. Our sexuality is ours; it's private within us, but at the community level, we're all human beings, and we're all entitled to respect, 'cause we all have our place in the circle.

M-S: When you were growing up, were you aware of your native background?

DTES: I was being made aware of it, but I wasn't really taught about it.

M-S: So your parents were not talking about it?

DTES: Never.

M-S: And they were raising you as Catholic?

DTES: Yeah, my mom is white; my dad is Red. And we were raised as Catholic. All that was said was that we were of indian descent. Never talked about it.

M-S: How did get involved with the High Risk Project?

DTES: It started about a year ago.

M-S: You really went back to your roots during the last year and a half. You reclaimed both your native and transsexual backgrounds at the same time?

DTES: Yes. Both. And it feels absolutely wonderful! I started to feel comfortable with myself and confident. I wanted to have a primary relationship with myself and learn about myself. So that was the hard part. When I graduated a year ago, as a registered psychiatric nurse from Douglas College, I wanted to do something for my community. When I cleaned up, I realized that there was nothing, that I was fortunate enough to be female legally, to have had my sex-change and to look like a female. I had seen the transgendered in treatment, and it's not always very nice. I saw how they were treated - the discrimination - so I wanted to do something for my community.

M-S: So you feel you're sort of privileged because you pass well as a non-transsexual and therefore don't get as bothered on the street or wherever as other people?

DTES: That's right.

M-S: And you wanted to do something for your own?

DTES: Yes. And that's how I got involved with the Zenith Foundation. They had started a support group on Wednesday nights called High Risk. With Barbara Hannon and April Valley. They had started doing that with First United Church. By that time, I had graduated. I joined High Risk because I wanted to do something for street people. I said: "This is who I am, and I am now a para-professional, and I want to incorporate both." So I got involved. They had a dispute with First United Church, so I started talking to agencies in the downtown east side. I had been working for a whole year in the downtown east side with some of the agencies so they knew me. It was easy for me to help that transition, and that's how we got the Thursday night group at DEYAS (Downtown East side Youth Association Services) -

I had a bit of trouble with being a transsexual but in our culture we're called Two-Spirited and everybody has a place in the circle

the needle exchange there. They said, "we'll support you, come along." They gave us a space in the back, and we started High Risk from there - Barbara, April and I. Then April dropped out and it was Barb and I. So High Risk went on for January, February, and March 1994, at which point the need came to establish something else, bigger. The girls said, "what about a coffee drop-in?" So I started talking to people. We went to Vancouver Native Health Society and they said, " Here's a space in our basement. Use it. Do what you want." That's when we started having a Coffee Drop-In on Mondays. It just grew from there. Barbara dropped out, so I got hung and I stayed with them.

M-S: And you tried to get volunteers around you?

DTES: Not right away. What happened is that I was left alone with the group. There was the support group in DEYAS and this drop-in thing that was catching on like wild fire. I was stuck. I had nobody. So Deborah who was with Zenith came on board to help. She's a good schmoozer. She busts everything for me which is good.

M-S: At the beginning, High Risk was part of the Zenith Foundation. When did High Risk become independent?

DTES: It separated about... hmm... September last year. By October it was announced that High Risk was going to be incorporated on its own. It became officially incorporated in January this year.

M-S: You probably also find that there is a lot of discrimination against transsexual prostitutes in most transsexual support groups, organizations, etc?

DTES: Totally. The transsexuals from the upper middle class, I call them the secondary transsexuals. They're the ones who have been fortunate to live long enough as men before to come out as women so that they didn't have to live through the poverty, through the discrimination, through the ostracization. They established themselves as men and then they became women.

M-S: I always found it interesting to see that most transsexuals who work the streets started living as women at a very early age.

DTES: Yeah, those are the primary transsexuals.

M-S: As opposed to the ones who came out after getting their houses, their wives, and their kids and who then put us down for not having taken advantage of hetero male priviledges. The bottom line is I couldn't even pretend half a day to be a straight guy. It was physically, emotionally, and sexually impossible.

DTES: And it's not our fault.

M-S: No.

DTES: But the problem is that we all suffer from low self-esteem. We all suffer from discrimination. We all suffer from segregation and from being ostracized by the community. We're always looking to validate ourselves as human beings. So we're all at high risk because we're all transsexuals and therefore part of a minority. You go in a bar, have a drink, and someone in front of you validates you by saying, "Oh honey you're beautiful ah-naa-naa-naa." You go, "oh yeah," and you get all flattered, flabbergasted. You bring the person home, be it male or female, whatever, you have a couple of drinks and the person says, "Let's not use condoms." You've put yourself at risk for HIV transmission, but they don't see that. It's not a question about whether or not they care about dying or getting HIV-infected; everybody cares about it. It's that disbelief factor: "It won't happen to me." Also there's the second part I emphasize which is the low self-esteem and the fact that you have someone in front of you validating you. I know this because I still once in a while have sex without a condom. And as a psychiatric nurse, I should know better than anybody else. I talk about it with the guy and say, "if you don't want to have sex with condoms forget it." I bring the guy home, put the condoms out on the table but in the heat of the passion and kiss kiss kiss - forget it. I say this because I want to emphasize it.

We're all at high risk because we're all transsexuals and therefore part of a minority

M-S: Do you find that all transsexuals are at high risk?

DTES: All transsexuals are at high risk. All minority groups and all cultural groups. When you've been discriminated against, when you've endured racist slurs and racism all your life, you're at high risk 'cause you suffer low self- esteem. But transsexuals are even more at risk, especially if they're on the streets. I say this because transsexuals are the lepers of this world. This is a harsh way to say it, but look at transsexuals in North America. Look at the people with low socio-economic means who are also on the streets -the IV-drug users, the prostitutes, the male and female prostitutes - look at all the service agencies out there for them. Not one specifically address-

es transgender issues. Not one of them. Transsexuals are still left out on the side. So we are on the streets at a higher risk than any other group, 'cause not only are we IV-drug users, not only are we prostitutes, not only are we drinking, not only are we suffering from all of that, but we're also suffering because of our transsexuality, not fitting in anywhere.

M-S: That should even be a stronger reason for the broader transsexual community to support transsexual prostitutes and street-active transsexuals.

DTES: It should. But have you ever seen a transsexual trying to help another transsexual? [hysterical laughter from both]

M-S: The first time I called a support group in Montréal, I asked if there was diversity in the group in terms of sexual orientation, cultural background, etc. The person answered something to the effect that there were prostitutes in the group and added some derogatory comments about them. I was so upset because I was already working as a prostitute boy, and I was very ashamed of it. Take this and add the insecurity of going to a transsexual support group for the first time and you can imagine how I felt.

DTES: It's unreal.

M-S: Who hangs out at the drop-in?

DTES: Street-active HIV+ transgendered. They come from various backgrounds, from very low socio-economic to rich people. I don't understand it. We have a lot of native transsexuals. The majority. And 72% of our girls are HIV+.

M-S: I supposed there's nothing in terms of AIDS prevention programs for transsexuals and transgendered people in Vancouver either?

DTES: No. There is absolutely no HIV/AIDS education for transsexuals. There is nothing, absolutely nothing. I'm publishing an article called: "Transsexuals: HIV and AIDS." I've been publishing more stuff like that because there's nothing, there's absolutely nothing.

M-S: Do you feel that the seroprevalence amongst transsexuals is stable or on the rise?

DTES: On the rise.

M-S: It's already high. I'm wondering when it's going to stop.

DTES: I've lost three girls last year and I'm so pissed off at the government because we have to schmooze them, and we have to write to them and lobby and lobby. But it's starting to change. Already after one year, we're seeing the changes. The agencies are calling us to go down and do some sensitivity training. Agencies are calling to refer transsexuals to us.

M-S: You think that behaviours have not changed amongst street transsexuals, that they are still practicing unsafe sex?

DTES: Listen, listen. The trick is there and you haven't eaten all day. You're coming off of a drug trip and he offers you 5 extras to take that condom off. What do you think you're going to do? You need that 5 bucks for your fix. You're going to take that condom off, that's reality. I don't blame the girls; I blame the tricks. And then they go home to their wives.

M-S: One of the greatest things there, is that it's going to be the first place run by transsexuals. It's not somebody else taking care of us.

DTES: It's transsexuals for transsexuals. It's totally run by volunteers and they're all street-active or IV-drug users. It's very cool. On our board, we have a couple of people that are not transsexuals. But they're not allowed in the drop-in. That's the rule. The girls in the drop-in have gotten together and made 10 safe house rules for themselves.

M-S: Which are?

DTES: No smoking in the building. No drugs in the building. You can be high, but if you come in and you're obnoxious, you'll be asked to leave. No working in front of the door and different things like that. But they've all agreed to that.They've all signed that. So that's cool. They police themselves.

M-S: What are the immediate and long-term goals

of the High Risk project?

DTES: The immediate goal is to address the primary needs of our girls. They're sleeping on the streets; they're sleeping in parking lots. They're HIV+, and they have malnutrition. They suffer all kinds of secondary diseases due to their HIV/AIDS status. To address those needs right off the bat, we'd like to build showers and install laundry facilities. The girls who are sleeping on the streets could come in, have a shower, and wash their clothes. Those are part of the primary needs that will help build some self-esteem. If you're clean, then you feel clean. Another thing is to build a kitchen and to have their nutritional needs met at least once a day. We could dispense vitamins and juice and do teaching about it. These are the immediate goals.

The long term needs are to establish an outreach program and an advocacy program for transgendered people. An advocacy program to tackle the legal issues, to advocate on their behalf at the government level, and to affect government policy changes or to represent transgendered in certain systems where they're being discriminated against. The outreach program. One night we were walking through the neighbourhood, and we thought it would be nice to serve hot chocolate in styrofoam cups. So we started going out to give out hot chocolate on the street. We walked out on the streets every night for a week or so, bringing hot chocolate to the street transsexuals. And it was needed. We saw transsexuals that were not coming to our drop-in, and we were able to reach them. And we pulled them into our drop-in too because of that. I'm sure that we could do a lot more. So we need that kind of outreach.

M-S: You need funding too.

DTES: We need money so that Deborah and I can leave our "regular" jobs and dedicate our lives and our energy to something that we want to do and that is needed.

The High Risk Project operates its drop-in at:
The Vancouver Native Health Society,
449 Hastings Street (rear)
Monday to Friday from 1:00pm–4:30pm.
for information: (604) 681-3202

*** High Risk Project Society is a registered charity and donations are always welcome.**

Transsexality: A Mental Handicap Or a Physical Disorder?

A position statement
by Sandra Laframboise and Deborah Brady
High Risk Project Society

In the press and other media, there has been a lot of discussion regarding the issue of Gender Dysphoria as a mental handicap. Transgendered activists are uniting to fight for justice and recognition.

In the United States, the organization Transgender Nation has been and is lobbying the American Psychiatric Association to remove transgenderism from the DSM III R's list of mental illnesses.

At High Risk we believe that transgendered people are not mentally ill. Furthermore, we also believe that as insured consumers within the medical health care system, as citizens and tax payers, we have a right to medical services specifically related to our gender needs.

Transsexuals are people who have the gender identity (psyche, mind or feelings) of one sex and the body of the other. Transgenderism has been an ancient and persistent part of diversified human cultures. Since the early 1800's there have been thousands of documented cases in medical journals (such as "Die Kontaire Sexualamp" findings — German journals). It is not surprising to us that Western European culture labels us as pathological when we transgress the rigid binary gender boundaries, since these boundaries attempt to enforce conformity to social norms. Before colonization, transgendered persons in North American society were highly regarded and considered shamans.

How then, can we claim to need medical services when we are not sick? In this country, an individual has the right to express their identity through non-coercive means and may alter their physical appearance as desired.

Our society needs to embrace this kind of diversity rather than concentrating on repression and conformity to a norm. Sex is what you are, sexuality is an action or preference, and gender is what you feel. It is essential that there be harmony between the body and gender identity for an individual to achieve happiness. For most transsexuals, sex re-assignment surgery is like liberation from a prison. The whole issue of transsexuality has to do with gender identity, the core feeling of who one is. Transsexualism is not a mental disorder.

However, there are few or no positive laws that establish exactly what legal rights and obligations transsexuals have when involved with our social services or medical services. This lack of recognition creates intense alienation and leaves the door open for discrimination in regard to access to those services. For the transgendered individual, even simple daily activities of life, such as going to the store and getting food, can be very difficult because people see transsexuals as freaks of nature.

Coping with intense discrimination, unemployment, poverty, lack of housing, and lack of medical care specific to our needs — these are the real issues we face. We, at High Risk Project, find it deplorable that the transgendered must ask, "please may we have the right to exist?" We are now demanding our rights.

In conclusion, to say that we are handicapped is as much a crime as to say that a person of colour is disabled.

I met Diane about a year ago. I was visiting my parents in Montréal and went to hang out at Cléo (a transsexual bar situated in the Red Light district, downtown) in order to meet with former clients and co-workers. I was chatting with a man when I saw Diane coming in with her backpack, distributing condoms and lubricant to the girls around. I was both surprised and excited. Having a transsexual prostitute finally being hired as an AIDS educator to reach out to other transsexual prostitutes represents a long awaited recognition of our specific needs in terms of AIDS prevention. I immediately asked Diane if she would be interested to be interviewed for gendertrash. Showing the enthusiasm of someone who realizes the importance of networking and who is dedicated to collaborating with others, she accepted. The following is a transcript of a conversation we had in April.

Reaching Out to the Unreachable:

an interview with Diane Gobeil from CACTUS Montréal

Interview and translation from French by Mirha-Soleil Ross

Mirha-Soleil: I would like you to talk about your background. At what age did you start working in the sex trade?

Diane: I am 32 years old. I started working when I was 19. I left for Vancouver, because I wanted to live there. I had friends there, and prostitution was better. We were not getting bothered as much by the police and all that. So I worked for 3 years in Vancouver, from 19 to 22. I was living with a man there, and he committed suicide. It gave me a big down, and I came back to Montréal in '86. Then I kept on working in the sex trade in Montréal while working in bars/clubs as a bar-maid. I also worked as a dancer in various clubs on the South and North Shores.

M-S: Have you always worked as a woman?

D: Always as a woman. I never worked as a man. Never, never, never. So when I came back to Montréal, I had an addiction problem. It started around that time, when my friend died and I got this big down. I ended up very depressed. But instead of going to see a doctor, I went to live with a girlfriend who said she would pump my morale back up. She showed me how to do coke and all that. I froze my emotions for eight years and lived all that time through some pretty turbulent and violent relationships with ex-inmates. I got stabbed four times once; I got shot twice in the back another time. I ended up in jail. I've been a prisoner's wife. I did the "pilgrimage" across Québec as a prisoner's wife. I was the first non-operated transsexual to have access to the "trailers" at the penitentiary. It had never been seen before. Two "same-sex" partners who would call the Canadian Ministry of Justice would be refused conjugal rights. We had to get civilly married and do papers proving we were common-law before. It took a very, very, very, very long time to get our first trailers. It took a year.

During that period, I exchanged needles with a man and became HIV+. I also spent quite a bit of time in jail, in men's jails, quite regularly.

M-S: So you did time in men's jail as a transsexual?

D: Yes. I was exactly as I am today, as feminine with breasts, etc. I was treated well, because I made sure that I would get respected. I was not doing prostitution inside. Because transsexuals in jail who go suck one and another are looked on badly. I had my little job at the laundry, pressing clothes. I was very respected.

M-S: Were you in a special section of the jail where all the transsexuals are sent?

D: At the beginning, yes. But then I met an *agent de classement* and I got put with people of my age (20-30), with everybody.

M-S: Did you have a boyfriend in jail?

D: Yes. I would get a boyfriend whenever I would get in, and it would last the time of my sentence. [*big laughter from both*] It would also keep me from being harassed for sexual services by other inmates. When they would know that I was with someone, those kinds of stories would completely stop.

Diane in les Bois de Boulogne, Paris 1994

M-S: How long did you spend in jail?

D: In 12 years of prostitution, I spent 2½ years in jail and did maybe another 2 years of parole. All for prostitution. I did 3 times 6 months. At a certain point, I did 6 months, got out and 2 days after got another 6 months for prostitution. So I did a complete year. I got out on parole many times. I was prohibited from certain areas, because I was a prostitute. They gave me a hard time during the last years to prevent me from going back on the street.

M-S: When did you finish your last sentence?

D: I got out the last time in February, '92. I kept on working through ads in the papers, but I stopped using in August, '92. I joined *AA*, *Cocaïnomanes Anonymes* and *Narcotiques Anonymes*. I started a spiritual 12 step program and since then I've abstained from all drugs, alcohol, medications, etc.

M-S: The percentage of transsexual women involved in the sex trade is much higher than the percentage of non-transsexual women involved in the sex trade. Why do you think that is?

D: I can talk about my own personal experience. I was 19 years old when I came out as a transsexual. With my papers that weren't changed, with an identity that wasn't well defined, I didn't have the courage to work in a straight environment, to get a job with male papers and look half and half, androgynous. Now I'm comfortable with who I am. I work for the Ministry of Health as an ex-drug addict transsexual prostitute. It's all my past that got me that job and this job is based on my personality. I developed my personality and I'm proud of it, because I'm now strong. I'm not ashamed of what I am. I'm proud to be a transsexual. I wouldn't want to be a "real" girl; I wouldn't want to be a man either. I'm proud. If somebody asks me, "are you a transsexual?" I say, "Yes of course I'm a transsexual." I don't have to be ashamed of what I am. I'm so comfortable with what I am. I'm so fine as I am. I can't see myself otherwise. I live in a small village close to Montréal. There are maybe 100 inhabitants here and I am respected. People have never asked me if I was a transsexual. And if they were to, I would tell them "yes."

M-S: When were you diagnosed with HIV?

D: In '87, but I was contaminated in '86. I had a partner who became sick at the time and we had exchanged needles. We also had unprotected sex because he said, "we won't put a condom on; I'm not a client." Et voilà! That's life.

M-S: How did you start working for CACTUS*?

D: I had been sick and went to live in a house for HIV+ women. I had met a nurse who was working for CACTUS. She said, "Diane, you're an ex-client, you stopped using, you're in good health, it's International AIDS Day; would you give a talk in Québec for doctors?" So I arrived there and introduced myself as HIV+, not as a transsexual, but as HIV+ for 8 years. I said I wanted to give a new orientation to my life. After I gave my

* Centre d'Action Communautaire auprès des Toxicomanes Utilisateurs de Seringues

talk, a doctor and a researcher came up to me and said that I should fill out an application for a government grant to work at CACTUS. And from there I sent in my application along with supporting letters from people writing that I was the kind of person they would like to see working at CACTUS. My project is called "Approche Novatrice d'Éducation Auprès des Femmes Prostituées par un pair" meaning by a person who lived in the same situation as them. After a six months waiting period, I received the response that my proposal was accepted.

M-S: I know that you work with prostitute women in general, but I also know that you give special attention to transsexual women.

D: Yes, definitely, because they're my people. It's my community. Working at CACTUS as a street outreach worker, I go in bars, restaurants, strip joints; I go and meet people in their working environment. I do the exchange of needles. I distribute condoms. I accompany them to the clinics, to the hospital. I take them wherever they need to go. I open the doors of already existing services for them. They often don't know about those services or are too embarrassed to go by themselves. Whether it's because they're transsexuals, or because they're drug addicts, or because they're prostitutes, they need special attention for their cases. What I can do is bring them to people who are going to take them as they are and who will treat them according to their needs.

Presently we are working on a project at the CLSC** Centre-ville to open a transsexual clinic for hormonal/psychological follow-up. There are lots of transsexuals and transvestites in Montréal who take hormones and buy them from the underground market. They have health problems that are related to that. So I'm in communication with a doctor and a nurse to start a clinic at the CLSC Centre-ville. We would have our little transsexual clinic at CLSC Centre-ville. Wouldn't that be interesting?

M-S: I left Montréal 3 years ago, and it looks like the world has turned upside down there. Things have really changed. [*both laugh*]

D: Well, when they let me in, they didn't know what they were doing. [*both laugh again*] Anyways, when I went to that conference in Toronto — Partageons l'énergie, on homelessness and prostitution — transsexual women were not represented at all. I was going there to represent prostitute women from Montréal. Another transsexual (from Montréal also) and I ended up being the only transsexuals there. So I went to complain to the organizers, stating: "You asked me to give a speech on the impact of marginalization, because after all who's more marginal than an HIV+ transsexual prostitute drug addict. You want to put all those labels on me, but I end up being marginalized by you." There were no connections, no one to take care of it. So they asked me to be on the advisory committee of the next conference. The first meeting is on the 29th of April at the Canadian AIDS Society in Ottawa. Starting from there, I'm opening doors. What I want to do is unblock some funds to go and do research on HIV infection amongst the transsexual community throughout Canada, probably starting with Montréal. For me, it's easy to get in communication with transsexuals. I asked people, "Why is it that nobody thought about doing a study about

Why is it that nobody thought about doing a study about transsexuals and AIDS?* Nobody could care less, nobody knows about it. It is easy to ignore a community that you don't know.

** Centre Local de Services Communautaires

* Until recently there hadn't been any studies done about TS's & HIV/AIDS in Canada. Thanks to Ki Namaste, this is no longer true. Ki has just finished compiling the results of a survey she conducted across Canada. See page 3 for details — *Mirha-Soleil.*

transsexuals and AIDS?" Nobody could care less; nobody knows about it. It is easy to ignore a community that you don't know. But now that I'm at the Ministry and that they know me, it is up to me to talk about my community. It is up to me to go and do research for the members of my community and offer them the services they have a right to, the help they need or maybe just to open new doors to something else for them. Can you imagine what it means for other transsexuals downtown to see me around; to see me on TV; to see me in the newspapers; to see me as a representative of prostitutes, of transsexuals and of addicts? It gives them hope that they may not only be good to freeze on the corner of the street, that maybe they can do something with their lives. I swear that transsexuals are really proud of me in Montréal. I open doors for them. Slowly, I find them jobs. If we have a transsexual clinic, maybe it'll give a job to one or two of them.

__M-S__: Why do you think AIDS organizations and AIDS prevention groups have neglected the transsexual community to such an extreme extent? How come they never thought about us? I've always had that question.

__D__: Try to take a census of the AIDS cases in Canada that are transsexual. It's hard because many transsexuals have male papers and are classified as male.

Diane with a few street girls in Lyon, 1994

__M-S__: Yeah, I know. They classify us as male if we are pre-/non-operative and as women if we're post-operative. And there's no way to keep track because there's no mention of transsexuality.

__D__: That's why it's important to have people like me doing the research. Not a little researcher coming out of university with her BA in research - she's very good the girl, but what the hell is she gonna do there? [*both laugh*] You know what I mean? She can come to listen to me and type. [*both laugh again*] That's my goal, because I don't want to be a street outreach worker my whole life. I just put a foot in the system, and my other one is coming. There's more to come. There are other women who will become street outreach workers, who will replace me, and I will move on to something else. It's a normal evolution. I'm 32 years old, and I have the intention to live until I'm 65. Minimum.

__M-S__: There are very few statistics related to the spread of HIV in the transsexual community, but the few that exist show that the incidence of HIV in our community is enormously higher than in any other community. What do you think accounts for that?

__D__: Lack of prevention. It's hard for existing services to go and do prevention, communicate with transsexuals. As I said earlier, it's easier for them to ignore people they don't know. I was talking about that with my boss last week. She said: "Diane it's not easy for straight folks to go sit with transsexuals and listen to them and try to help them." It's absolutely normal and most of the time they don't feel like doing it because for them, we're almost always sort of an attraction. They want to ***understand why.*** But me, when I go to meet a transsexual, I'm not there to understand why she is a transsexual. I couldn't care less 'cause I know why she's a transsexual - I am one. Right off the top, that eliminates 3/4 of the stupid questions. [*both laugh*] The ***Why?, Since when?, Have you always known?*** and ***How did your family take it?*** — we're sick of them and we don't want to be asked those questions anymore. [*both laugh again*]

M-S: People have been babbling the same questions for over 20 years. They should know the answers by heart now. Oh and what about: ***Are you going to get the operation?***

D: Or ***Are you sure you're going to be able have orgasms like a real woman?*** [*both laugh hersterically*]

M-S: Or ***Promise me you'll let me see it!*** or ***I want to be the first one to lick it***. [*both are laughing breathlessly*]

D: We are so tired of answering those stupid questions.

M-S: [*after a brief pause*] How has your HIV status affected your transsexuality?

D: First of all, hospitals refused to operate on me. I had finished my psycho-therapy in Vancouver. I was going to be operated but because I was HIV+, they refused. Today I don't care 'cause I don't want to be operated. I no longer have the intention to be operated. I accepted my situation as it is, and I'm fine like this.

M-S: What is the reason or argument the doctors gave you for refusing to perform an SRS on you?

D: They imagined that it wouldn't heal, that the immune system wouldn't be able to fight infection.

M-S: What I find very interesting is that they don't refuse other types of major surgery for that reason.

D: For them, other surgeries are emergency situations, whereas they imagine that for transsexuals, getting the operation is not an emergency.

M-S: That it's an esthetic issue.

D: Yes and I find this very stupid. I know some who constantly think about suicide because they can't get the operation. For them, it's a very urgent matter. But not for me.

M-S: Was any other aspect of your transsexuality affected?

D: Not really. Of course, I didn't accept it during the first years. I wanted to die. The only person I talked about it with was my mother. I thought my life was over. Ten years ago, it wasn't like today. They used to give us 2 years to live. Nowadays, it's different. But I have seen many transsexuals dying. I buried 2 last month. We were 4 living together when we were diagnosed with HIV the same year. We had shared needles together. They're all dead except me. So for me, right off the top, it's a heavy blow. I tell myself I may be the next one. But I've been in good health for 10 years. I take care. I took myself in hand. I consulted. I met a doctor with whom I'm comfortable, which is something very important for transsexuals, to feel comfortable with a doctor. To be able to say everything. Not to be scared to go and see your doctor. I refer all the HIV+ transsexuals I know to my doctor, and he's very comfortable with them, which is also very important.

M-S: Do you have hope that middle-class, non-prostitute transsexuals will one day change, getting rid of their own prejudices against transsexu-

Society treats prostitution hypocritically. People who dare to affirm themselves as prostitutes get fingers pointed at them by the same persons who use prostitutes' services. If there weren't clients, there wouldn't be prostitutes.

als who are prostitutes, IV-drug users and/or HIV+?

D: I would really like them to change, because there are a lot of transsexuals who are HIV+ and prostitutes who need help as much as others. Personally, I have the intention to work in that direction so that people have a broader attitude on that level. Society treats prostitution hypocritically. People who dare to affirm themselves as prostitutes get fingers pointed at them by the same people who use prostitutes' services. If there weren't clients, there wouldn't be prostitutes.

M-S: That's a very interesting point because I've met a lot of transsexuals who are very anti-prostitute but who at the same time admitted to me having used transsexual prostitutes' services when they were living as straight men. I couldn't believe it.

D: Exactly. Exactly. We're talking about people's right to live their lives as they wish and to be prostitutes if they want to. As far as I'm concerned, it's a life choice and I'm proud of it.

M-S: It's also a complete denial of reality to be against prostitution and to be uncomfortable with it, because the fact is that it exists, and that there are people from all walks of life who are prostitutes or who use prostitutes' services. That's the way it is and if you don't like it, too bad. That's reality so you better get over it or else move to another planet.

D: I was watching a TV show the other day and they were talking about a survey they had done of 300 Québécois-ses. The question was, "what is the oldest profession?" Eighty percent answered, "prostitution." [*both laugh*] It's considered a profession in people's heads. But still society prefers to close its eyes and live in hypocrisy. About two weeks ago, I was on a TV show and I made sure to specify that drug addiction and prostitution may be related, but not always. I said it 2 or 3 times on the show and had the hostess repeating it too. It's sort of an Oprah show in french. I was there to talk about my work as a street outreach worker for the homeless and the prostitutes. She asked me, "What brought you to do that job?" I answered that I had been a street prostitute for 12 years and that now I was there to make their lives easier and help them getting the services they have a right to in order to live their lives and do their jobs in dignity. They already work hard enough that they deserve to have adequate and decent services. Let's stop playing ostriches with our heads in the sand and let's stop looking in the neighbour's backyard. They are there, so lets work with them. Prostitutes are the best AIDS educators you can get. Not the clients. There are still a lot of clients who don't want to wear condoms. I just came back from an international conference. I was representing Canadian prostitutes in Paris. I did a TV show with other prostitutes from Holland, Switzerland, Marseille, Lyon, Paris, and Italy. We all face the same problems around the world. Clients offer you more money if you don't use condoms. It's the clients we need to educate, not the prostitutes. Instead of panicking in front of AIDS, we should teach people to take their responsibilities seriously. It is so simple to use a piece of latex.

Diane Gobeil can be reached c/o CACTUS Montréal, 1209 Saint-Dominique, Montréal, Qué. H2X 2W4 Tél: (514) 954-8869.

✱ Mirha-Soleil Ross is a sexually exhausted Québécoise who has turned enough tricks in her lifetime to be immune against crabs forever. Besides being gifted for giving celestial hugs and caresses, she is a vibrant soul, and a wholehearted vegan who recently welcomed 15 mice from a local shelter into her already extended animal family.

Recently, a great deal of controversy and discussion has arisen over the topic of who should be included in the New Women's Conference, the Michigan Womyn's Music Festival, as well as a few other events. These events are exclusionary in nature, accessible only to a priviledged few with the time and money to attend. While certainly fun, these events do little to help the vast majority of the Transgender Community.

Racism and Poverty

in the Transgender Community

by Christine Tayleur

While a few people run off and spend a $1000 to lounge around in hot-tubs or to protest transsexual exclusion at the MWMF, the majority of our population is excluded from basic human rights. Thousands are languishing in prisons because they don't have the money for a good defense, while many others are being assaulted and killed because of who they are. Many transgendered people are fighting for the right just to keep a job. While people are bickering over names, many are being locked up in psychiatric institutions for being transgendered. Thousands of our sisters and brothers around the world are living in poverty; they are turned away from shelters and must sleep on the street. Others are dying from lack of drug treatment, psychological help, medical treatments, and for lack of HIV treatment. Meanwhile, activists dine on steak and wine.

What are we doing as a community to combat racism, poverty, and other social ills in the community?

I have observed first-hand the effects of poverty and other social ills on our community. I have lived in the "skid-row" hotels, with cold and cold running water, cracked plaster, and bare light-bulbs. Too many of our sisters and brothers are still living in these places.

If you are poor and transgendered in San Francisco, you usually live in the Tenderloin or a similar neighbourhood. San Francisco's Tenderloin district (TL) is a densely-populated, multi-ethnic neighbourhood of some 24,000 souls, crammed into an area of 25 blocks. According to police statistics, the TL accounts for approximately a quarter of all the city's crime.

The TL resembles a war-zone, with boarded-up store front burnt-out shells of buildings, an economic disaster area, with people hanging out on the streets, drinking, and selling drugs openly. Violence is common-place. At any time of day or night one hears the sporadic, "Pop! Pop! Pop!" of gunfire.

A woman is several times more likely to experience violence here than a man — a transgendered woman is several times more likely than that to experience violence.

There are few employment opportunities in the "'Loin." Transfolk have even fewer. If you are a transgendered woman or man of colour, it's even more difficult. Most of the city's less expensive housing stock is located in the TL, thus people on fixed incomes are ghettoised into neighbourhoods such as the Tenderloin. Public assistance, the lowest form of cash assistance, pays $350 a month. Some are slightly better off with SSI payments which average about $600. The average rent in these «Welfare Hiltons» is about $400 per month. Hookers, both trans and non, walk the " 'ho'-stro' " (whore stroll) throughout which are scattered porn-shops and theatres. As in most poor communities, there is a high percentage of people on welfare. Women on welfare may hook because it isn't enough to live on.

Prostitution is hazardous work. It is fraught with many dangers from the "johns," the cops, and the people on the streets. More than a few transgendered sex-workers are murdered on the streets every year, their bodies often left in dumpsters. The police make little attempts to find the culprit. In 1993, Angel Lopez was found stabbed to death. In 1991, Lynn Tharrett was murdered 2½ blocks from the Tenderloin Task Force Police Station. It took four 911 calls and thirty minutes for the police to respond. Neither of these murders have ever been solved and there have been many more since.

Possibly 60% of the population of the Tenderloin are people of colour. They are mostly Southeast Asian, South Asian and Pacific Islanders. African-Americans and people from Central America as well as Mexico also make up a significant percentage of the population. Caucasian people are by no means monolithic and come from all over the country as well as some foreign countries. I estimate that transpeople comprise about 11% of this population. There are no accurate statistics.

Many transgendered immigrants, such as the Khmer and Salvadoreños, have witnessed or experienced torture first-hand from death squads. Transfolks have often been targets for this because they were/are not deemed "morally pure" enough to live. In Chiapas, Mexico, transpeople have been singled out for assassination by the military and police. These people arrive here to escape torture and repression. But they often have few job skills and speak very little English.

Life for people living in poverty is difficult enough for anyone. For the transgendered woman or man it is vastly more difficult. The shelters make impossible pre-conditions, such as staying in the men's section for MtF's or getting a doctor's or a TG community worker's statement confirming that you are transgendered (in other words, your identity is subject to someone else's "opinion"). The welfare workers treat everyone like dirt. They are full of self-importance and act as though one were trying to take the pittance, that the city gives, from out of their own pockets. If you're a transgendered woman, they call you "sir" or some other slur. Transgendered women walking down the street with groceries get rousted by the cops, thrown in the back of the police car, beaten up, and raped. They call you "Faggot," "Nigger," or "Gook." If you are poor and transgendered, you are a target for the police and other predators, particularly if you are non-white. If you report a crime, they act as if you are the culprit, or as if it is your fault. Last year, at the landmark 4½ hour hearing by the Human Rights Commission, a Native American transgendered woman gave testimony that the SFPD [San Francisco Police Department] refused to pursue a man who had sexually assaulted her and tried to rape her.

These atrocities are experienced in every major urban area across the country by our sisters and brothers. An FtM client of mine had his seven year old daughter taken away from him while he was in the hospital for tb. He had left her in the care of his lesbian pastor. Child Protective Service stepped in. While there were allegations, there were no formal charges laid against him for sexual abuse of his child. Despite the report of their own psychologist that this was unlikely, they chose to keep her.

Does the energy devoted to the NWC/MWMF controversies alleviate these injustices?

The recent elections were frightening. In California, as in many states, a homophobic governor was re-elected. In the previous election, he courted the Lesbian/Gay community. This time, he courted the Christian Right. He was also a major proponent of a "three strikes law" as well as the anti-immigrant measure, Proposition 187 (this racist proposition was supported by many members of the trans-community). Its ads depicted Latinos running across the frontier en masse and was coupled with dire warnings about how immigrants are destroying the economy. Instead of dealing with the real causes behind the failing economy, they targeted a powerless group, catering to xenophobia.

A few years ago, Dee Farmer, a young transsexual woman, was convicted of a minor crime. She was sentenced to 20 years. In prison, she was raped and denied adequate medical care for her transsexualism. Hundreds like her are languishing in prisons throughout the country. Most of these people's major crime was poverty. Poverty, which is brought on by social bigotry, is what prevents them from getting jobs, etc.

Where were the activists when she sued the prison system in the Supreme Court?

We activists have a duty to assist our sisters and brothers who are incarcerated or otherwise oppressed. Going to Michigan each year won't do anything for our people in poverty.

This country is now moving more towards the right than at any time since the '50s and '20s. An article, in the Autumn '93 edition of «DISSENT», describes the shift of Germany to the right after reunification because it hasn't effectively dealt with the legacy of Nazism. As in the US, racism is on the rise. Neo-Nazi groups and other fascist groups are gaining strength, just as in Germany in the 1920s, during Hitler's rise to power.

There may very well be a Republican in the White House in 1997. How do we fight this? If we are going to build a movement that will gain us any measure of respect and human rights, we must work together and set aside our personal differences with each other. Divide and conquer is the traditional strategy of oppressors. The Nazis played on the Poles' dislike of Jews, the Ukrainians' dislike of Stalin and so on. The right wing plays on economic uncertainty and xenophobia, as did Hitler. All one has to do is take a look at the ads promulgated by the right. They show crime on the increase, the economy in shambles, etc.

A few dedicated souls like Margaret O'Hartigan of Portland, Oregon and Kristine Holt of Pennsylvania are doing things that benefit many others. O'Hartigan spent $110 of her own money on a mass-mailing to help protect people's right to SRS under the state health plan in Minnesota. 10% of the cost to attend NWC or MWMF and well worth it.

Here in San Francisco, we managed to hold together a fragile coalition of diverse people to get far-reaching landmark legislation that will benefit us all. But just like we cannot do it alone, they cannot do it alone.

There are numerous TG organizations around the country whose express purpose is "educational." That's all well and good, but it's only one piece of the pie. If these organizations want to serve the community, they must do more than just educate. They must reach out to people of colour, the poorer members of the community, and our sisters and brothers incarcerated in psychiatric prisons, county jails and prisons. They must make connexions with every facet of our community, not just their friends and neighbours.

Labour organizer Saul Alinsky explains that activists have two equally important major functions. One: that the people and organizers must understand that organizing generates power to be controlled and directed for the realization of a programme. The second: that only by organizing can a programme be developed.

When we organize, we set aside our personal differences and petty ego trips to focus on the task at hand. We get to know and respect each other. We discuss problems we thought only affected us as individuals. We learn to compromise and come to agreement. Out of all this comes the common agenda, the people's programme. The other function of the organization then comes forth: the use of power in order to fulfill the programme.

Although organizers can state general principles during the initial stages, such as housing, medical care, jobs, educational opportunities; above all else, it's the opportunity to create a programme of their own. I have seen this in grassroots organizations such as the Transsexual Menace, Transgender Nation, Queer Nation, and other organizations, on a limited basis. What often happens is these groups wind up being controlled and dominated by a small clique. One sees this in the larger organizations in our community; they have become monolithic blocs of mostly white Anglo-Saxon men.

In 1989, at the IFGE Convention in San Francisco, I was chastised by a middle-aged TV, because I didn't vote with the otherwise-unanimous majority on some issue. I voted with my conscience, according to what I thought was in the best interests of the people I was representing — the Transgender Community of the Tenderloin. This was after a lot of fine speeches about federalism and liberty, etc. These ideas meant nothing to people who were worried about where they were going to sleep or eat that night. These power-brokers were staying in a deluxe hotel and eating prime rib.

Alinsky notes that it is hypocritical, paternalistic, and the worst kind of dictatorship for organizations to become dominated by small cliques of people, no matter how benevolent their intentions may be.

This then is our task if we are truly going to secure our basic liberties as human beings: we must organize at all levels of the community. It was Martin Luther King, I think, who said, "None of us are free until all of us are free." The words of pastor Martin Niemoller of Germany are also instructive: "First, they came for the Jews, I said nothing; I was not a Jew. Then they came for the Trade Unionists,... I was not a Trade Unionist... then... the Catholics... When they came for me, what could I say?"

The right is on the rise and nothing short of our very lives are on the line. If we are not helping the most oppressed members of our community, we are truly not helping anyone.

*✱ **Christine Tayleur is a transgendered activist originally from Fontainebleau, France. She is one of the original co-founders of Transgender Nation. She has been a counsellor/social worker providing counselling and other services to transsexuals and other transgendered people primarily in San Francisco's Tenderloin district for over 11 years.***

photo of Christine Tayleur by Loren Cameron

Bashing

Even "politically correct"
gay papers do it, vent
thinly veiled hatred, phrases
expected
from the Bush-whacked Right
but not from fellow travellers
on the road to personal freedom.
The voices that complain
long and loud at utterances
of a Jesse Helms,
are oddly silent,
as the same phrases
of hate and exclusion
come from the lips
of a radical sister,
making a mockery
of political correctness,
pariahs of our brothers
and sisters.

Michelle/Vernon Maulsby

✱ Michelle/Vernon Maulsby is just a princess trapped in a bear's body, a person with an addiction to the printed word. Despite her looks, a very shy and gentle soul.

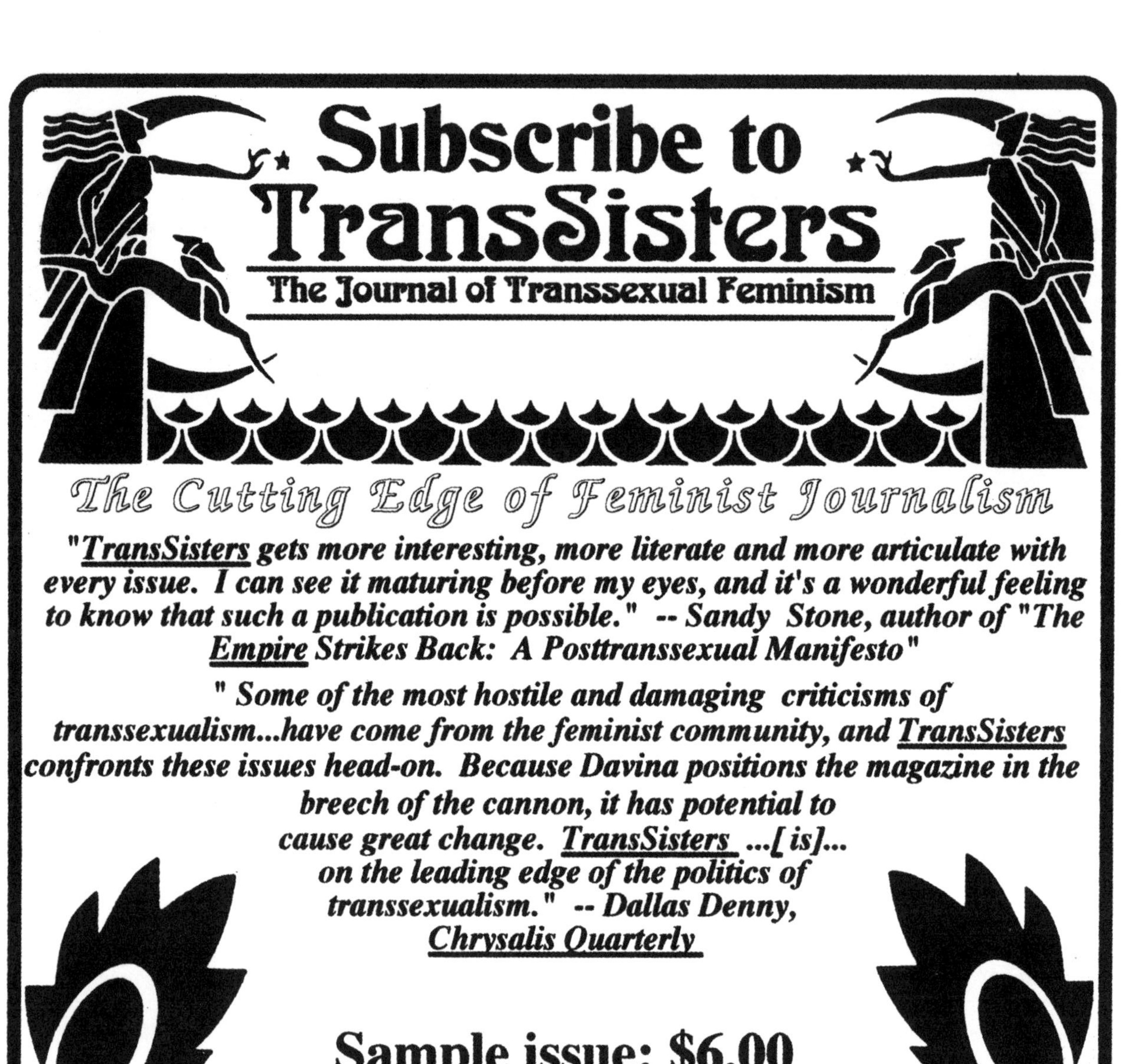

Sample issue: $6.00

One year (four issues): $24.00

Back Issues: $8.00 each;
any 5 for $35.00; 6 for $41.00;
all 7 for $46.00

To order use order form
on next page ☞

Issue # 1

Issue # 2

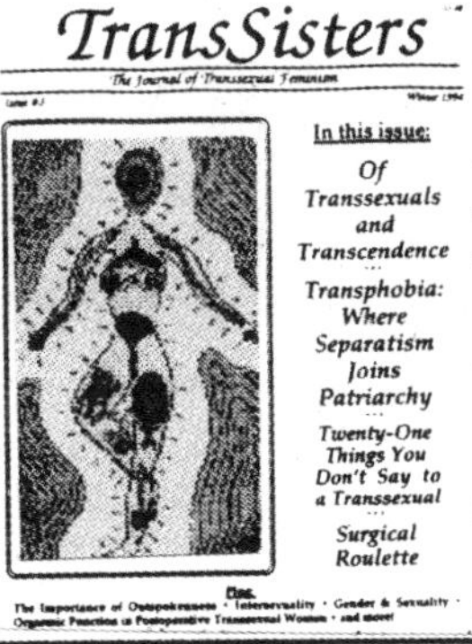

Issue # 3

Issue # 4

Fool's Paradox: An Interview with Kate Bornstein

Reviews of Her Book, Gender Outlaw: On Men, Women and the Rest of Us and Her New Play, Virtually Yours

Also: A Rose is a Rose: the Nomenclature of Sex and Oppression • Lesbian Separatist Identity Crisis • What Sex Are You? • Lesbians Who Date Transsexuals • Blossom of Boneheads • She Walks, She Talks, She Crawls on Her Belly Like a Reptile • The Grande Alliance • ICTLEP vs. HBIGDA • and more

Issue # 5

FIRST ANNIVERSARY ISSUE

TransSisters

The Journal of Transsexual Feminism

Should Preoperative Transsexual Women Be Allowed to Attend the New Woman Conference?: Conflicting Views

Plus: Transsexuals at Stonewall 25 • She's Baaa-aack!: Janice Raymond's *The Transsexual Empire* reissued • Transsexuals Allowed to Enter MWMF • and more

Issue # 6

TransSisters

The Journal of Transsexual Feminism

Transsexual Womyn At the 1994 Michigan Womyn's Music Festival

Plus: Leslie Feinberg on Making Sisterhood Real • The Power of Naming • Gordene MacKenzie's *Transgender Nation* • Beyond Patriarchal Power • Transsexual Theory vs. Reality • Transsexual Dykes to Watch Out For • Elitism • Transsexual Lesbians Expelled from Australian Lesbian Conference • and more

Issue # 7

$6.00

TransSisters

The Journal of Transsexual Feminism

Spring 1995

Interview with the Transsexual Vampire: Sandy Stone's Dark Gift

Current Issue

- ❑ **Please send me ____ sample issue(s) of *TransSisters* @ $6.00 each (current issue only)**
- ❑ **Please send me ____ one year subscription(s) (four issues) of *TransSisters*. @ $24.00 each.**
- ❑ **Please send me ____ copies of back issue # 1 of *TransSisters* @ $8.00 each.**
- ❑ **Please send me ____ copies of back issue # 2 of *TransSisters* @ $8.00 each.**
- ❑ **Please send me ____ copies of back issue # 3 of *TransSisters* @ $8.00 each.**
- ❑ **Please send me ____ copies of back issue # 4 of *TransSisters* @ $8.00 each.**
- ❑ **Please send me ____ copies of back issue # 5 of *TransSisters* @ $8.00 each.**
- ❑ **Please send me ____ copies of back issue # 6 of *TransSisters* @ $8.00 each.**
- ❑ **Please send me ____ copies of back issue # 7 of *TransSisters* @ $8.00 each.**

Any five back issues for $35.00
Any six for $41.00
All seven for $46.00

- ❑ **Enclosed is a contribution in the amount of ______________ to *TransSisters*.**

(New subscriptions begin with next issue. To receive current issue, order sample issue. Outside U.S.A., Canada & Mexico add $0.50 per single issue & $2.00 for each subscription ordered)

Total Amount Enclosed: $ ____________ (U.S. funds only)

Name ______________________________

Apt. or Suite # __________ **Address** ______________________

City ______________________________

State / Province ____________________ **Zip / Postal Code** __________

☞ **Please Make Checks or Money Orders Payable to Davina Anne Gabriel**

Mail to: Davina Anne Gabriel; 4004 Troost Avenue; Kansas City, Missouri 64110

subscribe to: gendertrash

a Canadian community & politically oriented publication for transsexual & transgendered persons

gendertrash	quantity	amount
gendertrash #2 $6.00		
gendertrash #3 $6.00		
gendertrash #4 $6.00		
gendertrash #5 $6.00 (Aug 1, 1995)		
gendertrash subscription $24.00/4 issues please specify starting issue: ____		
total amount (gendertrash)		

#	Buttons	quantity
B1	Stop Violence Against Transsexuals Now!	
B2	Don't touch me: I'm electric TS epileptic	
B3	Don't call me TRANNIE shitface	
B4	Maries Fight Back	
B5	Make Love not Steak	
B6	Bi Bi Love	
B7	We don't need balls to play	
B8	Drag King	
B9	This Transie's Angry	
B10	Sex Change	
B11	Blatantly BI	
B12	Trans Curious	
B13	100% TransGendered	
B14	Gender-Fuck Me	
B15	I love 'em butch	
B16	Feminists for TransGender Liberation	
B17	[no to] genderphobia	
B18	Just say No to transphobia	
B19	Butchy Femme	
B20	F2M Queer	
B21	TS Butch	
B22	Have a safe GenderFuck	
B23	Trans Dyke	
B24	Trans Fag	
B25	Gender Outlaw	
B26	Gender Queer	
B27	Transsexual Hooker	
B28	The Empire Strikes Back	
B29	Transsexuals get AIDS too	
B30	Transgender Fury	
B31	I love Transsexuals	
B32	TS lives under TS control Now!	
B33	Theory Mutilates Surgery Liberates	
B34	Only a Transsexual could love you	
B35	Employment Equity for Transsexuals	
B36	I have big feet - So what???	
B37	Woman-born Transsexual	
B38	I'd rather be dead than genetic	
B39	Transsexuals for Animal Liberation	
B40	Nobody knows I'm a Transsexual	

#	More Buttons	quant.
B41	Decriminalize Prostitution Now!	
B42	Pissed Off Transsexuals United	
B43	Gender Liberation	
B44	Polysexual	
B45	Poly gendered	
B46	Gender Oriented	
B47	gendertrash	
B48	Keep your theories off my gender identity	
B49	High Drag	
B50	High Femme	
B51	Switch	
B52	Clit Teaser	
B53	Top Femme	
B54	Baby Dyke	
B55	Small penises: anything more than a mouthful is wasted	
B56	Stone Butch	
B57	Bi-Curious not Bi-Confused	
B58	Veggie Queer	
B59	TS's Against Racism	
B60	Feminists for Prostitutes' Rights	
B61	Whining Works!	
B62	Hormonally Insane	
B63	Veggie TS	
total number of buttons		
price (buttons are 1/$2, 3/$5, 10/$15 or 25/$25)		
s/h ($1 on all button orders under $10)		
total amount (buttons)		

Booklets

HIV/AIDS and the TG Communities in Canada by Ki Namaste $5.00	
total amount (booklets)	

Donations to *genderpress*

donation (please specify amount)	
total amount (donations)	
Total Amount (add all totals together)	

Name ____________________

Address ____________________

City ____________________

Province/State ____________________

Postal Code/Zip ____________________

Send cash/money order/cheque (payable to genderpress) to: genderpress, Box 500-62, 552 Church Street, Toronto, Ontario, Canada M4Y 2E3

Let our buttons speak for you:

This sample is a black & white, 40% of the actual size version of some of our buttons.
See left hand page for ordering instructions.

I arrived at Pelican Bay Security Housing Unit (SHU) in July '91. This SHU opened in 1989 and is now a well-known Control Unit, sometimes called by the prisoners "Dungeon Pelican Bay." I informally call it "Treblinka."

The finer details of life in this SHU are not well-known. It is my intent to reflect on them, but first I believe some background is necessary as to how I ended up here.

This article originally appeared in Prison News Service (PNS), issue #39 (Jan/Feb 93). I have wanted to reprint it in gendertrash since then, because I feel that although a great many people have read it, very few transsexuals or transgendered people are even aware of its existence. I believe Lofofora's article to be a very important testimony of her experiences at Pelican Bay, (a state prison that is infamous for its abusive treatment of inmates), one that will hopefully open the eyes of the members of our communities to the realities of transsexual prisoners. The article is reprinted here with Lofofora's permission. *- editor*

I'm a male-to-female transsexual lesbian. I'm serving a life term out of Los Angeles and expect to die in prison, as opposed to begging the Board of Prison Terms for mercy. This is my first time in prison; I entered the system when I was 27. Since then, in 1980, I've rotated through seven California prisons, including San Quentin and Folsom (old and new). I'm a trained paralegal and jailhouse lawyer and am involved in extensive administrative appeals and litigation against conditions of confinement. I'm of American Indian and Mexican Indian lineage and have been deaf since age 15 from meningitis. My complaints and briefs highlight prison issues concerning Native American legal and religious rights, the rights of deaf prisoners, and medical treatment for transsexuals in prison.

In May '95 I defended myself against a bashing at Folsom, an attack that prison officials encouraged and deliberately failed to prevent in retaliation for my administrative complaints and legal activism. At the time of the incident I had a lawsuit pending against Folsom and the California Department of Corrections for treatment of transsexualism and a number of citizen's complaints against Folsom guards and administrative personnel for harassment and discrimination based on my gender orientation and exercising my legal rights to petition for a redress of grievances. Also, I and two other deaf prisoners (Louis Fresquez, a Mexican, and Thomas Brooks, a white, both of whom were most enthusiastic and steadfastly dedicated to the rights of deaf prisoners, whatever the consequences), had begun to assert our rights to equal treatment by requesting telecommunication devices for the deaf (TDD) to use the telephone with, and television decoders. Some deaf prisoners were also being forced against their will and on the threat of punishment to work in the factory, which due to their deafness poses a health and safety hazard to them and those around them and is violation of certain safety codes. We also filed paperwork for light-flashing alarms on the yard, and a computer readout screen on a wall to alert us to emergency situations in which the gunners gave everyone the order to "drop!", and other emergency instructions. This was a serious problem for us that could have easily turned lethal in the level-four Folsom setting, where there are always five gun towers covering the yard and signs everywhere give notice that "no warning shots will be fired — the first round will be for effect." Drop orders are often given and prisoners have been shot to death more than once. And more than once the order was given without my knowledge with the result that I ended up in the gunners' sights. Folsom officials did not like the fact that we were protesting such conditions.

In a disciplinary hearing at which a number of my due process rights were denied me I was found guilty of "battery with serious injury." A Folsom committee, which I had in court just weeks earlier, imposed a two-year disciplinary term to be served at Pelican Bay despite my claims of denial of due process, self-defense and the term being above the max. On July 23 I was shipped to Pelican Bay, shackled hand and foot and kept in a tiny cage at the front of the bus for the eight hour ride from Sacramento to the Oregon border.

At approximately 3 o'clock the next morning, while sleeping I was subjected to a violent, brutal "cell extraction" because I could not hear the guards calling me to "show skin" for count. This was Pelican Bay's welcome party and would be repeated two more times. The extraction team was in full riot gear, brandishing such weapons as a taser gun, weapons that shoot gas pellets, rubber bullets and wooden bullets, and their batons, visors and a shield. I had been shocked out of my sleep. I was brutally manhandled, my hands cuffed behind my back, ankles cuffed, and violently jerked out of bed. They stood me before them in my cell, naked, and played their flashlights on my breasts and privates, giggling like idiots. There were extraction team members and medical personnel, altogether about ten of them crammed in my cell.

A sergeant began to scold me; that's all I could gather. I couldn't understand a word he was saying. I was barely oriented and hadn't the wildest imagination of what was going on. I cut in by telling him that I'm deaf and could not understand him and could he slow down his speech so that I might read his lips. They all wore protective vests. The sergeant was small and his vest puffed up his size.

One of the biggest misconceptions about deaf people is that they can be taught lip reading like anyone can be taught to read and to write and thereafter can communicate with the greatest of ease. No problem, just read a person's lips as one would read a book. This is a myth. Lip reading is guesswork and everyone has their own way of speaking and no two pairs of lips are the same. A lip reader does not expect to understand every word but instead looks for key words that cue them. Thus most times things must be repeated because the person isn't able to key in on the message with the few words they think they understand. It contributes to the problem when the speaker makes no effort to speak slowly or consciously form words and instead speaks in a normal fashion as if the deaf person has normal hearing ability. Moustaches are also a hindrance.

The sergeant made no effort to effectively communicate with me and I indicated my hearing aid on the desk. It is a compact aid that fits behind the ear and serves to amplify sound. Hearing aids give rise to another myth — many people seem to think they "cure" deafness. Hearing aids do not restore normal hearing; they merely amplify sound. It is up to the individual to interpret the sound to the best of their ability with whatever remnants of hearing that remain in the damaged nerve, if it is a nerve deafness that they suffer from, as I do. I was struck with cerebral meningitis while in the youth authority, which caused as inflammation of the membrane surrounding my brain, damaging my ear nerves, and put me in a coma. I am medically diagnosed as profoundly nerve deaf without the faculties to hear adequately even with a hearing aid. Thus I must use a combination of lip reading and sound and even then it can be very difficult when a person is impatient and uncooperative in making an effective effort to communicate with me.

I asked to be uncuffed so that I could put on my hearing aid. They would not uncuff me. Instead one of them began to play with my hearing aid. He was obviously unfamiliar with it and was not handling it with care. It is a sensitive instrument. He immediately tried to place it on me and I had to tell him to insert the battery first. I didn't know why the MTA's, so-called "Medical Technical Assistants," did not take the medical responsibility of doing this themselves. The guard made a clumsy attempt to insert the battery, putting it in backwards. They got a kick out of it whenever I told them they were doing something wrong. I told him how to set the battery in and before I could tell him not to close the battery case he closed it. When this type of aid is "on" while not in the ear it emits a very loud, high-pitched piercing whistle that is offensive to persons with normal hearing but which cannot be heard by deaf persons. The result was that they all immediately recoiled and covered their ears with their hands and looked to be on the verge of stampeding back out of the cell. After turning the aid off the guard tried to put it in place. He failed, and just left it dangling from my ear. This appealed to their sordid sense of humour.

Eventually I was able to gather that I was expected to "show skin" for all counts, which include the 11 p.m., 1, 3, and 5 a.m. counts. I told them I would do so. A rereading the next day of the SHU orientation package showed no rule mandating skin counts.

At all times I was forced to stand shackled totally naked before them. My psychological process was strongly assaulted. I felt raped. To them I had no claim to dignity or defense. As a prisoner I was a non-person in their eyes and therefore had no rights, human or legal. I was inferior, I was debasement of debasement. Low. A judgement that gleamed in their eyes as they appraised me curiously in their puffed-up vests, sweating like swine. I a wakan, a holy image, a transsexual, was incomprehensible to these heathen. As a woman I was expected to be a physically and mentally shackled slave. Nothing more, perhaps less. Less than a non-person. Low. My scream is loud and long.

The next day the guards took an amusement in refusing to let me shave. This was a deliberate ploy to cause mental suffering to someone with a female psychological composition having to bear a 3-4 day stubble, since tweezers are not allowed here. I was allowed to shave after filing an administrative appeal. Razors are issued during showers only and showers are three times a week for ten minutes. My hair falls below my shoulders. To shampoo, shave and wash my entire body in ten minutes? Luckily sometimes a shower will run 15-20 minutes, or even longer if the guards are occupied. Sometimes I must compromise a shampoo to shave my legs or vice versa. Or I shampoo in my cell or take a birdbath, and so on.

Not all prisoners are receptive to or even neutral towards transsexuals. For the most extreme of this sort we seem to pose a threat to their sense of machismo and to their sexuality. And there are those who think that we must succumb to their whims. Bitch this, bitch that. This display is outright bullshit and is usually a case of male supremacy. And there's the omnipresent spectre of uneducated "peer pressure" for someone not to have anything to do with a transsexual or gay boy, not even convo. And in all cases these are the ones who don't want to struggle against their oppressor, who are from this crowd or that crowd and "we don't file appeals." Or don't want to educate themselves or see the light and that they are being the tools and the fools of their oppressor, who want to bury them just as deep as the rest of us.

Soon the guards told me I had to have a cellmate. I asked for a transsexual cellmate, if any, or a gay boy - someone with similar factors as mine or as close as possible in terms of my gender orientation. That same day a "straight" person was put in with me. He was in the cell no longer than 15 minutes when he expressed his displeasure at being celled up with me and asked for a cell move. He was told he could not have a cell move unless there was a cell fight, and when he tried to argue around this he was again told he could only move if he assaulted me. This is SHU policy, formal or informal. "Cockfights" are often set up by guards by placing known enemies together or persons they know will be incompatible and who know that there will be only one way out. This serves not only to keep prisoners divided and conquered but in SHU longer because they must receive a disciplinary write-up, lose good behaviour credits, TV or radio privileges, even yard privileges, for 30, 60, 90 days or more and could even have their SHU term extended for six months.

Realizing the futility of his verbal attempts my cellmate then immediately began to assault me in front of the guard, without pretext. I stumbled to the ground, and he began to kick and bang my head against the concrete bunk. I lost my orientation. When I could finally put things in focus an extraction team was assembled in front of the cell and my cellmate had his hands up. The door opened and he backed out. I was then told to bring his property out and set it at the pod door. They do this, hoping televisions or radios will be broken or letters kept for addresses and pictures or torn up and cosmetics kept. I didn't take the bait. I set all his property at the door, intact.

Pelican Bay SHU is comprised of C and D facilities. A and B facilities are the level-four mainlines. The whole SHU complex is about 100 yards from the mainline and appears as a giant X from above. Video cameras scan all four corridors of the X, at the centre of which there is a central control. C SHU has 12 units and D SHU 10 units. Each unit is comprised of six pods in a semi-circle, separated by walls. In a pod there are eight cells, four up and four down. There are no windows. The pods are totally isolated from each other and it is virtually impossible to communicate with someone in another pod. A control booth is at the centre of the semi-circle of pods, on the second-floor level, where the gunner has a view into each pod from his desk and makes announcements over the loudspeaker. They cannot see into the cells from control. There are two floor officers in each unit.

The yard or the "dog run," is a small space about 20 feet long and 10 feet wide, with 20-foot grey walls topped by mesh screen, half covered with plastic to block the rain, and a video camera by which control can observe you. There is nothing else out there but a drain hole, which some urinate into as there is no toilet. But this has stopped in most pods on unanimous agreement because it created a foul odour and also because prisoners talk to other pod yards through the drainpipe. Only a very limited portion of the sky can be seen from the yard. And that's all the direct visual contact we have with the outside world. "Dungeon" is an appropriate term.

A typical strip search is required before going to the yard and coming back in. Requiring us to spread our buttocks and squat three times is psychologically debilitating, which is its real purpose, not "security." Along with the other various blatant or subtle psychological techniques that Pelican Bay is all about, it has the effect of further depersonalizing prisoners and emphasizing the big me/little you guard complex. It's also meant to discourage us from going to the yard, which means less work for the guard and more time for them to shoot the shit and read our newspapers.

An assortment of weapons are used by the extraction teams. Not long after arrived in SHU a cell fight occurred upstairs. It broke our while the guard was up there, which is how they sometimes happen when solely done for a cell move. These two prisoners were heavyset and I could feel the vibrations of their rumbling. It was a fierce confrontation. The guard came running down the stairs, signalling the gunner to call the crew, and a short while later an extraction team entered the pod in full force. The lead guard carried a weapon that resembled a single-barrel 12-gauge sawed-off shotgun. Known as "Big Bertha" it scatters wooden shot. Close behind him another guard leaped up the stairs two at a time, carrying an Uzi that fires rubber bullets. A lieutenant with a taser ran by and a sergeant and other goons rushed up the stairs with a 5-foot plastic shield and a stretcher, wearing visors and carrying mechanical restraints and batons. Fortunately they did not use their weapons on the prisoners, but one was taken out on the stretcher.

It is especially difficult for me to communicate with the guard from my cell. The tiny perforated holes in the thick metal of the door (there are no bars) compound the problem. The doors are painted white inside and brick red outside. This combination of light/dark paint and tiny holes permits limited outward vision and maximum inward vision. Another little something. A guard at my door once expressed his annoyance at the resultant communication impasse. As it was later told to me, prisoners in other cells called to him and logically asked that due to my deafness why doesn't he simply write his comments on paper for me. At this point the gunner, a female, yelled into the pod, "You guys shut up and mind your own business!" Right, as if they were a bunch of heartless cowards. At which time they immediately cussed her out. The guard did eventually write his comments for me.

Nowhere in any SHU or CDC rule book does it say that prisoners in SHU must show skin for count. This arbitrary policy is a typical abuse of power, to wake prisoners in the middle of the night as a form of psychological harassment and to punish us. At times my intense bright light has been locked on all night by guards, and once for as long as three consecutive days, because I cannot hear them calling me. They will bang on the door with their batons at three in the morning knowing very well I can't hear it, just to annoy everyone in the hopes to get them mad at me. They'll yell, kick the door, slam my tray slot door open and closed, turn on all the pod lights. The second time I was extracted while sleeping the prisoners told them I can't hear them, that I am medically deaf. Some of them commented to each other, "Isn't [she] deaf? I heard [she] can't hear." But their leader ignored this. "Be sure to wear gloves. Continue to prepare." After the extraction, in which I was hogtied and taken out on the gurney, my sheets and blankets were taken away and light locked on all night. They pride themselves on this place being so high-tech, yet it is run by cavemen.

The jailhouse lawyers in SHU are very united. This is what uplifts me the most. Legal books and materials are shared. Case law is discussed through the air vents. Postage, paper, monthly canteen and even yearly 30 lb. packages are shared. The guards have attempted to break up such solidarity by arbitrarily and periodically moving prisoners around en masse or singly. They are especially concerned about the fact that other prisoners express protests over my treatment and I have been moved around many times. It is fair to say that I'm well known by prisoners in the SHU's as one who will stand up for my rights and the rights of others and will not hesitate to oppose the system with my mind in the fashion that many of them have taught me in ways that I never knew existed. In all my years of imprisonment I have never seen anything like the solidarity that can exist in this SHU. It has affected me profoundly. At certain times I'm not in a hurry to leave. I know that when I finally do leave my beloved friends here I will not forget them for one moment and I will miss them. We will continue to struggle together — that is certain!

"Oh Amazon... Tall babydoll..." The heathens have taunted me here. It would be a pleasure to oppose them on equal terms and lay to rest any myths they may have about women of whatever strain.

In the midst of all this madness, and lots more which has yet to be spoken, I had appealed the disciplinary guilt finding on due process grounds and a rehearing was ordered in October '91. It took until January '92 to have the hearing in SHU. I was again denied due process in the hearing preparation phase. I made a big issue out of this to the hearing lieutenant. To my surprise he agreed and entered a finding of not guilty. I was subsequently ordered released from SHU.

Instead of being released I was issued an indeterminate SHU term on the ludicrous pretext that there is no room for me elsewhere. Since being at SHU I had become one of the eight named plaintiffs in a class action suit against conditions at the prison and had filed a high rate of administrative complaints, citizen's complaints against SHU guards and ranking administrative personnel, and a civil rights action against Folsom. My illegal retention in SHU is retaliation for exercising my legal rights. Imagine being absolved of an unjust allegation and then issued an indeterminate SHU for absolutely nothing other than exercising my conscience.

There is a lot of work to be done and legal tools to be manufactured with which to kick these heathen in the seat of their pants as hard as one can and obtain what little more movement one is allowed under the "laws" of this corrupt system that is rent with contradictions and rotten to the core.

✱ ***Lofofora Contreras, alias Amazon Ice Queen, remains incarcerated in the California Department of Corrections.***

Pelican Bay Update

In 1990, prisoners at Pelican Bay initiated a civil rights suit against the prison with 300 individual actions. After deliberating for one year, Judge Thelton Henderson, (in ***Madrid v. Gomez****), ordered an end to "the pattern of needless and officially sanctioned brutality" at Pelican Bay, appointing a Special Master who will negotiate with the California Department of Corrections (CDoC) and the prisoners to end the violations within 120 days.*

However, some of the gross practises, (such as long-term solitary confinement, racial discrimination in the placement of prisoners, etc.), at Pelican Bay were left untouched by the judge and will probably continue. In addition, the CDoC, which is already in contempt of another judge's rulings (regarding changes for psychiatric care for all prisoners), has a long history of delaying and/or not implementing court orders that are in favour of prisoners.

Thus, this victory may be only a moral one with few or no non-trivial changes to the treatment of inmates. However, it is still an important step in the campaign to close down Pelican Bay.

For further information or to offer support, please write:

Pelican Bay Information Project*, 2489 Mission Street, SF, CA, USA 94110*
Prison Law Project*, c/o National Lawyers Guild, 588 Capp Street, SF, CA, USA 94110*
Prison News Service*, Box 5052, Stn A, Toronto, Ont., Canada M5W 1W4*

[source: ***PNS*** *issue #49 - Jan/Feb '95]*

Pretty Persuasion

BY SELENA ANNE SHEPHARD

Beginning

"The sky will split
and the planets will shift
Little sister, the sky is falling
I don't mind, I don't mind"

- Patti Smith

I skate around the mall with a walkman tuned into subversive sounds, I am in search of secret passageways, people of unusual genders, spaces of unabashed desire, the teenage girls w/nasty tongues never look at me, yet they tell me stories from afar, strange, exotic tales they could never have gotten from television, they dress in layers, in bizarre mosaic patterns indecipherable, I listen for simple truths yet hear only complex lies, which, of course, are much more trustworthy, I purchase working class lingerie (I mean, underwear) at Sears from a salesgirl who KNOWS but will never tell, I plead with her to scream it out, reveal the source of her despair, but she just laughs heartily and steals away into the hardware section, I call the security guards who arrest me for wearing plaid socks with a leather skirt, I manage to escape between the cracks, and return unscathed to the scene of the crime...

Middle

"Jesus died for somebody's sins, but NOT mine"

- Patti Smith

I light a cigarette though I don't know how to smoke, it seems natural at the time, I cross my legs, right over left, then left over right, I refasten my garter, smooth my skirt, fluff up my titties, I'm anticipating something but I'm not quite sure what it is, a recurring moment, perhaps, a (parenthetical thought), maybe, the merger of parallel lines, that's it, the merger of parallel lines, I remember vividly the secret dance I used to perform when I was nine and yearning — so awkward, so strange, so utterly incomprehensible — yet it couldn't be denied, it had a raw beauty to it that exhilirated me, I check between my legs to see what gender I am today, I find nothing in particular except an old beat up baseball mitt and two dozen rose petals, "I must be a guy, " I say to myself, though I can't be certain, I never am, but I never give that away, there are much better things to give away, imaginary kisses, telltale signs, sideways glances, I dream of climbing Mt. Everest in my Maidenform bra, I never reach the peak, I wake up in a cold sweat...

End

"Pretty boy, can't you show me nothing but surrender"

- Patti Smith

We make love in a vacant lot, as it was meant to be, cold asphalt below, full moon above, crickets chirping madly in the background, he is my dada daddy, I am his exotic drag princess in heat, when we kiss, our fantasies collide, explode, immersing us in minute particles of lust and longing, he touches me as if I wasn't there, when I cry out for more, he gives me less, the pleasure is all too much so I revel in the pain, he draws his sword and I my water pistol, we duel for hours into days, he backs me into a corner, I dive between his legs and make a run for the abandoned space between provocation and allure, between outrage and surrender, between perception and scandal, he calls for me, he pleads for me, he paints his face by numbers and recites nursery rhymes for me, remembering my name for the first time in weeks I reach out and pull him deep within, and hope he hasn't forgotten how to swim.

THE REAL WORLD

by Selena Anne Shephard

the real world is
a corset sucking in my gut
and a leather hood claiming my face
for its very own
the real world is
a $100 bill shoved between my phony tits
and the drop of his pants to the ground
the real world is
10 feet of chain dangling from my swelling balls
the real world is
a lacy petticoat & little girl sighs
and savouring "Daddy's" sweet thing
as if it was the last lollipop in the whole world
the real world is
a night drenched in skintight latex
the real world is
the sound of the whip coming down
upon my girdled bottom
the real world is a yellow raincoat
beckoning me, enticing me, seducing me
the real world is
legs split wide & a midnight cock plunging up the middle
the real world is
a kiss deep and long
yes, I do like to kiss

✷ ***Selena Anne Shephard/Andy Plumb is a writer/-collagist/photographer/cartoonist/videographer who enjoys discovering new ways and places to play betwixt and between (or, perhaps, above and beyond) the eithers/ors of gender and sexuality...***

Installment: Nightmare on Maitland. Part (ii)
TSe TSe TerroriSm ©1995 CaiRa

<u>On Maitland</u>. The car pulls up behind Turquoise (who still gives no sign that she is aware of what is happening behind her), about three or four car lengths behind her. Two people get out, each carrying something that looks like either a long pipe or a baseball bat.

<u>On Homewood</u>. In a house not far from the TSculturalcentre. On the second floor. Behind closed white lace curtains, Rhonda MacKenzie, respectable and local megalomaniac TS, is dreaming. And this is her dream...

<u>Rhonda's Dream</u>

all words & music & choreography © 1995 Cai-*I Really Do Know Best*-Ra - unless otherwise noted.

<u>Symbols Guide</u>

These symbols should make it easier to follow the action in Rhonda's Dream.

<u>The Forces of Good</u>

Symbol	
⌛	**Rhonda**
✂	**Her Imperial Ministers**

<u>Those Troublesome Transsexuals Who Won't Go Along With the Forces of Good</u>

Symbol	
🔔	**Willow**
📖	**The TransBackup Singers**
🕯	**The Audience**
✌	**Willow [*speaking*]**
☠	**Willow [*going from table to table*]**

<u>Other Symbols</u>

Symbol	
♌	**Intro**
●	**Original Melody**
♋	**Chorus**
⊛	**Middle 8 or Brand New Melody**
♍	**Slow or Slower Tempo**
♎	**Fast or Faster Tempo**

Rhonda is "singing" in her bad, overblown, yet distinctively operatic style (frankly sounding like something halfway between Maria Callas and Donald Duck):

<u>I Know Best</u>

⌛ I see
  Them out here on the street
With five inch heels
  Or knee-high boots upon their feet
Wearing clothes
  Made out of tasteless flash
And lingerie
  That belongs in the trash
And I see
  Too little; far too few
Who dress and act
  The way I want them to
Who wouldn't dream
  Of being indiscreet
In private
  Or simply out there on the street

And I know
  It's difficult to do
To live your life
  As I command you to
But I know
  Much better than the rest
I've seen it all
  I've passed through every test

I am Ruler
  Empress
Be-cause

<u>I</u>
<u>Know</u>
<u>Best</u>

choreography note: Rhonda starts singing in her bedroom (all in white) & moves to the windows (which are French doors of course) leading to a balcony in white and overlooking Homewood and a bit of Maitland. Rhonda opens the doors and plunges out onto the balcony at "I am" and gets there on "Ruler." There is a big orchestra dressed in white & powdered wigs down below at the intersection of Maitland and Homewood, accompanying her. South of the intersection, there is an audience seated facing Rhonda. And below them everyone in the street is watching and listening quietly. And if we look closely we can see that all the transsexuals are wearing ultrafemme makeup and apparel from 1950's American sitcoms.

In a cheap and gaudy underground café not far away, probably below a gay bar on Church Street (remember this is Rhonda's dream not real-life) where the lighting is black and the place is filled with smoke and everyone is wearing platform boots out of the '70's, tight and bright clothing and makeup and every wig that RuPaul has ever worn. It is quiet except for the hum of conversation and coffee cups on the table when Willow (wearing appropriate - for the dream and place - clothing and boots and makeup) enters. There is immediate silence. Willow begins singing the following song (while everyone listens - at least initially):

Auntie Rhonda's Coming To Town

(words © 1995 CaiRa,
the music & melody should be pretty obvious*)

Hey you transies there
I'm not fooling around
It's a real nightmare
Guess who's coming to town
That's right!
Auntie Rhonda's Coming To Town

She makes up a list — *No!*
She goes through it twice — *No Way!*
And lands on each trannie
Like a nuclear device
Get ready!
'Cause Auntie Rhonda's Coming To Town

The TransBackup singers (not quite as flashily dressed as Willow) now appear singing:

She doesn't care about your feelings
She doesn't care if you'll be missed
She doesn't care about your friends and family
Just as long as you're on her list

It may not sound real
That's just how it seems
But you'd better get ready
Even though it's a dream
Remember!
Auntie Rhonda's Coming To Town

So you'd better make plans
You'd better begin
It's time to get ready
And save your own skins
I'm telling you!
Auntie Rhonda's Coming
I said** Auntie Rhonda's Coming
Hot Damn! Auntie Rhonda's Coming To Town

with a splashy big band-type ending

* here's a great big clue for those of you who are still stuck - the original title is "S___ C___ is Coming To Town."
** the underlined words in this song are spoken/sung in a Frank Sinatra/Tony Bennett - type styling

Back on Maitland. Turquoise keeps walking. She is still angry, but for some inexplicable reason, turns around. She quickly takes in the scene; two people, each carrying something long, tubular and dangerous, coming towards her. She takes the plug out of her Echo™ (letting out an incredibly loud siren-type sound), and runs as fast as she can to Jarvis, screaming "Fire" at the same time.

Rhonda's Dream. Empress Rhonda is talking with (more like singing to or even at) her Imperial Ministers:

We Will Smash Them

You all know my Guidelines —
How a transsexual must be
They must be clean & white & pure
In short exactly just like me

I won't recite the Guidelines now
I know it's 20 volumes long
But there are some transsexuals who
Ignore Me & that is wrong

So - oh - oh - oh

We will catch them
And thrash them
And throw them far away

And we will smash them
Not just lash them
And leave them on display

We won't put up with
This rudeness anymore
We have more important things to do

These slaps in the face
Are a public disgrace
And a challenge to Your Imperial Rule

I know they can't help it
These unfortunates; these few
Maybe it was just an accident of birth

I feel saddened when I have to
Exercise my Moral Views
But I still must remove them from this earth

At this point the doors burst open and Willow and backup singers and band and a zillion non-stereo-typical transsexuals burst in singing:

TSe TSe TerroriSm continues on next page

continued from previous page

It's Over

●🔔 There were times
When we just went along
With whatever you told us to do
Well those days are gone

Things have changed
It's no longer the case
There's something we want to tell you
Right to your face

♋ It's over
Your reign is over

●🔔📖 Our lives are ours
And we're doing our best
No more Codes of Conduct
Like what makeup looks best

We're taking control
Right now today
Your grand plans are history
And that's why we say

♋ It's over
It's really over

✇ We won't be separated
Ever again
'Cause now we're all together
And this isn't the end

[immediately followed by well choreographed instrumental break and dance]

●🔔📖🕯 Yeah there once was a time
When we just went along
Doing what you told us to
Now those days are gone

We're controlling our own future
Right now today
We're not hiding anymore
And that's why we say

♋ It's over
Your schemes are over

☠ Don't you know that
🔔📖🕯 It's over
It's really over

☠ Can't you hear us?
🔔📖🕯 It's over
This dream is over

The chorus continues with everyone singing and dancing.

Back to Maitland (and reality). Turquoise runs really fast, not turning around to look (so she has no idea if the creeps are following or not) and still screaming her lungs out. She finally makes it to Jarvis, signals to a taxi (which surprisingly is there and is available) and gets in. She tells the driver to get out of the area and only then does she look back. There is no one there.

Return to **Rhonda's Dream**. Somehow through all this mêlée, Rhonda has managed to escape by climbing (in her big and now torn gown) out on the roof, waving her fist and quacking quietly (so that no one can hear):

This changes nothing
I'll be back
Sooner than you think
And it won't be pretty
It won't be pretty at all.

Rhonda turns and climbs along the roofs in a southerly direction towards Carlton, humming the chorus from We Will Smash Them to herself, while the sun sets in the west in the purple smog-filled haze of Toronto's evening sky.

end of this installment

💣 ***Of course all the characters in TSe TSe TerroriSm are created entirely from my imagination and do not represent any people living or dead. Any similarity is absolutely and entirely coincidental. Besides, I could never ever stoop to using real people in my stories, no matter how tempting.***

☺ ***Similarly all the songs (including lyrics, music & choreography) - with one obvious exception - are complete products of my imagination and are not copied from nor based on anybody else's material.***

— CaiRa

✷ ***CaiRa has been writing TSe TSe TerroriSm for what seems almost an eternity now. She hates pictures of herself, which is why there still isn't one here.***

Enterprises

6802 Ogden Rd. S.E.
Calgary, Ab., T2C 1B4
Phone (403) 236-7072

Greetings from Calgary and B&B Enterprises!

This is first and foremost a custom lingerie and streetwear shop. We help customers to figure out their clothing needs and for some customers, clothing for their fantasy's! We can create outfits from sketches, photos or imagination. We manufacture sequin ball gowns, shimmering evening dresses and casual clothes. Some of the fantasy clothes range from maids costumes to baby clothing to leather bondage outfits. Every idea can be custom fit and made here! As we are a custom shop we are only limited by your imagination....please feel free to write or call us!

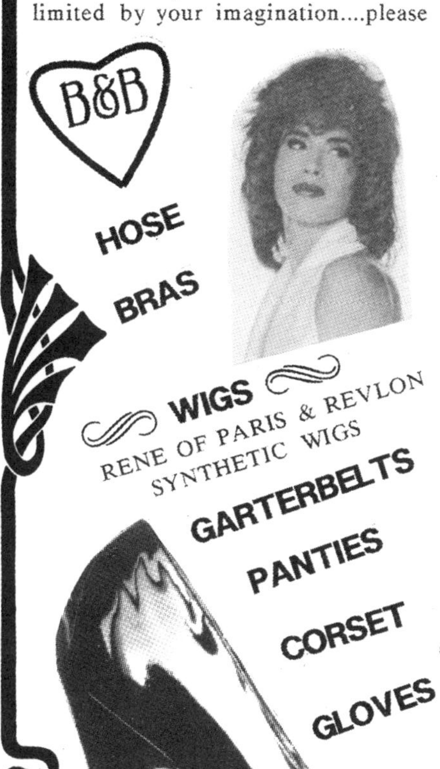

CATALOGS

Leather Catalogue $10.00
Leather Custom Clothing & Sub/Dom Equipment

Latex Catalogue $2.00
Latex Fetish Wear... Assorted Items

Sexy Lingerie Catalogue
70 page color intimate apparel $20.00
30 page color larger apparel......................... $10.00

Big Baby Catalogue $6.00
Sweet Clothing for the little girl in you!

Illusions Magazine..for the TV/TS Lifestyle
Back Issues .... $5.00 Current Issues....... $8.00

The Chatt $10.00
Adult Fetish & Contact Magazine

Make-Up and Beauty................................ $15.00
Makeup will no longer be a mystery!

Crossdresser's Quarterly................ $12.00

CD Int. Shopping Guide'94 .... $12.00

SHOES

These 4"heels are made especially for the Crossdresser. They are available in Red Patent #4504, Black Patent #4503, Black Satin #4533 and a Dyeable White Satin #4530. Sizes range from 4-14, AA to EE.

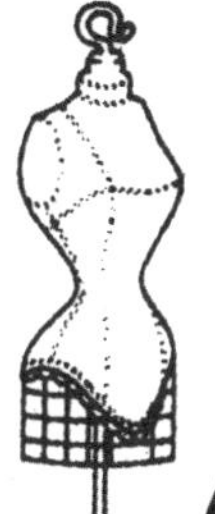

STOCKINGS
HIP PADS

Complete Your Fantasy

gendertrash
Canadian Directory of organizations, resources & services
for the TS/TG communities

Symbols List

- **NS** non-TS/TG/TV specific group
- **NP** non-TS/TG/TV specific group **with** a written policy prohibiting discrimination on the basis of gender identity
- 🕮 magazine/newsletter published by the group

The following was compiled to give as large a listing of Canadian resources as possible. Some of the groups/organizations listed are not specifically for TS/TG/TV persons but may still offer valuable services since they are known to be familiar with members of the TS/TG/TV communities.

The inclusion of any organization here does not necessarily stand as a stamp of approval by *gendertrash*. We believe that it is each individual's responsibility to decide for her/himself what is or isn't in her/his best interests. However, your comments about the quality, both positive & negative, of the services that you received from any of the providing groups would be appreciated & will be kept on file.

If you want your group, or any group that you know of, to be included in that listing.

Alberta

Calgary

Illusions Social Club

✉ **Illusions Social Club**, Box 2000, 6802 Ogden Rd. SE, Calgary, Alta, T2C 1B4

☎ (403) 236-7072

fax: (403) 236-1304

contact: Barbie & Christine

→ Illusions is a social club for support, outreach & self-education. They also run B & B Leatherworks & Lingerie by Barbie (a store catering to alternative lifestyles). Open to all gender gifted peoples & significant others. Meetings are 2nd Saturday & last Tuesday of every month.

membership: $40/year

🕮 **Illusions**

Edmonton

Crossroads (NS)

☎ (403) 474-7421

contact: Maureen Reid

→ provides various services for sex workers in general (AIDS education, safe house, pimp prevention, legal help, etc.) They have a big TS /TG clientele.

B.C.

Kimberley

Canadian Organization of Professional Electrologists (COPE) (NS)

✉ **COPE**, 410 Aspen Rd., Kimberley, BC, V1A 3B5

☎ (800) 665-COPE

fax: (604) 427-2573

→ COPE provides a registry of electrologists in Canada who subscribe to their high level code of professional and ethical conduct as well as standards of hygiene and sterilization.

Vancouver

Cornbury Society

✉ **Cornbury Society**, Box 3745, Vancouver, BC, V6B 3Z1

→ Non-profit support group for heterosexual cross-dressers & their families.

Foundation for the Advancement of Trans-Gendered People's Equality (FATE)

✉ **FATE**, 1-1727 William St, Vancouver, BC, V5L 2R5

☎ (604) 254-9591

contact: Jamie Lee

→ Promotes the well-being of transgendered individuals as well as public education & awareness. Provides advocacy for people on welfare. Registered as a non-profit organization.

🕮 **Destiny**

Centre for Sexuality, Gender Identity and Reproductive Health (NS)

✉ **Centre for Sexuality, Gender Identity and Reproductive Health** c/o Vancouver General Hospital, 715 West 12th Ave, Vancouver, BC, V5Z 1M9

☎ (604) 875-8282

→ Full gender identity clinic with several groups/ meetings, including Explorers, FTM's,etc. Child psychiatrist for TS parents. Drop-in & other services available.

Note: The clinic is moving

to a new address (which we don't have) very soon. Please call them to get their current address. Formerly known as **Gender Dysphoria Clinic**.

High Risk Project

✉ **High Risk Project**, 223 Main Street, Vancouver, BC V6A 2S7

☎ (604) 681-3202

contact: Sandy Laframboise or Deborah Brady

➔ The High Risk Project serves street active TS/TG/TV people. It operates a drop-in out of the Vancouver Native Health Centre (449 East Hastings Street - rear) from 1-4:30pm (M-F) & provides a free hot meal & support on Thurs night at DEYAS starting at 6pm. Donations are welcome & are tax deductible.

Note: See article (page 5) for more information on High Risk.

Zenith Foundation

✉ **Zenith Foundation**, Box 46, 8415 Granville St, Vancouver, BC V6P 4Z9

☎ (604) 261-1695

➔ Charitable non-profit foundation, whose objectives are to work toward improving the security & circumstances of people with gender dysphoria. Both FTM & MTF are welcome. Operates several committees. First contact by writing.

📖 **The Zenith Digest**

White Rock

Transsexual Support Group

✉ c/o Dr Angela Wensley, 14905 32nd Avenue, White Rock, BC., V4P 1A4

☎ (604) 536-2053

➔ Inclusive rather than exclusive support group for transsexuals and their families.

Manitoba

Winnipeg

Prairie Rose PRGR

✉ **Prairie Rose PRGR**, Box 23, Group 4, RR#1, Dugald, Man R0E 0K0.

contact: Beverley

➔ Club provides support, social activities & education. Write for info.

Village Clinic (NS)

✉ **Village Clinic**, 668 Corydon Ave., Winnipeg, Manitoba, R3M 0X7

➔ General health & STD clinic. TS/TG's welcome.

Nova Scotia

Halifax

Stepping Stone (NS)

✉ **Stepping Stone**, 2224 Maitland St., Halifax, N.S., B3K 2Z9

☎ (902) 420-0103

➔ User-directed street outreach programme for sex workers including transgendered youth.

Ontario

Cambridge

Society for the Second Self (Tri-Ess Society)

✉ **Tri-Ess Society**, PO Box 28002, Cambridge, Ont, N3H 5N4

➔ unconfirmed at this time

Haliburton

Intersex Society of North America (ISNA) Canada Chapter

✉ **Intersex Society of North America 'ISNA) Canada Chapter**, PO Box 1076, Haliburton, Ont., K0M 1S0

E-mail info@isna.org

➔ Group provides peer support, advocacy and counselling for intersexuals (ie hermaphrodites,pseudohermaphrodites), parents of intersexed children, and those who have (or have not) been medicalized and experiencing mutilating genital surgeries(y).

Mississauga

Monarch Social Club

✉ **Monarch Social Club, PO** Box 386, Stn A, Mississauga, Ont., L5A 3A1

➔ Social, support & info. group for TS/TG/TV people. Social dinner - last Saturday of each month. Focus is on those who are/will remain closeted.

membership: $40/year

Ottawa

Gender Mosaic

✉ **Gender Mosaic**, PO Box 7421, Vanier (Ottawa), Ont., K1L 8E4

☎ (613) 770-1945

➔ Social, support & info. group for TS/TG/TV people.

📖 **Notes from the Underground**

Friendship & Assistance for Canadian Transsexuals & Transvestites (FACTT)

✉ **FACTT**, PO Box 7421, Vanier, Ont., K1L 8E1

➔ TS/TV discussion group

St Catharines

TransEqual

✉ **TransEqual**, 165 Ontario St. #609, St. Catharines, Ontario, L2R 5K4

☎ (905) 688-0276

BBS (905) 358-5908 (N,8,1). Enter *TransEqual* when asked for name. Select Files from Main Menu, then Area 3 and then files can be previewed or tagged for downloading.

contact: Laura Masters

➔ TransEqual "hopes to ensure that each transsexual & transgenderist has appropriate legal recourse available to them... when their equal access to society is withheld". TransEqual is a TS/TG rights advocacy group.

Toronto

Canadian Crossdressers' Club

✉ **Canadian Crossdressers' Club**, 161 Gerrard St. E, Tor, Ont., M5A 2E4

☎ (416) 921-6112

➔ Provides a safe atmosphere for CD's & DQ's to dress up & meet others with similar interests/lifestyles.

📖 **DQ International**

Gender Identity Clinic (NS)

✉ **Gender Identity Clinic**, c/o Clarke Institute of Psychiatry, 250 College St, Tor, Ont. M5T 1R8

☎ (416) 979-2221 ext 2221

➔ To get an SRS reimbursed by OHIP, you must go through the Gender Identity's two year program & be approved by them for surgery. They also have a Wed afternoon support group for people in the program.

Hassle Free Clinic (NS)

✉ **Hassle Free Clinic**, 556 Church St, 2nd floor, Tor, Ont., M4Y 2E3

☎ (416) 922-0603 (M)
(416) 922-0566 (W)

➔ **Hassle Free** is a STD clinic, which provides anonymous HIV/AIDS testing & counselling (by appointment only). TS' are welcome at either clinic.

Women's Clinic - M,W,F (10-3), T & Th (4-8).
STD drop-in (no appointment necessary) - T & Th (4-6). Appointments required at all other times.

Men's Clinic - M & W (4-9), T & Th (10-3), F (4-7), S (10-2). No appointment necessary except for HIV/AIDS testing.

Human Sexuality Program(NS)

✉ **Human Sexuality Program**, c/o Student Support Services, Toronto Board of Education, 155 College St, Tor, Ont., M5T 1P6

☎ (416) 397-3755 (ask for the Human Sexuality Program)

contact: Tony Gambini

➔ This is primarily a counselling service for lesbian, gay & bisexual students, but they have included transgender students in their mandate. They have a support group for les-

(continued - next page)

*(**Directory** continued.)*

bian, gay, bi & transgender students (LGBST) who are experiencing personal difficulties, etc.

Maggie's Prostitutes' Resource Centre & Safe Sex Project of Toronto (P)

✉ **Maggie's**, PO Box 1143, Stn F, Tor, Ont., M4Y 2T8

☎ (416) 964-0150

→ A resource centre run by & for sex trade workers, providing condoms, legal info, AIDS info, referrals, etc. Drop-in (M&W, 12-6pm) at 298 Gerrard St E., 2nd floor.

Project Affirmation (P)

✉ **Project Affirmation**, box 1143, Stn F, Tor, Ont., M4Y 2T8

☎ (416) 593-9229
1 (800) 663-5530 (Ont. only)

fax: (416) 593-6697

contact: Ki Namaste

→ A research project investigating lesbian, gay, bisexual and transgendered people's access to health and social services.

ReproMed Ltd. (NS)

✉ **ReproMed Ltd.**, 2333, Suite 209, Tor, Ont. M6R 3A6

☎ (416) 537-6895

fax: (416) 537-4301

→ ReproMed Ltd. is a medically-oriented lab serving those who desire to have some measure of assurance against possible loss of their reproductive capabilities. They specialize in the cryopreservation of human spermatazoa for future clinical application and the providing of cryopreserved donor semen specimens to physicians (for artificial insemination).

Sex Workers Alliance of Toronto (SWAT) (NS)

✉ **SWAT**, PO Box 1143, Stn F, Tor, Ont., M4Y 2T8

☎ (416) 964-0150

→ A political action group working for the rights of all sex workers.

Sexual Assault Care Centre (NS)

✉ **Sexual Assault Care Centre**, 76 Grenville St, Tor, Ont., M5S 1B2

add (same as above - in Women's College Hospital)

☎ (416) 323-6040

→ The Sexual Assault Care Clinic provides services for the sexually assaulted.

Sistering (NS)

✉ **Sistering**, 525 College St. (admin). 220 Cowan St. (outreach).

add (same as above)

☎ (416) 926-9762 (admin)
(416) 926-1946 (drop in)
(416) 588-3939 (outreach)

→ **Sistering** provides support for homeless women (including TS/TG women).

Street Outreach Services (SOS) (NS)

✉ **SOS**, 622 Yonge St, 2nd floor, Tor., Ont., M4Y 1Z8

☎ (416) 926-0744

fax: (416) 926-9552

contact: Wayne Travers

→ **SOS** is an agency that assists youth, (16-24) involved in prostitution, to make informed choices in their lives, whatever their goals might be. They deal with TS/TG youth on a regular basis. Drop-in (M-F 10-6). Legal, medical, welfare & AIDS counselling available.

The 519 (P)

✉ **519 Community Centre**, 519 Church St, Tor, Ont. M4Y 2C9

☎ (416) 392-6874

→ All purpose resource centre for mostly lesbian/gay groups. Has other resources like free legal clinic, queer bashing hotline, etc which can be useful. People who work there are somewhat aware of problems that transgendered persons may face.

Toronto Rape Crisis Centre, now known as Multicultural Women Against Rape (NS)

✉ **Multicultural Women Against Rape**, PO Box 6597, Stn A, Tor, Ont., M5W 1X4

☎ (416) 597-8808 - this line may be picked up by their answering service, especially at nights

TDD:(416) 597-1214

business:(416) 597-1171

fax: (416) 597-9648

→ **Multicultural Women Against Rape** is a collective of non-transsexual women, providing support for victims of sexual assault (including TS/TG persons). They also run **Take Back the Night** & have no problems with TS', who identify as women, attending.

Transition Support

✉ Transition Support, c/o 519 Community Centre, 519 Church St, Tor, Ont. M4Y 2C9

☎ (416) 392-6874 (messages can be left only if necessary)

→ Support group open to all members of the transgender communities.

Voices of Positive Women (NS)

✉ **Voices of Positive Women**, PO Box 471, Station C, Toronto, Ont. M6J 3P5

☎ (416) 324-8703 (10-5), answering machine at other times

fax: (416) 324-8701

→ Community based non-profit organization directed by and for women living with HIV and AIDS in Ontario. Services available to anyone with HIV/AIDS who identifies as a women.

women's counselling referral & education centre (WCREC) (NS)

✉ **WCREC**,525 Bloor St. W., Tor., Ont., M5S 1Y4

☎ (416) 534-7501

→ WCREC has an extensive listing of feminist-oriented therapists. They try to match each client with the appropriate therapist. They also have a crisis line and seem to be receptive to TS women.

Xpressions

✉ **Xpressions**, PO Box 233, Station A, Toronto, Ontario, M5W 1B2

→ **Xpressions** is dedicated to serving the CD, TV, TS, TG and DQ communities by organizing a wide range of social activities for members and their spouses/significant others. **Xpressions** also aims to help and support transgenderists, especially those in the closet, to get out and enjoy all that our lifestyles have to offer.

membership: $35/year

🕮 **Xpressions**

Québec

Montréal

Association Des Opérées - és en Chirurgie Esthétique (ADOCE) (NS)

✉ **ADOCE**, CP 230, 5135 Jean-Talon est, Mtl, Qué., H1S 2Z2

☎ (514) 327-8148

contact: Rachel Boutin

→ cosmetic surgery info. & doc. centre. ADOCE provides extensive info on all types of cosmetic surgery. They also provide info on surgeons (both good & bad) in Québéc.

membership — $35/year

Association Québécoise des Travailleuses - eurs du Sexe (AQTS) (NS)

✉ **AQTS**, CP 5028, Succ. C, Mtl, Qué., H2X 3M2

☎ (514) 527-5320

contact: Claire Thiboutôt

→ AQTS is a support group for sex workers as well as a political organization of sex workers & sex worker rights advocates dedicated to the decriminalization & deregulation of prostitution & other types of sex work.

Centre d'Action Communautaire auprès des Toxicomanes Utilisateurs de Seringues (CACTUS) (NS)

✉ **CACTUS**, 1209 Ste-Dominique, Mtl, Qué., H2X 2W4

☎ (514) 954-8869

→ **CACTUS** is a needle exchange, condom distribution and AIDS information centre. A group of specially trained male & female nurses are on hand to offer support, references & first aid. Situated in the red-light area,downtown Montréal. Open from 9:15PM to 4AM.

Note: **CACTUS** will be moving after July 1 (new address unknown at time of printing).

Human Sexuality Clinic (NS)

✉ **Human Sexuality Clinic**, c/o Montréal General Hospital, 1547 Ave. des Pins ouest, Mtl, Qué., H3G 1B3

☎ (514) 934-8013

fax: (514) 934-8204

→ The Human Sexuality Clinic operates a gender identity clinic & offers various services including therapy, hormones & SRS referrals.

Fondation Nationale du Transsexualisme

✉ **Fondation Nationale du Transsexualisme**, PO Box 613, Stn C, Mtl, Qué., H2L 4L5

☎ (514) 526-5892

fax: (514) 526-1060

contact: Yvette Tétreault

→ The foundation exists to help anyone, experiencing gender dysphoria or dealing with transsexuality, to go through his/her transition in harmony with his/her values, beliefs & customs.

Dr Yvon Ménard, Chirurgie Plastique et Reconstructive (NS)

✉ **Dr Ménard**, 1003 Boul. St-Joseph est, Mtl, Qué., H2J 1L2

☎ (514) 288-2097

fax: (514) 288-3547

→ Dr Ménard offers a wide range of plastic & reconstructive surgeries, including SRS for both FTM & MTF patients.

Projet d'Intervention Auprès des Mineures - eurs Prostituees - és ("PIMP") (NS)

✉ **PIAMP**, CP 5028, Succ. C, Mtl,Qué., H2X 3M2

☎ (514) 527-1267

→ **PIAMP** is a team of street outreach workers, doing advocacy work for street youth. They also run a drop-in, in downtown Montréal.

Stella (Vivre et Travailler en Sécurité et avec Dignité/Making Space Safe for Working Women)(NS)

✉ **Stella**, CP 989, Succ. Desjardins, Mtl, Qué., H5B 1C1

☎ (514) 282-1563

contact: Natasha

→ Info/reference centre & drop-in for women working in the sex trade. Street outreach, socialization, clothing, food, showers, washer/dryer, etc. TS welcome & on staff. Drop-in times: 2-8pm(M-F). Call for location.

TRANS-PORS (Post Operation Residence Services) (NS)

✉ **TRANS-PORS**, 2006 Sherbrooke est, Mtl, Qué., H2K 1B9

☎ (514) 526-5892

contact: Delphée Martin

→ Community service created by Dr Ménard & the Fondation Nationale du Transsexualisme to provide room & board, with special care & support for people (both FTM & MTF) coming to Montréal for SRS or any other type of adjusting surgery.

Québec

Dr Denys Chabot (NS)

✉ **Clinique Dr Denys Chabot**, 1281 Place de Mérici, Québec, Qué., G1S 3H8

☎ (418) 682-8810

→ Dr Chabot is a cosmetic & plastic surgeon, offering several types of surgeries including MTF SRS. He is considering doing FTM SRS at a later date.

Québec Gender Identity Clinic

✉ **Québec Gender Identity Clinic,** 84 Boul. des Alliés, Québec, Qué., G1L 1Y2

☎ (418) 529-1152

contact: Mme Viviane Bélanger

→ Support group for FTM & MTF transsexuals. Provides referrals for therapy, hormones, etc. Works in close collaboration with the Centre Hospitalier de l'Université Laval. They also work with a local detoxification centre (Le Centre d'Aide St-Augustin) for people with addictive & compulsive behaviours.

Note: Formerly known as **Être Femmes.**

Publications & Newsletters

Boys Will Be Boys

Boys Will Be Boys, a publication for FTMs, can reached at: BWBB, PO Box 5393, West End Bris, Australia 4101.

Boy's Own
The FTM Newsletter

Boy's Own is published quarterly by the FTM Network, BM Network, London, UK, WC1N 3XX. Write for subscription information.
Provides a forum for FTM's to discuss issues of concern.

The Channel

The Channel is a newsletter published bimonthly, by ETVC, PO Box 426486, San Francisco, CA, USA, 94142-6486. Hotline: (510) 549-2665. Voicemail: (415) 334-3439. Membership is $20(US)/year, which includes 1 year subscription.
Available only to members, helping professionals or through club exchanges.

Les Chemins de Trans

Les Chemins de Trans is a newsletter published by Belgische Gender Stichting, Pluimstraat 48, 85000 KORTIJK-B, Belgium. Write for subscription information.

Chrysalis Quarterly

Chrysalis Quarterly is published 4 times a year by the American Educational Gender Information Service (AEGIS), PO Box 33724, Decatur, GA, USA 30033-0724. (404) 939-2128. Subscription rates: $36(US)/year - within the US; $46(US)/year - outside the US.
Publication dedicated to in-depth exploration of gender issues & designed for both consumers & caregivers.

City Lights

City Lights is a newsletter published by the Metropolitan Gender Network, 561 Hudson St., Box 45, New York City, NY, USA, 10014. (718) 461-9050. Write for subscription information.

Cross-Talk
The Transgender Community News & Information Monthly

Cross-Talk is published monthly. PO Box 944, Woodland Hills, CA, USA, 91365. (818) 907-3053, (818) 347-4190 (fax). e-mail: kymmer@xconn.com. Subscription rates: $54(US)/1 year - US, $96(US)/2 years - US. Non-US subscribers add $12(US)/year.
Contains many articles of interest to the CD/TV/TG/TS communities.

Cross Port

Cross Port is a newsletter published monthly by Cross Port, PO Box 54657, Cincinnati, OH, USA 45254-0657. (513) 474-9557 (Shelbi). Subscription rates: $8(US)/year.

The Crystal Chronicle

The Crystal Chronicle is a newsletter published monthly by the Crystal Club, PO Box 287, Reynoldsburg OH, USA, 43068-0287. (614) 224-1165. Subscription rates: $8(US)/year.

Destiny

Destiny is published quarterly by FATE, 1-1727 William St, Vancouver, BC, V5L 2R5. Destiny is free, but donations & postage are welcome.

Devil Woman

Devil Woman is a newsletter published by the Diablo Valley Girls, (DVG), PO Box 272885, Concord, CA, USA, 94527-2885.Phone: (510) 849-4112. Membership fees are $10(US)/year, includes subscription.
Available only to members, helping professionals & through club exchanges.

Dragazine

Dragazine is published two times a year and can be reached at: Dragazine, PO Box 461795, West Hollywood, CA, USA, 90046. Single issues are $5[95](US). Orders are by cheques, made payable to: Dragazine.
Dragazine attempts to cover small and big stories regarding the use of Crossdressing in Entertainment - Art, Politics, Music, Theatre, etc.

DQ International

DQ International is published quarterly by Canadian CDC. Canadian CDC, 161 Gerrard St. East, Toronto, Ont., Canada, M5A 2E4. (416) 921-6112. $20(Can)/issue includes tax & postage.

FTM Newsletter

FTM Newsletter is the world's most widely-circulated newsletter for the Female-to-Male crossdresser and transsexual (over 600 subscribers in 14 countries). The FTM Newsletter is the informal record of the thoughts and concerns of its subscribers. It strives to provide factual information for FTM TG/TS people so they may make informed decisions. It also provides a forum for expression/exchange of views and a medium through which FTMs may find support. Published quarterly (January, April, July, October) since 1987 by FTM International. **Subscribe!** $15/4 issues. $20 for international (to cover additional postage), and $25 for professional subscriptions. All cheques or money orders ahould be in US funds, payable to: FTM or FTM Newsletter. Contact: FTM, 5337 College Avenue #142, Oakland, CA USA 94618. Voicemail: (510) 287-2646. Fax: (510) 547-4785 (24 hours). E-Mail: JamisonG@aol.com.

Hermaphrodites with Attitude

Hermaphrodites with Attitude is a newsletter published by the Intersex Society of North America (ISNA), PO Box 31791, San Francisco,CA ,USA, 94131. E-mail: info@isna.org. Subscription rates: $12/year, $50/year (institutional). All cheques/money orders payable to ISNA.

Gender Quest

Gender Quest is a newsletter published bi-monthly by Phoenix Transgender Support, Phoenix, PO Box 18332, Asheville, NC, USA, 28814. (704) 259-9428. Subscription rates: $7(US)/year.

Girlfriend!

Girlfriend! is available for $4(US)/issue. Send money to Box 191781, San Francisco, CA, USA 94119.
Girlfriend! is a drag zine. The **Girlfriend!** calendar also available for $7(US).

Illusions

Illusions is a 40 page magazine published by the Illusions Social Club and is included with membership. Otherwise it is $8/issue for non-members. Please send money or write to Illusions, Box 2000-6802 Ogden Road SE., Calgary, Alta T2C 1B4. (see Resource Listings for further information)

In Your Face!
The Journal of Record of Transexual & Transgender Activism

In Your Face's mission statement is to cover all actions by transpeople and friends around the country. It is published 2or 3 times a year. Free. Contact: IYF, c/o Riki Anne Wilchins, 274 W. 11 St. - #4R, NYC, NY, USA, 10014. E-Mail: Riki@PipeLine.com (to reach Riki) or nm@world.std.com (to reach Nacny Nangeroni).

IXΣ

IXΣ is a newsletter published monthly by IXΣ(Iota Chi Sigma or Indiana Crossdressers Society). IXΣ, PO Box 20710, Indianapolis, IN, USA, 46220. Membership is $23(US)/year, which includes 1 year subscription. Back issues are $2(US)/issue. Checks should be payable to "cash" or "bearer".

Journal of Gender Studies

The Journal of Gender Studies is published twice a year by the Human Outreach and Achievement Institute, 405 Western Ave., Suite 345, South Portland, ME, USA 04106. Subscription rates: $16(US)/year.
This is the official publication of the Institute.

Ladylike

Ladylike is published quarterly by Creative Design Services. Subscriptions are: 4 issues for $32 in the US/$35 in Canada/$50 Overseas. All prices are in US currency. Each issue is 48 pages (with 8 in colour) featuring real people from the transgender community, articles, humour, cartoons and lots more. Contact CDS, PO Box 61263, King of Prussia, PA USA 19406. Phone: (610) 640-9449. E-mail: cdspub@omni.voicenet.com

Lipstick and Lace

Lipstick and Lace is a newsletter published by Girl's Night Out. Write for subscription information to GNO c/o Barbara Fortune, POB 350369, Brooklyn, NY, USA, 11235-0007. (201) 794-1665, ext 202.

New Men And Women of Minnesota

New Men and Women of Minnesota is a newsletter published quarterly by the New Men and Women of Minnesota, PO Box 6432, Minneapolis, MN, USA, 55406-0432. Membership fees are $25(US)/year which includes 1 year subscription.

Notes From the Underground

Notes From the Underground is published bi-monthly by Gender Mosaic. PO Box 7421, Vanier, Ontario, K1L 8E4. Phone/Fax: (613) 741-3007. E-Mail: bz247@freenet. carelton.ca. Subscription rates: $20 (Cdn)/year.
Contains various articles relevant to the gender communities.

PPOC Girl Talk

PPOC Girl Talk is a newsletter published monthly by the Powder Puffs of California (PPOC), PO Box 1088, Yorba Linda, CA, USA, 92686. (714) 779-9013 weekdays, 9 to 9 pm (pacific time) & leave message. Subscription rates: $30/year for non-members.

Reflected Images

Reflected Images is a newsletter published quarterly by Reflections, PO Box 4002, East Dedham, MA, USA, 02026. $4(US)/issue. (617) 323-6082.

Renaissance News & Views

Renaissance News & Views is the monthly newsletter of the Renaissance Education Association, Inc., the national open-membership support group for all transgendered people. Subscriptions are $16/year. Contact Renaissance, 987 Old Eagle School Road, Suite 719, Wayne,PA, USA 19087. (610) 975-9119.

The Southern Belle

The Southern Belle is a newsletter published monthly by Sigma Epsilon, Tri-Ess, PO Box 272, Roswell, GA, USA, 30077. They don't sell their newsletter, but are willing to trade it with other newsletters.

Tennessee Vals

Tennessee Vals is a newsletter published monthly by Tennessee Vals, PO Box 92335, Nashville, TN, USA, 37209. (615) 664-6883 voice mail. Membership $25(US)/year includes 1 year subscription.

TNT
Transsexual - News - Telegraph
The Magazine of Transsexual Culture

TNT, 41 Sutter Street, #1124, San Francisco, CA USA, 94104-4903. (415) 703-7161. Subscription rates: 4 issues for $18(US) within the US & $23(US) within Canada.
TNT is a political publication that aims to cover the many issues affecting TS/TG persons (besides shopping and make-up), while promoting transsexual pride.

TOPS
Newsletter for Transsexual Sex Industry Workers

TOPS is published quarterly by the Ongoing Network - Transsexual Outreach Project (ON TOP). All correspondence should be addressed to ON TOP, PO Box 11-412 Manners St.,Wellington, NZ, phone 64-9-3666-106. Write for subscription rates.
Provides a forum for transsexual sex trade workers to communicate with each other about their various issues & concerns.

The Transgenderist

The Transgenderist is a newsletter published monthly by the Transgenderist's Independence Club (TGIC), PO Box 13604, Albany, NY, USA, 12212-3604. Membership is $40(US)/year which includes 1 year subscription. Contact TGIC at the above address for further information.

TransSisters
The Journal of Transsexual Feminism

TransSisters is published quarterly by Skyclad Publishing Co., 4004 Troost Avenue, Kansas City, Missouri, USA, 64110. Phone & fax (call first by voice to set up the fax): (816) 753-7816. E-Mail: davinaanne@aol.com. Subscription rates: $24(US)/4 issues within US, Canada & Mexico; $26(US)/4 issues outside those countries. Back issues available for $8(US) within Canada, US & Mexico; $8.50(US) outside those countries. All checks payable to Davina Anne Gabriel.
Provides a forum dealing with issues of transsexuality from a feminist perspective & exists to promote dialogue, understanding, co-operation & reconciliation between the feminist & transsexual communities.

The TV\TS Tapestry Journal

Tapestry is published quarterly by the IFGE. Box 367, Wayland, MA, USA 01778. Phone: (617) 899-2212. Fax: (617) 899-5703. Individual copies: $12(US). Subscription rates: regular subscriptions are $40(US)/1 year; 1st Class, Canadian & overseas surface subscriptions are $55(US)/1 year; overseas air subscriptions are $65(US)/1 year; Two year subscriptions (US bulk mail only) are $72(US)/2years. Subscribers receive a personal listing free of charge for the duration of their subscription and are considered voting members of IFGE.
Primary publication of IFGE.

Xpressions Xplorer

Xpressions Xplorer is published monthly by Xpressions, PO Box 223, Station A, Toronto, Ontario, M5W 1B2. Free with paid membership. Please contact Yolana or Laura (editors) for further details.

The Zenith Digest

The Zenith Digest is a newsletter published quarterly by the Zenith Foundation, Box 46, 8415 Granville St., Vancouver, BC, Canada, V6P 4Z9 (604) 261-1695. $3 (Cdn)/issue, payable to the Zenith Foundation.

Gee!!
I Used to
Wish I
were
a Woman!
But
I didn't
Think
It was
Possible!

Dragazine
LANA
LUSTER
The Cycle Sluts
Ethyl Eichelberger
Jim Bailey
Pagan Holiday
DRAGAZINE!
for Halloweeners and Inbetweeners!
$5.95 for the current issue.
Complete this form and send your check or money order to:
DRAGAZINE • PO BOX 461795 • DEPT X
WEST HOLLYWOOD, CA 90046
NAME
ADDRESS
CITY
STATE
ZIP

PERSONALS

HOW TO PLACE AN AD

It's free!!! Just send us your ad with your name, complete address & phone number. All of these will be kept in our strictest confidence, babykins. And then all you have to do is wait by the mailbox for tons & tons of letters requesting your personal (& we're talking very personal) attention.

TO ANSWER AN AD:

Place your letter in a sealed & unstamped envelope. Write in pencil and in the top right corner of the envelope, the drawer number of the ad you are responding to. Next put the envelope(s) plus $5.00 for one contact or $10.00 for three contacts (in cash or cheque/money order payable to genderpress) in another envelope & mail it to us at:

"*gendertrash*/personals"
box 500-62,
552 Church St,
Toronto, Ontario
M4Y 2E3

Please remember: no money no response. *gendertrash* can't live only on good intentions.

The editor & publishers of *gendertrash* assume no responsibility or liability for any meeting(s) resulting from these services.

❦❦❦

A Satisfied Personals User's Testimony

"It was an intriguing & mysteriously erotic correspondence, leading from sheets of parchment to sheets of 50/50 poly/cotton. Thanks gendertrash personals"

- DA

Amazonian TS Woman
Strong & sincere Amazonian Transsexual woman seeks a playful and aware baby bull, bambi or Minotaur with whom to co-mingle- *Toronto #220*

Bi-Curious
Post-op TS woman, single, french speaking, socially active, good natured, early forties, curvaceous. Recently found myself attracted to women. Would like to practise my english and explore my bisexuality with transsexual or genetic women. - *Québec City # 170*

French Man
Straight, but open-minded French genetic man, late 30's, attractive, business type, seeks good-looking & intelligent MTF TS for ongoing relationship. Discretion & respect a must. - *Toronto # 230*

Gender Oriented Genetic
I am a gender-oriented genetic man who is drawn to TS's. Also am a bit of a crossdresser. I would like to find a cute, smart TS who seeks a lover/friend/or relationship. I have many cultural interests from A to Z (abnormal psychology to art to avant garde novels). My favourite author is Jack Kérouac, father of the beat generation and son of French Canadians - pacifist, Zen seeker, jazz disciple, etc. - *Pennsylvania area # 100*

Girlboygirl
Gender dysphoric girlboygirl seeks butch of any sex/gender/sexuality for torrid affair. - *Montréal # 250*

Hazel Eyes
Romantic Pisces. 35, 6', 200 #, all muscle. Hazel-eyes. German-Irish nationality. Professional chef. Homeowner. Desires feminine post-operative for marriage. Pre-ops also write! I'll provide home, security, all my love. Write soon! Thank you! - *Florence, Arizona # 190*

In Search of a FTM
Genetic woman, french, 25, red-head, mature & insightful, seeks sensitive, politically aware, intelligent, sexy FTM with a sense of humour, who likes children, for friendship and more...- *Montréal # 120*

Party Girl
French crazy smoking, drinking, wild partying genetic girl wants to meet TS/TG girls with a brain for friendship, watching TV, eating junk & nights out. - *Toronto # 270*

Sexy Femme TS
Beautiful model-type transsexual, 25, tall, slim, sexy, feminine figure, long curly brown hair, blue eyes. Seeks cute young (18+) guy for friendship plus ? - *Toronto # 190*

True Friendship
I sincerely would like to meet someone with whom I can share and exchange ideas, thoughts, dreams, and experiences with. Someone who will and wish to explore the essence of true friendship and wish to develop a meaningful relationship. - *California #240*

TS Angel
Young but mature MTF Angel. Very beautiful, soft, sweet and sincere, but strong and assertive. Seeks unattached, intelligent, pro-feminist, non-smoker, vegetarian, attractive man for stable long term relationship, based on affection not garter belts... - *Toronto # 130*

TS Lesbian Wanted
Non-transsexual lesbian, trans-curious, presently living in Montréal but planning to move to another planet soon. Would like to correspond with and/or meet a soft-core feminist transsexual lesbian. Must be open-minded and love travelling. - *Montréal # 110*

TS Man Wanted
Would like to meet a masculine, confident, passable, open-minded, caring, politically aware FTM for friendship and/or more. I'm a very attractive TS woman in her late 20's. - *Toronto # 140*

TS Woman Wanted
40 years old TS woman would like another intelligent, mature, political, vegetarian, non-smoker, non-drinking, quiet TS woman, 30-40, for friendship. Operative status unimportant. No makeup sessions nor lingerie parade, please. - *Toronto # 180*

Weltschmerz Fin-de-Siede
Sassy, sincere, weltschmerz, fin-de-siède, MTF, transgendered person of the feminine but not necessarily passive persuasion seeks pen-pals, not necessarily penis-pals - *Toronto # 260*

Le Babillard

- <u>GIRLCULT/GIRLKULTURZINE</u>, a zine "celebrating girls, grrrrls, women, dominatrixes, wymyn, drag queens, femmes, butches, dykes, trannies, bi's," wants submissions (prose, poetry, cartoons or artwork). Artwork must be less than 8"×6" (20cm×15cm). Send to: 48 Craig St., London, Ont., N6C 1E8 (include a S.A.S.E. if you want it returned). Accepted material gets free copies of magazine.
- <u>PROJECT AFFIRMATION</u>: Ki Namaste is doing research on Ontario transgendered people's access to health care and social services (including hormones, HIV/AIDS, relations with police, prisons, psychiatrists, welfare, FBA, etc.) and would like to interview transgendered people, especially FTMs and/or TS/TGs in prison. An honorarium is available. For further information, please call Ki Namaste c/o Project Affirmation, (416) 593-9229 or 1-800-663-5530 (Ontario only). Fax: (416) 593-6697.
- <u>FTM CONFERENCE</u>: **A Vision of Community:** The First All-FTM Conference of the Americas, will be held August 18-20, 1995 in San Francisco. Workshops, seminars, panels, exhibitions, networking and socializing for FTMs, their partners and friends. Registration information can be obtained from: FTM Conference, 5337 College Ave., #142, Oakland, CA, USA 94618. See the ad for the conference (page 32)
- <u>BRANDON TEENA MEMORIAL FUND</u> needs donations to help pay for a headstone for Brandon Teena (an FTM who was brutally beaten, raped and murdered in Lincoln, Nebraska last year - the trial of the accused murderer starts May 15). Send donations to: Teena Brandon Memorial Fund, 1204 WO Street, Lincoln, NB, USA 68528.
- <u>MWMF</u>: Plans are already underway for next year's protest against the Michigan Womyn's Music Festival. For information & greatly needed donations please contact Davina Anne Gabriel, 4004 Troost Ave., Kansas City, Missouri, USA 64110; phone: (816) 753-7816; e-mail: davinaanne@aol.com (Internet) or DavinaAnne (America Online).
- <u>TRANSGENDER PRIDE PROJECT</u>: Leslie Feinberg (author of **Stone Butch Blues** & **Transgender Liberation**) is soliciting tax-deductible donations to publish her historical & cross-cultural research on transgender, tentatively titled **Transgender: A History of Resistance.** Checks ahould be made payable to the Column Foundation, c/o William Sachs, Esq., Suite 830, 7 Penn Plaza, New York City, NY, USA 10001. Please clearly mention that this contribution is to be used for the Transgender Pride Project.
- <u>ICTLEP</u>: The International Conference on Transgender Law & Employment Policy, Inc., is holding its 4th annual conference June 14-18, 1995 in Houston. They are also looking for donations. For further information, please contact them at 5707 Firenza St., Houston, TX, USA 77035-5515; phone: (713) 723-8368; fax: (713 723-1800.
- <u>2ND INTERNATIONAL CONGRESS ON CROSSDRESSING, SEX AND GENDER ISSUES</u> will be held in late Spring, 1997. For further information regarding costs and location, please contact JoAnn Roberts, Ph.D., c/o CDS, PO Box 61263, King of Prussia, PA, USA 19406; phone: (610) 640-9449; e-mail: conff2@cdspub.com.
- <u>THE TRIANGLE PROGRAM (aka "GAY HIGH")</u>, an alternative high school for lesbian, gay, bi and transgendered youth (grades 10 & up) is starting intake now. It will open in September, 1995 at the MCC on Simpson Avenue. For further information contact Tony Gambini c/o Human Sexuality Program, Student Support Services, Toronto Board of Education, 155 College Street, Toronto, Ontario, M5T 1P6. Phone: (416) 397-3755 (ask for the Human Sexuality Program).

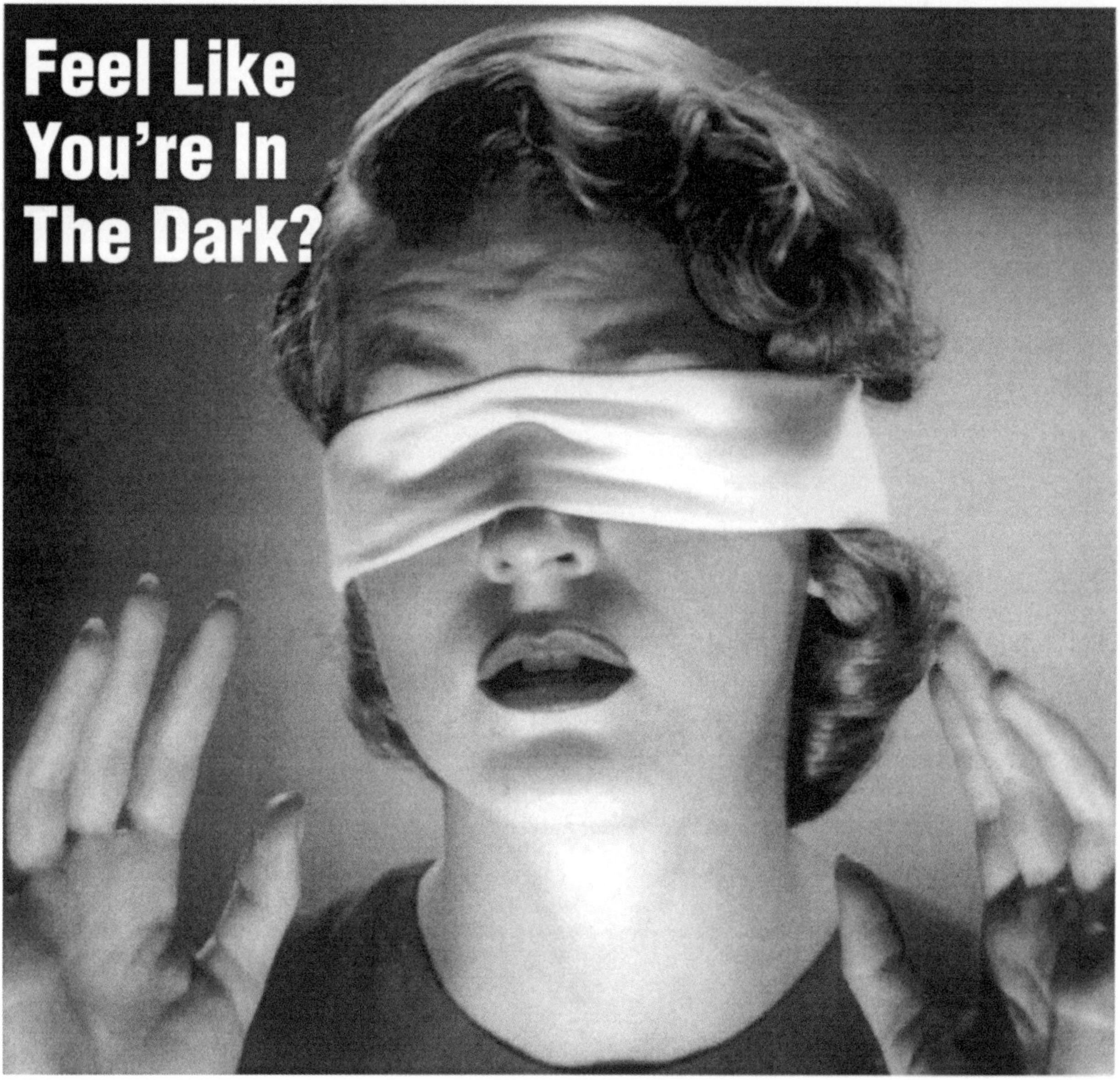
Feel Like
You're In
The Dark?

GENDERTRASH

ISSUE 5

1995-1996

[A note on the back of this photo of a mannequin in a shop window at night in Danforth, Toronto, circa 1995 indicates it was intended for use in Gendertrash #5. *It seems an appropriate emblem for this reconstruction of an issue.]*

issue # 5

Gendertrash #5 was originally slated to come out in August 1995, and then later at some time in 1996. It was to be a major step forwards for the publication: the plan was to publish it on newsprint paper, in an edition of 2000 copies, in comparison to *Gendertrash* #4's 500. This change was particularly motivated by a desire to, as Mirha-Soleil Ross says in contemporary correspondence, "keep on distributing *Gendertrash* to transsexual prisoner and street active transgendered for free" [*sic*].

However, *Gendertrash* #5 was never finished. This reconstruction is guided in the first instance by a provisional handwritten *Gendertrash* #5 table of contents from 1995. Some items mentioned are provisionally laid out, others only exist in draft typescript, or in preparatory materials, others still do not exist at all. What does exist has been reproduced here.

Also included are two other classes of items that are not listed in the table of contents. First, items that contemporary correspondence indicates were accepted for *Gendertrash* #5, and second, items that Mirha-Soleil Ross has personally indicated were intended for publication in issue #5.

This second class of items includes several documents from the *Gendertrash* archives, and two documents (an interview with Jamison Green and an interview with Viviane Namaste) that do not survive in physical form in the archive, but which do survive in Ms. Ross's personal computer files.

As a precaution, a few personally identifying details in the documents (telephone numbers, prisoner numbers, addresses) have been blurred out.

Taken together, there is at least an issue's worth of material here, indeed rather more. It is unlikely that all of this material would have made it into the hypothetical version of *Gendertrash* #5 that went to the printers in 1995 or 1996. What this material does faithfully represent, however, with only a few small gaps, is the range from which a final selection would have been made.

– gendertrash #5

– review Rothblatt & Castle
INK Tantrum
– review Walking the Dead
– human rights article
– Premarine article
– Health confer. press release & pamphlet
– short version of survey,
– Interview w Wendy Rose
– Interview w Peter
– Beacon press protest against.
– News Items.

[the only items on this list to which nothing in the Gendertrash *files corresponds are "INK Tantrum" (a comic strip by the cartoonist Diana Green) and a few practical items that were never written up: the "short version of survey," the "Premarine article" and the "News Items."]*

Gendertrash #5

- review Rothblatt & castle
- review Walking the Dead Ink Tantrum
- human rights article
- Premarine article
- Health confer. press release & pamphlet
- short version of survey
- Interview w Wendy Rose
- Interview w Peter
- Beacon Press protest against
- News Items.

V

Letter to the Editor

A copy of a letter from Mirha-Soleil Ross dated July 22, 1995, in response to this letter from Michelle Maulsby, shows Ross asking for permission to reproduce Maulsby's letter specifically in issue #5. A further letter from Michelle Maulsby grants that permission. The ink in the original letter is green.

Mirha-Soleil Ross,

Greetings. I wanted to thank you for the issue of Gendertrash that arrived today, it is truly great, the Christine Tayleur piece did much to change my attitude about my priorities. Even though I point to the events that occured at the MWMF as the catylyst to my own "emergence", Ms. Tayleur's piece has given me back a sense of perspective, one I hope to use to aid my sisters in here. This may sound somewhat ironic, considering that I grew up poor and black...

Printing my poem was very kind, considering that it's no where near as moving or wonderful as the Selena Anne Shephard poem, for example. It means much to me, as it is the first time a "Michelle" poem has ever been printed. It is a validation of who I truly am, one made even more special by my present surroundings, there are not many ways I can show myself as Michelle, your kind inclusion of my poem was a way to share who I am, and I am grateful.

Your interview with Dancing To Eagle Spirit made me cry, to read about someone who has gone through so many of the things I have, and has emerged so strong, gave me hope. I'll briefly explain, I was a "bed warmer" to two of my uncles until the age of 15, my body was theirs to screw or beat, whatever took their fancy at the time, I also hustled for a while after I ran away from home (since I was big and black, I always got picked up by those in need of rough trade), and just ten years ago managed to kick my addictions to booze and downs. The interview helped me believe that even someone like me can change and grow better and stronger.

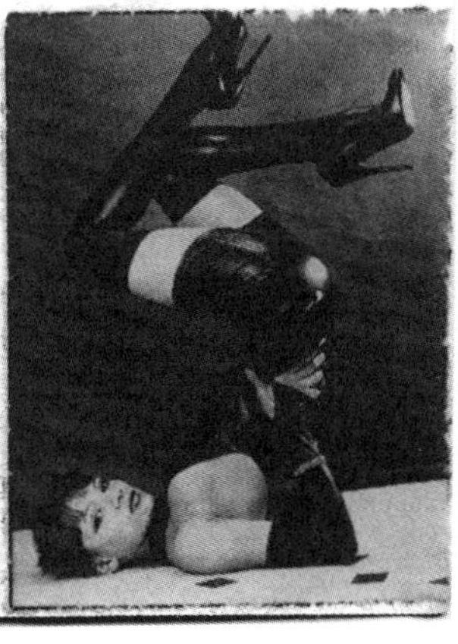

One other thing I thought that I should mention is that when you begin publishing inmates names and IDs at the end of their personal ads, their prison mailrooms

②

may sieze it as a chance to forbid entry into the prison of Gendertrash. Let me explain; many prisons forbid (in some degree or another) communication between prisoners, and so, if inmate names and numbers are printed, they very possibly might forbid the zine because of the possibility (however slight) that a prisoner could communicate with another. To give you an example of how far this insanity can be taken, ~~the editor of Prison Life Magazine is a former PA prisoner, now~~ on parole, the PA prison mailrooms used the fact that he had an Editor's Page, with his comments, to forbid allowing the zine into PA prisons. I just wanted to mention that.

I close now, again expressing my thanks.

Sincerely,

Michelle

Vernon Maulsby [blurred]

[blurred] Prison

Box 244

[blurred], PA

[blurred]

Letter to the Editor

This letter from Dallas Denny responds to the article "Racism and Poverty in the Transgender Community" by Christine Tayleur in *Gendertrash* #4. Mirha-Soleil Ross wrote back asking to publish it in *Gendertrash* #5, commenting that "I find that far too many people in our communities can only see things as either right or wrong and your letter is a perfect example of the opposite."

Denny also submitted an article to *Gendertrash* on "Race and Class in Transgender Communities" which Mirha-Soleil Ross indicates she intended to publish in *Gendertrash* #5 under a different title. Unfortunately it does not survive in the *Gendertrash* archives.

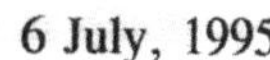

AEGIS
American Educational Gender Information Service

A 501(c)(3) Nonprofit Corporation

Ms. Dallas Denny, M.A.
Executive Director

P.O. Box 33724
Decatur, GA 30033

404-939-2128 business
404-939-0244 helpline
404-939-1770 FAX

aegis (e'jis), n. ***1.*** *in Greek mythology, a shield or breastplate used by Zeus and later, by his daughter Athena; hence,* ***2.*** *a protection.* ***3.*** *sponsorship; auspices.*

6 July, 1995

Mirha-Soleil Ross
Box 500-62
552 Church Street
Toronto, Ontario
M4Y 2E3 Canada

Dear Mirha-Soleil:

Congratulations on issue #4 of Gender Trash. I especially like the articles by Lofofora Contreras on the conditions at Pelican Bay SHU and Dancing to Eagle Spirit (formerly Sandra Laframboise). Each was very powerful in its own way.

I'm enclosing a letter I wrote to Lofofora Contreras, a copy of a recent press release, and a copy of an article I have submitted to TransSisters about the recent protest in Minnesota.

I would like to comment on Christine Tayleur's article, "Racism and Poverty."

Having had a foot in each of the two "transgender communities," I am well aware of the lack of concern shown by many affluent transexual people and crossdressers. Having been on the street myself, I am also aware of the difficult choices and dangers faced by those with nowhere to turn.

I am also aware that there are very great needs in both communities, and that much work is needed in all areas. There needs to be effort made to educate women at the Michigan Womyn's Music Festival, there needs to be outreach to the HIV-positive, and there needs to be education of caregivers so that they do not mistreat us or turn us away because of ignorance. There need to be transgendered and transexual lobbyists on Capitol Hill so we will be included in bills like the Employment Non-Discrimination Act, which will prevent us from being discriminated against in the workplace. There need to be places for us to safely come out, and places where we can go where we are shattered.

At this time, there isn't even an easy-to-find place where we can go so we can find out what the hell is going on with us. Many organizations have their own agendas, and either steer people towards or away from certain decisions about their lives. Other organizations exclude many because of high costs for membership and activities. Those organizations which provide unbiased educational materials for free, like AEGIS, are handicapped by low budgets which limit outreach efforts.

In short, there's plenty for all of us to do, and many of us are doing as much as we can in as many areas as we possibly can.

When an organization or individual is deliberately or through oversight not addressing the needs of a certain segment of the community, action is definitely indicated, and I support it. At March, at the IFGE convention in Atlanta, for example, members of the activist group Transexual Menace leafleted attendees, asking why the organization was not addressing important health concerns. More recently, the Human Rights Campaign Fund was protested for their deliberate decision to exclude transgendered and transexual people from the Employment Non-Discrimination Act. With Terry Murphy, I coordinated the Atlanta action against HRCF.

It's important to realize that helping our brothers and sisters can occur in all sorts of ways, hands-off as well as hands-on. While I certainly do my share of hands-on work, counseling transexual people on the telephone, calling and visiting friends who are depressed and suicidal, letting those who are down on their luck crash on the floor, going to the bars so I can hand out my card, participating in benefits and fundraisers, I also appreciate that even greater benefit can accrue from less direct efforts. Mounting the effort to get San Francisco's nondiscrimination act passed magnifies the efforts of those who worked on it a thousandfold, as does publishing a magazine like <u>Gender Trash</u>, which you have by now no doubt discovered for yourselves. Whether it is educating health care professionals who then go back to their home cities and treat transexual people with more respect and greater competence, educating lesbians at the Michigan Womyn's Music Festival, having a booth at Pride, as the Atlanta community recently did, writing a book, doing a radio show, or starting a support group-- all of these endeavors, and more, affect people we never see or hear, in ways we will never learn about-- but affect them it does.

The contention of Christine Tayleur that spending money or effort in any activity which does not directly address issues of discrimination, violence, homelessness, and prejudice is an extravagant waste is an unfortunate one. Christine claims that "going to Michigan each year won't do anything for our people in poverty." Well, if transexual people had been going to Michigan longer and in higher numbers, educating lesbians, then perhaps Filisa Vistima, whose mistreatment at the hands of lesbians contributed to her taking her own life (Filisa certainly lived in poverty), would still be alive today; and perhaps also, the lesbians who kidnapped and tortured a transexual in Pittsburgh would have been among the thousands who were educated by transexual people at Michigan.

I attended the second New Woman's Conference-- due to the generosity of a friend, I might add. It was my chance to come to terms with a body altered by surgery and to recharge my batteries after years of activism. There, alongside those who came only for private purposes, were Sister Mary

Elizabeth, who has been active in fighting discrimination since before there was a transgender community, and who continues today with the world's largest free HIV bulletin board; Merissa Sherrill Lynn, who started organizations which have quite literally saved hundreds of lives, and who has saved hundreds personally, with her own two hands; and Anne Ogborn, who was brave enough to wear a t-shirt through the same Tenderloin Christine writes about, proclaiming herself a sex change-- long before Christine had a Transgender Nation t-shirt to wear.

There are terrible problems facing transexual people, and the ones which affect people in sex work and people on the street are the ones most likely to be unaddressed or underaddressed. We are getting beaten and murdered, catching viruses from sharing needles and unprotected sex, being forced out of our homes and churches and away from our jobs, turned away by shelters and treatment programs, and exploited by health care practitioners. There are ideological enemies too-- those who would deny us the right to change our bodies with hormones and surgery. And nowhere in all this is there a place where people of color feel welcomed or comfortable.

Many of us, myself included and Christine included, are addressing those issues, to the detriment of our pocketbooks, our sleep time, and our health. It's unfair for Christine to tar those of us who do care with the same brush she uses for those who don't care, or to intimate that by doing any sort of outreach other than that which has her seal of approval, we are failing our brothers and sisters. The bottom line is that those who are doing nothing, those who complain but do nothing constructive, and especially those who interfere with those of us who are working, are the ones who are really letting down their brothers and sisters.

Incidentally, AEGIS is an organization for all transexual and transition people. We have addressed and will continue to address issues like HIV and silicone injections, discrimination, and murder head on. Our next public service advertisement will address the lack of people of color in many of the community's organizations.

Sincerely,

Dallas

Dallas Denny
Executive Director
American Educational Gender Information Service, Inc.

pc Lofofora Contreras
TransSisters

review Rothblatt & Castle

This seems to have been a projected review of Martine Rothblatt's *Apartheid of Sex: A Manifesto on the Freedom of Gender* and Stephanie Castle's *Feelings: A Transsexual's Explanation of a Baffling Condition*. It was never written, and it is even unclear who was slated to write it, but this Letter to the Editor from Margaret Deirdre O'Hartigan, which suggested the idea, sheds light on the kind of approach it might have taken.

Margaret Deirdre O'Hartigan
P.O. Box 82447
Portland, OR 97282 USA

July 3, 1995

GenderTrash
Gender Press
P.O. Box 500-62
552 Church St.
Toronto, Ontario
M4Y 2E3
CANADA

Letter to the Editor:

After observing Martine Rothblatt June 18 at the United States' 17th National Lesbian and Gay Health Conference in Minneapolis, I am increasingly discomfited through her co-optation of the Black African experience under the obscenity of apartheid for the title of her book.

As one of the three transsexual activists to free the "Transgender Health" symposium from the control of its non-trans organizer and moderator in order to open the panel to participation by the many segments of our community which had been excluded, I found Rothblatt extremely disrespectful of the others in speaking first and then stalking out -- particularly given the fact that every trans man and woman on the panel has contributed far more and far longer to our community than has Rothblatt.

Rothblatt's originally scheduled 30-minute presentation was shortened to 10 to accommodate additional panelists, including transsexuals of color -- none of whom have experienced the decades of white, middle-class male privilege which Rothblatt has enjoyed. While I imagine Rothblatt was rather disappointed to suddenly find less time available for her presentation than originally planned, her obvious willingness to participate in a symposium panel so racist in make-up that without our intervention it would have totally excluded participation by trans people of color makes it difficult for me to sympathize with her.

Rothblatt's obvious insensitivity to people of color is not the only issue I take with her, however. The proposed Standards of Care of her Health Law Project, re-defining transsexualism as "not in itself a medical illness or mental disorder", as well as her call for "providers of health care (including surgical) services to transsexuals...to charge reasonable fees for their services, <u>to be paid in advance</u>" (my emphasis), will remove access to sex-reassignment for all but the privileged few. As almost all government-funded health care in the United States is paid after services are provided, and a similar situation exists with employer-provided health insurance, Rothblatt's stance clearly singles out trans people for even greater discrimination than they currently experience. Minnesota's 17-year-history of publicly-funding sex-reassignment, for example, would have been impossible were Rothblatt's standards in effect at the time.

The danger which Rothblatt obviously poses to the impoverished, disenfranchised and downtrodden is not to be over-estimated -- and the divisiveness which threatens our community rests not upon those of us who object to her tactics and goals but with herself.

Sincerely,

Margaret Deirdre O'Hartigan

Margaret Deirdre O'Hartigan

review Walking the Dead

This review was written under the pseudonym "Anne Archie" by regular *Gendertrash* contributor and researcher kiwi.

Review: Walking the Dead

Written by Keith Curran. Performed at the Canadian Stage Company, Toronto, May 19 - June 10.

~~by kiwi~~

Reviewed by Anna Archie

The promotional material for this play proclaims that this is a theatre piece about "fags, dykes, and tranies." Well, the fact that the word "trannie" is misspelled in the publicity indicates just how much work the company has yet to do, to really *get* transgender issues.

The play ostensibly centres around Veronica/Homer, a female-to-male transsexual involved with a genetic woman named Maya. Secondary characters include a gay male neighbour and his new love interest, Homer's mother, and a rather annoying film director who plans to document Homer's transition.

The character Maya is one of the best developed. She struggles with her own identity as a lesbian, who is romantically involved with a female-to-male transsexual - a man! At one point, she tells Homer that going through a transition may be difficult for him, but at least he knows who he is, and is making decisions to live as such. To be involved with someone going through a transition, Maya points out, puts her own identity as a lesbian into question. This theme is explored in depth throughout the play, with a great deal of thoughtfulness, insight, and reflection.

The gay male next-door neighbour is a rather comic character. He's totally insecure, and always searching for love. And he supports Homer 100% throughout his transition. He gets involved with an obnoxious, bitter old queen who hates everything and everyone in the world, and who understands little about Homer's particular situation.

Homer's mother is one of the best aspects of the play. She refers to Homer as Veronica throughout. The writers exploit her insipid racism as well, with constant references to "the darkies" and the fact that she herself has chosen to be remarried to "a little Mexican." In the context of the play, her remarks are humourous, rather than offensive. Indeed, the writers demonstrate that just as the mother does not quite fully understand Homer's gender, nor does she really appreciate the racially and ethically diverse society in which we live.

These supporting characters create a supportive, if somewhat comic, network around Homer. Ironically, however, Homer's character is the least developed. We follow him through srs, for instance, yet there is no mention of any complications which resulted from the surgery. As if phalloplasty is a perfected technique! Likewise, Homer yells at the director of the gender identity clinic during their very first meeting. While it's true that many of us may despise our shrinks, not all of us choose to interact with anger and aggression from the very start. This section of the play revealed its weaknesses, in my opinion.

*ask Kiwi for ~~self~~ descr. Bio for A-archie.

There was very little understanding of the control psychiatry has over our lives, and therefore of how we conduct ourselves in the clinical setting.

When Homer attends his mother's second wedding, he puts on a wig, heels, and a green taffeta dress (thereby looking like a drag queen). Upon his return home, Homer is stalked by two men, who plan to rape him. Upon discovery that he is a man, they assault him, cut off his penis, and kill him.

This incident left me quite perplexed. Now, I understand the compromises we all make around the self-presentation of gender within our family settings. But it just didn't seem realistic to me that after living as a man for years, Homer would simply don a dress and show up to his mother's wedding ceremony. Again, Homer's feelings were not explored.

The play concludes with a community of people - Maya, the gay neighbour, his boyfriend - united to both mourn for Homer, and to work for social change. They get involved in an activist group, Queer Anger, which focuses on issues of violence and discrimination against queers.

This group, Queer Anger, serves as a nice, tidy resolution to all the ugliness and hurt in the play's narrative. At the same time, it offers a too-easy coalition between transgendered people and lesbians and gay men. There is virutally no discussion of how transgendered people are excluded from lesbian and gay communities. Likewise, the writers don't address how activist groups like Queer Nation (the obvious model for this Queer Anger thing) often were incapable of responding to violence against women and people of colour, let alone transgendered people. As such, Walking the Dead offers a distorted, revisionist history of Queer Nation: a collective entity where trannies, lesbians, gays, bisexuals, young, old, and everyone who was somehow *different* got together, got along, and got things done.

Well, I'm sorry, but it didn't quite happen that way. At least not in San Francisco, New York, Toronto, Los Angeles, or Montréal. In case the writers of the play have forgotten, Homer wasn't the only one that died. The utopian ideal of Queer Nation is also a thing of the past.

human rights article

This was an interview conducted by *Gendertrash* editor Xanthra Phillippa MacKay with "DR," an official at the Canadian Human Rights Commission. The initials DR, according to Mirha-Soleil Ross, likely stand for an official job title, not a personal name. The piece has been provisionally laid out for publication. Mirha-Soleil Ross also notes that this "was a piece Xanthra was very proud of."

XP: The other thing is I wanted to split it into three sections. The first one was a history and background of how the Canadian Human Rights Commision (CHRC) got involved with transgendered issues and how that occurred. The next part would be who's covered, who isn't covered. The third part is making a claim. Does that sound okay?

DR: Sounds reasonable to me. I'll do the best I can to answer them. When it comes to the history, there may be a few holes here and there. If you find that's the case, I'll try my best to fill them later. So why don't we get started?

XP: Okay. You remember you were telling me about the history? If you wouldn't mind go back over that?

DR: Sure, not at all. Well I'm not going to back too far but I mean obviously the Canadian Human Rights Act (CHRA) itself was put in place in 1977 and then our Commission was created in 1978. And there were a prohibited grounds of discrimination listed in the legislation. I won't go through them all because there's 10 plus an eleventh that the courts added - that being sexual orientation.

Of course one of those is: sex. For the purposes of the transsexual and transgendered community, that's the one that's probably the most relevant. Over the years we haven't received what I would call a large numbers of complaints from people in the transsexual or transgendered community- I'm not sure for whatever reason. But I did a check last week and apparently the number of complaints we have, could be numbered on the fingers of one hand. We've had five or less - in that ballpark.

About three years ago, four ago, there were some discussions about the most efficient and I guess the most appropriate way to take a complaint from your community. And it was decided that sex was the most appropriate ground and that a policy was developed in that area. And it's since then that's been the course that we've decided to follow is that when a complaint is recieved, it's taken on the ground of sex and from then on, treated like any other complaint, basically. That is the investigators look into the matter to determine whether or not discrimination has taken place and then decide the best way to proceed.

XP: Can I ask what sparked that, the need for the change? Because a lot of people aren't aware of the transgendered communities - we're not extremely well-known.

DR: .What sort of prompted all this? Well, having not been a the Commission at the time, it's a little difficult for me to be certain. But I know that some discussions were initiated twofold:

One, as a result of some complaints - I understand that there were a number; one of those five or so that I mentioned. Taken from people. So it was decided that the Commission needed to look at an effective way of dealing with the complaints.

And then secondly there was a discussions with a member of an advocacy group, by the name of Laura Masters and she wrote a lot of letters to the Commission and dealt with someone in our Policy branch, so I think it was a twofold reason behind it. At least that's my sense.

XP: One thing I just wanted to make clear: this is official CHRC policy?

DR: Yes that's right.

XP: 'Cause that was one thing that I just wanted to clear up, just make it clear for the readers that this is official; this isn't...

DR: That's right. I mean I think if you go looking for a document that says "this is how we deal with the transsexual or transgendered community," you won't find it. However what was decided, I mean there were discussions that went on for some time actually and if you were to ask our Director of Policy and ask the investigators and so on, that's the ground on which these types of complaints are being dealt with. It is official.

XP: That covers what I had in the "History and Background", so I'd like to move on to sort of like "Who's covered/Who isn't and What areas are covered and What isn't covered. As far as the coverage - I just had a few areas. Obviously as we were talking before, it's federally mandated businesses or institutions that are affected by the Canadian Human Rights Act?

DR: That's correct. So falling under that would be things like federal government departments, federal agencies like ours - for example we fall under our own act. It would also include Crown corporations like Canada Post and Atomic Energy of Canada for example. It includes federally regulated businesses like trucking companies; uranium mines I believe come under it; the nuclear industry; bus companies that cross provincial borders; broadcasting, telecommunications, radio and television stations.

XP: In addition things like banking?

DR: Yes, exactly. Banking's another one.

XP: Via Rail?

DR: Right. I mean if it comes under the federal jurisdiction, then it falls under the authority of our act.

XP: That's an area that I wanted to go into. There are several programs that are funded in part either directly or indirectly from a federal source, for example Health and Welfare and daycares?

DR: As far as Health and Welfare goes, the federal Health and Welfare department and their programs that would be us. If you were talking about hospitals, that would be the provincial jurisdiction, because the hospitals fall under the authority of the provinces and therefore it would be their provincial human rights commissions as well.

XP: So even if they're getting pertly funded by the federal people, it depends on the legislation?

DR: That's right. Actually that happens a lot in education as well. For example universities come under the authority of the provinces; however they do receive quite a bit of federal funding. But for the purposes of human rights, they would come under the provincial jurisdiction.

XP: So it's not a case of who gets funded or how it gets funded, it's a case of looking the legislation?

DR: Yeah and who has the authority for looking after it.

XP: That's really important. Some areas that are really important to transgendered people are the birth certificate registration - would that fall under provincial or federal legislation?

DR: I'm just thinking for a moment. That's an excellent question. My instinctive reaction is to say it's federal, however I'm not certain; I'm going to have to check that to make sure that I'm correct.

XP: Then again the same question comes for passport and the SIN number.

DR: Those would be federal.

XP: Okay this is the question then: for those passport and SIN number, to change one's gender on either one of those, at the moment they require that you've had the surgery and etc, etc, etc - you prove it that way. Could that not be seen in terms of the other stuff as being discriminatory against those who are transgenderist, who are transsexual but non-operative or who can't afford the surgery, but who still identify as the opposite gender?

DR: I understand. To be honest, it's almost impossible to say, just because each case is different for the purposes of the law; each case is different. You'd almost need a test case to find out whether or not that was so. I suspect that if someone in your community - transsexual/transgendered community - chose to file a complaint, they might have the basis - certainly it would be looked into. As to what the outcome would be; it's always hard to say.

XP: That is something I wanted to talk about later on. ?

DR: My first reaction is that I'm sure that somebody would look into it and very likely the possibility that there would be grounds for a complaint. However, as I said, not being an investigator, not knowing all the facts of each individual's case, it's really impossible to say. It's like asking you know about a traffic violation almost - I mean I'm not trying to trivialize your situation, I'm just saying since each incident is different, it's always impossible to say what the outcome would be.

XP: That's sort of it and I expected something like that and of course even if you were an investigator, there's no way you could pre-judge a case and say "oh yeah it will take this long" or "this would be the outcome."

DR: An investigator would probably be in a better position than me to determine whether or not there was grounds to go ahead. I mean, based on what I have seen over the years, I would say that the complaint probably would be taken and it would be investigated. But as I said a moment ago, the outcome, who's to say.

XP: I think that sort of my questions about coverage - Who's covered/who isn't covered/ what's covered/what isn't covered - ?

DR: Yeah I mean it can be a little confusing certainly, because there's so many overlapping juridictions - I mean when you start throwing in the federal, provincial, then start thinking of things like university harassment codes, I believe a few municipalities have their own employment equity, you know there's so many overlapping jurisdictions it can be a little confusing. But the thing to keep in mind and I think your readers might find interesting as well, is that the vast majority of areas that they can think of where they might be discriminated against - and this is not just the transsexual community, it's everyone - fall under provincial jurisdiction. For example if you go into a store and you get tossed out; that's provincial because most retail stores come under the provincial human rights codes. Schools, hospitals, universities, again that's all provincial. Most private-sector companies, provincial again. We're a much more limited organization in that we deal only with the federal sphere.

XP: I think this is something that our readers - one of the biggest things that we have found is that the people in the transgendered communities really don't have any idea of the impact on them or any effect on their lives. Quite frankly they feel excluded from a lot of this stuff.

DR: Well I think it's probably important to mention that people in the transsexual community have the same rights that any other Canadian has and they have the right to be free from discrimination based on their sex, in this case, as well as all the others. And if there are refused goods or services from the federal government - or the provincial if it goes to the provincial commission - they have the recourse to file a complaint with their human rights commission. If they're fired from from their jobs, again they don't have to sit back and take it, I mean they can grieve it and there is a recourse in the form of the various provincial human rights commissions that will look into their case and decide whether or not they've been discriminated against. Again like anyone else who files a complaint it doesn't mean that the commissions or the tribunals will necessarily always rule in their favour. But it means that they do have a place to go and their rights are just as secure as everyone else's.

XP: That's one of the aspects I wanted to get into. A lot of transgendered people see them in the sense as much more long term and therefore have no effect on their immediate short-term.

DR: In terms of the complaints you mean?

XP: Yeah Like for example say I was thrown out of a store, by the time I went and did the complaint and the complaint was judged and everything was gone through?

DR: It could be years.

XP: It could be years. The problem is that a lot of us have more of us have - especially those of us with AIDS. Now I don't know if you've got a - do you have the fast-track thing for people with AIDS?

DR: Well, the complaints are dealt with very quickly. Yes and that's a policy that we've put in place a couple of years ago now as a matter of fact. And by the way, for people with AIDS, AIDS is considered - if someone discriminates against you because you have AIDS, in fact that comes under the grounds of disability. So in fact a complaint can be filed there. To address the point about the length of time involved: well certainly that's true. I mean I guess I would respond in two ways: I'd say first of all that unfortunately the time delay is not something that is directed particularly at the transsexual or transgendered community; it's simply because in the case of our federal commission we receive about 1500 complaints a year and each one has to be thoroughly investigated and dealt with and something that takes time. However, having said that we've had some success as have our provincial counterparts I believe at least in most provinces, in reducing the amount of time that it takes to deal with a complaint. At one time the average time frame would have been about 18 months, 24 months before a complaint was dealt with and that was average. That's since been reduced to about a year. So we have seen some improvements in that area.

XP: Sorry to interrupt, when you say the complaints are dealt with - does that mean the complete process or is that just the initial part?

DR: No that's the complete process on average. Some of course will continue to take longer. If for example a case winds up and not many do, but if it winds up going all the way to the Supreme Court of Canada, that's not going to be done within a year; that's takes on average about 5 or 6 years to happen.

XP: That's more like say, a test case?

DR: Yeah. But many of the complaints that we get now, in fact don't even go to a tribunal any more. For example if someone's discriminated against, what we always try to encourage is, we'll bring the two parties together - the person who has been discriminated against and the employer or whatever - and try to find a way to bring the parties together so that they can find some kind of solution without ever stepping foot in a courtroom. And we've had some measure of success doing that, so that's also included in our statistics as having dealt with the complaint as long as both parties walk away happy.

XP: That's good to know.

DR: We don't always want to put peeople through court. In fact only a very small percentage of our cases actually go to a tribunal; I would estimate it's actually 5% or less. We try to deal with it as quickly and effectively as possible in other ways. As to people having better things to do, I'm not sure quite how you phrased it, but they had to get on with their lives. Of course that is also true. I guess the only thing that I would say to those people is that if they feel that they've been honestly aggrieved, that they've been discriminated against, then they may wish to pursue it, just on the matter of priciple. I mean, you're right, when someone's pitched out of the Bay at the Yorkdale Mall in Toronto, it's not going to help them a lot to call their human rights commission 'cause nobody's going to show up to allow them back in that afternoon. But what it does mean is if the commission does find that if they were discriminated against, then it means that they can go back there later and know they're not going to be thrown out or more importantly the mall knows that that's not acceptable behaviour. So there's some measure of progress made. And quite frankly that's how all of our human rights advances have come about; in these slow steps. It's discouraging though when you're the person involved and your complaint is going on for years and years and years.

XP: I mean sure you have had to deal with this - they want justice to be done and fast and quick and unfortunately that's just not the way it happens.

DR: That's true. And sometimes it might not always go the way you want to either. It's the same at our tribunals and it's the same at the provincial - they're like court cases; they're *quasi-judicial*, which means there are lawyers involved and it means you know most of the same rules of any other court will apply, so you might not always win. At least not on paper, but it doesn't mean the case has been a failure by any means.

XP: One of the things as you point out they're quasi-legal like courts. Does that mean that you can get your own advocate to come in with you?

DR: Sure. You don't have to though. Part of the way the commissions have been set up so that they're accessible to everyone. And if the commission decides that your case has some merit, and in fact should go right to the tribunal level, the commission will provide the lawyer to argue the case. You are of course at liberty of case to hire your own lawyer if you want but you don't have to.

XP: I think the most important thing is that a lot of transgendered people just do not understand at all, they just see it as something, but they don't understand how it works, so it's just a case of giving them the information so they know how it works.

DR: Before I let you go, I'll get your address again. I'll send off a packet of information. One of which is a brochure called **Filing a Complaint** and it tells sort of the steps on how things are dealt with and through a lot of the bureaucracy

XP: Well I guess we're sort of on "Complaints"?

DR: Well I can give you in a nutshell how the process works - I'll send you the brochure as well - but basically what happens when someone calls the commission and they feel they've been discriminated against. The first step of course is someone takes the particulars, the details, the person's name and the circumstances. Then an investigator is assigned to the case. They'll talk to the person to get the full details of the alleged discrimination. Then they'll talk to the other side, of course, to find out what their view on it is. After all the facts are gathered, the investigator then makes a recommendation on how the complaint should be dealt with. She or he may decide that the best way is to bring the two parties together; you know they can talk it out and a solution is reached - and of course if possible that's the first choice. They may decide that they need even more investigation, so they'll go back and get more facts and then make a decision later. Or they may pass that information up to the seven people who sit at the top of our organization - the commissioners at the Canadian Human Rights Commission, the head right now being Mr. Max Yalden. Once a month those people meet and they look at all the various cases that have reached this point and they decide how they should be dealt with. They may decide that the complaint doesn't look it has any basis and dismiss it; they may do like the investigator did and decide that they need more information before they can make a decision, in which they'll request the investigators do that. Or they may decide that there seems to be evidence to suggest that there was discrimination and it should be dealt with by a human right rights tribunal and they'll send the case to the tribunal.

Once that happens it's virtually out of the commissions's hands, because the Human Rights Tribunal is a separate organization from our commission; they're two different bodies. The Human Rights Tribunal does all the work in organizing the hearings, setting the location, making sure everybody's in place and so on. The commission sends a lawyer to argue on behalf of the person who filed the complaint. The respondent or the person who the complaint is against, has the option of also having a legal counsel and then there's a legal hearing like a court hearing and a decision is reached. Once that decision is reached then either pary, either the complainant or the person who the complaint is against, has the option of appealing the decision. And we don't have too many of those, but they can in fact be appealed right up to the Supreme Court of Canada. And we've had a few go that far.

XP: Yes I know. I'm aware of them in other areas. ?

DR: Not many, but as you've said when theydeal with a very important social issue and they're new in some way, then yeah they will go that far.

XP: Yeah test cases. There was just one other thing - is lack of financial assets - is that considered - when you're discriminated on that kind of a basis, like for example someone who has $100,000 can easily afford an SRS, etc,etc and the other things, whereas other people who are say on - I'm talking about who's transsexual - someone who's transsexual but on welfare cannot afford an SRS?

DR: Sorry I don't know what an SRS is .

XP: Oh that's the actual operation - that's the quote *sex change* - it actually stands for **S**ex **R**eassignment **S**urgery. In Canada it costs about $7000, but if you're on social assistance, $7000 is a lot of money?

DR: I thought OHIP covered it?

XP: I don't think you deal with OHIP.

DR: No not at all. I'm just curious

XP: OHIP sort of does. They reimburse. They have it right in the front of their guidelines - they will reimburse anyone who the Gender Identity Clinic at the Clarke approves, they will reimburse. And the Clarke has an arrangement with a doctor in Britain. Like so in other words you have to come up with the money initially anyways and then OHIP will reimburse you. As far as I know that's the only procedure that's done like that and it's specifically for transsexuals and that's something else. But I assume that health insurance or health coverage is a provincial matter.?

DR: That's correct. Getting back to your original question about financial, there really isn't a ground under our act to cover that one. I mean a lot of provincial jurisdictions have that you can't discriminate against someone because they're on social assistance. To be sure I'm not sure if Ontario's one of them or not - I'd have to look it up. But there are a few, but there's nothing really quite that in our legislation; we have the pretty much standard 10 grounds plus sexual orientation.

XP: So does this mean that if someone came to the Canadian Human Rights Commission, say it was something that was covered federally, like for example the SIN number. For someone who has the money it's much easier to get an SRS, to get the surgery and therefore they're not going to have a problem - once they have the surgery, Employment Canada will switch the gender on the SIN card. But for someone who's on social assistance it's very diff-, almost impossible to get that money, so that it's impossible to get that gender changed on the SIN card?

DR: So it's the domino effect - one thing leads to another. That's a hard one to call. I now that we haven't had a case like that before. Again I know that it wouldn't fall under a specific ground, however one could file a complaint based on sex as we discussed at the outset and? Obviously the transsexual/transgendered community's been around for a long time but from a legal point of view and particularly when it comes to human rights, this is a relatively new area. Relatively unexplored at least, so we'd almost have to see where it goes; it'd be interesting to see but at this point I'm not sure.

XP: That exhausts all my questions - is there anything that you'd like to add?

DR: Well only that I don't know well or much you've interacted with Laura Masters in the past, but I've become somewhat familiar at least with the issues when she's called me over the years and that I guess I would say is that the human rights mechanisms at the federal and provincial levels are in place and they were designed to protect people's rights and to make sure or least as much as possible ensure that all Canadians have equality of access and opportunity in our society, so that if someone does feel that they're being discriminated against, then by all means they should avail themselves of the commission and hopefully they will find some redress if they've been wronged.

XP: ?

DR: .

Health confer. press release & pamphlet

More than one version of this press release exists, but the edits in pen mark this as the most revised version. The associated pamphlet exists in only one copy. The original is shocking electric pink.

(June 18, 1995, Minneapolis, Minnesota) --

FOR IMMEDIATE RELEASE

TRANSSEXUALS STAGE NON VIOLENT COUP D'ETAT AT SYMPOSIUM ON TRANSGENDER HEALTH AT

17TH NATIONAL LESBIAN AND GAY HEALTH CONFERENCE

Frustrated by six weeks of fruitless negotiations with the non-transgendered white male moderator of a symposium on transgender health, three transsexual activists DISRUPTED THE AGENDA AND CAUSED Dr. Walter Bockting, coordinator of the University of Minnesota Program in Human Sexuality, TO STEP DOWN as moderator shortly after the symposium began at 6:30 p.m. Sunday, June 18, at the Hyatt Regency Minneapolis.

After first distributing briefing packets explaining the action, the three activists -- Christine Tayleur of Transgender Nation, San Francisco and Rachel Koteles and Margaret Deirdre O'Hartigan of Portland, Oregon -- strode to the symposium stage as Bockting began introductory comments. Seating herself in the chair Bockting had just vacated in order to speak from the podium, O'Hartigan interrupted the proceedings to denounce the fact panel participation had been completely determined by Bockting, head of a surgery program which has received extensive criticism by transsexuals for nearly two decades, and cited the existing panel's omission of transsexuals/ transgendered people of color as well as the exclusion of trans youth, trans elders, disabled transsexuals and trans people living in poverty.

As conference security guards moved towards the dais, Koteles and Tayleur shouted "Remember Stonewall", and O'Hartigan appealed to the approximately 150 gay, lesbian and bisexual health professionals present to support the addition to the panel of all trans people who chose to participate.

As transsexuals and transgenders left their seats in the auditorium to approach the dais, the audience broke into applause -- and Tayleur began adding chairs to the raised platform to seat the additional panelists. Seated were Kiki Whitlock of San Francisco's Asian AIDS Project, Jamaican-born ~~Migel~~ Mecole Little of Action AIDS Philadelphia and Rebecca Durkee, director of Boston's Gender Identity Support Services for Transgenders.

Tayleur and O'Hartigan replaced Bockting as moderators of the suddenly revamped symposium, which saw Martine Rothblatt and Dallas Denny, two of the three original panelists, shorten their presentations from 30 minutes to 10. The sole exception to the 10 minute limitation was Armand Hotimsky, a transsexual health care activist of Paris, France, who retained the 30 minutes originally allotted him in recognition of the fact he was the sole female-to-male transsexual on the panel.

Also retained was the originally scheduled 30-minute period for questions from the audience at the conclusion of presentations by Rothblatt, Denny, Hotimsky, Little, Whitlock, Tayleur and Koteles.

At the conclusion of the two-hour symposium, O'Hartigan thanked Bockting, Rothblatt and Denny for acceding to the activists' ~~call~~ demand for inclusion.

"The reception to our protest by those health care professionals in attendance was gratifying," Koteles stated in an interview. "It leads us to hope similar action will not be necessary at next year's conference in Seattle -- but that presumes conference organizers will recognize that responsibility for formulating and articulating trans people's health needs rests primarily with ourselves and is not the prerogative of non-trans people.

"The depth of knowledge and experience of the trans professionals added at such short notice, and their expertise, illustrated the contributions to be made by segments of our community if they are only given the opportunity," Koteles continued. "Just as other queers have empowered themselves by demanding to define their own health needs, it is time trans people be acknowledged as the experts in their own health care."

Commented Christine Tayleur: **"Trans people have a large enough community, we have reached a critical mass where ~~and~~ there are enough health/GAPP professionals in our community now, to enable us to take charge of defining our own health care issues."**

- 30 --

For further information contact: [redacted]

Christine TAYLEUR
Transgender Nation
SF CA

encl.: protest flyer from action

Rachel KOTELES

Margaret Deirdre O'HARTIGAN
P.O. Box 82447
Portland, OR 97282

SILENCE = DEATH

A death warrant for Minnesota's transsexuals was signed last month with passage of legislation abolishing state-funded sex-reassignment services -- and Walter Bockting and his University of Minnesota Transgender Services program were shamefully silent.

But such silence is nothing new -- in the 1970s the University program sat on the sidelines as two transsexuals sued for the right to receive adequate health care -- just as it remained silent while transsexuals fought in 1978 and 1994 to defend those victories.

A different sort of silence is being perpetrated today -- the silence of censorship.

The "Transgender Health" symposium panel is NOT comprised of representatives of our community, despite claims that it is. Transsexuals are not just white, middle-age and middle-class. We are disabled. We are young. We are old. We are people of color and people living in poverty.

Where on the panel are transsexuals of color? Where are our youth? Where are our elders? Where are veterans of the decades-long struggle to advance the rights of our people, who can speak from hard-won experience? Why are female-to-males outnumbered two to one?

Where are the representatives of our community on the panel?

They are excluded from the panel purporting to address our health needs, shut out by Walter Bockting, who avoided speaking out as our health care funding was demolished, only to usurp the legitimate voices of the transsexual community today.

The majority of transsexuals are excluded for the very same reasons they are always ignored: they are not college graduates and career-oriented professionals. They are rejected for not having decades of white, male professional privilege to legitimize them.

They are silenced because they are runaways -- or throw-aways. They are blue- and pink-collar workers. They are whores, exposing themselves to AIDS in a desperate gamble to earn the money for surgery before getting sick. They are living on the streets. They are drinking and drugging themselves in a futile attempt to alleviate their pain.

We are living in war time. Our health care repealed, we can not -- we must not -- tolerate "business as usual." The same university program which denied impoverished transsexuals health care until forced to relent by court order must not be allowed to continue its shameful history of abuse and neglect by deciding who should be heard from and who should be silenced.

Help us open the panel so we can speak for ourselves!

STOP THE SILENCE!

Interview w Wendy Rose

This interview with "Church-Wellesley superstar Wendy Rose" was provisionally laid out, and several printed versions survive. The one reproduced here includes some edits in pen to the original transcript made at Wendy Rose's request, which mark it as the most revised version.

Wendy Rose is a transsexual performer, singer, songwriter, and guitar-player who is most well-known for her street corner performances in the gay village in Toronto. She has been hanging around there for over a year now, singing on the street as well as at local clubs, parties, and other events. She has written a lot of original material and hopes to create and produce an album of her songs later this year. ~~A documentary about her music and her lifestyle is in the works as well~~. She feels the sky is the limit as far as opportunities are concerned, and where they do not exist, she will make them.

M-S: Where are you from?

WR: Good question. I grew up in an Armed forces family. I lived all over the country. I'm not really from anywhere. Two years here, two years there. I lived in Winnipeg, Vancouver, Victoria, Ottawa, Toronto, and Halifax. My ethnic background is French, Scottish, Irish, English and Micmac, Canadian Indian: a typical Canadian mix.

M-S: Are you still in contact with your family?

WR: Yes I am. I'm pretty much on good terms with all my family.

M-S: How many children are in your family?

WR: Four.

M-S: Are you the only musician?

WR: ~~Yes, I would say so~~. MY SISTER PLAYS PIANO AS WELL.

~~**M-S:** Are there any other artists?~~

~~**WR:** No, I guess I'm pretty much the only artist of the family.~~

M-S: When did you move to Toronto?

WR: Two years ago now.

M-S: Why did you decide to move here?

WR: Well, I started playing on the street in Halifax because I had lost my job and I couldn't find another one. I have been playing guitar for twenty years, but I was too shy before to play in public. So I started playing on the street because I needed money really bad. I did fairly well. A friend of mine was coming down to Toronto and he paid my bus ~~fair~~ FARE down. He said that I probably would do a lot better in Toronto. So I came down and started playing on the street here.

M-S: Is it indiscreet to ask how old you are? [Both laugh]

WR: Not a good question. Twenty-nine on a good day; nineteen on a really good day. [Both laugh]

M-S: You started playing guitar right away when you arrived here?

WR: Yes 'cause I had no job. I applied for welfare and got a cheque, but then they cut me off right away. So I played guitar. It was a real struggle when I first came here. I was starving. I lost my room and was homeless for a while. The first year was really a big struggle, but the past year has been great. I was playing as a guy when I came. I was living half and half. I was confused about my gender so I was playing as a guy, but I was dressing up as a female in my off time.

M-S: Have you always played in the gay village?

WR: I tried the gay village to play 'cause I was gay, but I couldn't make any money there. So I went to play in the straight parts, along Yonge Street and along Bloor. I had a lot of trouble because people knew that I was gay; I looked gay. I had that appearance, so I used to get teased a lot.

M-S: It wasn't working even in the gay village, as a guy?

WR: No it wasn't working as a guy at all.

M-S: I know many transsexual women (and that includes myself) who were very unpopular as boys in the gay community.

WR: I was never very comfortable as a guy.

M-S: So you think it's a matter of being comfortable with oneself, ie: if you like yourself, others will too?

WR: Yes I think that it's a question of perception.

M-S: Is it also what accounts for the fact that you are more popular as a woman in the gay community then when you were living as a gay guy?

WR: Well, I'm comfortable being that way and expressing myself that way. I just wasn't comfortable trying to do it as a male. Just wasn't comfortable at all. So I had to make the switch, I guess. Actually I made the switch to being a full-time female about a year and a half ago, because the Clarke was prodding me to work as a female. The only job I really had was playing guitar, so I started playing guitar as a female. I told them that I was going to do that.

M-S: And they were fine with that?

WR: Yup! They said: " If you can make a living, do it!"

M-S: Do you think that your being more successful as a woman in the gay community has something to do with the absence of sexual tension between you and gay guys?

WR: Yeah it is, I guess, because they're not attracted to transsexuals. But there's a big mix of different people who like me for different reasons. The gay guys like me because they find me campy and outrageous. They like that kind of thing. I'm kind of wild and a bit like a drag queen and gay guys really go for that. I also have a lot of lesbian fans. They like me because of the fact that I'm female, singing my own original songs and expressing my feelings. I think they like me for that reason. And straight people find me really bizarre.

M-S: So being a transsexual has really played in your favour?

WR: Yes it has. And in a big way too. I wanted to succeed as a singer/songwriter and I couldn't as a guy. But when I made the switch, it started working well.

M-S: You just pointed out that gay guys like you because you're a little bit of a Drag Queen. So how do you think they perceive you, as a transsexual or a Drag Queen?

WR: I think most people perceive me as a transsexual. They perceive me as being an original transsexual kind of performer. That's different, and they like that idea.

M-S: How do you handle being a transsexual who "is a little bit of a Drag Queen"? For many transsexuals, that would be too much to deal with. Don't you find it confusing?

WR: No I don't. I'm definitely a transsexual. I don't fit with the Drag Queens at all. I tried to be in Drag shows and all that. Drag queens are basically guys who live as guys during the day and dress up as women for the showcase at night. And It's mainly a lip-sync thing. It's a campy, performing glamourous kind of thing. It's all show business. For me, there's a whole lifestyle involved. I'm singing my own original songs; I sing live with my own voice, with my guitar. I'm expressing a lifestyle, so it's completely different from the drag thing. I just want to point out that as far as being an entertainer, I use a lot of Drag Queen things in my shows. That is allowed. As an entertainer, I can borrow things from anywhere and incorporate them into what I do. I feel comfortable doing that. I've been known to wear wigs now and again, and some pretty wild make up and looks that Drag Queens use. I feel like I have to reinvent myself to be different, in order to be interesting on the street all the time. I can't come out looking the same, people will get bored and I would make less money. So I have to keep on reinventing myself.

M-S: What kind of music do you play?

WR: I try to play mostly all my own songs that I wrote. If I'm not playing my own songs, I'm playing songs from old Broadway musicals. But I play electric guitar so I've really souped them up a lot.

~~M-S: Do you always play solo?~~

~~WR: Well I was playing with my friend, Kenny. We had a show called: "The Kenny and Dolly Show." And we've just disbanded a few days ago. It wasn't working for me in particular. Basically Kenny sings country rock and I'm more rock, pop style. We were trying to mesh the two styles, and it wasn't working. We tried to do the street thing to see if we could make a few bucks and instead of getting better, it was losing popularity, so we had to drop it.~~

M-S: Here's something that a lot of people probably want to know: do you make money?

WR: Yes I make a lot of money. It pays the rent. Lots of people ask me that on the street: "How are you doing there? You know, are you making good money?" I have to admit: "yeah, it's getting better all the time." I play on the street, at clubs, bars, and parties. I do all kinds of things. Anything lucrative that comes along, I'll try, like art show openings. Some artists put on shows and they want live entertainment for the first day.

M-S: Sometimes it's hard when you're a street entertainer to interact with people. It can get rough and tough. Do you ever get into trouble?

WR: I'm very good with people of all descriptions. And I know all the street people. I'm the street social worker. I've seen all kinds of crazy things happen, and life goes on. I'm very comfortable with playing on the street, in fact, I enjoy it. I enjoy it because it's real life. You're really in real life, and people tell you right away what they think about you whether they like you or not. Their feelings come out right away. It's not like when you're in a club and you're on the stage, you have a built-in acceptance factor. But on the street, they tell you right away or you know immediately if you're not singing in the right key or your guitar's out of tune or you're not looking great that day. [big laughter from both] They let you know. I mean, you can't be too sensitive about all this.

M-S: How do you handle it when somebody, for example, throws a tomato at you ?

WR: I have a sense of humour. I don't let it get to me. If I have a bad hair day, I make a joke about it. Life's too short to be serious.

M-S: Do you need a permit to play on the street? Have you ever gotten into trouble with the police?

WR: No, you don't need a permit, but I've had some problems with the police lately, with making too much noise. Anybody who doesn't like me, it seems, can phone in and complain. Even the police agree with this. It's not so much that I'm making noise. It's the fact that if someone doesn't like me, they can phone the cops and the cops pretty much have to make me move. So it's just a nuisance. They're going to make me move ~~off~~ up or down the street here or that way or whatever.

M-S: Does it happen a lot?

WR: . It did for a period of time. These things kind of happen in a bunch but I haven't had problems lately at all.

M-S: Have you ever received a ticket?

WR: They threatened me with a fine one day so I had to go home. See, it's a matter of what kind of cops approach you too. They're anywhere from good to bad. And one day I got a couple of really bad ones. They gave me a shake down and ran my name in the computer and all this routine. He said that if he came down one more time and saw me, he would give me a fine. So rather than taking a chance, I just went home and waited until the next day.

M-S: How do you find the city here? A lot of people who come from elsewhere, including myself, find this city and the people who live here very cold.

WR: I myself like it very much here. Much more than

Halifax 'cause I find Halifax very conservative. And the gay scene there is very much in the closet. It's a whole different scene from here. I couldn't really get away with doing what I'm doing here over in Halifax. Little places like Halifax are still fighting the battles for acceptance for gay people. It's not the same as here, so I'm glad to be in Toronto.

M-S: What are your immediate and long term projects?

WR: Okay, well right now I'm just taking it easy because summer's here and I'm just playing on the street. That's what I like to do most of the time. I have a resumé, and I try to get club work, but right now I'm kind of laid back. I'm just taking what comes along.

M-S: Do you play in straight clubs?

WR: A friend of mine approached me a couple of weeks ago and asked me to play in a straight bar on Queen Street as her opening act. So I agreed. She's a transsexual performer and a guitar player too. I went there and dressed myself up looking like a classical guitar player, looking like I was going to play in an orchestra. It was hysteria. I looked like Fiona Boyd. I had this long, black evening gown on. I went up and performed rock with my electric guitar and everything.

M-S: Did it go well?

WR: Oh very well.

M-S: Was it the first time you played in a straight environment?

WR: The third time. I played at the Cameron House and the Winchester Hotel. They're both basically straight. It's a different kind of atmosphere, totally different from playing in gay bars. And I enjoy playing for straight people. Actually I find them not quite as demanding as gay people as far as showbiz and all that. I feel more relaxed. I can just kind of get laid-back and play. Any fine jobs like that that come along, I'll take 'cause I keep on looking for new challenges.

M-S: Like doing an album?

WR: Yes, I want to do an album. Of course it's finances that are always the problem. It's expensive to make an album. So I'm going to make a mini-cassette with five or six original songs on it later in the year. I'm looking for a grant. I've got a lot of money saved up. I'm going to do it myself, but I'm going to try to get a grant If I can't got a grant, then I'm going to go make it myself. I'm also going to market it myself. I'm hoping to get something out for Christmas.

M-S: Are you going to sing "Silent Night"? [both laugh]

WR: No, I'm going to sing up-tempo dance-type numbers that people know me for on the street. I actually have people coming to me and asking to sing original songs that they've heard and that they like. It really pleases me a lot when people come up and ask me to sing my own songs that they've heard. So I'm going to include some of them on the album.

M-S: People are really getting familiar with your songs?

WR: Yes, some people are. There's a fellow who wants to do a documentary about me. And we've talked seriously about this. He's going to shoot some footage and apply for a grant too. We're hoping to have this out later in the year. The documentary will be out and hopefully it will coincide with the album release. I need something right now. I'm kind of just in one place, and I'd like to move on to something else. It's stable, but it's not going anywhere. So I have to do new, different things.

M-S: Try to break the status quo?

WR: Exactly. Not just playing on the street. I'd like to get more work in clubs and bars.

M-S: What do you think of alcoholism and addiction problems in the transsexual community?

WR: I've had these problems in the past. I used to be quite a heavy drinker at one time. I never dabbled much into the drug scene. I guess I just want to tell other transsexuals that it's possible to be drug-free and alcohol-free. I don't drink anymore, and I don't smoke. It's been quite a few years, and you can cope with life without drinking and drugs. I don't need five beers before I go on stage and everything. I'm quite comfortable. You can get comfortable with your life and not have to abuse [illegible] a lot of things. It's obviously related to not being comfortable with yourself and the world around. It can be very hard for transsexuals, as I've found, to live day-to-day. Especially if you live every day as a transsexual, and you're trying to cope with things. It can be quite a strain. Sometimes people are rude with you and prejudiced. You have to learn to cope with these things without being too sensitive and realize that [illegible] things are going to happen.

M-S: What do you have to say to transsexuals who probably look at you and think: "Oh God! I would like to have the guts to do what she's doing."

WR: Well, I like to encourage people to do what they want to do and not let things hold them back. I was too shy for 20 years to play in public, and it's too bad because I could have gotten a lot of things. I missed a lot of years that way, so I would say: "You should do what you want to do and not let shyness or what people will think hold you back."

Interview w Peter

This interview with Peter Dunnigan, which exists in provisionally laid out format, was also recorded, and this recording was later edited by Mirha-Soleil Ross and released as a videocassette.

Original unedited version

M-S: Ottawa appears to me to be a conservative city. How was it growing up there?

PD: Ottawa is a conservative anal retentive city. And if you're not wearing polyester and a straight three piece suit and tie, you don't fit in, o.k. So that answers that so you can imagine how I fitted into that norm not to well.

M-S: Was everybody like that there or you had a group of friends that didn't fit in either?

PD: I grew up in a straight gang. They just accepted me as I guess a Tomboy at that point right. That was from 14 to 19. I never changed from 14 until now so this has always been my look except that I have more facial hair. So to them, I was always just being me.

M-S: Were you already dating girls then and if yes did it cause any problem with the gang?

PD: Yeah, and as far as tension yes there was. Especially at parties when I was with a woman because they didn't know how to react to it right.

M-S: So they were ready to accept Pete as a tomboy, but they were not ready to deal with him fucking girls around too.

PD: Yeah because they were all straights so I mean I was introducing them to something that they were not familiar with. I understood their own uncomfortableness as much as I was uncomfortable being there with my girlfriend. Both parties felt that.But in the long run we didn't feel thar way in the end cause we all stayed together for pretty well 20 years.

M-S: When did you meet another transsexual for the first time?

PD: I wasn't aware that there were other transsexuals out there and for the longest time I believed I was the only one. It was a real lonely feeling. My first contact with another transsexual was with someone that I met in a Doctor's office that dealt with transsexual. That was my first introduction to "someone being like me." That was in my early twenties.

M-S: Was there such a thing as a transsexual scene then?

PD: There wasn't really much of a transsexual scene. There was more of a Queen scene or Drag scene or gay scene. There was more of that activity going on than there was exposure to transsexuals. I wouldn't even have known if there were a few lost transsexual around cause I was that naive. I wasn't very educated in that area.

M-S: This person you met in the doctor's office has been you main transsexual contact?

PD: Yeah, I remain with her for two and a half years. We were together for two and a half years. It was love at first sight in the doctor's office. It was like bonding you know what I mean.

M-S: Did you know some lesbians at the time and how was your relationship with them?

PD: Yes, I knew quite a few lesbians and bisexual women. I knew more bisexual women than I knew lesbians. The only type of women who had problems with me were the older dykes. They probably would be now in their fifties. I always hung out with a much older crowd of bisexual and lesbian women. They had a problem with me because they couldn't accept me being who I was yet I didn't have a problem accepting them for who they were.I believe it was just their own insecurity and ignorance. I think they were very unhappy and unstable people to judge me. That's what it comes down to when anybody judges you.

M-S: There is that idea in the lesbian community that in the good old days butch/fem lesbians were more receptive to transsexuality in general but to ftm's in particular. Did you find that too?

PD: What I found was that I was considered too masculine at the time.

M-S: Even too masculine to be a very butchy dyke?

PD: Yes, and butch dyke didn't like it nor did the feminine women because then I looked like a male. So that turned them off. I really did not realistically fit in with them. I didn't. Where I fitted in the most was with the bisexuals.

M-S: From the moment I left my parents place, I lived and socialized almost exclusively with lesbians. I was open about my transsexuality at the time and I have found most of the women I was close to to be receptive and understanding even if I was living as a boy. But their attitude, I found out, would change when it would come to the subject of female-to-male transsexuals. I mean they would sort of accept me claiming a lesbian identity but would freak out at a female-to-male claiming a heterosexual identity. Words like internalized lesbophobia would fly around the room when talking about a straight transsexual man. Did you also encounter that kind of attitude?

PD: Yes, I have. I have encountered that. A lot of: "Why don't you just stay a woman? Why do you want to be a man?" It's because of their own ignorance. Being who I am brought a lot of insecurity because then maybe it meant that their girls were going to be looking at me. I don't want to single out a whole group of women like that but the ones I was circled in were very unhappy and insecure. And also, there was a lot of jealousy. Maybe I just hung out with the wrong group of women.

M-S: At that time, you also got involved in a relationship with a transsexual woman. How did they react to that? I mean you were kind of a queer straight couple. [both laugh]

PD: At that point they became irrelevant. For me they were not existant and not important because I was in love and I stopped going out to clubs. I wasn't living in that environment or very little. I also don't think it would have been important what they would have thought of me and Chantale because the way that I felt about Chantale is nobody could have said anything bad against her cause I would have punch them out. They were not important. She was important.

M-S: Do you identify as a feminist?

PD: I consider myself a feminist and maybe it's because I was a woman that I've been able to see both sides. And I believe that there is really not a gender issue. We make it a gender issue.We place parahierarchy in a dominant role and I don't believe we have a dominant role in society that we're all equal. I believe in that we're both equal we're one. I believe being a feminist is very important to help women who are being mistreated in the workforce and to fight laws that are not protecting women who are being beaten and violated. And I think feminist just means a compilation of a lot of things. Not that you're a man hater. I think there's been a lot of stereotypes about that. I think it's a balancing out of both. So I consider myself a feminist as much as I would consider myself on the other side.

M-S: There is that myth (encouraged by gender identity clinics and even some transsexual activists that a real transsexual should have zero investment in the genitals. It is almost like we should always be standing in front of the mirror with a razor blade or a knife in our hand. A while ago you told me something that was very touching about the way you looked at and treated certain parts of your body before surgery. Do you mind talking about that?

PD: No. Well When I had my mastectommy I prepared myself on all three levels: mentally, physically and spiritually for the operation. Since I never had an operation prior to that, I had to let my body know that it was o.k. and that it was going to be o.k. I wasn't removing my breasts because I hated my breasts. My breasts were part of who I was. It was just not part of my make up of who I am today. I had to go through this ritual of a mourning of a loss cause after all I had them until I was 24 years old. so I mean they were part of me whether or not I was strapping or not. They were a part of who I was and they were a part of my identity. I had to honor that and respect that in oreder to move forward. Just before the surgery, I cried and I touched them very gently, stroke my breasts and sais you know, it's not because I hate you. I had to let my body know that so it wouldn't be traumatised cause I knew the surgery enough would be a former traumatisation because I had never been operated on. Normally people get operated on because they're sick, well I wasn't sick. So for my body to be healthy and go through this, my body would have been confused. So I had to talk to my body and to myself. I had to allow myself to be at peace with the desision I was making because once I made that decision I knew that I was not going back. So I had to really really in my heart know mentally, physically and spiritually what I was doing.

M-S: Did you go through a similar thing when you had your hysterectomy?

PD: No, I went through nothing. I told them I would prefer to have my hysterectomy cause I was in college at the time. And they agreed with me and I went in and had it. I would have prefer to have been prep as to the outcome when I woke up and realized that certain things were going on after the surgery with my body that I wasn't aware of. I had to find out in kind of a frightening fashion. You know when you wake up from the anasthetic and realized that certain things are happening to you. So I would have prefer to have been prep. Cause I didn't know what the outcome was going to be.

M-S: I have seen some non-transsexual women litterally freaking out when learning about ftm's getting mastectommies and hysterectomies. For many of them, it represent total mutilation of a female body. Doesn't even matter if the person is a guy. It just is inconceivable to them as women. What do you have to say to these women?

PD: Get some education! [both laugh] I can understand that because they're not educated enough to know what it's like to be in my skin and in my head. So I understand their ignorance but at the same time I take the time to acknowledge their ignorance so I would like them to aknowledge where I'm coming from, my situation to have the same consideration. After a while you get tired of worrying over what other people think because if I had to think about what everybody thought I don't think I'd be sitting here having an interview today I think I'd be dead. When you walk alone it's a long/lonely road. So what I would have to say to these people is: "lighten up, have sex with me then we'll talk after then you'll know exactly what I'm all about." [both laugh]

M-S: You told me before that you are much more comfortable aknowledging/accepting your feminine side, that you are now much softer, gentler, that you can cry, that you are finally reaching a balance between your feminine side and your masculine side as a transsexual man...

PD: I think when you're placed in this disposition for myself being a transsexual and you have to really become very intent about on how a male role is out in society you start to imitate that role now what happened with me was that I was imitating this role to fit in society. But it still wasn't me per say as Peter. I was imitating the norm that was out there. And I didn't like what was out there in terms of how men were to begin with but I lived that life for a long time. It was a very unhealthy, very destructive life. And I got to a point where I just wanted to be myself and be in touch with me and that meant accepting my masculine my feminine side and appreciate both qualities and not say oh in ordre to be a man you can't cry. In order to be a man I can't ask for a hug or I can't prefer my wife to fix my car. It wasn't a question of gender at that point, it was just a question of being me.and once I succeeded to be me I waqs much more able a lot more at at peace with myself. a lot less angry at the world, I was able to move forward. because I wasn't trying to fit in I fit in today but I don't knowI don't know what I was trying to live up to then. It was a role that I wasn't comfortable in.

M-S: For how long have you been in AA?

PD: I've been a member for four and a half years. I'm not saying within that four and a half years I haven't relaps which is a terminology used when you go to drink cause that's part of the disease that I have. I drank for 18 years before I mae into the programme. I was diagnose as a chronic alcoholic in my early twenties. I was not aware of that ubtil a year ago. I happened to find that in my doctor's file. So they hid that from me. I drank on a daily basis. It was the norm in the seventies to go out party. It was sex drug and rock and roll right we lived well unfortunately a lot of us didn`t came out of that era of the seventies and it became a lifestyle. Unfortunately it's a lifestyle that has killed many of my friends. I've been fortunate enough to walk out of it. with no health problems or psychological problems for that matter I'm lucky to be intact as they say other than just have to deal with the disease itself. So I consider myself very fortunate. I originally started off as a social drinker. I had no intentions of being an alcoholic. It just ended up that way. Before realizing it, what started out as aThursday, friday, and saturday night thing became a seven day a week thing a way to live and a way of coping. After a while of being rejected by the whole fucking world you kind of get down on yourself. You lack a little self esteem a hell of a lot of self esteem. I didn't feel I had a purpose in this society and a reason to be here. I think drinking was kind of a tool for me cause it kept me alive in a very unhealthy way. I think If I wouldn't have drink I wouldn't be here I would have killed myself because of the disposition of being who I was. And being the only out there whom I knew of.There weren't many option for transsexual supprt group.

MS: What made you decide to go to AA. What was it that made you say that's enough.

PD: I ended a relationship with somoeone I was going to get married to. and that relationship really emotionlly brought me down.It really gave me a lot of time to reflect upon myself on why I was so unhappy, what could I do to change it. It took a year before I ended up in treatment. By then I was anorexic, because my desire to live at that point was not there. I was punishing myself for the people I had hurt in my past and I was punishing myself cause I didn't know how to get out of being me anymore. I guess the best way to do it was to hurt myself. I realize it was inconscient. cause I think consciently if I would have been aware of it I don't think I would have set out to hurt myself the way I did but I was not o.k. Obviously I was dying and I couldn't see that I was not o.k. So it was hitting rock bottom that brought me into the program. And knowing that I would have died. I don't even second guess. I was that close to it. The disease had progressed and it brought me down.

M-S: I supposed it also caused problems in your relationships...

PD: It caused problems in my personal relationship because I was aggressive. I was verbally, physically and spiritually abusive to women because of my own unhappiness. I inflicted my pain on them. It reflected in my work, in my attitude and behavior. If I was having a particularly bad day because I had a hang over or I hadn't drank. I was insufficient in some of the job that I held because I was drinkink on the job. I was not able to operate on a quote sober fashion or state of mind. it interfered in just everyday living, in everything I did. It prevented me from doing things that I always wanted to do.

M-S: What about relaps?

PD: The relaps weren't negative relaps. They were very positive because what they indicated to me that they were always happening at a time in my life when I was dealing with issues of intimacy and getting close to another human being. I usually became very frightened, very insecure. I'm not exactly sure why but I always felt that it was related to my gender issue. Being tired of always explaining that I was atranssexual, going through the motions of it. It got pretty tideous and tiring. So anytime I got close to anybody, the best way to deal with it was to be drunk cause that way I could have suppress how I feltand have the casual sex or whatever it is that I needed to have with that person. I'm not saying that it made the situation better but it was a pro way of dewaling with something because I didn't know how to. At this point today I no longer need to get drunk to be intimate which is a big accomplishment. It was the hardest thing for mew to accomplish.

M-S: How did your life improve in general after becoming sober?

PD: The rewards were great. fears that had bounded me and robbed me of being who I was in general as a person dissapeared. The chains started to come off and I became freer within who i was as a person. I was able to speak my mind and defend myself . I devellopped self confidence and self respect, self love for who I was. I started defending my needs and my desires that needed attention and I realized that I had a Voice and that my voice was important, that it carried, and that I wasn't irrelevant, I was relevant, and that I played a major role in this community and in this society as a whole, like anybody else. So AA gave me back me. It saved me. So, I can only say [that] I tried different religions, geographical cures, different jobs, different relationships, different drinking patterns. Nothing worked. They all failed. The only thing that has worked up to this point is the AA program. Like they say, like they told me for a diabetic they need their insulin, for an alcoholic you need your meetings. So, in that sense that`s what AA has been for me - it`s my insulin and it`s a second goal and get healthy. And it`s a simple program. And once you learn to accept things in life that are out of your control or you learn to accept who you are instead of trying to always change who you are. Coming to terms with being who you are, enables [you] to deal with the personal issues and the problems that I grew up in. It gave me an opportunity to accept Peter more as Peter. It gave me the opportunity to get in touch with emotions that have been suppressed for eighteen years - I was able to feel again. I was able to cry and I think crying is probably the greatest healing gift I`ve been given because it allowed me to be human and it allowed me to feel. And I needed to feel, to be human because for a long time I didn`t feel human `cause being a transsexual made me feel inhuman. Made me feel indifferent. And I was portrayed and seen as different. And the program allowed me to be comfortable as being Peter.

M-S: One thing you mentioned though is that you can`t talk about the fact that you`re a transsexual and the program and that`s a problem.

PD: Yeah I know there are a lot of people in our group that are gay and that`s fine and dandy but I see as being gay as being more acceptable than a transsexual still up to this point. And I think society as a large has more of a constant dose of what a homosexual is as opposed to a transsexual.

M-S: And especially a transsexual man.

PD: So it warrants less information and knowledge. Whereas if I was to say that I was a transsexual people would be very intrigued and it would be time-consuming because they would want me always to define who I am and why I am and I`m tired of that `cause I`ve done that for thirty-five years. You know for like the time that I`ve been who I am. And I`m tired of defining me. I just want to live and be me. You know I don`t ask straight people to define themselves or gay people or bisexual people. But I find that there`s always a tendency if you`re a transsexual there`s a curiosity, you`re a novelty. You know "tell us how you came about being who you are." And a novelty gets tiring. It really does. You just want to live. You just want to say "look that`s just a small part of who I am." And that`s all there is in reality. Me being a transsexual is just a small part. But unfortunately to an ignorant society it is brought to my aware[ness] that it became the major theme.

M-S: I feel a contradiction in what you`re saying `cause on one hand you say it`s a very small part of who you are; on the other hand you say it`s a big problem `cause you can`t talk about the fact that you`re a transsexual in the AA group because you would have to constantly if they would know you would have to constantly to explain yourself.

PD: I would have to define yeah out of their curiosity. `Cause people are curious.

M-S: You couldn`t talk, you couldn`t like spend your energy on talking about your issues and your outcomes in relation to your transsexuality. You would have to explain your transsexuality to them.

PD: Yes because I would always have to explain where it stems from because there`s so little information out there on female-to-males or I don`t know transsexuals in period but I can only assure you that I don`t want to spend the rest of my life in a program that I`m trying to maintain my sobriety defining my gender issues to people. You know if that`s the case I`d rather just go and sit in front of a shrink who has some knowledge and be able to talk freely without having to always define myself. I`m tired of defining myself.

M-S: Does your sponsor know?

PD: No he doesn`t.

M-S: He`s a guy?

PD: Yeah.

M-S: And he doesn`t know?

PD: No he doesn`t know.

M-S: That`s a big chunk.

PD: I`m having a problem with that right now. I`m a bit uncomfortable with them. I`m not sure why I am. This may be one of the reasons I`m probably agitated because I think I`m tired of keeping myself in the closet. And if I would have had it my way I would prefer to have a sponsor who was a transsexual. Someone that would be able to identify with what I`m saying and not try to identify. It makes a really big difference in the way that they can offer suggestions or help for your needs. So again once again I`m in a program that is serving my need as an alcoholic but it's not serving my need in relation to other issues that reflected the alcoholism, that were a part of...

M-S: So what do you think can be done about that? Do transsexuals have to start AA groups?

PD: Well we don't have a group. The gay community have a group. I'm not interested in going to it, a gay group. I'm not anti-gay, I'm just not gay or lesbian and don't fit in. I actually probably fit in more in the heterosexual community like I have all my life than I do a gay community. But there's still a need that's not being addressed and that's still the gender issue because that does play a role in your alcoholism. And so yeah we need meetings. We need a meeting group started for transsexuals in AA. And I wouldn't recommend an open meeting where we have to [noise] figure there's probably enough transsexuals to come in on a weekly basis and tell their story. But I do suggest that a twelve step program or a Living Sober book program where you read and then discuss a chapter or share whatever it is that you need to express that's upsetting you at that point.That type of meeting I think would be healthy for transsexuals. But I'm not aware of the need within the community because I'm very oblivion to the community because I've been in the mainstream heterosexual world for so long that I don't know what the transsexual community needs. But I know being a transsexual I know what I need and I think a program as such would benefit not only myself but other transsexuals. And that's all **he** wrote.

M-S: What?

PD: And that's all **he** wrote. I think being a transsexual and having to be out of place with who I am, for being who I am. I think society needs to be educated so that we can be re-integrated into a heterosexual community if we wish to be a part of it. That's what I mean like introduced to. I think awareness and education really needs to be out there because there is a large population of transsexuals in our community you know or in society as a whole. And I think we're past the Dark Ages; that our needs up to this point are not being met by the government. It has recognized that we are born this way and we are not being treated accordingly promptly. And that's in terms of education, programming, in terms of operations, cost factors, the legal system, having to go about properly obtaining legal name changes for your cards and what not, the overall agenda is up to this point I would believe very poor, the statutes are not up to par.

M-S: There's especially very little for female-to males in Canada for example and for example in your experience you've me t very few female-to-males, how many did you meet in your entire life?

PD: One. Only because he was a friend of mine and I helped him get to where he needed to go.

M-S: It was at the beginning of his transition?

PD: We met in high school and we remained buddies and

M-S: Did you know about what you were in high school?

PD: No, which was ironic that I expressed...

M-S: Was he tomboy too?

PD: Very. Very tomboy. Very good looking man. And he was the only one I ever encountered. So that was kind of nice.

M-S: That encounter?

PD: Yeah.

M-S: At the same time it's very important to meet when you're either beginning to transition or you're starting to know that, it's important meet people who have experience behind them about that. And it's sort of, it's probably frustrating sometimes for you that you couldn't find anybody who?

PD: No, I was always alone and I guess that's why the drinking progressed part role because it knocked out the loneliness and the isolation I felt being who I was and that way I didn't have to think about it; I could just exist. I wasn't living, I was existing. Today I live I don't exist anymore. But I only existed for a long time and that is an awful way to live just because of your gender identity. It really is. It's appalling and it's a shame the way society looks upon transsexualism and the way that we're treated because of the lack of education out there. I'm as human as the next person and I feel the same way as the next person and to be treated differently, I almost feel like I'm a minority. And I am a minority, a very small minority. Whose needs aren't being met you know in the community. And I shouldn't have to be ashamed of who beinng who I am. And I shouldn't have to hide. I should be proud of who I am.

M-S: Oh you said that you sort of came out to a woman in your AA `cause you were wearing a button right? Or omething like that? So you come out to people once in a while you told me some stories sometimes.

PD: Yeah, I just came back from the Gay Pride Day and I had a button "I love transsexuals." There was another one "only a transsexual could love you"

M-S: What was the other one?

PD: "Genderphobia" or something like that and she kept staring at them and I was so full of pride that day and she was looking at them and I said "you know these really mean a lot to me" and she said "are you one" and I said "yes I am." And she said "that's fine Peter I love you just the way you are."

M-S: Did she went to chat with other people about it?

PD: I don't care. I seem to be coming out more and more and more. I told my teacher in school at some point this term. Only because my teacher was sarcastically rude to me. She said oh, the only reason you were able to accomplish this is because you`'re a man. And the only reason I didn't is because I,m a woman. I said excuse me honey I used to wear shoes like you. And I said don't give me this gender bullshit. I said if you have something to say and it has to get the message across it doesn't matter what your gender is if you have to say it just get the message across. There was equipment in my course that wasn't getting repaired in my english media course. She apparently had tried it and it wasn't sucessful. Because there was a discrepancy - whatever problems there was between the two parties, I took it initially upon myself to take the equipment home 'cause the electrician said these equipments were disfunctioned. And I brought 'em home and I bought the parts and repaired them and I brought it back. And then I fixed a stand in which at that point a Panasonic camera be on so you could glide across the room when you were filming. So I went over her head to the two departments that were supposed to repair these and both being male when they realized that my needs were not being met as a student they said that they would do anything at that point for me and I could call them because I showed an interest in my education in the course that I was taking and so when she found out that I addressed these issues she more or less said that it was because I was a man and I became very defensive at that point and told her that don't give this gender issue and at that point I said "I wore shoes like you" and she looked at me and I said "you know like I'm a transsexual, so look honey I know where you're coming from and I've been in your shoes and when I was female I could speak my voice just as well as I can today as a male." So it's not a question of what gender you are; it's a question of how assertive you are.

M-S: What did she say? She was shocked?

PD: Well, yeah, she went into shock at that point like I mean she goes "you must have experienced a lot in your time. And yeah I guess I could say as an old-"

M-S: Was she a dyke?

PD: No, I don't know what she is. She's a little fucking [laughs]. Okay. Oh I don't want to get into what she's done to me but anyhow that's another story. But all I can tell you is that

M-S: Good story. Whatever.

PD: Well there's been lot of them.

M-S: Oh yeah?

PD: Yeah. I had another teacher that wanted to train me for four years 'cause I had potential as a writer and she was a Pisces like me so we got along very well and we had a lot of characteristics and interests that were much the same and she was just very fascinated with who I was and at the same time I think she was angry because she had liked me for so long and she didn't know so she already got hooked - line and sinker type thing and then when I said I was a transsexual, well I guess that was kind of a shock to know that she could have any feelings for a transsexual. I really get shocked when people like me for who I am and then they find out and sometimes they become really shocked you know. "Oh my God, I could actually love somebody that's indifferent [*should be* different]" you know and in actual fact you know I'm not any different. I'm probably more than... But they just don't have the intelligence to know that because they're so insecure with their own gender you know what I mean and that when I expose mine it's a...And then on the other side it's very positive. I haven't really been rejected per se because of my gender. In terms of relationships, because people that have come into my life have left me for me and not my gender. And they tell me that 'cause I'm the one that's insecure. You know I don't think that I'm good enough or that I can please them enough, because at that time I didn't feel that way about myself. And they basically would just say that we love you for who you are; it's not what you have between your legs. And it was kind of nice to hear that, when you don't feel that, you know. So there's been a lot of positive to date a transsexual in terms of enlightenment seeing two sides of role-playing or whatever you want to call it, I mean I guess it's kind of unique in itself given that kind of mentality but in terms of what's out there for us I'm not impressed at all with our community. No I'm not impressed. There's not enough. Where is our community? Where are our voices? We're voiceless still and...

M-S: And the ones that have voices spend more time bitching and trashing each other than to do something...

PD: That`s what I mean. I mean we need a healthy community and with a community that's getting well that's becoming spiritual that's becoming strong that's becoming proud. Not as a community that's going to insult their own community and compete against their own community.

Beacon Press protest against.

A variety of materials relating to this protest are preserved in the *Gendertrash* archive, and it is unclear precisely which ones were intended for publication. For this reason, they are all reproduced here.

In 1979
the Unitarian-Universalist Association
published the most hate-filled,
anti-transsexual literature
ever to see print --
Janice Raymond's
*The Transsexual Empire**

Janice Raymond, writing in *The Transsexual Empire*:
"I contend the problem of transsexualism
would best be served by
morally mandating it
out of existence."

Lon Mabon agrees, including transsexuals in his
anti-homosexual initiatives.

Unitarian-Universalists refuse, to this day,
to acknowledge their contribution to the climate
of prejudice and hate towards transsexuals
Lon Mabon exploits in his campaign
against transsexuals, lesbians, gays and bisexuals.

Unitarians who fail to condemn their own organization's
role in promoting hatred against transsexuals
have abandoned any moral basis on which to criticize
the politics of hate.

They are the pot calling the kettle black.

* Beacon Press, Boston, Massachusetts, 1979

For Immediate Release

P*R*E*S*S R*E*L*E*A*S*E

Strains of pipe organ music had barely begun to ring through Portland's First Unitarian Church for the 9:30 service Sunday morning, July 23, when transsexual activists Rachel Koteles and Margaret Deirdre O'Hartigan began distributing flyers to church members denouncing 17 years of anti-transsexual literature produced by the Unitarian-Universalist Association's Beacon Press. Citing transphobic works by Beacon Press authors Mary Daly, Janice Raymond and Walter Williams, the flyers were distributed to nearly all in attendance before the activists were forced to cease distribution by church ushers.

Entitled "J'Accuse", the flyer began: "For the past 17 years the Unitarian-Universalist Beacon Press has borne false witness against transsexuals. We have been dehumanized, demonized, denigrated and dismissed -- the transsexual struggle to survive made immeasurably more difficult in a society encouraged to heap abuse and scorn upon us as a result of the lies and half-truths directed against us by the Unitarian-Universalist Association through Beacon Press."

The flyer quoted passages from Beacon Press publications characterizing transsexuals as "eunuchs", "necrophiliacs", "Frankensteinian", and "rapists".

"Nearly 100 years ago," the flyer stated, "Emile Zola wrote: 'It is a crime to misdirect public opinion and to pervert it to the extent it becomes demented. It is a crime to poison small and empty minds, to arouse intolerance and reaction through the exhalation of that miserable anti-Semitism...' And what was true of French anti-Semitism a century ago is as true today of the Unitarian Universalist Association's fomentation of transphobia through the Beacon Press."

After the service -- which Koteles and O'Hartigan made no attempt to disrupt -- the activists engaged in conversations with congregation and board members, providing additional examples of transphobic writings from additional Beacon Press authors, and urging First Unitarian Church members to support the flyer's call for action:

"Transsexuals call upon all people of good will, who value and work for peace and social justice, to join their voices to ours in demanding an explanation for the years of vilification and slander Beacon Press has perpetrated against us. We ask that you join your voices to ours as we call upon the Association to acknowledge the harm it has inflicted upon transsexuals. And we ask your support in demanding from the Unitarian-Universalist Association an official, public apology for the role it and Beacon Press have played in fostering transphobia."

In a letter to the First Unitarian Church Board of Directors, O'Hartigan stressed the action was a last resort after failed efforts urging Unitarian ministers, Association headquarters in Boston, Massachusetts and Beacon Press itself to renounce the Association's 17 year history of disseminating transphobic literature. O'Hartigan noted in her July 24 letter that transphobic works published by Beacon Press authors Mary Daly, Janice Raymond and others "have been routinely offered for sale at Unitarian churches across the United States -- including First Unitarian Church here in Portland."

"At the front of every one of Beacon Press' anti-transsexual publications is the statement: 'Beacon Press books are published under the auspices of the Unitarian-Universalist Association of Congregations'," states O'Hartigan. "Considering the impact on transsexual civil rights, health-care and well-being these works have had, an apology seems little enough to ask for from the Association."

* * *

For further information: [illegible]; P.O. Box 82447, Portland, OR 97282

Margaret Deirdre O'Hartigan

J'Accuse

For the past 17 years the Unitarian-Universalist Beacon Press has borne false witness against transsexuals. We have been dehumanized, demonized, denigrated and dismissed -- the transsexual struggle to survive made immeasurably more difficult in a society encouraged to heap abuse and scorn upon us as a result of the lies and half-truths directed against us by the Unitarian-Universalist Association through Beacon Press.

In 1979 the Unitarian-Universalist Association's Beacon Press published the most virulently anti-transsexual propaganda ever to see print -- Janice Raymond's *The Transsexual Empire*. In this book, Raymond demonized transsexuals, demanding an end to our hormone therapy and sex-reassignment surgery, and calling for an end to recognition of transsexualism as a medical condition deserving of treatment: "I contend that the problem of transsexualism would best be served by morally mandating it out of existence."

The Transsexual Empire contained such incredible claims as "All transsexuals rape women's bodies by reducing the real female form to an artifact" and equated the transsexual "empire" -- the medical professionals treating us -- to the Nazi-perpetrated Holocaust, claiming we are part of a partriarchal plot to genocidally exterminate women.

Yet *The Transsexual Empire* is only one of many transphobic books produced by the Unitarian-Universalist Beacon Press. In 1988 Beacon Press published Walter Williams' *The Spirit and the Flesh*, which denigrated the transsexual experience as "bodily mutilation", characterizing our sex-reassignment surgery as "a heavy price to pay for the ideology of biological determinism." Ten years earlier, in 1978, Beacon Press published Mary Daly's *Gyn/Ecology*, which castigated transsexuals as "eunuchs", "necrophiliacs" and "Frankensteinian".

Nearly 100 years ago Emile Zola wrote: 'It is a crime to misdirect public opinion and to pervert it to the extent it becomes demented. It is a crime to poison small and empty minds, to arouse intolerance and reaction through the exhalation of that miserable anti-Semitism..." And what was true of French anti-Semitism a century ago is as true today of the Unitarian-Universalist Association's fomentation of transphobia through the Beacon Press.

It is beyond comprehension how an organization which so consistently speaks out against injustice and oppression, can take exception to transsexuals and levy such calumny against us. And yet organizations all-to-often fail to represent their own membership.

Transsexuals call upon all people of good will, who value and work for peace and social justice, to join their voices to ours in demanding an explanation for the years of vilification and slander Beacon Press has perpetrated against us. We ask that you join your voices to ours as we call upon the Association to ackonwledge the harm it has inflicted upon transsexuals. And we ask your support in demanding from the Unitarian-Universalist Association an official, public apology for the role it and Beacon Press have played in fostering transphobia.

Lest we be morally mandated out of existence.

For further information please write: P.O. Box 82447, Portland, OR 97282 ( )

Interview with Petra Chevrier

This interview, conducted by both Xanthra Phillippa MacKay and Mirha-Soleil Ross (going by the name Janou), survives in not easily legible handwritten form in the *Gendertrash* archives. Mirha-Soleil Ross has indicated that she hoped to include it in *Gendertrash* #5. It is therefore transcribed here.

Petra Chevrier is a filmmaker and arts journalist who, in the mid-'90s, was working at *Fuse* magazine. She was the cover model for *Gendertrash* #2 and, according to Mirha-Soleil Ross, "did a lot of work to support the production side of the zine."

Janou: So Petra, when did you start thinking about going through a transition?
Petra: I think I remember first thinking about it when I was about 11 or 12, and many years went by before I acted on it or did anything real about it. So probably sometime when I was 22.
Janou: And since that time you've been around [laughter].
Petra: Well I think I arrived in Toronto in 1991 and I really started making a break with my past at that point and making a break from being completely in the closet. Because really I was in the closet for 10 years from the age of 12 until 22, and I guess at that point I came running out of the closet [laughter].
Xanthra: That's an interesting way to put it, "running out of the closet." Where did you go running to? [laughter].
Petra: Well, there was nowhere to run to, but I guess I just had to start to do things that have been in my mind for a long time and it's partly coming out but it's also seeking a way of changing, a way of gaining control over my physical development.
Xanthra: When we say "coming out," for us do you feel it's much different than coming out for someone lesbian and gay?
Petra: It's still a matter of being able to tell people. For me it's a question of being able to say to somebody "Yes, this is what I want, this is who I am," and not be afraid to say that to people, you know. Because before that I couldn't tell anybody and that's the problem.
Janou: What has been your relationship with psychiatric institutions during all those years? You probably have lots of things to say about them.
Petra: I waited for a while before I went to see anybody at the gender clinic and then at that point I felt that I needed to get some sort of formal assistance and that was the only place I knew about, so I went there and basically left very disappointed, feeling like I have been sent through a very intense period of examination and then dumped back out at the other end of the machine, left with no more resources than when I went in and no more assistance than when I went in. So I felt "well what was the point of that?" and a long time went by before I was able to go back there and you know, through insistence, and through honesty and truth, trying to get them to listen to me, and trying to get them to take some actions to help me
Janou: Do you think things have changed in the gender clinic during the last years?
Petra: I think things changed. Between 1983 and 1990 there was a lot of change in there, both in their own conception of what they were doing and also in their realization that things were changing very quickly in the outside world, that TS's were following very different paths, and were not fitting into the same kind of models that they had experienced or seen during the 60s and 70s. Our stories were changing. It took them a while to realize that we maybe were just being a bit more honest or perhaps just that there were more of us than they realized.
Xanthra: And that maybe we wanted more options than what had been given us!
Petra: Also I think, with the gay revolution, the urban landscape was changing very very quickly, and what it was like to live as a TS coming out in 1983 or 82 was very different than, for example, 1975. The options were multiplying, and the whole thing of androgyny influences what possible choices we have.
Janou: One of the big things people in the GIC had to realize, I think, is the variety of sexual orientations transsexuals now choose to embrace. If we're male to female,

for example, we don't have to pretend to be heterosexual women in order to get on hormones, SRS etc.
Petra: This was a big issue with them because I was quite open about the fact that I am attracted to women and that I see myself and I identify as a lesbian, and they sort of put a hold on me because of that. I was penalized because of that, in a sense, and I ended up having to work completely on my own independently and go along my own path.
Janou: But you went back to them after?
Petra: I did eventually, to see what the attitude would be. And at that point it had changed completely, in 1991 – So they understood that maybe that's OK if TS's are lesbian [laughter].
Janou: They don't have the choice, I think, because some say that in some GIC programs up to 50% of them identify as lesbians or gay men. So they've got no choice to deal with us, otherwise they'll have very few people in their GIC and eventually lose their job [laughter].
Petra: I think that it was much more difficult for TS's in the earlier history of the clinics to be able to say they identify as lesbians. It was common knowledge that if you would tell them that you would be penalized, and therefore a lot of people would simply not talk about that or lie outright to the psychiatrists in order to get into the programs.
Janou: We talked about the psychiatric establishment. What about socially? People around you, friends, etc. How did they react? The usual reaction is "you wanna be a woman, be a real one, be straight."
Petra: Some people are really surprised by that, because they still associate transsexuality with homosexuality. They think we're that kind of branch subsections of homosexual men. I think people who have more life experience are usually a lot more accepting. Even within the lesbian community things have changed.
Xanthra: Yes, you must have seen big changes in the lesbian community.
Petra: Things changed, but gradually. When I had lesbian friends in the 80s, there was a bit more attention, a bit less sense of acceptance, although they wanted to understand, but it was always a barrier there that was always a little bit more difficult to overcome. And I think that those barriers have come down gradually, and I think that lesbians are, I don't want to generalize, but I know a lot of lesbians who are very accepting and completely open about it. They're not troubled by that at all, they don't feel I'm taking over.
Janou: I'm glad to see more and more MTF lesbian and FT Gay Male cause I think it's a relief. It breaks down this idea so many people had that we're just homosexuals who can't handle our orientation, and that we get a sex change to legitimize our sexualities, and this idea was going on all over in the gay lesbian communities as well as in the psychiatric field, etc. etc.
Petra: I wouldn't say the acceptance is completely universal. I have to be honest about the fact that a lot of lesbians tried to call me "he," as other people do, and you know, I have to make corrections. I have to come out and say to them that I'd really rather not be called "he" and sometimes it becomes quite deliberate. Sometimes it's not…
Xanthra: …an accident!
Petra: They don't even think about it. They say "well I'm sorry, I just wasn't thinking about it."
Xanthra: How does that affect your personal relationships… emotional, sexual relationships with other women?

Petra: Well that has meant I've gone through a whole transition, of course. Because initially most of my relationships with women were with straight women, and during the course of changing my life, I guess that's a good way of putting it, my orientation changed from straight women to lesbian women, and of course, along the way there is bisexual women, Dyke-identified bisexual women [laughter]. You know there's a whole gamut that you could consider being possible sex partners, so it's not simple. It gets very complicated sometimes, and I've actually had a girlfriend who has at some point decided she didn't want to be a lesbian anymore and that created a great deal of tension in the relationship. So it's taken a long time to sort that one out. I wouldn't even dream to think that's over because that's something that's ongoing. It's like a continual process for anyone who tries to follow their own path in that kind of transition to be able to arrive at relationships that work on all different levels.
Janou: Thank you, Petra. Merci, Petra.

Negligees Never Sleep

A copy of a letter from Mirha-Soleil Ross to Selena Shephard, dated June 19, 1995, during the period when *Gendertrash* #5 was being worked on most intensely, indicates this poem was accepted for publication "in gendertrash or somewhere else."

Selena Anne Shephard
P.O. Box 5112
Larkspur, CA 94977

Negligees Never Sleep

They've altered the text again
Blackened my I's
Sold my tongue at discount
Stolen my fantasies
Slandered my genitals
Stamped a Universal Price Code on my ass
Sliced open my belly and buried secrets deep within
They've made me happy in spite of myself

"Which way to the Pope's Boudoir?"
scream the men in baby drag

To Provoke Thought Is To Create Life...

In a letter to Heather Hatfield, dated February 6, 1995, Mirha-Soleil Ross says "I really appreciate your poetry and will include some of the poems you sent me in a future issue of *Gendertrash*." The poems are taken from Hatfield's zine/chapbook *When Clothes Are Not Enough*.

To Provoke Thought Is To Create Life...

The Voices, The Other Side

I find myself, day by day, facing life from the other side.
Wishing the voices would lie quietly,
would quit calling to me,
would quit waking me in the middle of the night
to tell me all deaths are suicides.
To tell me all deaths are suicides is dangerous.

Creator/Destroyer

If you can be both, why can't I?
My life is the dagger you plunged into my heart...
...the way you have taken everything from me, stripped me naked, and then
even took that. Why? Why would I owe you anything but my contempt?

Creation

Above the storm urges ran like water in his garden spring.
    They would
            pound
                beat
                    boil the sea
so he could see below the surface of the sea of sad shadows.
            And he did
            And I was born

Homelessness and the Transgendered Community

This essay, by Christine Tayleur, seems to be a companion piece to her essay "Racism and Poverty in the Transgender Community" on pages 17–20 of *Gendertrash* #4. Mirha-Soleil Ross has indicated she intended to include this essay in a future *Gendertrash*, and that she "would be happy to see it in #5."

The essay exists in complete, submitted form, but has not been laid out for publication or edited, as witnessed by the fact that its final paragraph repeats material from its first.

Homelessness and the Transgendered Community

(The Problem We Never Talk About)

by Christine R. Tayleur, ASC

Tenderloin Self-Help Center, San Francisco

The Tenderloin Self-Help Center is a non-traditional, alternative mental health programme, targeting residents of San Francisco's "Tenderloin" neighborhood, who would otherwise not be able to utilize more traditional programmes. A project of Central City Hospitality House, a community resource agency, serving the Tenderloin's many diverse populations for the past twenty-five years, the Tenderloin Self Help Center provides peer-oriented counselling, referrals for food, shelter, clothing and other resources. Additionally, we provide benefits advocacy services, services to the Trans-gender Community, volunteer training, peer-counselling training, and community organizing. We were founded in August 1986, as a result of community pressure on the city. Since opening our doors, we have served over 300,000 people, approximately fifteen to twenty thousand trans-gendered people, and perhaps ten to fifteen thousand lesbians and gay men.

The Tenderloin is a densely-populated, multi-ethnic, inner-city neighborhood, with all the attendant problems of inner-city neighborhoods. The Tenderloin has a population of 27,000 people crammed into an area of twenty-five blocks, of whom approximately 1,500 are trans-gender. Crime, drugs, homelessness, poverty, prostitution and violence. Always a rough neighborhood, since its days as the Barbary Coast, in recent years it has gotten even worse. Crack cocaine has become a real scourge, and now "ice" (smokable amphetamine). Along with homelessness, domestic and street violence, and all the other attendant problems of inner-city neighborhoods, many impoverished members of our community who live here succumb to these social ills.

Life in the Tenderloin, or T.L., as it is sometimes called, is often hectic. Crime and violence are a daily occurrence. For trans-gendered people living here, it is frequently even more hectic. Because of its reputation as a "gay Mecca," trans-gendered people come here from all parts of the country, the Caribbean, Central America and Mexico, as well as from countries of the Pacific Rim. They come here with all sorts of personal, emotional "baggage," so to speak. Most of these people are impoverished and feel disenfranchised and alienated from society. A great many of them have histories of physical, emotional and sexual abuse, as well as severe psychological dysfunctions. Because they are poor, they wind up in the T.L. They often become homeless, because the cost of an apartment or even a "skid-row" transient hotel room is outrageous. A one-bedroom apartment in San Francisco averages between $600 and $700 per month, a cheap hotel averages $325 to $360 a month. A General Assistance grant is $360 a month, plus a food stamp grant of around $70. The hotels have no cooking facilities, are often filthy, insect and rodent infested, are fire-traps, and have no heat. Further, they are often crime- and drug-ridden.

The transgendered folks living in San Francisco's Tenderloin neighborhood have an extremely difficult time, just making ends meet, just walking down the street to the store for milk. They may experience verbal or physical harassment from the police, street people or drug dealers. Like many inner-city neighborhoods, violence and crime are a daily occurrence. If you are homeless, you are ten times more likely to be either a victim of violence or a witness to violence. If you are transsexual and homeless, you are a hundred times more likely. Western society's homophobia shows itself in its most virulent form: "transphobia." The police, drug dealers, sex-workers, drug and sex-customers, pimps and other hazards are real. People get killed because they get "read."

San Francisco, because of its reputation as a "Gay Mecca," attracts thousands of trans-gendered people a year. They come here from all parts of the country, Central America, the Caribbean, many countries of the Pacific Rim and Asia. They come seeking help for their gender issues, social and economic justice, and to escape war, domestic violence, gripping poverty and persecution. What they find are:

1) High prices and a dearth of low-cost housing
2) A lack of social services and lack of access to adequate health care
3) Lack of employment opportunities and lack of educational opportunities
4) Lack of shelter space available to homeless trans-gendered people
5) Absence of counselling and safehouses for trans-gendered victims of domestic violence
6) Absence of any inpatient substance abuse treatment facilities that will accept trans-gendered people
7) Lack of access to legal services
8) Prejudice and bigotry

In 1989, we started the "Transgender Addictions Group," for trans-gendered people dealing with addiction issues. As far as we know it was one of the first of its kind. Not a twelve-step group, it was founded because people were saying that they would want to speak about how their gender issues affected and were intimately related to addiction. They were saying, "When I get read, it makes me want to go out and use or get drunk."

People in the Twelve-Step groups they were going to, told them that gender wasn't a recovery issue, etc. Not confined to chemical dependence, the group also deals with relationship addictions (co-dependence) and any issue anybody identifies as an addiction issue.

Another of our services is that we train peer-counselors. Over the years we have had numerous sisters and brothers go through our peer counselor's training and have had great success. Many transgendered people prefer talking to transgendered peer-counselors rather than non-trans-gendered counselors because they understand; "they are there, have been there, they know what we are going through."

Although we recommend some kind of waiting period before hormones, we do not follow the Harry Benjamin "Standards of Care." We agree with Sheila Kirk, when she says hormones just aren't that dangerous when taken with adequate medical supervision, we don't feel that three months is necessary. Instead, we offer counseling along with the referral. This is just to give the person a chance to think about the socio-economic ramifications of hormone therapy, i.e., "Can I work as a female/male? How will this affect my future? Is this really the key to my own happiness?" etc. Besides, we know that they can get them off the street through the black market or just go into numerous doctors' offices and get them. Also, we feel that people will find out soon enough whether they want hormones; as one gentleman I worked with expressed it, "It put junior to sleep." Finally, hormones are reversible. Believing that it sets up a better dynamic of trust between counselor and constituent, we refuse to act as "gatekeepers;" we view it like needle exchange and abortion: it saves lives. Moreover, we advocate a revision in the "standards," because they were written by "Nons" (non-transgendered people).

Transgendered people in general, we believe, are best qualified to determine their own treatment. Just as non-transgendered women are best qualified to determine whether they should get an abortion.

In the next year, we hope to establish an employment program for transgendered people. This should help get them off of the streets, improve self-esteem, reduce crime, lessen the strain on an already over-burdened mental health system. Additionally, it will have the added benefit of causing a reduction in the welfare rolls. Unemployment of course often causes homelessness. Transgendered folk in the shelters frequently have a difficult time because the shelters require them to have i.d.; in order for a transgendered person to get i.d. in the opposite gender, they must see a doctor.

Last year, the Transgendered Community of the Tenderloin celebrated a memorial service for a transsexual constituent who got killed walking to dinner at some friends' apartment. We also remembered the death of a sister and friend who died from a combination beating by her boyfriend and drug overdose, as well as several other people who had died that people remembered. This year we have at least two more passages to remember. The Tenderloin Self Help Center donates space to this function.

The Center tries to work with anyone who walks in the door. The population we work with is people who cannot utilize the more traditional services. This may be for any number of reasons: they may be too "out of it" to be able to make and keep appointments; they may be in crisis; they may be too drunk, or high; if you become homeless it's even harder to make ends meet. People living on welfare or disability often run out of money by the end of the month; in the last week before the end of the month, people become desperate. Transgendered people are often perceived as easy targets. They know that the police will often treat them worse than the criminal(s). Should they get mugged, the police have been known to blame them. If the trans-gendered person is an ethnic minority, then life is that much harder. Many customers ("johns") of transsexual sex workers will pick a caucasian trans-gendered woman sooner than a woman of color, thus causing competition and in-fighting and further oppressing them.

Our non-traditional, alternative approach to mental health, and our belief in advocacy on behalf of our constituency led us to conflict with the city's mental health department who use to fund us. They did not like our non-traditional approach. They didn't appreciate our emphasis on homelessness and substance abuse. This led to serious conflicts with them, culminating in a major funding battle.

In 1990, the Tenderloin Self Help Center underwent the most serious struggle for funding since we opened. We were slated for a three hundred thousand dollar cut, which would have effectively shut us down, by eliminating seventy-five percent of our program. This would have eliminated the peer-counseling program, thus eliminating the availability of peer-counselors and peer-counselor training, outreach and group facilitator training to the community. Several courageous trans-gendered women and men joined us when we set up shop on the steps of city hall, providing services there and still managing to serve at least half of our normal constituency. We held a trans-gender support group on the steps of city hall, with about twelve people and a number of brothers. We also carried pickets and informational leaflets, giving them to all who would accept them. This showed people in the most effective way what we did. It also helped them to see that if we were defunded, where would these people go? This was scary to a lot of folks who didn't like the idea of all these homeless people without a place to go for help and time on their hands. It would have been devastating to the Gender Community here.

The protest took place over several weeks on several different occasions. We won our funding battle with no cuts. We experienced minimal disruption in service delivery and we were able to prevent long-term service interruptions. The center was able to get our funding source changed to a more sympathetic city department, which believes in our program. With our new contract, we are specifically funded to do community organizing, a point of contention between us and Community Mental Health Services before.. Over the past two years, we have been able to concentrate on the development of the program generally and the transgender component of the program, and organizing people to fight for their political rights, and take charge of their own community. We feel that empowerment brings self-esteem, reduces crime and mental illness. In our view, the medical/psychiatric colonization of our community is a major problem. Of course, people want and feel the need of counseling, from time to time, but the medical/psychiatric industry is not only getting rich off of our sisters and brothers' misery, they perpetuate the dependency. Along with the police, we feel that they contribute to oppression. The psychiatric and medical industry (in my view) has never been a friend to us. One only has to look at the history of the transgender movement, psychiatrists label us (e.g. mothers feminized phallus, failure to make Oedipal separation, masculine protesting, etc.). Unfortunately, we need many of their services. Trying to get them out of the shelters, helping them build self-esteem and lessen their contacts with the mental health system and police. Shelters are not an answer to homelessness, jails are not an answer to crime, and institutions are not an answer for mental illness.

The center also provides assistance with entitlement rights, identification, information on homeless rights, as well as a host of other rights. We have helped trans-gendered folks get name-changes and referred others to where they could get legal advice and help. We look forward to expanding our services further. Although next year, we anticipate another major funding battle, due to a hostile ex-police chief mayor who believes that homeless people are criminals and that more jails and police are the best answer. Also because of an anticipated unprecedented major budget short fall created by politicians in Sacramento and city hall (the mayor spent untold millions to save a baseball team, while people are without homes). In spite of this, we will survive and continue to give free, non-traditional, alternative services and even to expand our services to reach other underserved population groups.

To supplement General Assistance, some trans-gendered people resort to prostitution. Drugs, alcohol, domestic and street violence, frequently go hand-in-glove with prostitution. In addition to drug addiction and alcoholism, many trans-gendered people in the Tenderloin suffer from a variety of mental illnesses and homelessness, or any combination of these problems. The past three years have seen a dramatic increase in the number of trans-gendered people who are either sero-positive or living with AIDS. They have the additional burden of being trans-gendered, along with HIV, which carries special concerns and problems.

These are the people that the Tenderloin Self Help Center seeks to serve. We presently have several trans-gender employees and volunteers. The Center has two on-going transgender support groups, one for general support and a trans-gender addictions group, that is nearing its fifth year of operation. The general support group provides a safe, supportive atmosphere for trans-gender people of all persuasions to discuss issues of relevance, such as: passing, dealing with family and friends, sexuality, domestic violence, street life, life in the shelters, and other issues that people bring up that they have concerns about. Several times a month we have speakers. We host full-time successful living speakers, some of whom are post-operative. We also feature providers who come in to do presentations, a few times a month. In the Transgender Addiction Group, we discuss chemical dependency issues, and how they relate to trans-gender issues. For example: many group members have stated, "When I get read, it makes me want to go out and use or get drunk." We work to build self-esteem, thereby sobriety and stability, by discussing not only our issues, problems and histories, but also philosophy and how other cultures view and treat their transgendered people (e.g. the Hijra of India, the Mahu of Polynesian cultures and of course, the berdache of indigenous Native American and Asian cultures). We've found it's often helpful to know that in many cultures transgendered people are highly respected. Since we are not a twelve-step group, we can use material that is not "conference approved," and discuss topics that are not just recovery issues.

A project of Central City Hospitality House, a community center for San Francisco's Tenderloin neighborhood, the Tenderloin Self Help Center is a non-traditional, alternative mental health program targeting residents of the Tenderloin, who would otherwise not receive such services from existing resources. The Tenderloin is a densely populated, multi-ethnic inner-city neighborhood near the Civic Center. In addition to peer-oriented counseling and community support/education groups, the Center has been providing benefits advocacy services, referrals for shelter, food and clothing, telephone and mail services, general survival counseling and substance abuse counseling, as well as volunteer training since 1986. We serve a diverse population, which includes: transsexuals, cross-dressers, gay and lesbians, bi-sexual, hetero-sexual, African-Americans, Asian-Americans, Asian-Americans, European-Americans, Native Americans, Latin-Americans, as well as other minorities.

Interview with Jamison Green

This is the first of two interviews Mirha-Soleil Ross conducted in October 1996 and broadcast in December of the same year as a special feature on CIUT 89.5FM's *Gaywire Radio*.

Though conducted significantly after the initial slated (and missed) release date for *Gendertrash* #5, Mirha-Soleil Ross indicates that at this point she still hoped to complete the fifth issue, and intended to include this interview in it.

The interview does not survive in the *Gendertrash* archive, but the following transcription has been provided by Mirha-Soleil Ross from her own files.

Jamison Green was, in 1996, the Director of FTM International, and had previously been the editor of the *FTM Newsletter*. He is also the author of the seminal transmasculine autobiography *Becoming a Visible Man* (2004).

Mirha-Soleil Ross: It's really frustrating trying to explain to people that transsexual men didn't "change sex" for socio-economic reasons or because they're self-loathing women/lesbians. It's one of the most pervasive misconceptions around, despite a number of FTMs appearing in articles, books, and videos, clearly stating that those are not the reasons for transitioning. Could you be more eloquent than me at explaining it?

James Green: Well I can try. I think people have a misconception that it's going to be very simple for us to suddenly get male privileges and that's why we do it, when exactly the opposite is true. We are still transsexuals and we still have all of the social conditioning that we had prior to transition. So we still have our own self-esteem issues and fear issues about being accepted as men or even as human beings because of being transsexuals. And also you don't automatically join the Old Boys' Club just because you happen to have a male body. You have to be born into the Old Boys' Club to be a member of the Old Boys' Club. Not all men belong to the Old Boys' Club. And we [transsexual men] certainly don't automatically get membership in it. And I would say that probably 99.9% of FTM transsexuals are aware that social status is not an automatic thing. I think very, very few of us are women-loathing. I think many FTMs are attracted to women sexually. There are certainly plenty of gay-identified FTMs. Many of them have actually been lesbians and very feminist-conscious lesbians prior to transitioning but found themselves with a transitioned sexual orientation as well. This is one of the surprises that can happen to people as they transition. These things are not written in stone. But again, it's not about getting something that you don't have. Transitioning is about being something that is already inside of you. It's not even about being something that you want to be. It's being something that you are.

Mirha-Soleil: I also tell people that it's very problematic to say that a whole community of men "suffers" from internalized sexism especially when so many of its members come from a lesbian-feminist background and are, as you said, very feminist-conscious.

James: Certainly. We have not internalized sexism. I have seen FTMs, especially younger ones who have not been through the feminist movement, who are too young for that, who are starting hormones much closer to their original biological adolescence. Some can end up with some sexist behaviours and a lot of it is just acting out the adolescence stuff that happens. A lot of it is biochemical and they usually wake up after a few years. But I haven't seen many older FTMs who are all that sexist.

Mirha-Soleil: One underlying idea in all of this is that it's easier to be a transsexual man than to be a lesbian.

James: [Laughter] That's an incredibly naïve statement. I mean that's a lot less expensive to be a lesbian. If you have a female body you certainly don't risk losing your social status. And lesbians certainly have a social status that is probably higher than transsexual men. Because at least most people in this culture understand that gay and lesbian people are pretty much o.k. whereas people are very prejudiced against transsexuals.

Mirha-Soleil: A FTM friend of mine told me that one reason it took him so long to transition was because he had a hard time reconciling his feminism with his wanting to change his body and live as a man. Have you met many transsexual men with similar experiences?

James: Absolutely. I think a lot of people who have come of age in a feminist-consciousness do have difficulty with reconciling transsexualism and feminism. It's a very, very difficult thing to do. I personally knew I was a transsexual when I was 20 years old but I was scared to do anything about it. And by the time I was absolutely compelled to do anything about it, in my mid to late 30's, I was scared to death to lose my entire history. I had done a great deal to advance the cause of feminism myself and I certainly don't want to pretend that never happened.

Mirha-Soleil: I read somewhere that you really flipped out when you were 18 and your lover suggested that you should have a sex change?

James: Yes. I just said, "Don't ever talk to me about that again. I have enough problems in my life. Only crazy people do that."

Mirha-Soleil: When I was younger, I decided to live as a gay boy because it was at least a valid and recognized identity. There were also positive gay role models out there. All the images I had of transsexuals were horrible. I had all those negative scary stereotypes in mind.

James: I had exactly the same thing. I thought there were only crazy people who did it. I also wasn't sure that you could do it if you had a female body. And I knew that because I had a female body and that I was attracted to women, there was a social role for me called "lesbian." And they were young burgeoning communities. I thought,"This has got to be it; this must be where I fit."

Mirha-Soleil: Especially at that time, it's not like there was a very strong FTM community to belong to.

James: There was no FTM community; there was nothing. There were isolated people but they were really, really difficult to find.

Mirha-Soleil: Do you think that many people who are now living as lesbians want to transition but are scared of being rejected by, stigmatized by, and to lose a community they have strong links with?

James: I suspect that there are more latent FTMs lingering in the lesbian world, yes.

Mirha-Soleil: I know that there are transsexual men who have strong links with the lesbian community and want to remain part of it even after transition. How do you feel about that whole issue?

James: Well personally I think that it is extremely problematic. I think that those people need to cultivate communities that will accept them. They shouldn't expect to walk into any lesbian space or situation where people don't know them personally already and expect people to understand who they are and where they're coming from. I think there's a lot more developing tolerance and acceptance of FTM people within lesbian spaces now in San Francisco at any rate. But I personally would be very much against a blanket recommendation that all lesbian spaces should be open to any FTM. Because I think there are very distinct differences. Once you've been taking testosterone for a long period of time, even a couple of years, your thought processes are different. You may still have the consciousness and may still have all the memories of your past, but your way of dealing and being in the world is different. And some people don't want to admit that.

Mirha-Soleil: There seems to be an increasing interest within the lesbian community about transsexual men. Do you think that it is just a phase or a sincere interest that might eventually lead to a better understanding?

James: Well I hope that it's not just a phase. I hope that it is a sincere interest. I think it is part of the exploration of gender and what does gender mean and what is the place of butch and what is butch-femme and all of that. It's a very complicated thing. I personally never encourage anyone who is butch to be FTM. That's not what I or my group is about. We offer space for people who are butch to see how it feels but without any kind of pressure whatsoever. I believe that people who are butch often will have conflicts about their bodies but that does not necessarily mean that they are transsexuals. And those things can be worked out for many people. Some of them may be transsexuals, for some of them it may be more appropriate to live the rest of their lives in a male body with a feminist-consciousness.

Mirha-Soleil: Another misconception is that TS men were the"butchiest" when living as women. But as you said in an interview in *TransSisters*, you were very androgynous compared to the butch lesbians who identified as women. They had an attitude and mannerisms that you didn't want to have.

James: Yes, that's correct. And I think that there are certainly many FTM transsexuals who you would never pick as being butch at all. I certainly have met women – especially who have not come from the lesbian world – who you would not ever suspect as having a butch cell in their body. They just look feminine, act feminine, and yet as you talk to them and as they open up, you begin to see the masculine side. There are people who have told people like them, "Oh, you'll never make it! You won't make it as a man. You will not transition well. You won't look good." And that isn't necessarily true. …

Mirha-Soleil: You went to Camp Trans in Michigan in the summer of 1994 to support transsexual women's protest for the right to participate in the Festival.

James: I was invited by the Transsexual Menace and tangentially by the Lesbian Avengers to speak and hold a workshop at Camp Trans and to support the inclusion of lesbian- identified transsexual women. I think that what lesbians are afraid of with respect to transsexual women is that they may have penises. And they're afraid that the penis they might have makes them behave or think in certain ways, that they're going to perpetrate male violence against women or try to take over the women's spaces. I would counter that by saying that most transsexual women, while having had male bodies, have grown up with a kind of oppression that is very much similar to that women female-bodied people experienced as outsiders and as not men. And that women have nothing of that sort to fear from transsexual women who identify as lesbians.

Mirha-Soleil: I think it's particularly true for the ones of us who grew up visibly transgendered. While some transsexual women were able to pass as straight men for 20, 30, 40 years prior to transition, some others like me were stigmatized, ostracized, and physically assaulted on a daily basis as feminine boys. And in the patriarchy, being a feminine boy is certainly not better than being a woman.

James: In fact, it's probably worse because you are made responsible for holding the image of male where as women aren't responsible for holding the image of male so you don't get beaten up.

Mirha-Soleil: It's also that you can't defend yourself and have no recourse. You're not strong enough to fight back and you can't get support because it's considered socially legitimate for men to beat up feminine boys and men. We are considered to be the ones at fault. So you're stuck.

James: I feel for you and other people who have experienced that. I just think that it is such a painful thing. I also was a very androgynous child and suffered for that. I was visibly transgendered as well and it was very difficult. But certainly as a female-bodied transgendered child, I didn't have it as hard as male-bodied children. But it is still not easy because even though the system comes down really hard on a feminine boy much earlier than on a masculine girl, there comes a point when she is now suddenly made responsible for holding the feminine image as much as the feminine boy is made responsible for holding the masculine image. And the girls start giving you trouble for being inappropriate. And the boys start giving you trouble because they think after puberty, "Ah-hah, here's a girl and we can use and treat her like a girl. She's available because she's here with us."

Mirha-Soleil: We always hear transsexual women talking about *The Transsexual Empire.* But do transsexual men talk about it too? Did it have any impact on your community?

James: The original edition of the book had virtually nothing in it about transsexual men. The second edition of the book had a revised introduction in which transsexual men were mentioned as simple dupes of the system and pretty much dismissed. Because we haven't been in a battle with Janice Raymond, no it's not a book that FTMs refer to and talk about to the extent that the rest of the gender community does. Those of us who are making general arguments about how transsexuals are viewed will of course refer to *The Transsexual Empire* because it's such a seminal work [laughter]. But for the men's community as a whole, it doesn't have that much impact. But we have a book in the FTM community that MTFs never talk about and that is *Female-to-Male Transsexualism* by Leslie Lothstein. That is our nemesis book. [The next sentence is distorted and can't be transcribed.] While that may be true for some people, it is certainly not true for all FTM transsexuals. Not all FTMs come from families that are abusive. Not all FTMs have been abused or raped or have had violence perpetrated against them or observed that happening to their mother or sisters. And many female-bodied people in our culture experience that kind of abuse and do not become transsexuals. So I think this is a false syllogism and Lothstein based his entire study on this. In fact many of the people who came to his clinic were brought by their homophobic parents. And in the face of homophobia, some people do think that the only way to be normal is to have a sex-change. And that's one of the reasons why I think gay people react to transsexuals. Because they think that we are the traitors, that we are trying to become normal, that we are unable to deal with homosexuality, and receive transsexualism as a cure. And this also is not true. All of this is from the point of view of blaming the victim. It's a way to say, "Of course they want to do this, they are crazy." And Lothstein's book is the only book entirely about FTMs that has ever been published.

Mirha-Soleil: What people should understand is that there are probably as many transsexuals who decide to live as lesbians or gay men because it's a way to avoid having to deal with their transsexualism. Something else that is bad about that kind of analysis is that you can't be a transsexual man just because you are a transsexual man. You must be doing it because of internalized sexism, lesbophobia, or because of abuse in your family. It can't be just a condition in itself like for MTFs. Do you think transsexual men and women have a lot of knowledge that can be extremely precious and beneficial to feminism in better understanding the complexity of oppressions based on sex, gender and sexuality?

James: Absolutely! And I don't know how I can put it any better than what you just said [both laugh]. I think we bring something not just to feminism but to all human understanding because we have been through this transition. We have walked/lived across the bridge between cultures that are male and female. We still don't really fit into either one even after we transition. We are still different. Many transsexual people say, "No we're not... " or "No I'm really a woman... " or "No I'm really a man." Now that may be the way they live but personally I feel that we are still different because we have shared this transition that very few people go through. We can observe gender in ways that non-transsexual people simply do not see. We have the capacity to make observations that are enlightening about what gender is and what those systems are that bind us down. And we can choose to break those because we choose to walk across that bridge. For instance, men say, "Men are not emotional and they can't cry." And many FTMs also say, "Since I've taken testosterone, I'm not as emotional. I don't cry as easily." For me personally that is not the case. I still am very emotional and I can cry at a good Hallmark card commercial. I'm embarrassed about it [both laugh]. I think, "They manipulated me again." And I can bring that as a man. I can bring that "emotionalism" to other men.

Mirha-Soleil: That leads to my next question. Do you think that pro-feminist transsexual men have something important to contribute to the anti-sexist men's movement?

James: Absolutely. I have personally participated in a pro-feminist men's group of about forty men for a period of five years. And I'm still very close to a number of the men in the group. The reason I stopped participating was because my transsexual activism was taking more and more time. And also I needed to have time with my girlfriend and my daughter. But the fact is I was in that group for over a year before I came out to anyone as an FTM. And in the year when I was perceived as a man, I sort of rose to a leadership position in the group. A lot of the men in the group looked up to me as a role model. I was very comfortable in my body and I had a very easy masculinity that other men, who had various insecurities about themselves, admired. When they found out that I once had a female body, some of them were literally shocked. Well most of them were shocked but only a couple of them were actually upset and only briefly. They realized that their experience of me had been so real and so true that they had to call into question what they had thought of as meaning masculinity and meaning men. It actually gave them a new perspective. First of all, they realized that they can't make assumptions about anyone anymore and that made them more aware of everyone around them. Not that they were suddenly worried about being betrayed or worried about somebody trying to pull the wool over their eyes. But they realized that people are much more than what they see, than what someone observes about them. That people are much richer than that. And they wanted to be open to experience that richness about other people rather than just judge them on their experiences, on appearances.

Mirha-Soleil: You said something that really touched me once. You said that you really worked on being a woman and a lesbian. I feel that I worked very hard on being a good gay boy prior to transition and therefore I think that we both earned our membership in the queer community, even if our sexual orientations are somehow heterosexuals.

James: Yes, definitely. I feel that I will always be a queer person even though I am completely acceptable and accepted as a man. And even though I appear to be in a heterosexual relationship, my partner is bisexual. One of the things that I was worried about knowing that I was going to be a heterosexual man was, how am I going to deal with heterosexual women who have no feminist-consciousness? Am I going to have to train people that I become involved with? I was so fortunate to find a woman who already had that consciousness and was interested in being in a relationship with me. Maybe it's an expression of a bias that the queer community has against heterosexual women which probably is unfounded but still, it is something that you think about. And I'm certain that there are heterosexual women who are feminist-conscious but still, you panic when you think: "I'm enculturated in this way and how am I going to relate to somebody who hasn't shared this culture with me."

Mirha-Soleil: Now what about heterosexual privileges? I've got to admit that when I walk hand in hand with a guy on the street, I'm not going to get the same look, attitudes that a gay male or a lesbian couple would get. But I think they're just superficial heterosexual privileges, don't you think?

James: Yeah, and I mean what does it get you?

Mirha-Soleil: It doesn't get you the right to be married if you're pre- or non-op and in certain places, even when you're post-op.

James: Yes, that's right and it doesn't get you a better job.

Mirha-Soleil: There is at least something great that you have, that MTFs don't have and it's a support group for partners of FTMs.

James: To tell you the truth, I think that consciousness to develop a group for partners came out of people's lesbian history, came out of the feminist background, came out of that consciousness about other people that you have when you are socialized in a female way. We don't lose that. Not that we are female. We are not female. But we have consciousness that we gain from years of socialization, some of which worked and some of which didn't. There were lots of things that I was socialized to do as a female that I couldn't do, that simply would not work for me. I was incapable of behaving in certain ways that were expected of me as a female-bodied individual. But I have not changed my behaviour or my attitudes now that I have a male body. The way I walk is the same. The way I move, use my body, the way I express myself is exactly the same.

Mirha-Soleil: Don't you also think that the way or the extent to which you internalize the male or female training that was imposed on you as a child varies a lot not only depending on each person but also on your environment, how you perceive yourself, how people react to you when you walk on the street, etc. For example, a masculine girl probably doesn't internalize socialization the same way a feminine girl does.

James: And people have different family dynamics, as Dr. Lothstein noted. Some families are more tolerant than others, tolerant of different aspects of masculine behaviour in a female-bodied child. For instance, I was very much encouraged to be athletic and very physically active but we also fought a lot about clothing that I had to wear but only at certain times. So to me it seems like there was a mixed message. One day I'm allowed to be who I am and the next day I'm supposed to be somebody else. So I had to learn to adapt to different things. I've talked to other kids who grew up in a much more rigid environment where they were literally in a gender gulag with respect to how they were forced to behave 100% of the time.
Mirha-Soleil: James, thank you very much.

Interview with Viviane Namaste

This is the second of two interviews Mirha-Soleil Ross conducted in October 1996 and broadcast in December of the same year as a special feature on CIUT 89.5FM's *Gaywire Radio*.

Though conducted significantly after the initial slated (and missed) release date for *Gendertrash* #5, Mirha-Soleil Ross indicates that at this point she still hoped to complete the fifth issue, and intended to include this interview in it.

The interview does not survive in the *Gendertrash* archive, but the following transcription has been provided by Mirha-Soleil Ross from her own files.

Viviane Namaste, a previous *Gendertrash* contributor, went on to produce some of the most crucial works of trans scholarship of the twenty-first century, including *Invisible Lives* (2000) and *Sex Change, Social Change* (2005).

Mirha-Soleil Ross: Can you talk about the difficulties you encountered when starting to do research on transsexual and transgendered people's access to healthcare and social services?
Viviane Namaste: I think the biggest difficulty was the fact that there was nothing available in the past. So when I would speak with people who were unfamiliar with the issues at different agencies, they would not have any kind of information. So people would often say: "Oh well, are there many transsexuals in Montréal or in Toronto?" Also people would assume that gender and sexuality were the same thing. That transsexuals, transvestites, and transgendered people are a subsection of the gay male community and that the gay male community takes care of us. So that was just sort of an automatic thing – people would constantly refer me to lesbian and gay groups.
Mirha-Soleil: I think another problem you had to face was that you couldn't include the whole transgender spectrum?
Viviane: Oh absolutely! (laughter) Yes, when I started doing research on HIV, I wanted to do research on HIV and transgendered people. And what I found, which seems fairly obvious in retrospect, is that as transgendered people we live our lives in very different ways. Especially for people who are invested in any kind of body work. We organize our lives very differently to change our bodies. People with middle-class resources organize their lives through gender clinics, through savings, or investments to pay for surgery, electrolysis, etc. And people who don't have those kind of educational, financial, capital resources often do sex work to pay for their transition. So I found that people had very different relations then to HIV and to sexuality in general. Cross-dressers didn't want to have anything to do with the work I was doing on HIV. They didn't see themselves as in any way at risk for HIV because HIV was something that affected gay men, that affected drug users, that affected sex trade workers.
Mirha-Soleil: So how do you account for the diversity of transsexual and transgendered people's lives both when doing research and when trying to implement social services for them?
Viviane: I think there are a number of different strategies. I think in terms of both the research that you do and the social services that you develop, you begin with what people are living. You begin with where people are in the world. Because if you begin somewhere else, you're not going to get people's confidence. They're not going to want to talk to you about their lives for your research and they're not going to want to come to your programs. So people have to be involved in that process and feel a part of that process. And that takes a while to sort of do. Also I think that you have to look at diversity and differences within transgender communities. So understanding that not only will there be splits around class but also there may be splits around race and different cultural communities. For instance here in the context of Montréal, Haïtian transsexuals or Native transsexuals may not even negotiate the same kind of spaces that transsexuals who are white or québecoise "de souche" might negotiate. So those kinds of issues are important when wanting to address diversity.
Mirha-Soleil: You said earlier that there was nothing done before and that was one of the biggest difficulties when you started doing research. It must have been very frustrating?

Viviane: It was incredibly frustrating. What I actually found to be the most frustrating experience was walking into mainstream AIDS services organizations and realizing that in every city I went to in Canada, they were all located in the downtown area, they had nice offices, computers, phones, and nothing for transgendered people. Nothing in Montréal... Nothing in Toronto... Nothing in Vancouver. I was just like – fuck! What the hell is happening here! And when I went to needle exchange programs, they didn't necessarily have specific services for transgendered people but they didn't flip out when I walked in the office as a visibly transgendered person. Some of the agencies had already been collecting statistics using categories of male, female, and other or male, female, transgendered. So that to me indicated that already they knew this population existed. Then the other thing that was noteworthy is that these were often located in the poor section of the cities and they often had funding for the next 6 months, one kind of old MAC classic computer from the eighties hobbling on some table, and one phone for four people. So it really struck me around the politics of AIDS, AIDS funding, and how AIDS gets managed. And what that means then for addressing HIV concerns for transgendered people and especially for transgendered people who live and work on the street.

Mirha-Soleil: Have you found it hard to get transsexual and transgendered people to talk about their issues?

Viviane: Yes to talk about their issues for sure. I think that the only discourse we really have ever been allowed is one of autobiography. It's one of saying: "Well when I was 5, I always played with dolls... and I've always been this way... and I'm trapped in the wrong body." That kind of thing. Everything from talk shows to books to even psychiatry. If you see a doctor who had no experience with transgendered people, that will be one of the first questions that's asked: "How long have you known?" And if you say: "Oh well when I was 5, I remember this happened," that serves the function. So I think that transgendered people often speak that line but I don't think that we have the skills—

Mirha-Soleil: Yet!!!

Viviane: Yet... exactly! (laughter) Exactement! – to get back and analyze our situation. I think people know that there's a lot of injustice out there. People understand what it means to live with that harassment, discrimination, and absolute denial of access to services. But I think that we're just beginning to articulate what that means. And we're just now as transgendered people – especially those of us who don't come from middle-class backgrounds and who don't come from a history of NGOs – beginning to figure out how NGOs work, how the government gives money, and say: "Oh this money is for populations which haven't been serviced by other agencies. Well that's us!"

Mirha-Soleil: There's something I always tell transsexual and transgendered people who are not academics like me... I always tell them that it's very important to be able to understand what academics are saying about us because they're the ones who are taken seriously when it comes to making decisions that affect our lives.

Viviane: Absolutely.

Mirha-Soleil: And I think we need to be able to train our own people to be politically articulate.

Viviane: I think so as well. I was just reading some historical stuff on transgendered people this week. Once they had operations happening in the early forties, in this case in Switzerland, they realized there was a huge problem with civic status and with legal status. And none of the lawyers or the government representatives knew what to do. So they just turned to the doctors and said: "O.k. what is this person?" And the doctors said: "This person is a woman." It was a male-to-female transsexual. So they classified the person as a woman legally. But they didn't turn to that person and say: "How do you identify and how do you describe yourself?" What does this mean? It's always experts who are invoked in that way. And I think that yes we do need to train our own but I also think we need allies who are non-transgendered people and are willing to engage in collaborative research methods with us. Who are willing to sit down and document what the problems are and who say: "What kind of services do you want to see. What would be useful for you?"

Mirha-Soleil: When we say training our own, we mean training our own to be able to analyze and understand how transsexual and transgendered people are oppressed in this culture... But I also think that we need to be present and work in social agencies because I don't think that sensitivity training is enough. I think we need to have our own people out there too.

Viviane: Yes. Also there's something about "présence permanente" that makes us always there which means that people have to deal with it on a regular basis. And non-transgendered people have to deal with the situation of a pronoun fuck-up whether it's them who mix up a pronoun with a transgendered co-worker or a transgendered client or whatever. Because people make pronoun mistakes all the time. And that could be a really painful experience for us as transgendered people to go through. But what I actually find the most interesting thing now is to see how people deal with that. And that for me is a really important reason why we as transgendered people should have positions in social service agencies and represent our own interests.

Mirha-Soleil: In *Access Denied: A Report on the Experiences of Transsexuals and Transgenderists with Health Care and Social Services in Ontario*, you talk about the discrepancies you found between what transsexual and transgendered people and the staff at social agencies would tell you.

Viviane: The point of the research was to give a survey of what transgendered people's experiences were with healthcare and social services in Ontario, primarily Toronto because there wasn't really a lot of money allocated to transgender research within Project Affirmation. So when I spoke with transgendered people, they told me horror stories of showing up at youth shelters and being told: "No you can't stay here because you look like a freak and it wouldn't be safe for you so go away and stay out on the street" because that's apparently safe for you. To people who were left in halls of hospital emergency wards, who were literally ridiculed by the emergency room staff, who were referred to with the word "it." Things like that. And then when I would call the different hospitals or shelter workers, people would always say: "Oh no no no! There's no discrimination here." So then I would sort of push it and say: "Oh well do you have an anti-discrimination policy which includes transgendered people?" And 9 times out of 10 people would ask me to define what "transgender" meant. Then we would sort of get through that and find out that no, there was no anti-discrimination policy. And I would push further and ask if they had training on transgender issues for the staff. And again I'd find out that no, that hadn't happened. So I think that was a huge discrepancy within social services. Workers were saying: "Oh no there's no discrimination here; we're here to help." And transgendered people were saying: "Oh my God it was a total nightmare!" And the upshot of that is that transgendered people just don't access those services. The transgendered sex trade workers that I interviewed for Project Affirmation, when I asked them if they've ever used women's or youth shelters, they just laughed at me. They were like: "No way! They totally don't want us so why would we go there? We'll go to the bathhouse, or we'll go to the crack house, or we'll find a friend's place to crash, but no we would never ever consider going there."

Mirha-Soleil: Can you talk about the importance of addressing the issues of transsexual and transgendered people who are sex workers, homeless, ex-convicts, HIV+, IV drug users in particular.

Viviane: There's one thing that I really noticed especially when I was dealing with shelters and shelter issues. Women's shelters would often have different criteria for who could come although none of it was written down. But when I would interview people, they would say for instance: "We'll accept some woman here at our women's shelter if she's post-operative or if she doesn't look like a man." I was also told by numerous people who work at different agencies: "If she's not a problem because we don't want any disruption and we want the other women to feel safe." And what the criteria of someone having had sex reassignment reinforces is a division between good transsexuals who are post-operative and bad transsexuals or not complete transsexuals who aren't post-operative. I talk about this in the report for Project Affirmation, about how that actually denies the realities of transgendered people who are living on the street. For instance if you're a seropositive transgendered person, you can't find someone who's going to do surgery on you even if you want it. So in effect these women's shelters are saying that they'll accept male-to-female transsexuals but they won't accept implicitly male-to-female transsexuals who are seropositive. The invocation of appearance is the same kind of thing. If somebody is living on the street, they don't have a lot of financial resources. Then they might not have a lot of money for electrolysis which can cost from 40 to 80 bucks an hour. So they might have a bit of visible facial hair and they might not pass as non-transsexual women. They might or they might not. So again, that type of criteria doesn't really respond to that. Or if someone's just gotten out of jail where they couldn't do electrolysis, where they may not have gotten their hormones. So all those kinds of issues aren't being addressed. So in a way street agencies are saying: "We're here and we'll serve transgendered people and there's no discrimination." But when it comes to the nitty-gritty reality of street transgendered people's lives, they're not being served.

Mirha-Soleil: In *Genderbashing*, you look at the relation between sexuality and gender in violence against sexual minorities. Can you talk about what you found out?

Viviane: What I found out in *Genderbashing* are two things. One is that most of the documented incidents around violence against lesbians and gay men is often violence against people who violate normative sex/gender relations. So basically what I found out was that most of the people who are hit, who are assaulted, or who are harassed in any kind of way are harassed because they're not fitting into expectations of gender. The second thing that I found out is that in community-based responses to what is colloquially referred to as "gay bashing," gender isn't really discussed at all. So not only the community-based responses to violence don't address the situation of transsexual and transgendered people, both female-to-male and male-to-female, but in point of fact, they don't even provide a really complex response to violence against lesbians and gay men. Because lesbians and gay men who don't violate normative sex/gender relations, while they may still be subject to verbal and physical harassment, are subject to that much less than lesbians and gay men who do violate sex/gender relations.

Mirha-Soleil: Are any lesbian and gay activists/community workers starting to take that knowledge into consideration?

Viviane: Specifically around transgendered people?

Mirha-Soleil: Yes.

Viviane: I think that there are a few. But I know that in presenting the work at different conferences, a couple of people who self-identify as lesbian and gay people and who've been working in anti-violence stuff have come up to me and asked for copies of it. I also know that when the article was published, I went down to "Dire enfin la violence" which is the anti-gay and lesbian violence project here in Montreal and got them a copy. I said: "This is what I am and this is what the article is about. If you would like a workshop on transsexual 101, it wouldn't have to be specifically violence, I would be more than happy to do that. We should work in collaboration." The article also concludes with specific methodological issues like if a transgendered person doesn't perceive him or herself to be part of lesbian and gay communities, then they're not going to call the lesbian and gay bashing hotline to record the incidents of aggression. So there's a whole methodological problem around the way we collect statistics – how could we better understand this violence and the gendered nature of that violence if transgendered people don't become involved in lesbian and gay communities. So I spoke with the outreach worker about that and that was in July or August 1996 and I've heard nothing. So to me that kind of experience arises often particularly within the context of Montréal and if ever they're questioned on it in the media people will say: "Oh well the transgender community is a closed community and we haven't been able to access it."

Mirha-Soleil: This is the usual argument to legitimize their lack of action on the issue.

Viviane: That's it. But the reality is that I've said: "Look I have all the stupid academic credentials and I'm willing to give of my time to do a 101 thing or to sit down and chat with you." And I didn't even get a follow-up phone call of politeness. So I don't want to trash all lesbians and gay men but . . .

Mirha-Soleil: But "point de suspension..." (both laugh loudly) I find that a lot of lesbians and gay men working in community organizations and social services often assume that they can deal with transsexual/transgender issues. What do you think this assumption is based on?

Viviane: I think in some ways it's based on this assumption that lesbians and gay men know what it's like to live with difference, to be persecuted for having a marginalized sexuality, and even a marginalized gender position because gender and sexuality do get collapsed in this culture. And I think the whole "Queer" thing... God I totally wish that would have never happened because I think it has totally erased differences around different kinds of non-heterosexual people. Particularly when lesbians and gay men use that term because I think that they often apply the coming out model to everything, to their political work, to social services and social organizing, and to youth programs. And in the case of transgendered people, coming out isn't appropriate because we don't have the luxury of staying in. You can't change your gender on the job and not tell people because gender is a really public thing. If your landlord lives in your building or right behind you, it's really hard to change your gender and not have her/him know. So coming out and being proud to me has no relevance. I want to survive the fucking day without being hit. For me when I was in the middle of my transition, that's what I would always think about all the time. And I think that lesbians and gay men don't often sit back and think about how things may be different for transgendered people or for other sexual minorities for that matter.

Mirha-Soleil: For the ones of them who have really good motivations, sincere ones and are really meaning well and are ready to learn and work on it...

Viviane: And there are many...

Mirha-Soleil: Yes there are many... What would be your piece of advice?

Viviane: Keep doing your homework. And when I say doing your homework, I mean much more than reading Kate Bornstein and Leslie Feinberg. Read our media. Read *Transsexual News-Telegraph*, Female-to-Male Newsletters. Read our autobiographies. Watch our videos...

Mirha-Soleil: I think sometimes people feel it's a lot of work for a percentage of the population that is still considered small. And that it's not worth all the efforts and energy. I think it's for the same reason that only recently have social agencies started to offer honoraria for transsexual/transgendered people to educate them. Before they expected it for free. It was not worth it financially. I want to talk about the academia. You criticized some people who are referred to as social theorists and who write about transsexual/transgendered people for being insensitive to and disengaged from the experiences of the communities they theorize about. Can you explain that, give examples?

Viviane: Mostly I was talking about Marjorie Garber who wrote this book called *Vested Interests*. *Vested Interests* is a really scandalous book. She just grabs on to this thing "transgender/transvestite" and then every time she sees transvestism happening she cites it with very little historical context, no social context, no real discussion. So she moves from David Bowie to Kabuki theater in Japan and goes: "Wow yeah! Transvestism. And you know why? It's because the phallus was always hidden because Lacan, the French theorist, says the phallus only works when veiled. That's why David Bowie was so successful because the phallus was veiled and that's why the Kabuki theater is so interesting because the phallus is veiled." So you read it for 400 pages and you go: "What? Where's your editor?"

Mirha-Soleil Ross: Yes I know. She really needs an editor. In one of your articles you said that academics can produce knowledge that is useful to community activists. I think she's a good example of someone who's not producing very useful material.

Viviane: Also she moves between transsexuals and transvestites without ever looking at how those terms get used and defined and pitted against each other within transvestite/transsexual/ transgender communities. So in that sense she's not grounded. And she kind of stops on page 4 and says: "Oh yeah... transgendered people are also political because they're organizing around the right to shop. Because they want access to women's clothes in large sizes." So for her in *Vested Interests* that sums up transgender politics.

World's Greatest Cocksucker

These interviews were conducted by Christine Martin. They have been fully laid-out, and Mirha-Soleil Ross indicates that she hoped to include them in *Gendertrash* #5. A letter from Martin, dated September 11, 1994, also verifies they were indeed accepted for publication. It also indicates the illustration to be included on page 13, sadly not preserved, was a drawing by Danny entitled "that's a good boy, suck daddy's big hard dick." Portions of the text on the third page of the article (marked as p. 9) are overwritten by the words "FTM Queer", so a transcription of that page has been provided after the facsimiles.

c:\xpress\gtrash4\vern.

"World's Greatest Cocksucker"

interviews with two female-to-gay males
by Christine Martin

These interviews were taped respectively in March & April 1991 and were originally part of an art installation at the Whitney Museum Independant Study Programme. Since then, they have been published in a variety of places including, "Fuzz Box" (a gay fanzine from Montréal), the gender issue of the New York dance magazine "Movement Research", and a literary journal "Fiction International" from the University of San Diego Press.

"World's Greatest Cocksucker" *illustrates how "Danny" (a female to male transsexual hustler and gay male chaser) cannot fully be represented by identity politics but can only be understood of in terms of libidinous flow. Libido flows stronger than the categories of sexual preference and gender. Female to male transsexuals who love men, and male to female transsexuals who love women are not merely "gay transsexuals." The libidinous flow has a survival mechanism like a river finding its way to the ocean. It will overcome obstacles, flowing over and around rocks, hills and mountains; it is drawn to the source.*

C.M. Sept. '94

Vern

Christine: ***What did you mean when you said that there is genderphobia in the gay community and homophobia in the gender community?***

Vern: "Genderphobia" is my term. I made it up because there is a clone movement in the non-heterosexual community to make everybody look just like heterosexuals who sleep with each other. The fact is that there is a whole large section of the gay community or the sexual minority community who is never going to vote republican. There are drag queens, there are transsexuals, there are transgenderists, and there is a real groundswell in the "gay community" to try and pretend that these people don't exist and it drives me crazy.

C: ***Sounds like an attempt to "clean up" the gay community.***

V: Yeah and to make the gay community look like the straight community. If you want to just be straight and sleep with other straight people of the same gender, well, that's your own business, and I'm not going to tell you not to do it, but what Stonewall and all this other shit is about, is the freedom to be who you are, and if you are a crossdresser or a transsexual, or if you are a three-eyed monster from Mars, it's nobody else's business to tell you not to be that.

C: ***Is there prejudice in the gay community against transvestites, either in the bars or in the bedrooms?***

V: There is one real asshole bar owner here in Buffalo — he's a real scumbag. His name is John Little — please feel free to publish his name. All of his bars restrict entrance to crossdressers. Most of the gay community's transvestites don't have any lack of sleeping partners, but they do lack the respect they should get. These are people who deserve the same rights and privileges as everybody else. Human rights should be equally applied to everybody. You can't just point fingers at people who are not just like you, and say, "You aren't as good as me so you don't get the same rights that I do."

C: ***I heard that 40% of male-to-female transsexuals are lesbians, and I was wondering about the percentage of female-to-males who were practicing gay men.***

V: There was a show taped for Geraldo, on transsexual gays, but they cut it; they never showed it. It was too controversial. Nobody wants to talk about it, especially the gay community. People want to be able to say, "You're a transsexual so you must do this," and straight people especially think that transsexualism is just an extreme form of homosexuality. It makes everyone much more comfortable to believe this. It's a nice and tidy way to understand the world.

C: ***Have you gained male privilege as a female-to-male?***

V: In that video by Johnny Armstrong, "Linda Les and Annie," Les Nichols says he feels like a spy, and that's true. It is amazing the amount of respect you get as a man. In my tenth grade auto shop class the mechanics would pull the men out onto the floor to show them the parts and explain what they were doing, whereas if you were a woman they would assume you were a complete twit. I'm 26. This time last year I was "Miss." Now it's "Sir." It didn't go from "Miss" to "Son" or "Ma'am" to "Sir." It went from "Miss" to "Sir."

C: ***That is a step up in terms of respect. All the F2Ms I have met have been very attractive, very virile guys, and I was wondering how that masculinity is being invented. I see gay male codes influencing their style.***

V: Last night I was at an overdressed activity, which was crawling with crossdressers, and there was this meta-crossdressing there: genetic males who were transvestites who were dressing like women in men's clothing. Some people analyze it too much. People want there to be neatness and tidiness, and there isn't. Transsexuals make a big scrap heap out of everybody's tidy life. If they can file us some place they are happy, but when they can't they are tormented.

C: ***You sleep with both men and women. How does this happen?***

V: Actually, I'm not sleeping with anybody lately because I don't do relationships very well.

C: ***Neither do I.***

V: I just broke up with somebody really badly and have felt like a swine for weeks.

C: ***I wanted to talk about F2Ms who sleep with men (even if their preference may be for women), and how man-to-man sexual experiences differ from other sexual experiences for you. What's the difference?***

V: One of the big differences is the power relationship. Between men there is more of a power parity than there ever can be in any heterosexual relationship. As a woman I dated men whom I was perfectly capable of beating to a pulp, but there was no power parity, and this goes for even the most egalitarian "fluff ball" of guys. There are women who are my friends who recognize this and are even bothered by me now, and I'm still the same "fluff ball" I always was. In this society, just being perceived as male increases your power relative to your partner. The difference with lesbian relationships is that you are two of the disaffected. Two white males in this society are almost the "aristocracy" because you have the trappings of the power structure.

if nothing else, transsexuals in this society shake things up a little

C: ***Are you a top or a bottom, and does that change if you are with men or women?***

V: I'm sort of fluid, and it varies with who I'm with. People want to stick me and everyone into a little pigeon hole, and I, more so than most, don't have one. Most people don't, but there are a lot of people who will try to fit into one anyway. There is so much less struggle that way. It's good to be shaken up. If nothing else, transsexuals in this society shake things up a little.

C: ***The gay and lesbian community needs to be shaken up, too. For example, the separatism that lesbians have been practicing just doesn't make sense any more, especially now that there are no guarantees regarding gender.***

V: I tend bar at a lesbian bar one day a week. A few weeks ago there were these two women there who were real men-haters. They were upset at the fact that I was tending bar there. They were making anti-man comments all night, and what was I going to say? It wasn't worth the effort to get into it all. After they left, I was alone in the bar, and these three men came in. They had come from the strip bar up the street. They were real assholes. They were everything the women before had believed all men to be. What it is that these women hated about men does exist out there. It's easy to generalize. Those men had perceived as a guy and didn't get heavy with me, but the power play was interesting because if they had perceived me as a woman things would have been very different.

C: ***Are you ever concerned with the threat of violence?***

V: No, not really, because I pass very well.

C: ***Even though you have now gained a certain amount of male privilege, couldn't you now be subjected to [illegible] violence which threatens gay [illegible]***

V: I don't wo[illegible]ch. I really live on the fringe.

C: ***Are you out as a tr[illegible]sexual?***

V: I'm really o[illegible]all town. There isn't a bar w[illegible]ere I don't know someone. H[illegible] usually have no clue because they [illegible] read the gay papers.

C: ***Most of my political associations have been with gay me[illegible]ifically through ACT UP and the AIDS cri[illegible]), my roommates are always gay men, and I th[illegible]ity, desire and fantasies ar[illegible]ion of the gay male commu[illegible]ommunity. For example, my [illegible]rt and my sexual partners are frequent. These practices and tastes are typ[illegible]lly associated with gay men.***

V: In Buffalo [illegible] no gay community as separate from a l[illegible] community. There are some "women-only dances" but mostly it's a very integrated gay and lesbian community. There isn't enough vol[illegible] on its own to support the [illegible]e need, so we really need t[illegible]

C: ***How do y[illegible] you are sleeping with that you are not a genetic man?***

V: That hasn't really come up. People usually know me. There have been a few sort of frenetic things where it wasn't a genital thing. But so far that hasn't been a problem.

C: ***What is more essential to masculinity: testosterone or a penis? What are some of the different priorities F2M transsexuals have when choosing the different phalloplasty operations available, for example, urination, erection, orgasm, or ability to penetrate?***

V: I will probably never have a phalloplasty. Maybe if I was really rich and had a long vacation...

C: ***I guess it's pretty expensive equipment.***

V: I have fully functioning equipment now. I know men who have equipment that doesn't work or don't have equipment, and it doesn't make them any less men. I have a lot of connections with the handicapped community or the differently abled community (I hate that term). I know a lot of peopl[illegible] through car accidents or meningitis or wh[illegible] don't have functional equipment, it does[illegible] make them any less of man. No one says [illegible] Steve, "You're not a man anymore"[illegible]

C: ***A lot of people [illegible] that there is a sexuality to anyone who is handicapped.***

V: Both of my parents [illegible] disabled. My mother had acute arthritis. S[illegible] two artificial knuckles, two artificial kn[illegible] an artificial ankle. I have dated people [illegible] handicapped. You don't stop being se[illegible] certain equipment doesn't work. Y[illegible]op being sexual because you stop looking like a *GQ* ad. We are sexual beings from cra[illegible] grave. To deny that is to delude oneself[illegible] is more to sex than orgasm. I hope pe[illegible]lize this, and maybe some of them don'[illegible]an interaction. There's a whole w[illegible]cal manifestations of personhood ([illegible]eve I said that). There is physical stuff that doesn't involve genital contact of a spe[illegible]re is it written that "This is the act[illegible] should engage in"?

C: ***I agree.***

V: I read an article[illegible]st 'zine. They were talking about[illegible] our children and youths, as if th[illegible] insulated away from all sex or sexuality. Then, suddenly at some specified age w[illegible] to be conversant and compete[illegible]d when they are not, [illegible] mental insecurities [illegible] regarding sex.

C: ***There are [illegible]ing on all the time. And th[illegible] to talk, write, and make pictu[illegible] avoid these accidents. Sex is too important to keep in private "behind closed doors".***

V: Sex is about life, and everybody wants to make it unrelated to the everyday. As if our genital life, our sexual life, our late night activities are somehow unrelated to the person who walks around on the street. As long as we keep this mythical dichotomy, we are going to doom ourselves.

C: ***I often attempt to talk about sex in my classes. I often get ridiculed for having a "one-track mind". If people think sex is "one-track," they are thinking a singular orgasm-oriented, penis-oriented, vagina-oriented "track". Well, that is NOT the only thing to talk about. That's so limiting. No wonder they want to change the subject.***

V: You can describe almost anything for hours, and people won't think anything of it, but if you describe any kind of sexual pleasure, people think you're a pervert, for example, if you like such and such a person for oral sex because of the musky smell of their genitals.

C: ***I don't mind if people think I'm a pervert.***

V: Fitting in is less work than dealing with the fallout from not fitting in. No one has been beat up in a subway for being an accountant.

C: ***There is that line from Kate Bornstein's play that "When it comes to gender, how come we can't count higher than two?" People get scared when you talk in numbers more complicated than one and two.***

V: People like easy answers.

C: ***When did you decide you were a transsexual?***

V: I told my family when I was six. But I didn't do anything about it until a few years ago. It's not that uncommon that people in their 30's and 40's find out that their parents had guessed wrong about their genders. Changing gender doesn't change who people are for the most part, you just remove certain parts, and everything can go on happily.

C: ***What did you do first?***

V: First you have to go to counselling, so I went to counselling, and after the minimum 90 days I got a blood test and couldn't go on hormones because I had elevated testosterone levels. It explains a lot because I am relatively muscular (underneath the fat) and I have a lot of body hair.

C: ***So you don't do any hormone treatment at all?***

V: I do now, but at first I had this condition which was confusing them. I've been on hormones for about a year most of the time.

C: ***I've heard that testosterone increases your sex drive.***

V: It does, but I already had a pretty active libido.

C: ***Are you considering any surgery?***

V: Well, I'll probably get a hysterectomy pretty soon for unrelated reasons, and I think my insurance will cover it. If nothing else that will allow me to reduce the level of hormones that I'm taking.

C: ***What about the long-term health effects, a few men in the group (especially the young ones) were complaining about hair loss and the possibility of liver damage.***

V: I come from a fuzzy family, so that's not a problem for me. It's difficult to say whether cardiovascular risk in transsexuality is due to hormone treatment or eating hamburgers, the sample size is still too small to make decisions. I am concerned with other health worries, but suddenly being on the male side of the risk pool is not something I worry about.

I really understand why female-to-males would want to be gay, to reject femininity totally

C: ***I want to go back to this notion of genderphobia.***

V: O.K.

C: ***There is a big movement in the gender community (transvestites, transgenderists, crossdressers and transsexuals), the ones that aren't gay, to cut themselves off from the gay community. Many crossdressers are heterosexual, probably most. If there was ever a natural coalition it's among the gender community and the gay community. If you're a straight genetic male wearing a dress in the subway you are going to get beaten up by the same punks and the phrase they will use is faggot. The people who aren't us don't differentiate so it's silly for us to. There was only one person from the gender community on the New York State pride agenda committee.***

V: We are all Queers.

C: ***As far as the straight world is concerned we are Queers. If we don't work together, it's stupid. Why is the Queer alliance so difficult?***

V: You have the gays saying, "Sure, we want domestic partnership and anti-violence rights but just leave us alone we're not like those queer ones, we're just regular folk, we want to be left alone in our condo". And you have the transsexuals saying, "We're not queer, we have our own thing and we just want to be left alone". It's a war zone out there. "Always vigilant" should be the slogan for the gay community. You have to always be watching out. A gay man was killed in Buffalo recently, and the killer got away with it. The jury bought the excuse that the killer was acting in self-defense. A big strapping 19 year-old beats up and kills a 40 year fat guy who was drunk. Self-defense? The jury bought it. We have to be aware that these things are happening, and we have to stick together

C: ***We can't believe that by becoming conservative we may integrate into straight society.***

V: No, you can't, because some day you will let your guard down, or someone will see you through the windows. Do you want to live the lie: "We're good neighbours we're just like you"? We're *not* just like you. This is about being who you are and not being ashamed or afraid of who you are. Brenda from Brenda and Glenda said to me, "It would be great if tomorrow every gay person woke up with lavender skin because then people would have to confront it." The teacher that is teaching your second-grader whom you really like and trust, your pediatrician, your next door neighbour with the nice roses, your cousin Kathy. Holy mackerel! This would be great, but it isn't going to happen.

Danny

Christine: ***What percentage of F2Ms sleep with men after the change?***

Danny: It's really hard to say exactly, because until about three years ago it was totally unacceptable to present a gay male identity, so people didn't really present it (outwardly).

C: ***Do you mean people weren't "out" about it?***

D: Yes, and I think the numbers are going to end up being a lot higher than people would even think. It makes sense to me. It's the same as male-to-females wanting to be lesbians. I really understand why female-to-males would want to be gay, to reject femininity totally.

C: ***You've told me that while you prefer to sleep with women you do occasionally sleep with men.***

D: I don't know about *sleeping*.

C: ***I think the readers would be interested in the details... where you pick your potential partners up and what you do.***

D: Well, I write my name on men's room walls, and I distribute these little cards.

C: ***Can I see one?!***

D: *Sure!* Here's a good one. Each one is a little different.

C: ***"World's greatest cocksucker 353-3810" These are great! I love them!***

D: I leave them in various places — bathroom stalls, and phone booths. If I went to bars, I would hand them out, but I don't go to bars because I don't drink.

C: ***So mostly people phone you or you meet them anonymously?***

D: I also cruise. Wherever you are, you can seek out the cruise spots, porno houses and parks. All parks are fair game. This is funny because this is just the standard gay shit.

C: ***So the methods so far are standard, but when you've picked the person up, is it also standard from then on?***

D: Well, no. That's when things change. Well, actually on *one* side it's exactly the same. On the other side it's not the same at all. I *only* have "one-*sided* sex," and it's actually very easy, because most guys don't give a shit; it's fine with them.

C: ***They just want to get off?***

D: Look, I don't want to make a generalization. There are *lots* of guys who are into more than just getting off. There are guys that want more. There are guys that try to do more than that. They may want to see and do stuff to me, but that's the key. I am always totally in control of the situation. It's funny because sexually I am submissive, but nonetheless I am completely in control of what's going on.

C: ***I was going to ask if you are a top or bottom and if it changes with men and with women.***

D: Absolutely. With women I am dominant, with men I am submissive. There you go. That's the difference. It's probably terribly sexist and awful.

C: ***Not at all. I think I am the same way.***

D: From my point of view, though, it's pretty sexist because I'm the *man* so I am dominant over the woman. But with men they are the man (I mean I am the man, too), but they can dominate *over* me. I respond submissively to older men. It's like they can dominate me, because they're "above" me.

C: ***What's so different about man-to-man sex?***

D: This may not be true for everyone, but for me it's really a good affirmation of masculinity. It helps me to affirm my masculinity, to be accepted as a gay male in the gay male community. I really like that. When I used to hang out with women I really liked the feeling of community with just one gender, you know what I mean, even though I felt like an imposter. But I could appreciate that sense of community which was there. It was really nice. Sisterhood *is* powerful. So is brotherhood.

C: ***Are there prejudices in the gay male community against F2M gays?***

D: In terms of being gay I am not out about being a transsexual. Forget it. No way! In fact, there is this transsexual group meeting at the gay centre, and I was considering going but then I thought, I don't want to be known in the gay community as a transsexual. It's difficult. Well, I shouldn't say that, because it's not difficult. It's actually quite easy, and that's the way I like it.

C: ***You don't want to blow your cover?***

D: I don't want them to know. I worked really hard to attain my manhood, and I don't want the integrity of my masculinity in any way compromised. There was a support group a while back called "Group Integrity". That's really important to most transsexuals, the integrity of their chosen gender identity. There are some transsexuals who want to be out, about their gender situation. I think that's really great, and I support them wholeheartedly.

C: ***I guess that's a different sense of identity, if someone wants to identify themselves as one chosen gender or as a transsexual.***

D: People who want to identify as transsexuals... but most of us want to be just the one gender. The support group is great because those who aren't out can get together one day every few months and accept the past, and I think that's very healthy. But I can understand why people don't want to be recognized as transsexuals.

C: ***You've told me before that the final test of "passing" was to be able to go into a gay male bar where men scrutinize each other much more closely.***

D: Yes. You see, they have a more refined sense of gender. They are so much more sensitive to the nuances, the variations, and the differences that are within the male gender. They know through experience that there are transsexuals, crossdressers, and variations of gender. Gays and lesbians know that a woman can look like a man just as easily as a man can look like a woman. So they look to the core when they see you.

C: ***They are more sophisticated in gender,***

D: They've seen a lot of butch women. So if you can go into that community and pass, that's a really good test.

C: ***Why is transsexual sexual desire so unintelligible to heterosexuals?***

D: If you haven't ever experienced gender confusion, you can't imagine what it's like. Gender is immutable. No matter how feminine a man is inside, he knows he's a man. Even transvestites know their core identity is male. They *feel* male, and know they are male in their hearts. If your core identity is female, you *feel* female. You can take hormones and grow a beard, but that's not going to make you a man. In fact, many women are androgenized by natural hormone imbalance, and yet they remain female-identified. No one can change your core gender identity. People think that transsexuals change their gender, but they don't. If you're a true transsexual, your gender identity is unchanging. Any transsexual would say that if they could be "normal" they would. No one *wants* to go through this, but if your core gender identity is at odds with your body, then you *have* to change your body because you cannot change your core identity. No one can. That's the way it is, in general. All the gender experts agree with that, too, for what it's worth.

> ***Most transsexuals are totally hung up on their partner's perception of them***

C: ***At one of the meetings it seemed that the lovers of F2Ms were mostly bisexual women, why is that?***

D: Many are also straight women, but they'd be having "one-sided sex". Most transsexuals do not involve their genitals in sex because it's too incongruous.

C: ***You talked about a man who had been castrated in a car accident. He's still a sexual being.***

D: Which is what we are. We really are castrated men — castrated by God, if you will. Of course unfortunately we have some *other* parts which have to be dealt with here. We are not *just* castrated.

C: ***What's the most important thing to a sexually functional masculinity, penis or hormones?***

D: Well, a bottom line is that *hormones* make you male, physically. As far as *surgery*, it's different for different people. There are a lot of surgical alternatives for reconstructing the genitals. People have different choices, and what you choose must reflect of your own personal priorities. It really varies. For some men it's important to have a penis that can urinate. For others it depends. Many female-to-male transsexuals feel that the only way that they can be men is to have a full sized penis, functioning to some degree, what ever that may mean — ability to achieve intromission or orgasm (in the penis)

C: ***What does intromission mean?***

D: Penetration.

C: ***When it gets down to the possibility of genital interaction, when do you tell them that you are not a genetic male?***

D: It depends. As I said before, I try to be in control of the situation, and if I *am* totally in control of the situation then they will never know. I'm talking to *whatever* degree, even anal sex.

C: ***You're the bottom?***

D: I'm the bottom. It just requires that I don't get totally undressed, and that's why I have to be totally in control of the action. I have to have at least a jockstrap on. That's as naked as I can get, but that's easy to achieve. I've had hundreds of sexual encounters and most of the time, no one finds out what's in my jock. Most of them are not that overly curious. Even though I'm sexually submissive, they respect my limits and allow me to be in control. But if someone really wanted to get nosey they would find something out, I mean, *I have a sexual response too!*

C: ***What 's the difference in having sex with men now and having sex with men before?***

D: I didn't really... if I did it was oral sex... it was already gay sex... umm... that's a grey area. It depends on your partner's perception. If a man thought that I was a woman... we didn't do it. *Now* I know that it doesn't *matter* what my *partner* thinks. *My* perception is the true one, but it took me a really long time to get to that point. Most transsexuals are totally hung up on their partner's perception of them.

C: ***You've talked about having a virtually bionic cock, and I think that is such a powerful image.***

D: Yes, that's one of the *positive* aspects. But that is not really a factor in gay sex, I wouldn't use the bionic cock except with women.

C: ***Well I'm really interested in both those things.***

D: You, like most women, are different than men in that way. In general, women are more flexible in terms of what they will accept. Most men feel that biology is destiny.

C: ***Whatever is between the legs.***

D: Right. The average jerk thinks that, but the average women is more flexible. Maybe this is just in my own experience, because I know more feminists and lesbians. But I think on the whole, *enlightened* women are more flexible than enlightened *men*.

drawing by Danny

C: ***All the F2Ms I have met have been very attractive, very virile guys. I perceive a style of masculinity which is not unlike gay codes of masculinity. You know leather and denim, well built, and macho!***

D: You've seen a lot of F2Ms who are great examples (there *are* those who aren't so well balanced). You're talking about some pretty self confident people.

C: ***What is that swaggering style?***

D: I guess it's self-confidence and a little overcompensation for the fact that you are a castrated man; maybe we have to be more "cocky." Also if you show that you're not confident, that's when people start to question you.

C: ***Why these gay male codes?***

D: Well, maybe *they* are over-compensating, too, you know, proving they're a man, and all.

C: ***Well I guess everything's a construction.***

D: That's true.

C: ***Do you think the gay male community has its own prejudices about masculinity? It seems that everyone loves a drag queen at the bar, but they all only sleep with the butch boys and macho men.***

D: Yes, and that type of limited acceptance is exactly what we would get if we were out. But I want to go back for a minute because we didn't talk about the part of my gay male sexual encounters when they find out, when I'm not in control of the situation.

C: ***Has that happened yet?***

D:It's really interesting. I've gotten different reactions... Well, I don't go to bars (except The Spike). Usually I cruise the parking lot of bars (in the suburbs). On this one evening, nothing was happening, so I figured I'd leave. Then this other guy came in a car and made some signal. He was a really big guy (I mean fat), but I'm not prejudiced. So we both drove down this dead-end street, and I pulled up beside him to talk. You know, the usual horny remarks and, "Hi, how are ya doin?". So we decided to go to this motel. I don't remember how it happened, but something happened. Somehow he grabbed me the wrong way and knew something was up. I said my standard rap for when this sort of thing happens. Usually I can anticipate things and say this *before* anything happens, but this time was different, and I think that is why I got the bad response. So I say, "I'm not *like* other guys. Do you know what a hermaphrodite is?" They usually say no, and I say, "That's what I am. A hermaphrodite is someone with both genders, part male and female." Well this guy could not deal with it. He kept giggling (he was pretty young). I said, "Don't worry about it." I tried to make light of the situation instead of making it a really heavy thing. Anyway, I think I ended up giving him a blow job or something just to get it over with, but that was the only time I got a negative reaction. In general, people are pretty accepting. I think I've been found out maybe 10 times out of a thousand (I've had lots of sexual encounters). A couple of times there were gay guys who had never been with a woman who wanted to penetrate me vaginally. I'm not into that at all, but I let this one guy do it because it was such a revelation to him. It was what he had been looking for all of his life, only he hadn't realized it. When he saw me all of a sudden it was like "Wow, I want a man with a vagina." The same way that some guys want a "she-male" (a woman who has a penis), but I was what he wanted. This has happened twice. They were both totally gay guys, and neither of them had ever had sex with a woman. The first time was in the park at 3 in the morning. It was incredible. It was so risky, so scary, but that really adds to the whole thing, too. This totally gay guy was really turned on. He had never even allowed himself to think that *this* was what he wanted. I hope that some guys reading this article might recognize something there. Maybe one or two guys will say "Oh shit!" It's just like the guys who are attracted to she-males. Unfortunately, I'm not really into it.

C: ***Are there many gay men who seek pre-op F2Ms as lovers?***

D: I've spoken to three other gay guys (genetic males) through the network who are totally homosexually identified but are attracted to this concept of a man with a vagina. One, I remember, told me that he and his F2M lover would go to gay male bars, and this guy would get off on putting his hands down his lover's pants and getting them *wet*, and then deliberately getting his hands near someone's face, or rubbing them on someone's beard, so they would smell it, just to see their reaction. He was somewhat of a rebel.

Christine Martin is a fully libidinal woman who lives near Times Square in Manhattan.

Because the text on the third page of this interview (marked as p. 9 in the original layout) is partly overwritten by the words "FTM QUEER", a transcription is provided below. It begins with the last question at the bottom of the second page (marked as p. 8) and runs to the first line of the fourth page (marked as p. 10).

C: *The gay and lesbian community needs to be shaken up too. For example the separatism that lesbians have been practicing just doesn't make sense any more, especially now when there are no guarantees regarding gender.*
V: I tend bar at a lesbian bar one day a week. A few weeks ago there were these two women there who were real men-haters. They were upset at the fact that I was tending bar there. They were making anti-man comments all night, and what was I going to say? It wasn't worth the effort to get into it all. After they left, I was alone in the bar, and these three men came in. They had come from the strip bar up the street. They were real assholes. They were everything the women before had believed all men to be. What it is that these women hated about men does exist out there. It's easy to generalize. Those men had perceived me as a guy and didn't get heavy with me, but the power play was interesting because if they had perceived me as a woman things would have been very different.
C: *Are you ever concerned with the threat of violence?*
V: No, not really, because I pass very well.
C: *Even though you have now gained a certain amount of male privilege, couldn't you be subject to the homophobic violence which threatens gay men?*
V: I don't really worry about that too much. I really live on the fringe.
C: *Are you out as a transsexual?*
V: I'm really out. Buffalo is a small town, there isn't a bar I can go to where I don't know someone. Heterosexuals usually have no clue because they don't read the gay papers.
C: *Most of my political associations have been with gay men (specifically through ACT UP and the AIDS crisis), my roommates are always gay men, and I think my sexual identity, desire and fantasies are as much a product of the gay male community as the lesbian community. For example my relationships are short and my sexual partners are frequent. These practices and tastes are typically associated with gay men.*
V: In Buffalo there is no gay community as separate from a lesbian community, there are some "women-only dances" but mostly it's a very integrated gay *and* lesbian community. There isn't enough volume of either group on its own to support the social services that we need so we really need to keep it together.
C: *How do you tell someone that you are sleeping with that you are not a genetic man?*
V: That hasn't really come up. People usually know me. There have been a few sort of frenetic things where it wasn't a genital thing. But so far that hasn't been a problem.
C: *What is more essential to masculinity: testosterone or a penis? What are some of the different priorities F2M transsexuals have when choosing the different phalloplasty operations available, for example, urination, erection, orgasm, or ability to penetrate?*
V: I will probably never have a phalloplasty. Maybe if I was really rich and had a long vacation…
C: *I guess it's pretty expensive equipment.*

V: I have fully functioning equipment now. I know men who have equipment that doesn't work or don't have equipment, and it doesn't make them any less men. I have a lot of connections with the handicapped community or the differently abled community (I hate that term). I know a lot of people who through car accidents or meningitis or whatever don't have functional equipment and it doesn't make them any less of man. No one says to my friend Steve "You're not a man anymore".
C: *A lot of people want to deny that there is a sexuality to anyone who is handicapped.*
V: Both of my parents were disabled. My mother had acute arthritis, she had two artificial knuckles, two artificial knees, and an artificial ankle. And I have dated people who were handicapped. You don't stop being sexual because certain equipment doesn't work. You don't stop being sexual because you stop looking like a *GQ* ad. We are sexual beings from cradle to grave. To deny that is to delude oneself. There is more to sex than orgasm. I hope people realize this, and maybe some of them don't. There's human interaction, there's a whole wealth of physical manifestations of personhood (I can't believe I said that). There is physical stuff that doesn't involve genital contact of a specific sort. Where is it written that "This is the activity that you should engage in"?
C: *I agree.*
V: I read an article in an anarchist 'zine. They were talking about how we treat our children and youths as if they should be insulated away from all sex and sexuality. Then suddenly at some specified age we expect them to be conversant and competent. Then we are surprised when they are not and we are surprised at the mental insecurities that most of them have regarding sex.
C: *There are sexual accidents going on all the time. And that is why we have to talk, write and make pictures about sex to avoid these accidents. Sex is too important to keep in private "behind closed doors".*
V: Sex is about life and everybody wants to make it unrelated to the everyday. As if our genital life, our sexual life, our late night activities are somehow unrelated to the person who walks around on the street. As long as we keep this mythical dichotomy we are going to doom ourselves.

Trannies Speak Out

This is a second, much longer version of the feature "Trannies Speak Out" from *Gendertrash From Hell* #1. Janou is a pseudonym of Mirha-Soleil Ross. As the document indicates, this was originally laid out for *Gendertrash* #4. Although it does not feature in the provisional table of contents, Mirha-Soleil Ross indicates that she also hoped to include it in *Gendertrash* #5, and an incomplete second attempt at a layout, presumably for issue #5, also exists. Additionally, a note in the *Gendertrash* archives indicates it was intended for "a future GenderTrash issue."

Trannies Speak Out!!!

I'm always excited about going out with my micro-cassette recorder. It makes the night a little less boring for me and for the girls working out there. After years working as a prostitute, I have partially lost interest in the bars where we (TS/TG prostitutes) hang out and the streets where we work. This is especially true since I no longer depend on them to earn a living (I am now a respectable indoor girl). I go back when I want to relax, have a drink, chat with old co-workers/friends and nostalgically remember the time when I was a young chick, hanging out 7 days a week, drinking, dancing, cruising and working hard in the parking lots until 6 or 7 am (I talk as if I were a 70 year old Madame writing her memoirs in 12 volumes).
Anyways, with the loud music in the bars and everybody working hysterically on the street - this is not the time or place for long, tiresome and introspective interviews covering their lives from conception onward and discussing the why's of who and what they are.
So I went on with this light and entertaining question:

What is your ideal client?

Here are some answers and excerpts from conversations I had that evening with some of the most prominent girls of Toronto's nights.

Janou: one-two, one-two...can you hear me... I'm at Colby's and I'm talking with...
Corky: Corky... to answer your question - the best client I like is one that knows what he wants, who is specific over the phone or on the street, whatever... The money's up front and he's very nice. He's satisfied, he can become a regular and he doesn't turn into an asshole. He won't change his mind, he won't try something else and won't try to talk me to do something I don't want to do.
Janou: What about when they ask what kind of men you're into? Does it matter?
Corky: Actually, I don't care if they're old, ugly or good looking. As long as they have money... but it's nice if they're good looking.
Janou: What about when they want you to be horny?
Corky: Never. I always tell them I'm on hormones and I can't get it up. Sometimes I do. I put a video or think about my boyfriend.
Janou: Okay, I'm still at Colby's and I'm now with the extravagant and grandiose Charlene. Charlene, tell me, what is your ideal client?
Charlene: My ideal client is someone that carries a VISA gold card, drives a Jaguar Sovereign and has a beautiful house in Rosedale. He will take me to 5th Avenue in New York City and I will live with him for the rest of my life as long as he gives me $2000 a week.

Jennifer: The ideal perfect client is somebody that treats me like a real woman, that doesn't treat me like somebody off the streets. He treats me with a lot of respect for what I want to be treated like. I like somebody that dosn't just look for a good time but walk away and will remember the good qualities about the woman he met.
Janou: Thank you.
Jennifer: You're welcome baby.
Janou: OK inquisitive readers, I'm now down on Maitland, *the Street of Iniquity* and am asking Marcia: what is your perfect client?
Marcia: The ideal client is sort of experienced, between 19 & 22 who has a fantasy and it's his first time. You let them know that you're actually getting off on them so they should be flattered that you're enjoying them rather than just being a client. And then you sort of massage them and you sort of play right up to them and you make them feel that they're with the most beautiful woman who really knows how to be a very hot woman and then you get paid for it which is probably the most important thing - I like them very hot & very young, they want to live a fantasy so you help them.
Janou: So you're a saviour, the Mother Teresa of the street?
Marcia: Yeah, they have a lot of energy and they ejaculate very fast and very hard.

photo by Janou

Janou: So that you can go back to your little things (life)?
Marcia: Well a bit yeah...
Janou: What about you Lisa?
Lisa: A thousand dollars with no sex!!!

Janou: Wham, bam, thank you ma'am! That was fast 'n' easy.

Janou: I'm gonna go a few feet ahead to talk with my dearest Christy...Hi Christy,could you tell me what is your ideal client?

Christy: Agewise? 30 to 35 years old. That's the age I like. He respects your wishes and follows your order. I like that. And money of course. Not a lot as long as you don't get in trouble...

Kim: (with an obviously overly pussy cat voice) The one who looks like Richard Gere. He's a nice... (oops she is now deserting me for a client) Hi, are you looking for company? (back to me) Can you hold for one second, I'll be back.

Janou: While she's doing her business, I'm with Marisa, who already knows the question.

Marisa: He treats me like a lady. Good money, good pay!

Kim: (who's back after screaming "fuck off and move" at the four studs/clients in the red sports car) Executive guy with nice ties, suits with lots and lots of money. And so much stress at work that he comes to pick me up after work 'cause I can relieve his stress and give him the best. Yeah, you know... And he pays me like about $\$150^{\underline{00}}$. And also the one who looks like Richard Gere.

Pretty woman (somebody yells from the other side of the street).

Janou: Here's an I'm-cute-innocent-&-fuck-anything-that-moves-type guy. Let's ask him a couple of questions.

Guy: Where are you from?

Janou: Gimme your name?

Guy: John Doe, with a capital "D".

Janou: So what are you doing here?

John: I'm passing by 'cause I just got off work and I'm on my way home.

Janou: So how come come you're cruising the girls here?

John: (on the defensive) I'm not cruising girls, I'm just walking. This is my flight back, thank you very much. (big laughter from everybody on the street)

What do you like? If you ask me questions...

Janou: No, I ask the questions. I'm the top here! So you're straight, gay or bi?

John: Straight.

Janou: So how come you're cruising girls who have penises?

John: No, you missed the last one. I'm on my way home.

Janou: Oh yeah, yeah, I've heard it before.

John: (trying to sound innocent) But it's true.

Janou: You can still keep your straight identity intact and cruise girls here you know. You just need to take my workshop "<u>How To Suck Cocks and Stay</u>

Straight and Proud of It For the Rest of Your Life".
John: Where are you from?
Janou: Montréal.
John: Boston's going to kick your ass.
Janou: What?
John: Boston's going to kick Montréal's ass.
Janou: What do you mean?
John: Hockey.
Janou: Oh I don't follow that. I know everyone in Québec is supposed to follow hockey, but not me.
So you've never slept with a transsexual?
John: Yup!
Janou: Finally, it's coming out...
John: No we never slept.
Janou: You did things. What kind of things? Tell me about it.
John: All the kinds of things that two people who get along can do.
Janou: Whooo, what does that mean?
John: It means that if you have that chemistry & things transpire, well things transpire.
Janou: So it didn't threaten your straight identity?
John: No it strengthened my human identity.
Janou: Human identity? That's nice.
John: Is that sweet? What paper are you from? You're a bad girl...

Janou: Here's my last one for tonight... Akina, tell me from the bottom of your heart, what is your ideal client?
Akina: Good money! Yeah, personality and good money.
Janou: And physically? Does it matter?
Akina: Well, if you're working like a hooker, it dosn't matter young or old, right? If you're looking for sex, of course you'll mind what kind of person you'll want to be your partner, right? If you do the job, everything is a fake. So it doesn't matter, young or old, as long as they have the money. As long as they pay good.

❤ ***Janou** is a very sexy political transsexual prostitute who has practised in both Montréal & Toronto. The back alleys, the parking lots, the bars, the agencies, the newspapers, the peep shows… name them — she's worked them.*

Splash Pages

Three unpublished splash pages, one attributed to Xanthra Phillippa MacKay, the other two very much in her style, survive in the archive. They resemble splash pages like "Transsexuals Get AIDS Too" in the earlier issues of *Gendertrash*, but their style (laid out in a desktop publishing program, not by collage) marks them as having been intended for a later issue of *Gendertrash*.

Anti-transsexualism isn't "cute"...

Anti-transsexualism isn't "funny"...

Anti-transsexualism is gross...

Anti-transsexualism destroys lives...

Anti-transsexualism has to be stopped...

Immediately.

Our lives

are

worth it.

Stop anti-transsexualism now.

End the hate now.

Pointing out transsexuals,

publicly,

for any reason

is

an Act of Violence Against Transsexuals

It's time

to fight back.

Our lives

are

worth it.

Stop anti-transsexualism now.

End the hate now.

"The most important event for transsexuals & transgendered people in the last 25 years, is happening right now: the emergence of a Transgender Liberation movement. We are finally speaking out & standing up for ourselves. We want complete control over our own lives and bodies and We Want It Now. No more shit from anyone whether lesbian, gay, straight or feminist."

Xanthra Phillippa

Afterword

by Leah Tigers

"We didn't relate to most of the other transsexual and transgender magazines out there," Mirha-Soleil Ross once admitted. She was young then, about twenty-four, speaking alongside her girlfriend and co-editor Xanthra Phillippa MacKay for a local queer radio program. "Traditionally," she hazarded, "a lot of transsexual and transgender magazines were not very political, and were not very politically articulated." Their magazine would be different, part of a new crop. Their magazine would be *Gendertrash From Hell*.

The feminist resurgence of the early 1990s, a so-called "third wave" of which *Gendertrash* was undoubtedly a part, had a punkish, anarchic spirit. What media it produced (the good stuff, anyway) was typically shaped like *Gendertrash* was, when Xanthra and Mirha-Soleil printed its first run for around $600 in 1993. Cheap, slim volumes, or "zines," were photocopied, with limited circulation, grassroots appeal, and independent, low-budget production. In terms of perspective and content, even high-end offshoots, glossy alternatives like *Bitch* and *Sassy*, were at least a little bit queer. For the low end of zine culture was, make no mistake, very queer, explicitly so, with tremendous variety. From *Homocore* to *J.D.s* to *Diseased Pariah News*, almost every niche of gay and trans counterculture in those years was archived on the page, though few readers got to see it. From a distance, *Gendertrash* looks to be just another thread in this tapestry, a transsexual publication, "devoted to the issues and concerns of transsexuals."

Among the easiest ways to close this distance from *Gendertrash* is, then, through its network, this wonderful tapestry. The network was sometimes indirect. A poem took inspiration from the witchy spiritualism of 1980s lesbian writing ("the sun was a cunt"); a transcribed speech referencing "transsexuals, drag queens, passing women, hermaphrodites, the intersexed" took inspiration from the "big tent" of contemporary bisexual activism. The heaviest, most consistent influence of this sort was community bulletins on the AIDS crisis, which provided the first major springboard for queer zine subculture. *Gendertrash* was not a zine "about" AIDS, yet its pages never stray far from that crisis. It belongs to a time when it still felt necessary to clarify for trans women that "there have been no recorded cases of HIV... through electrolysis." One full-page spread reads "Transsexuals get AIDS too." Pessimistic certainty of getting AIDS pervades Mirha-Soleil's earliest video document, the drunken confessional *Chroniques* in 1992. Retraining this pessimism as activist defiance, she was surely responsible for a majority of this coverage. This was a consciousness-raising publication, whose political message was spurred by the urgency of the plague.

Other times this network was literal. Davina Anne Gabriel's *TransSisters: The Journal of Transsexual Feminism* and Riki Wilchins's *In Your Face!* were sister publications, trading advertising space between one another. From the academy, Viviane Namaste, future writer of *Sex Change, Social Change* and *Invisible Lives*, was a direct contributor (as Ki Namaste); and kiwi, who penned another zine titled *Queer Tapette/Queer Terrorist*, contributed reviews of academic conferences. The transgender activist world was small enough, back then, that its writers and editors generally knew each other, crossed bylines, and published on the same topics. Doing so was classic movement-building work, with the largest movement-building endeavor for trans activism in those years, the Camp Trans protest against exclusion at the Michigan Womyn's Music Festival, figuring prominently in all their journals.

Between the plague, protest actions, and combative rhetoric, the trans zine subculture, if not zine culture in general, may be read as a sustained argument for minority communal existence. This was a time when even more of trans language was idiolect, or at least, subject to rapid change. The word "cisgender," for instance, coined in 1994, appears nowhere on these pages; nontrans people were "genetics," an archaic term rotating in and out of circulation since the early '70s. Needless to say, Xanthra's idea to call trans women "gender described wimmin" did not catch on either. The word "transgender" is also used in its early, activist sense, including any and all kinds of gender variance, from cross-dressers to intersex persons. As tempting as it is, with hindsight, to regard such definitions as private flights of fancy, they were born, in the moment, of a pressing need to establish a shared vocabulary, or, as the authors liked to say, a "heritage."

Regarding media about but not in community with transsexuals, *Gendertrash* took no prisoners. *The Crying Game* earned a warm review because "the writer... got [this information] firsthand"; the lesser-known *Le sexe des étoiles* was excoriated on the grounds its writers "used a minority they know little, if anything, about." This tendency was most ambivalent in regards to the academy, where, kiwi wrote, "I feel embarrassed to be an academic." At that time, transsexuals were written about academically, the academy was written about transsexually, with the two methods firmly disjoint. Academic realignment from "gay studies" to "queer theory" felt slow and, as Viviane Namaste, who cut her teeth on *Gendertrash*, spent her academic career explaining, insufficient: "queer theory and much transgender theory do not respect transsexuals because they do not understand transsexuality on its own terms."

Surely it was no coincidence that pioneers of this generative, outlier minority culture developed a tendency to fall in love with each other. In an exactly analogous process to that by which radical feminists of the 1970s, having lived, organized, and protested with other women for years, slowly recognized they had been lesbians "the whole time," Xanthra, at least, came to believe attraction to trans people was "definitely an orientation," which she, naturally enough, had. The rhetoric behind this was confrontational. "Trans dykes," Xanthra defined, were distinct from "transsexual lesbians" in that their foremost attraction was to "other gender described wimmin."

Yet the rhetoric was also multiple; Mirha-Soleil's short biography in *Gendertrash* describes having to "juggle her attraction to men and her love for TS women." In their video work from the period, she went into more detail: "I'm sexually attracted to men, physically, period. Nothing else... I'm attracted to genetic women on every other single level, spiritually, emotionally, politically. Like, I've been living with women, all my friends are women, my life is with women, period. Not with men. I don't have one male friend... I suppose what I needed to have those two things together was someone of my own gender."

By 1997, the last issues of *Gendertrash* were long complete, and the couple had split. Mirha-Soleil was again dating a man, Mark Karbusicky. But even the end of this trans romance had a tender, queer cordiality. "Xanthra is my ex-girlfriend," Mirha-Soleil announced at a live event, "and Mark is my current boyfriend. We all live together!" All three were onstage, laughing.

Who knew, back in the early 1990s, that trans people could love one another like this? Who knew that what the academy published on transsexuals was not representative? Who knew, most pressingly, that transsexuals got AIDS too? Education can literally save lives, or at least bring joy to them. It is a good reason to remember this little counterculture, in general. But this is not enough. There is something special about *Gendertrash*, specifically.

Perhaps it was that *Gendertrash* was a Canadian publication. American comrades *TransSisters* and *In Your Face!* occasionally mentioned domestic sex worker orgs like Margo St. James's legendary COYOTE (Call Off Your Old Tired Ethics), and vaguely gestured towards decriminalization, but they never exactly gave sex workers pride of place. Not so with *Gendertrash*, whose second issue proudly awarded trans woman Justine Piaget "Hooker of the Year." Much of this writing was done by "Jeanne B.", a pen name for Mirha-Soleil, who identified herself as "a long-time prostitute" and "an unrepentant whore."

For decades in Canada there had been an especially strong tradition of sex worker activism, in which transgender women were routinely leaders. "If there's any trouble with guys," remembered one sex worker for the 1984 Vancouver documentary *Hookers on Davie*, "they [the queens] will come and back you up, no problem." Michelle, the trans star of the film, worked with the homegrown Alliance for the Safety of Prostitutes, delivering the earliest "bad trick lists" to fellow workers around Davie Street, warning them off dangerous clientele. Warnings published in *Gendertrash*, "to all the TS/TG/TV/she-male/she-boy/he-she prostitutes in Toronto," were direct descendants of these lists. While the primary locus of activism had been Vancouver, word traveled fast; Michelle and her friend Tiggy practiced their French to visit Montreal, where "it's very cheap [to live]."

Those golden days of Davie Street were a few cities away and years before Mirha-Soleil took up sex work, in Montreal, 1990, aged twenty. Her friends and mentors in activism, however, remembered.

Vancouverite Jamie Lee Hamilton, who was the first Canadian to receive adolescent transition care in 1969, had turned tricks in the West End in the '70s. Her life on the streets turned into a life of politics: in '96, she ran for city council; in '98, she camped out for over a week outside city hall, demanding a grant to run a safehouse for sex workers; in the 2010s, she joined a research group at the University of British Columbia on "The Expulsion of Sex Workers from Vancouver's West End, 1975–1985," contextualizing her own past.

Together, in 2001, Jamie, Mirha-Soleil, Viviane Namaste and Monica Forrester formed the "National Committee on Prostitution, Transsexuality, and HIV," releasing an extended address to "Social Service Agencies and Transsexual/ Transgendered Organizations." "We are a group of transsexuals with a history of prostitution," they wrote. "We consider that a history of transsexuality is a history of prostitution."

Major trans zines of '90s America were not saying this, at least not so loud. *Gendertrash* was, especially by the end of its life cycle, eager to point that out. In its final volume, Christine Tayleur of Transgender Nation contributed a refutation of even their own magazine's earlier coverage: "While a few people run off and spend $1000 to lounge around in hot-tubs, or to protest transsexual exclusion at MWMF [Michigan Womyn's Music Festival], the majority of our population is excluded from basic human rights... These events are exclusionary in nature, accessible only to a privileged few." This was as severe and potent a critique of '90s trans activism as any participants then dared. So too in the early 2000s, when Mirha-Soleil rebuked the widely adopted Transgender Day of Remembrance as a "shameful example of political appropriation... if you take a moment to look at the long list of victims, you will clearly see most of them were prostitutes."

When it came to the sex worker orgs themselves, Mirha-Soleil judged less harshly, but still with her critical eye. For her 2002 one-woman show, *Yapping Out Loud*, she "went back to the beginning of the contemporary prostitutes' rights movement in North America" to discuss COYOTE. "There was a parallel to be drawn between how coyotes are blamed by rangers for all their problems, and how prostitutes are blamed for everything wrong with our neighborhoods... I had to explore that metaphor more profoundly." Bringing her lifelong animal rights interests to bear, she revealed the hyperbole of the metaphor with literalist humor: "There have been reports of prostitutes taking small men away from their wives, even when on a leash."

When speaking about the murders of prostitutes she knew as real people, however, her tone was evidently sober. "We live in a small transsexual prostitute world," she said. "I can go to Montreal, Ottawa, or Vancouver, and I'll reunite with girls I worked with a decade ago." These girls fill the pages of *Gendertrash*, in spirit and name. They are its lifeblood.

As a matter of direct proximity, sex worker activism became a focal point of *Gendertrash*, but not only for this. It was part of their general moral imperative. "I didn't become politically active because I wanted to improve my own life circumstances," Mirha-Soleil specified, "but because I cared about other animals, human and non-human." This entailed a special attention for at least one group of transsexuals who were already, as far back as the 1970s, writing in to gay liberation periodicals declaring themselves "the forgotten ones." Two decades later, they wrote in to *Gendertrash* too.

"I have just received two issues of *Gendertrash* today and I was so happy to hear from you," one such message ran. "Hear [*sic*] on 'Death Row' it gets very, very lonely." The Ross fonds, held at the ArQuives in Toronto, are filled with these letters, all preserved. Another began, "Ms. Soleil-Ross, greetings. I have been experimenting with creating cosmetics my sisters and I can make for ourselves while in prison… I do not know how many transgendered prisoners are lucky enough to read *Gendertrash*." "I'm a 31 year old transsexual slut," said yet another, "who is reading a review of your *Gendertrash*, can totally relate. I am pretty active within the community as best I can while I'm still locked up."

From the heirs to movement leaders at Walla Walla, who founded the first prison chapters of Gay Liberation Front and Men Against Sexism, to the practically unknown Clallam Bay Corrections Center, to infamous addresses from San Quentin, prisoners were reading and responding to *Gendertrash*. They were, quite possibly, its majority audience.

To obtain such a readership, one had to recruit. In the March '95 issue of *Prison News Service* #50, the editors placed a brief ad:

> *Gendertrash* is a political and community-oriented magazine for transexual and transgendered persons. Subscriptions are $24/4 issues, free to transexual/transgendered prisoners. Write:
> *Gendertrash*
> Box 500–62,
> 552 Church St
> Toronto, Ont M4Y 2E3

To this, there were perfunctory responses. ("Please send me a copie [*sic*] of Gender Trash 3 that you send prisoners free.") There were even requests for lewd photographs. But beyond these, a deliberate archive was extricated, from the obscurity of prison, of a forgotten transgender subculture. "Greetings Kindred-Spirits," opened the most activist-minded among them. "I/we was taken aback to hear that there is a publication that addresses our concerns. I'm a 3rd yr. gender-re-assignment the op isn't finished, but its well on its way. I'm very involved in the gay community behind these walls (N.Y. State prison-system). There are about 40 real swishy-queens who are livin with hopes of goin thru the whole procedure. They've lived as females for yrs. on & off a host of reasons brought them to prison, but almost to a person it was economics many times to raise money (for hormone-shots, the full op, etc.) I am the legal-beagle for the majority of gays here and across the state so if at all possible I try to play into any & all groups/persons who are sensitive to the plight. Please send us (via me) regular issues of this publication…"

When letters of this quality came to Mirha-Soleil's hands, she did not withhold her true intentions. "To go right to the point," she returned in one letter, "yes we would really really really like you to submit articles, letters, short stories, etc. about your experiences in the prison system with regards to transsexuality… I also have to admit that we have a bias in favor of material from transsexual/transgendered prisoners because we feel it is an area that has been neglected in ts/tg publications." "Do you really want know!☺" a prisoner wrote back, smiley face and all. "I will be more than happy to submit articles of this nature…"

These interactions were the result of a growing activist vocation, but also, and more importantly, an affinity. Xanthra and Mirha-Soleil had never been to prison, it was true. Noting this, Mirha would add, "knock on wood." Her separation from the prison system, as a trans woman and sex worker, struck her as contingent. Her conversations with prisoners were not laden with the duty-bound weariness of pure activism, but the authentic charms of companionship. "Send us something about how wonderful, extraordinary, and amazing we are," she wrote out to one prisoner, concluding with "Hi! Hi! Hi!!!"

Honest gender historians may find these positions of *Gendertrash* on sex work and the prison system – to say nothing of its less overt advocacy for animal liberation and Indigenous (Métis) justice – to be upstanding and noble, but we cannot claim they have been especially influential. They were influential, to be sure, but only for equally local, marginal countercultures that followed in their wake.

Small, insular scenes of trans women dating one another today, for instance, often have their resident historian or artiste, who goes out searching for instances of this behavior from before they called it "t4t." Such women often stumble upon the video *gendertroublemakers* by Mirha-Soleil and Xanthra Phillippa, made in the prime of the *Gendertrash* years. "Look at this SOV flick from THIRTY YEARS AGO!" Canadian filmmaker Louise Weard posted to her socials in 2023. "Glimpse this sublime t4t scene shot in 1993… I want more movies [like this] that explore the beauty and resilience of transsexuals." Of its influence on her recent five-hour SOV epic, *Castration Movie*, there is no doubt.

While this sexual influence has been the most obvious, in terms of artistry, it would be reductive, even offensive, to suggest the influence of *Gendertrash* was purely sexual. Queer zinesters, particularly out of Canada, look to the mag as a matter of course. "As someone who spends a lot of time in both Montreal and Toronto," wrote Lee P, intern at Queer Zine Project and publisher at Sheer Spite Press, in 2024, "I regard *Gendertrash* and its authors as a vital part of the trans culture of both of those cities." Mirha-Soleil and Xanthra had helped found Counting Past Two, a trans arts festival in Toronto, in 1998, frequently reported as the first of its kind in the world. Simply in terms of organizing and maintaining a public audience in that city for trans art, they proved invaluable. Confining this influence to a city may also be too restrained. Just last week Jackie Ess, author of the gender-questioning romp *Darryl*, who spent only a few years in Canada, reflected to me with her typical severity, "For a few years it seemed to me Mirha, Xanthra, Viviane and Trish were the only ones talking sense."

Inside the academy, scholarly offshoots of *Gendertrash* in the work of Viviane Namaste "largely went unremarked in queer writing on transgender," as Trish Salah tactfully put it in 2007. Yet here was Trish nonetheless remarking on it, in a piece titled, moreover, "Undoing Trans Studies." But Trans Studies has not been undone, at least not by the productive alternative proposed by *Gendertrash* and its descendants, which "insists upon the importance of discussing the lives of transsexual prostitutes, prisoners, and drug users," with humane empiricism closer to a field like sociology.

In the world of activism, we may have the highest hope of impact. In *Gendertrash*,

Mirha-Soleil and Xanthra discovered their activist voice; activism became their community, their way of life for the next twenty years. Mirha-Soleil co-founded Meal Trans, a drop-in program for poor, homeless, and sex-working trans people at The 519. It still exists today. Xanthra ran a local radio show, *Psychopathia Transsexualis*, defending and informing trans people up to the week of her death. Her lengthy interview with Rubert Raj, and Mirha-Soleil's with Peter Dunnigan, provide some of the best video records of early trans male activism in Canada. Together, Mirha-Soleil and Xanthra would sell back issues of *Gendertrash* at the Toronto Vegetarian Food Fair; all activism bled together. Morgan M Page – writer, historian, all-around transgender Renaissance woman – wrote in 2019 that she "had taken my own turn running the services [Mirha-Soleil] had created and launched my artistic career in her image." What could be greater influence, within one life, than this?

Expanding scope, however, increases our pessimism. Sex worker and prisoner rights have not been taken up *en masse* by the wider public, or even just the mainstream gay and trans rights movements. Animal liberation, Mirha-Soleil's true later passion in her activist life, was so heavily despised and suppressed in the early 2000s as to be almost laughable, though this lack of respectability was something Mirha-Soleil seemed to value. As she recalled: "When I was elected Grand Marshal for the annual Toronto Queer Pride Parade [in 2001] in recognition of my work within the trans and sex workers' communities, I decided to use that opportunity to celebrate my own favorite group of heroes: the Animal Liberation Front. I organized a contingent of activists who carried placards that highlighted ALF actions spanning two decades. So while irritating leftwing radical queer activists kept complaining about how queer pride had become too corporate, too mainstream and too apolitical, we led the parade celebrating an organization that is identified as a domestic terrorist threat in North America!"

Hearing this sort of exclamation, one is tempted to break out a phrase that has not been used for a queer person in many decades, and label Mirha-Soleil Ross an "actor, martyr, and saint." These were the words used by Jean-Paul Sartre in 1952 about another French-speaking queer sex worker closely associated with prison life, Jean Genet. "There begins the systemic turning of the positive into the negative and the negative into positive," Sartre wrote, "which later, carried to the extreme, will lead Genet to 'saintliness.'" By this Sartre means that Jean Genet, like Mirha-Soleil Ross, consistently chose to criticize mainstream society and celebrate unpopular causes.

I have meditated on this comparison often while composing this afterword. I think it is just off the mark. Genet was anti-moral: murderers became icons to him, simply because they were hated by society. Mirha-Soleil Ross, by comparison, has an extremely consistent, demanding moral code. She was not in the activist game to be one among the hated and despised. She was in the game to win it. Of course, she and the acolytes of *Gendertrash* did not win it: animals are not liberated; sex work is not decriminalized; human rights abuses in prison are rampant and growing. She has not won, yet, but she has left a mark. It is a mark we can observe, appreciate and expand on, if we so choose. This essay has been my attempt to do so. What's yours?

New York, 2025

Works Cited:

- **Cole, Janis, and Holly Dale, directors.** *Hookers on Davie*. Spectrum Films, 1984.
- **Cunningham, Sidney.** "Subscribing to *gendertrash*: The Radical Subcultural Transmissions of Toronto's Original 'TransZine.'" 2019. *Papers of the Bibliographical Society of Canada / Cahiers de la Société bibliographique du Canada*, vol. 57, pp. 13–41.
- **Hoolboom, Mike.** *Mark*, 2009. https://vimeo.com/139616710.
- **Irving, Dan, and Rupert Raj, eds.** *Trans Activism in Canada: A Reader*. Canadian Scholars' Press, 2014, p. 108. See pp. 27–32 for memories of Jamie Lee Hamilton, including mention of ASP.
- **Kempf, Christina (as C. Chris Wheeler).** "The Forgotten Ones: Gays in Prison," July 1971. *Gay Sunshine* v. 7, pp. 1–2.
- **Kitching, Heather.** "Gay Show" interview with Mirha-Soleil Ross and Xanthra MacKay, 1993. Queer FM on CiTR. Archived at https://open.library.ubc.ca/collections/citraudio/items/1.0132975.
- **kiwi et alia.** *Queer Tapette / Queer Terrorist*, 1991. Vol. 1. Archived at https://archive.qzap.org/index.php/Detail/Object/Show/object_id/374.
- **Namaste, Viviane K.** *Sex Change, Social Change: Reflections on identity, institutions, and imperialism*, Women's Press, 2005. See especially Ch. 6.
- **P, Lee.** "Zine of the Gay: *Gendertrash From Hell*," June 7, 2014. https://gittings.qzap.org/gender-trash-from-hell.
- **Page, Morgan M.** "The forgotten legacy of trans activist and artist Mirha-Soleil Ross," Feb 12, 2019. *Dazed* Digital. https://www.dazeddigital.com/art-photography/article/43093/1/mirha-soleil-ross-morgan-m-page-chelsea-manning-trans-art.
- ***Prison News Service,*** Mar/Apr. 1995. Nr. 50, p. 20. https://prisonfreepress.org/Prison_News_Service.htm.
- **Ross, Mirha-Soleil.** *Chroniques*, 1992. Thanks to Vtape for providing preview viewings of the Ross and MacKay video archives free of charge. See https://vtape.org/ for details.
- **Ross, Mirha-Soleil, and Xanthra MacKay.** *Gendertroublemakers*, 1993.
- **Ross, Mirha Soleil, and Mark Karbusicky.** *Yapping Out Loud: Contagious Thoughts from an Unrepentant Whore*, 2002.
- **Ross, Mirha-Soleil, and Mark Karbusicky.** *Proud Lives*, 2002. Document of Animal Liberation Front Pride March.
- **Ross, Mirha-Soleil, et alia.** Mirha-Soleil Ross fonds (f0033) at the Toronto ArQuives. See https://digitalexhibitions.arquives.ca/collections/show/16.
- **Salah, Trish.** "Undoing Trans Studies," 2017. *Topia* vol. 17, pp. 150–5.
- **Sartre, Jean-Paul.** *Saint Genet: Actor and Martyr*, trans. Bernard Frechtman. Plume Books, 1962.
- **Sorfleet, Andy.** "Alliance for the Safety of Prostitutes (1981–1987)" for *The Naked Truth*, Dec. 16, 2018. https://walnet.org/csis/news/vancouver_2018/nakedtruth-181216.html.
- **Vaughan, Claude.** "Shaking Things Up: Queer Rights / Animal Rights" interview with Mirha-Soleil Ross, 2003. *Vegan Voice*. Archived by Satya at http://www.satyamag.com/oct03/ross.html. For more information regarding '00s domestic terrorist charges against Animal Liberation Front, see *Green is the New Red* (2011) by Will Potter.
- **Weard, Louise.** https://twitter.com/weardjupiter/status/1665072040943190016.

About the Editor

Mirha-Soleil Ross is a legendary trans activist and performer. She was the editor of *Gendertrash From Hell*, the organizer of the first-ever trans film festival, Counting Past Two, and the creator of multiple one-woman performances, including *Yapping Out Loud: Confessions of an Unrepentant Whore*. Her work since the early 1990s in Montreal and Toronto has focused on transsexual rights, access to resources, advocacy for sex workers and animal rights.

About LittlePuss Press

LittlePuss Press is an independent feminist press run by trans women. We believe in intensive editing, printing on paper, and throwing lots of parties.

It is also central to the purpose of LittlePuss Press that we are an intergenerational project. We therefore offer some brief reflections on what this project means to us as individual readers of these zines across several trans generations.

Cat Fitzpatrick

I first read *Gendertrash From Hell* in 2013. This was a dozen years after I'd come out, in an England where the main sources of information about transsexualism had been salacious articles in *The Sun* and perhaps, if you looked really hard, the Press for Change website. Everyone I knew of, cis or trans, seemed to agree that the purpose of being a transsexual was to try to become as much like a "normal person" as possible. I certainly believed this implicitly for many years.

So when I downloaded those PDFs back in 2013, the thing I couldn't stop thinking was, what if I'd known about this in 2001? What if I'd encountered slogans like "I'd rather be dead than genetic" or "we're just as queer as dykes and fags"? What if I'd been confronted by the idea that what trans people really needed to do was not disappear (or become "more visible" either) but *organize*? It would have terrified me (even Sandy Stone terrified me) but it would have changed my life.

It's now over a decade later still. By the mayfly standards of trans generations I am a decrepit old crone bitch, but I am still learning about how to organize from *Gendertrash*. I also think any transsexual coming out now will still find much to learn from it too. Yes, some parts, especially the adverts and poems, have the prurient tingle of nostalgia. But so much of it, after thirty years, still hits with the shock of the new. We have not yet caught up with the bald directness of its demands, both on us and for us. There is still, simply, nothing else like it.

Casey Plett

In moodier moments, I'm given to think trans people have to learn (most) things the hard way, that when we do learn from the mistakes of our forebears, it's more exception than rule. One melancholy side effect of reading *Gendertrash* in 2025 is witnessing the same responses hashed out to the same problems – both intra-community issues and the bullshit that wider society forces on us – that we oft find ourselves with today.

In contrast, something I'm moved by: In the never-published 5th issue, Mirha-Soleil Ross had planned to print a letter from Dallas Denny taking issue with Christine Tayleur's characterizations of trans activists in the 4th issue, even as elsewhere in *GT* Ross expresses opinions more in line with Tayleur's (opinions I largely share). Ross wrote to Denny: "I find that far too many people in our communities can only see things as either right or wrong and your letter is a perfect example of the opposite."

I love the idea that we could be angry and unapologetic while also nurturing collaboration and disagreement, live pluralism without both sides-ism, be welcoming without being mealy-mouthed. What could we do if trans people – any group, of any trans people – got really good at living this way? It could be fun to find out.

Emily Zhou

Trans people have a funny relationship to history — not least because we tend to become history while we're still alive. 1993 wasn't too long ago, but neither was 2013, and when I first arrived in New York in 2021 I became acutely aware that I was surrounded by several different life-worlds that were in the process of disappearing as their members dispersed to private life or other cities. So, when I first started reading these zines, I was in awe of them (I remain so). They felt like an antidote to the subsequent failures of the movement, a vision of a path not taken. Mirha and Xanthra and their writers were laser-focused on the potential we have if we work together, something still downplayed by a culture industry committed to a particular vision of transition as a heroic struggle against the world – and that at best. Reprinting them is a sort of corrective. But of what kind?

We've all been awash lately in reminders that "we have always been here," as the assaults on our basic dignity ramp all the way up. I could imagine asking the readers of this volume to think of the past and gather strength from it. But strength isn't all we need. When I look around me at the outrageously productive flourishing of trans cultural production – and, especially, its collaborative character – I see another opportunity to get it right. Our continuance isn't assured, but our burning need to "express ourselves in our own languages / phrases / words / ways" – that's never going anywhere. I encourage the trans readers of this volume to see yourself as a part of this unfinished project. Work at something, and do it together. Do your ancestors proud.

Sasha Karbachinskiy

Gendertrash fills me with a strange sort of regret; had these discussions taken firmer root in the '90s, maybe we wouldn't have to be having them today. These zines stake a firm claim in declaring a "trans culture" which does not stipulate our existence from the margins, but where we get to be the centers of our own universe. It shoots right past the liberal "we're people too, please tolerate us" and straight to "we're here, we're queer, and we have a list of demands." Everything feels grounded in concrete and material needs for our communities while also forerunning conversations around things like "good representation."

They also go a long way to contextualize that the current moment is not as novel as it may feel to those of us in it. That our fight is not only precedented, but steeped in a rich history of resistance and care. Most of us know this in the abstract, but it's a different thing to hold it in your hands and see the specific dimensions of it, in what specific ways it is exactly the same and in what ways it is different.

Gendertrash is vulnerable and even intimate yet it's also abrasive and resentful. That's what's so brilliant about it; it is the earnest and sometimes contradictory nature of these zines that most illustrates our humanity beyond any trite pleas for compassion. It is above all truthful and honest and in that sense has not aged a day because it speaks to the core of both our strengths and our needs as people. Messy, silly, beautiful people struggling not only to survive, but to make meaning and find fulfillment in our existence.

Typographical Note

The sections of this book that are not facsimiles are set in Aktiv Grotesk, a sans serif designed by Dalton Maag Design Studio in 1991. Aktiv is a contemporary descendant of Akzidenz Grotesk ("multi-purpose sans serif") released by Berthold Type Foundry in 1891.

The titles are set in FF DIN, a digital font designed in 1995 by Albert-Jan Pool. FF DIN is derived from DIN 1451, designed in 1931 for purposes of public signage by Ludwig Goller at the Deutsches Institut für Normung ("German Institute for Standardisation").